WISH YOU WERE MINE

KINGS OF EDEN FALLS

WISH YOU WERE MINE

JUDY CORRY

ALSO BY JUDY CORRY

<u>Eden Falls Academy Series:</u>

The Charade (Ava and Carter)

The Facade (Cambrielle and Mack)

The Ruse (Elyse and Asher)

The Confidant (Scarlett and Hunter)

The Confession (Kiara and Nash)

<u>Kings of Eden Falls:</u>

Hide Away With You (Addie and Evan)

Say You Remember Me (Maddie and Ian)

Wish You Were Mine (Lucy and Owen)

<u>Rich and Famous Series:</u>

Assisting My Brother's Best Friend (Kate and Drew)

Hollywood and Ivy (Ivy and Justin)

Her Football Star Ex (Emerson and Vincent)

Friend Zone to End Zone (Arianna and Cole)

Stolen Kisses from a Rock Star (Maya and Landon)

<u>Ridgewater High Series:</u>

When We Began (Cassie and Liam)

Meet Me There (Ashlyn and Luke)

Don't Forget Me (Eliana and Jess)

It Was Always You (Lexi and Noah)

My Second Chance (Juliette and Easton)

My Mistletoe Mix-Up (Raven and Logan)

Forever Yours (Alyssa and Jace)

<u>Standalones:</u>

Protect My Heart (Emma and Arie)

Kissing The Boy Next Door (Lauren and Wes)

*For anyone who knows falling in love isn't the hard part—
it's the fear that this time will break you just like the last.
I hope you find the courage to risk it anyway...
and the joy of realizing it was worth it.*

"Lie with Me" by VOILÀ & NERIAH
"Catch" by Brett Young
"LOST IN THE CITADEL" BY Lil Nas X
"Don't Tell My Mom" by Reneé Rapp
"One Man Show" by Andi
"24/5" by Mimi Webb
"Can I Call You" by David Archuleta
"I've Seen Forever" by Dani Sylvia
"Lonely In Love" by Mimi Webb
"Beauty and the Beast" by Royal Philharmonic Orchestra
"twilight zone" by Ariana Grande
"In Case You Come Home" by Hanniou
"Some Things I'll Never Know (feat. Maren Morris)" by Teddy
Swims
"Like No One Does" by Jake Scott

1

______

LUCY

THE NEON LIGHTS of the club pulsed, flashing to the beat of the music as my best friend, Nora, and I made our way toward a table in the corner where our friends from the university hockey team had decided to gather for the night.

Usually, the guys held their after-game parties at the big house just off campus where a bunch of them lived so they could celebrate their win with the other students at Eden Falls University. But since it was the middle of winter break, and most of their fan club was home for the holidays with their families, they decided to take their celebration to The Garden.

"This place is amazing," I told Nora as I slipped into the booth beside her, wondering why we'd never been here before. We didn't drink much, since we were both on the university gymnastics team and tried our best to stick to our meal plans, but we did enjoy a good party on the nights we weren't studying or training.

"I know, right?" she said, glancing around at the main level of the upscale club. "I heard this place was meant to look like the Garden of Eden or something, but I didn't really believe it would look this good."

"I wonder if all the plants are real," I mused, eyeing the leafy vines creeping along the balcony above and the botanical arrangements filling every corner. It was full-on winter in Connecticut, but here, with the lush foliage and columns wrapped in vines and leaves to resemble trees, I could almost pretend that summer was right around the corner. In this ethereal ambiance, I could almost forget that my final semester of college was looming on the horizon, along with the reality that I'd have to start acting more like an adult soon.

Yeah...I had mixed feelings about graduating this coming May. Sure, as a senior I was thrilled to be almost done with my bachelor's degree—it had been a grueling few years working to keep my grades up while trying to be in top shape for gymnastics. But even though things got crazy at times, I was also a bit overwhelmed about what came after.

My life had revolved around gymnastics since I was three, and with my final season ending in just a few short months, I didn't know what I'd do with myself once it was all over.

Hopefully, I'd find a job I liked in marketing...since changing my major for the fourth time was not exactly an option at this point. Not unless I wanted to come back for a fifth year of college.

"So, what are you wearing to my brother's New Year's Eve party?" Nora asked, breaking me from my thoughts.

"I haven't decided yet," I said, tossing a lock of my blonde hair over my shoulder. "I've never been to a party at a famous pop star's house before. Do you think everyone there is going to be crazy rich?"

"Probably." Nora shrugged. "Ky doesn't exactly have normal friends these days."

That was an understatement. Nora had come from a

normal middle-class family, but after her older brother, the famous Ky Miller, won a Grammy for *Best New Artist* for his debut album a few years ago, everything changed. Now Ky had a huge place in the Hamptons, where Nora invited me to stay with her for New Year's.

"I'm just hoping Miles will be there," I said, thinking about Ky's NFL quarterback friend who had been at Ky's Fourth of July party a couple of summers ago.

"Oh, *definitely.*" Nora's eyes lit up. "He's always fun to flirt with."

"And not too bad to look at either." I winked, picturing the tall guy with broad shoulders who was the sole reason Nora and I now tuned into the New Haven Sentinels games on Sunday afternoons. "Hopefully, he gets a night off with their big game against the Dragons coming up on Sunday."

Though, since New Year's Eve was on Friday, there was probably a low chance of him sneaking in time for a party.

I was about to ask if she and I would be sharing the same room at Ky's house when a familiar raised voice caught my attention.

"I wouldn't be saying that if I were you," the angry voice of the hockey team's captain, Josh Rallison, cut through the club's upbeat music. "I saved your butt out there, and if it wasn't for me, you'd be sitting out our next game."

I turned toward the sound of his voice, my heart giving an involuntary thud. Josh was standing a few feet away, speaking to another guy on the team, his jaw set and his body tense.

And even though we were *trying* to stay friends after our breakup last spring, my stomach still rolled at the memory of his temper.

But before I could get too worked up, Josh's eyes immediately softened and his lips curled into a grin as he slapped

Andrew on the back, laughing. "Just kidding," he said, his tone suddenly light. "Let's just not make a habit of it, okay?"

I exhaled, the tension leaving my body as I watched the two guys laugh together.

So he was just joking around this time?

"You okay?" Nora asked with a raised eyebrow.

"Yeah," I said, shaking my head with a small, relieved smile. "Just...old habits die hard, you know?"

"Oh, I know..." It looked like Nora was going to say something bad about Josh. But her expression softened instead. "I think it's cool that you and Josh are getting along better this semester. After everything that happened."

"We're getting there." I nodded slowly. "It's definitely... complicated, but we're making progress."

"Well, I still think you need to find another guy tonight, like we were talking about earlier." She smirked, her tone turning light. "You know, before you're tempted to fall back into that 'on-again, off-again' cycle with Josh."

"I've learned my lesson," I said, sounding less sure than I intended. "We won't be getting back together."

"Good." Nora gave me a satisfied smile. "You deserve someone who knows how lucky they are to have you. Someone tall and strong and sexy..."

"Are you sure you're not daydreaming about Miles Hawthorne again?" I grinned into my glass, the starry-eyed look in my best friend's eyes all too familiar. It was basically the same expression she had on Sunday when the cameramen zoomed in on his face during the Sentinels game.

"No..." She shoved my arm and shot me a look. "You know my brother's best friend is off-limits."

"Yes...but that hasn't stopped you from having steamy dreams featuring him and you in a hot tub now, has it?"

She rolled her eyes. "I knew I never should have told you about that dream."

I laughed. "I mean, it did sound like a really good dream. I certainly wouldn't mind a good hot-tub make-out sesh right about now."

She raised her glass. "You and me both."

"For real." I clinked my glass with hers.

"Which is why our dating drought *has* to end tonight," Nora said, turning in the booth, her eyes scanning the club like a hawk. "I mean, we're hot, talented seniors on a Division I gymnastics team. We're catches. And even if none of the guys at school were smart enough to snatch us up fall semester, surely there's someone here who could be our perfect knight in shining armor...for at least one night, right?"

"I guess," I said, glancing around at the various men in the club. "I mean, there has to be someone here for *you* at least."

Nora's brow furrowed. "But not you?"

I shrugged, my gaze drifting over to Josh, who was standing a few feet away chugging a beer with a few of his hockey friends while the other guys chanted "chug, chug, chug" in unison.

"It's probably not the best idea for me to hook up with some random guy in front of my ex..." I sighed, looking back at Nora. "Especially when I already agreed to be his designated driver tonight."

"Ugh, why do you always have to be so considerate of his feelings?" Nora tsked, shaking her head. "I mean, he's the one that messed up."

"I know." I sighed, the familiar knot of confusion tightening in my chest. "I just don't want to risk messing up the truce we have going right now."

When she opened her mouth to protest, no doubt ready to accuse me of being too considerate of my ex, I quickly added,

"But he won't be at Ky's party, right? So we can focus on finding my knight in shining armor on Friday instead."

"I'm gonna hold you to that." Nora's face lit up with a mischievous grin as she pointed a finger at me. "Because after dating the same *dud* for three years, you deserve to have at least a little fun during your last few months of college."

"So true."

"All right, let's get serious," Nora said, shifting in her seat again. "Time to scan the room for potential candidates."

With that, the playful energy between us kicked back in. But as I glanced around the club, I realized I wasn't exactly sure what I was looking for, since I had no clue what type of guy Nora would be in the mood for tonight.

But apparently, Nora was more decisive than usual because she quickly pointed toward the bar.

"Okay, I've got a contender," she said, her voice low with excitement. "Oh, he's a major hottie."

I followed her gaze and froze as I took in the guy she was looking at. He had dark hair, was tall and broad-shouldered, and looked...surprisingly familiar.

I blinked my eyes a few times, wondering for a split second if I was seeing things.

Was it possible the bartender had slipped me the alcoholic version of a Moscow Mule instead of the virgin one I'd asked for and the alcohol was messing with my eyes?

But when I focused on the guy and recognized the button-up shirt I'd given him for Christmas, I knew I couldn't be mistaken. Because I was ninety-nine percent sure the guy my best friend was pointing at was none other than...my older brother, Theo.

"Umm, Nora..." I started to say when Theo turned his head sideways just enough for us to get a better view of his face.

And I knew the moment Nora recognized him, too, because her face immediately went beet-red.

"Oh my gosh!" She gasped, covering her mouth with her hand. "That's Theo! I can't believe I just called your brother a major hottie."

I burst out laughing. "Apparently, your subconscious wants you to end this year with a bang by having you go after all the forbidden people in your life. First, it's your brother's best friend, then it's your best friend's brother... Who's it gonna be next? Are you gonna go after Josh? Your best friend's ex?"

"Never!" She crinkled her nose. "Ew. No."

"I mean, you and Theo would be pretty cute together." I waggled my eyebrows, teasing her. "And just think...we could be sisters."

"He's way too old for me." Nora rolled her eyes dramatically. "Plus, I know you think your niece is the cutest, but I'm nowhere near ready to be trusted with raising a child anytime soon."

"So it's only because he's almost thirty and has a daughter?" I grinned, raising an eyebrow. "Because if you think my brother is hot...I can go up to him right now and ask if the attraction is mutual."

"Oh no you won't!" Nora's eyes widened as she grabbed my arm, yanking me back. "You will not walk over there and tell your sexy corporate lawyer brother that I think he's hot."

"Oh, so you think my brother's *sexy*?" I grinned even wider.

Her eyes narrowed, but I could see the pink creeping up her neck. "I'm not blind. But that doesn't mean I'm going to make a fool of myself tonight. Plus...isn't he still grieving?"

I sighed, my expression softening as I thought about Theo. "He'll probably always miss Alisha," I said quietly, referring to my brother's late wife who had died in a car accident a year and a half ago. "But he's gone on a few dates lately, so I think he's ready. Come on, let's go talk to him. We've always said we should have been sisters."

"No." Nora chuckled, shaking her head. "I get why you'd want this but...roommates, teammates, and best friends will have to be it for us."

"Fine." I pouted playfully. "I guess I'll try to be okay with that." I was about to say something else when my gaze shifted back to the bar where Theo was now talking to one of the bartenders—and my breath caught.

Because...wow. The bartender was *mega* sexy. Dark hair, huge biceps that looked like they'd been carved from stone, and when he smiled at something Theo must have said, his whole face lit up, creating this instant magnetic pull.

"Holy crap," Nora muttered, leaning in closer to get a better look. "Who's that?"

"I..." I blinked, feeling my pulse speed up. "I have no idea. But wow."

"Well, it looks like he and your brother are friends." Nora grinned, raising a reddish-brown eyebrow. "Maybe we should forget about your plan to spare Josh's feelings tonight and ask your brother for an introduction?"

I glanced over at Josh, who was now sitting in the booth with his back to the bar, and for a moment, I considered Nora's suggestion. Maybe it was okay to say hi to my brother.

But just as we were standing from the booth, Nora winced and placed a hand on her lower stomach. "Can we hit the bathroom first? Because I really need to pee."

"You and your tiny bladder." I laughed, shaking my head.

We headed to the bathroom, but as we were making our way back toward the bar, Josh was standing there, already getting another drink. When he saw us, he waved us over to him.

"You two are still planning to be our DDs tonight, right?"

he asked when we reached him, putting a muscular arm around my shoulders.

"Yes." I nodded, trying not to feel that familiar warmth and safety that always came when he had his arm around me. "We're just getting waters now."

"Good. 'Cause I'm about to get *wast-ed*," he said excitedly.

And even though he seemed happy, a flicker of concern flashed through me. Josh wasn't the best at knowing his limits, and he sometimes got into trouble because of it.

But he's not your responsibility anymore... I reminded myself.

Plus, he really did seem happier tonight than he'd been last spring, so hopefully, things were better now and would stay that way.

The bartender finished preparing Josh's drinks—one shot of clear liquor, probably vodka, and a beer—and set them down on the bar. "Looks like my drinks are done," Josh said, giving me a quick kiss on the forehead before grabbing them. Then turning back to Nora and me with a grin, he said, "Enjoy your waters, girls."

"What was that?" Nora asked, looking perplexed. "Do you think he's already drunk enough that he forgot you're broken up?"

"I have no idea," I said, feeling as confused as she looked. "But at least we're getting along?"

I watched Josh head back to his buddies, relieved that he seemed to be in a good mood at least. Then Nora looped her arm through mine, pulling me farther down the bar to where we'd seen Theo sitting earlier.

Just as we approached, two seats next to Theo became available.

"Hey, bro," I said, sliding onto the barstool next to him. "Fancy running into you here."

"Oh hey, Lucy." Theo looked up from his glass of scotch, clearly surprised to see us. "What are you doing here?"

"Came with Nora and the hockey team to celebrate their win." I shrugged. "We saw you from our table and thought we'd say hi."

And yeah...hoping to flirt a little with the bartender, too. But my brother didn't need to know about that other motive.

"Well, what a great surprise. Never thought I'd see the day when my baby sister would be grown up enough that I'd run into her at a club." Theo was eight years older than me, so we hadn't hung out much growing up. But after Alisha died, I'd moved in with him to help with Charlotte during my summer breaks from college and we'd grown a lot closer because of that.

"And it's good to see you as always, Nora." Theo leaned forward to smile at my friend. "I trust you're keeping my sister out of trouble."

"Of course," Nora said, and I noticed the faintest flush creeping up her neck when she met my brother's gaze.

Was she blushing?

When our eyes met, I could've sworn I saw her shoot me a warning look, as if telling me to keep our earlier conversation about how attractive she thought my brother was just between us.

I turned back to Theo and asked, "What are you doing here all alone on a Sunday night anyway?"

"I met a girl for drinks earlier." Theo took a sip of his drink, leaning back in his seat. "Walked her to her car, then decided to come back and chat with my friend Owen." He gave a subtle nod toward the bartender Nora and I had been eyeing earlier. "Charlotte's at Mom and Dad's tonight, and I just didn't feel like heading home yet."

"Ooohh, you had a date?" I asked, raising an eyebrow. "How was it?"

"It was all right." Theo shrugged. "Someone I met on a dating app, but I don't think there'll be a second date."

"Ah, dang," I said, frowning.

"It's okay," he said, turning his wrist to adjust his Rolex. "Owen and I were actually just talking about how it's all a numbers game. As long as we keep at it, it's gotta work out sometime."

"Oh, so you're on the dating apps, too?" Nora turned toward the bartender, who had just walked over from the other end of the bar, clearly picking up on the fact that Owen was the friend Theo had been talking about.

"Yeah." Owen gave a half-smile, leaning slightly against the bar. "I caved about a month ago and signed up."

"But you're still single?" Nora raised an eyebrow, and I could feel my cheeks heat up when Owen's gaze shifted between me and Nora.

His eyes lingered on mine for a heart-pounding second, seeming to inspect my face, and I couldn't help but wonder if he could somehow sense why we might be interested in his relationship status.

Hopefully, he didn't think we were trying to hit on him... *even if that was exactly why we'd come over.*

"Yeah, I'm single," Owen said with a shrug, a playful glint in his eyes.

It looked like he was about to say something more, but then Theo patted me on the back and said, "Lucy here has no idea how bad online dating is these days."

"Never had to sign up, huh?" Owen asked.

"Nope," Theo answered for me. "She met her long-term boyfriend at their freshman orientation and that was that."

And with those few words, my heart dropped because Theo made it sound like Josh and I were still together.

Which we definitely weren't.

I cleared my throat to clear things up. But before I could say anything, Owen said, "I'm guessing the long-term boyfriend is the guy I just saw you with? The one I gave drinks to down the bar?"

"Yeah," I muttered, tension creeping up my neck as I shifted in my seat.

But before I could explain that Josh and I were just friends, Owen glanced at us again. "So, are you two just here to chat with my fancy lawyer friend, or would you like me to get you something to drink?"

"Can I get a water?" I asked, trying to keep my tone casual though my words came out too quickly.

"Me too," Nora added.

"Sure thing." Owen nodded and turned to grab our drinks. His movements were smooth and confident.

And as he filled our glasses, I couldn't help but watch the way his muscles flexed with every motion, his biceps subtly stretching the fabric of his black T-shirt. He was different from the guys at school—a few years older, obviously. But I also sensed a confident maturity that was so attractive after dating a dude-bro for so many years.

When he returned with our waters, a guy in a business suit approached the bar, and instead of lingering to chat like I'd hoped, Owen quickly shifted his focus to the new customer.

"You and Nora still heading to Ky's party on Friday?" Theo asked, bringing me back into our conversation.

"Yeah," I replied, trying to focus on my brother, though my thoughts wanted to keep slipping back to his friend. "What about you? Were you able to get a babysitter for Charlotte?"

"Alisha's parents are keeping her overnight. So I should be able to make it," Theo said with a smile. "I don't know what I'd do without all the family around to help."

"I know," I said. "We're the best."

"And humble, too." Theo chuckled and took another sip of his scotch.

"Of course." I grinned.

As we continued to talk, a guy who looked to be in his mid-twenties stepped up to the bar next to Nora, striking up a conversation with her.

"Think Nora's gonna give this guy a chance?" Theo nodded over at the light-haired guy who had started chatting with my friend.

"I don't know." I looked at the guy briefly and then to Nora, studying her body language. "She seems interested right now, at least."

"Yeah?" Theo raised a dark eyebrow. "I can never tell with her."

"Why do you say that?" I asked, curious what my brother thought about my best friend.

"I don't know." He shrugged. "I've just seen her with so many different types of guys since you've been friends that I've always been curious if there's a common thread among any of them."

"I have no idea," I admitted, since I'd been equally puzzled about Nora's tastes in men. "But I think a lot of it is the chase."

"The chase?" Theo furrowed his brow.

"Being pursued," I said. "You know, having someone woo her. It's nice to feel wanted."

At least, I wouldn't mind feeling *wanted* for a change. *Desired*. Instead of as someone's backup plan.

"I guess I can see that," Theo nodded thoughtfully. "We all want to feel wanted." He looked back at Nora and seemed like he was about to say something when his phone buzzed. After checking the notification, he sighed and said, "My ride just pulled up out front. I better head out."

"Got another early morning meeting in New Haven?" I

asked, knowing my brother's high-powered law firm kept him busy. He was one of the youngest junior partners in the firm's history and was hoping to make senior partner before too long.

"My client wants to meet before his deposition."

"Sounds exciting," I said, still not fully understanding what my brother's demanding job entailed.

"Very," he said with a wink, grabbing his suit coat from the back of his chair and slipping it over his shoulders.

"Well..." I stood and gave him a quick hug. "Take care, bro."

"You too." After returning my hug, Theo tapped Nora on the shoulder to say a quick goodbye. "See you Friday." And just like that, he was gone.

I slipped back into my seat. Since Nora was still happily chatting with the guy next to her, leaving me the third wheel, I let my gaze wander over to Owen while I sipped on my water. He was wiping down the counter with a dishrag, and maybe it was because I hadn't kissed anyone in months, but dang! The way the muscles in his forearms flexed as he moved the cloth...it was so hot. Almost hypnotizing.

I'd never seen arms like his before.

Did he just lift weights all day?

As a bartender, his schedule was probably pretty open for a nice, long mid-morning workout at the gym...

He had a great torso, too. Nice pecs. Toned shoulders and back.

The sleeve of his black T-shirt rose just enough on his bicep to reveal the bottom of a tattoo. *Dang.* Tattoos were hot.

Did he have any others? Maybe something on that well-defined chest of his? Or on his back...

Too bad I wasn't drunk right now. If I was, I might be able to get away with flirtatiously asking him to show me more of his tattoo.

Okay, Lucy...you're getting way too carried away, I chided myself. Since when did I objectify guys like this?

Since you saw the sexiest man alive wiping down the counter like he had plans to lick something right off of it.

I found myself imagining him walking around the bar, his eyes locked on mine, the space between us pulsing with tension. He'd step closer, his strong hands gently lifting me up on the counter, setting me there as if it were the most natural thing in the world. The cool—now sparkling clean—surface beneath me would send a shiver through my body and then his hands would thread through my hair, tilting my head back just enough for him to press his lips to mine.

It would start soft, tentative—because, of course, he was a gentleman—but then heat and hunger would rush in, and before long, I'd be wondering if I was about to burst into flames.

I closed my eyes, imagining the feeling of his mouth against mine, the way his kiss would send a shiver down my spine, the way his strong hands would press into my back and pull me closer to him and—

"...Now to see if that guy actually texts me," Nora's voice entered my mind.

And just like that, I was snapped out of my fantasy and back to sitting in my seat—sadly, not in the bartender's arms.

"Sorry, what?" I blinked, looking at Nora who was watching me.

And that was when I realized that the guy she'd been chatting with was no longer at the bar.

My cheeks instantly burned. *How long had I been checked out for?*

Nora grinned, clearly aware of what was going on. "I was just saying that I wonder if that guy will actually text me or if he was just being nice."

"He asked for your number?"

"Yeah," she said, glancing over at Owen briefly before raising her eyebrows at me. "But I think you might need to exchange more than just phone numbers with our sexy bartender before you internally combust."

"Was my daydreaming that obvious, then?" I gasped, covering my eyes with my hands.

"Only because I know you." Nora chuckled.

"Sorry." I shook my head. "I don't know what has come over me tonight. I just... I don't think I've ever found a guy so physically attractive in my life."

"Well..." Nora laughed. "He is *way* hot and your exact physical type. Almost as if that guy from your favorite Korean drama and Theo James had a baby..."

"Two guys having a baby?" I cocked an eyebrow. "Do I need to give you a biology lesson?"

Not that I'd ever been great at science. I was, after all, the girl who had put off getting her required chemistry credits done until her last semester of college.

"Oh, you know what I mean." Nora waved it off.

"I know, I was teasing." I laughed nervously, feeling jittery as I glanced back to Owen and considered Nora's description. And realizing that she was spot on, I said, "And yeah, that's actually the perfect description. Like Kim Soo-hyun and Theo James had a baby that grew up to be a hot bartender."

Almost as if his ears had been burning, said bartender looked down the bar at us. When his eyes briefly locked with mine, my heart skipped a beat. And as he walked back toward us, his confidence practically radiating off of him, a rush of heat flooded my cheeks.

Get yourself together, Lucy, I told myself. *Just because he's walking your way doesn't mean you can slip into another fantasy.*

"Do you ladies need anything?" he asked, his voice smooth,

deeper than I remembered. "Another water? Or perhaps something stronger?"

And suddenly, I was tongue-tied.

Which had never happened to me before.

"I'll take another water," Nora answered first. Then with a smirk, she added, "And your phone number for my friend here."

"Nora!" I gasped, my eyes going wide before I elbowed her in the side. "I can't believe you just said that."

But Owen's eyes sparkled with amusement as he glanced at me and said, "Didn't our mutual friend Theo mention you have a long-time boyfriend?"

2

______

OWEN

"OH NO, THAT'S NOT…" the cute blonde sitting at the bar started to say, clearing her throat. "I mean, I used to—"

But before she could finish her sentence, a sudden commotion erupted behind her. And when I looked to see what was going on, the guy I'd seen with his arm around the girl I was currently talking to suddenly wound up his arm and threw a punch straight into another guy's face.

Oh no. This is definitely not happening.

"Excuse me, ladies," I muttered. "I need to go take care of that."

But before I could take even two steps, the chaos exploded even further as the two guys, probably drunk out of their minds, went at it.

And by the time I reached the altercation, there were a few other guys trying to break up the fight. But the bigger guy—the one who had thrown the first punch—was belligerent, looking like he was out for blood.

I hadn't had to break up too many fights since I started managing The Garden two years ago, but I should have known that a team of college hockey players coming in after a big game would make for an interesting night.

The noise was almost deafening as the two guys continued to throw punches at each other, completely oblivious to the chaos they were causing. My heart rate kicked up as I made my way through the mess, my eyes scanning the crowd for a way in.

"Hey, guys, you need to break it up!" I shouted, trying to make myself heard above the ruckus. But my voice was lost in the sea of shouting and the clinking of glass.

I pushed forward, trying to get closer to the fight, but one of the hockey players grabbed my arm like he thought I was about to join in.

"Hey, I work here," I said, shaking him off.

"Oh, sorry," the guy muttered, releasing my arm just as my security team showed up.

"Josh, calm down!" a female voice shouted through the chaos. "You're gonna get kicked off the team if Coach finds out about this!"

I froze for a second, looking toward the opening in the crowd where a woman had stepped forward. It was the girl I'd just been talking to at the bar. I think Theo had said her name was Lucy. My mind raced as I watched her shout at the guy who was obviously at the center of the fight. The guy whose name, I assumed, was Josh.

It had seemed like she'd been about to tell me that the guy I'd seen her with earlier—the one she was currently yelling at—wasn't her boyfriend. But from the way she was going after him, I couldn't think she was anything but his girlfriend.

Either that or she was his sister.

The bouncers had a grip on both guys now, but Josh—big, angry, and way too drunk—was still fighting back, struggling to break free. And instead of staying on the sidelines where it was safe, Lucy was right there, pushing her way closer like she was trying to stop the fight.

She's gonna get herself hurt. Sure, she was probably pretty strong for a girl—I had noticed how toned her arms were in her sleeveless dress as she'd been sitting at the bar with her friend. But strong as she might be, she was still tiny. From the looks of it, she was barely five feet and could easily get hurt if she got too close to a guy that was enraged.

"Hey!" I called, stepping forward, my hand reaching out for her. "Let my security team handle them, okay?"

Lucy looked up, her gaze going to my hand on her shoulder before meeting my eyes. "Are you guys gonna call the cops?"

"If he doesn't start cooperating, we'll probably have to," I said, eyeing her boyfriend who was still thrashing against the bouncers.

"Josh," Lucy yelled, stepping out from my grip and pleading with him. "Please just calm down. He's not worth it. Whatever is happening isn't worth it."

I wasn't sure her boyfriend could even hear her over the noise and the adrenaline pumping through his veins. But then —thankfully—he noticed her and seemed to snap out of his rage. And with a deep, ragged breath, he gave in and let the security team guide him out of the bar.

Lucy stood there for a moment, watching them. Then she turned to me, a tight, apologetic smile forming on her lips before she said, "Sorry about all this. I don't know what happened." She shook her head, and then seeming to speak to herself, she added, "He was in such a good mood earlier."

"It's not your fault," I said, but before I could say more, she was already darting off toward a nearby table and grabbing a white puffy coat.

She shot me a look I didn't understand over her shoulder,

and then she was off, chasing after the security team and the two guys they were escorting outside.

I stood there, watching her leave, feeling a strange sense of concern for her.

I really hoped she was going out there to break things off with him. Because if not, well...I didn't want to think about what might happen if she found herself on the wrong end of his temper.

Hopefully she'd be okay.

I turned back to the area where the fight had broken out, scanning the space for any signs of broken glass or damaged furniture. There was a lot of noise and frantic energy, but thankfully, everything seemed to be intact.

"You guys okay?" I asked, quickly checking in with the few people who'd been nearby. "Anyone get hurt?" They shook their heads, and thankfully, everyone seemed to be okay.

"Sorry again for the disturbance," I said. "Hopefully, that's all the excitement we'll be having tonight."

When I turned to head back to the bar, my eyes caught on the girl Lucy had been hanging out with. She was grabbing a black coat from the booth Lucy had just run from. *Good.* Hopefully that meant she was going to help her friend.

With a deep breath, I walked back to the bar to check in with Irina and Malik. They were chatting, glancing at the aftermath, but their eyes met mine when I approached.

"Everything good here?" I asked, trying to shake off the tension from the scene.

They both shrugged, looking at each other. "I think we're fine," Irina said, giving me a half-smile. "That was...intense."

"Yeah... Man." Malik let out a low whistle. "That was crazy."

"It was." I let out a breath, running a hand through my hair. "I knew I should've kept a better eye on the hockey team."

"Sorry about that." Irina winced. "The big guy told me he was getting drinks for him and his girlfriend, so I didn't realize how much he'd had already."

"It's okay," I said, shaking my head. "His girlfriend was only drinking water, so I think he played us."

"Should I add him to the blacklist?" Irina asked, eyes already flicking to the computer.

"Yeah." I nodded. "Put him on it."

I turned back to the bar, my eyes scanning the room. It was just after midnight and the busiest part of the night was past, so I decided to take a few boxes from the back room out to the dumpster.

The cool night air hit me as I stepped outside, the gentle fall of snowflakes brushing against my cheeks. I opened the lid to the dumpster and tossed the first two boxes in. I was reaching for the next box when I heard voices coming from the parking lot.

"You can't drive like this," an all-too-familiar voice said. "You're way too drunk."

I froze. It was Lucy again. And I had a good idea who she was talking to.

How did such a seemingly bright girl end up with such a loser?

I quickly tossed the last box into the dumpster and jogged toward the voices, careful not to slip on the ice. When I rounded the corner, I saw Lucy tugging at her boyfriend's arm, clearly putting all her weight into her attempt to stop him from getting behind the wheel of a sleek sports car.

Her friend was nowhere to be seen. Had she taken the other guy from the fight home, then? The girls had been drinking water, so maybe they were the hockey team's DDs for the night.

I looked around to see if my bouncers were still outside, but they must have already gone back to their posts inside.

I shook my head. I should've called the cops on this guy earlier. If he was trying to drive in this state, he clearly needed someone to lay down the law. Before he put anyone else in danger.

I picked up my pace and when I reached them, Josh was already pushing Lucy off him, mumbling something under his breath about him being fine and that she should stop getting in his way.

When he tried to get into the car, swaying on his feet and with his balance all off, I could see the panic in Lucy's eyes. And I was suddenly twelve years old again, back in my parents' driveway and trying to keep my mom, who suffered from addictions of her own, from driving off in the middle of the night.

I shook the memory away and tried not to think of all the things I'd lost, the tragedies that came from bad decisions. Because I knew all too well what could happen if Josh got behind that wheel. The kind of consequences that could wreck everything in an instant.

"Is there a problem here?" I asked, stepping forward. And when Lucy turned to see me, I saw that flash of relief in her eyes.

"I'm just trying to stop him from driving," she said quickly, her voice wobbling. "I was supposed to be his DD tonight but he's not listening to me."

"I'm fine," Josh slurred, leaning against the car now, thankfully not sitting down in the driver's seat, looking at me with bleary eyes. "You can go back to your bar. You don't need to worry about me."

"You're in no condition to be getting behind the wheel tonight," I said, my tone firm. "Let your girlfriend take you home."

"My girlfriend?" Josh scoffed, an edge of bitterness in his voice. "Yeah, right. She doesn't care about me anymore. And I said I'm fine."

"Clearly, you're not." I crossed my arms, standing my ground. "And if you get behind that wheel, I'll have to call the cops."

Lucy's eyes darted between us, her desperation clear, silently begging him to listen. "Come on, Josh. Coach will kill you if your dad has to bail you out of jail again."

This guy had already been bailed out of jail before?

I glanced at his sleek, expensive sports car, and everything clicked. I knew his type well: entitled rich kid with parents who cared more about appearances than anything else, letting him slide by without facing any consequences for his actions.

Josh sighed heavily, muttering something under his breath about his coach. After what felt like an eternity, he reluctantly pushed away from the car, swaying as he stumbled toward the passenger seat. With an exaggerated huff, he collapsed into it, throwing himself in with a grunt. "Happy?" he grumbled, slamming the door so hard it rattled the vehicle.

I stood there for a moment, watching Lucy. She was still visibly shaken, her hands trembling slightly like it was taking everything within her to keep it together.

"You gonna be all right?" I asked, dipping my head so I could look into her eyes. "Because if you don't feel safe driving him home, we can take his keys and find another way to get him back."

"No, I'll be okay." She wiped a stray tear from her cheek, her eyes avoiding mine as she let out a shaky breath. "Thanks for stepping in."

"Are you sure you don't want to find someone else to take him home? Maybe one of his teammates is sober?" I glanced over at her boyfriend, now slouched in the passenger seat like a petulant child. "He doesn't look like someone you want to be around when he's like this."

"I'll be fine," she said, her voice steadier now. "I just need to get him home."

"Okay." I nodded, though I was still concerned. And since I couldn't help it, I added, "Just take care of yourself, okay?"

"Thank you for your concern," she said, her voice soft but firm, her tone telling me that I was starting to cross a line and she just wanted me to stop inserting myself where I didn't belong. "I appreciate you worrying about me, but I'll be good now."

So instead of saying anything else, I just watched her for a second longer, feeling a sharp ache in my chest that I couldn't quite explain. And when she climbed into the driver's seat and started the car, I shook my head and sighed, turning to head back to the bar.

It wasn't my place to get involved further, and she wasn't my responsibility.

But dang if it didn't feel like this girl needed a little saving.

3

———

LUCY

THE HUM of music downstairs drifted up through the floorboards, signaling that Ky's New Year's Eve party was starting to pick up. Nora and I stood side by side in the bathroom attached to the bedroom we were sharing at her brother's beach house in The Hamptons, putting the final touches on our hair and makeup.

"So, did Josh ever end up telling you why he punched Brody in the face?" Nora asked, adjusting the strap of her black dress over her shoulder. Her lips pressed together as she studied herself in the mirror.

"No." I blinked, pausing my mascara application as I recalled the last message I'd received from him. "The only thing I've heard from him since Sunday was the 'sorry for being a butthead' text he sent me the next day."

"Classic Josh," Nora said, her voice dripping with sarcasm. "At least he kind of apologized, though?"

"Do you believe Brody's side of things?" I asked, genuinely curious if Nora believed what Brody had told her when she'd driven him home from the club.

"That Josh went ballistic just because Brody joked about asking you out?"

I nodded, meeting her gaze in the mirror's reflection.

"I mean, it wouldn't really be out of character for Josh to do something like that, would it?" Nora said with a shrug. "Even though you're not together, he's still pretty possessive of you."

"Hence why I didn't want to flirt with other guys that night," I replied, shaking my head. The situation still felt like a tangled mess I didn't know how to navigate.

I mean, I still cared about Josh. I knew he was a good guy deep down. But I also deserved to move on and be happy. And continuing to get sucked into his drama was not going to help me do any of that.

Nora nodded, her expression softening. "And since he messed up our attempts to get you that hot bartender's number, it's only right that you find someone else to have fun with tonight."

"I did notice your brother's hot tub is all set up out back." I smirked. "At least one of us should put it to good use."

Nora chuckled. "I like the way you're thinking."

I raised an eyebrow. "I mean, if Miles doesn't show up to make that steamy dream of yours come true, there's always my brother."

"I'm never going to live that down, am I?" Nora shook her head. "You didn't tell him that I thought he was cute, did you?"

"I think the exact phrase was 'Major Hottie,'" I teased.

She glared at me.

I laughed. "Of course, I didn't tell him."

"Good." Nora fluffed her hair, adding volume with a quick push of her fingers. "But speaking of your brother, do you think Theo is here yet?"

"I would think so. I'm pretty sure he said he was leaving Eden Falls around five." I grabbed my phone to check the message Theo had sent earlier, but a frown crept across my face when I saw he'd sent another text that I hadn't seen. After reading it, I sighed and said, "Looks like he's not coming after all."

"Really?" Nora's face fell.

I nodded. "He said Charlotte ended up with a fever, and with how quickly hers can spike, he decided to stay home with her instead of leaving her with Alisha's parents in Manhattan."

"Oh, that's too bad." Nora's expression softened. "But that's good he's being a good dad. Tell him we hope Charlotte gets better soon."

"I will." I quickly typed out a message to my brother. Once my message was sent, I looked at my reflection in the mirror. My bleached-blonde hair was in soft waves around my shoulders, and the strapless burgundy dress that I'd picked out on a whim—the one that made it look like I actually had some cleavage—looked good on me.

"You ready to head down?" Nora asked with a grin, eager for the night to begin now that we were officially glammed up and forty-five minutes late to the party.

"Yeah." I nodded, taking in my reflection one more time. "Let's go see if we even know anyone here."

With that, we both headed out of the room to go downstairs.

We made it to the main living area of Ky's beautiful home a minute later and weaved through clusters of people, all of them much taller than Nora and me.

At just five feet one, we both fit the gymnast stereotype perfectly—short and strong. But with most people a head or more taller than us, it almost felt like we were wading through a sea of long legs and high heels.

I recognized a few faces as we walked around. Alessi Holland, the singer who opened for Ky during his European tour, was standing by the fireplace chatting with some of Ky's backup dancers.

"So, does Ky just spend all his time off with everyone he takes on tour with him?" I asked, genuinely curious since I still wasn't used to the whole "celebrity lifestyle" her famous brother lived.

"Pretty much." Nora shrugged, tucking some hair behind her ear. "I think it's hard to know who to trust when everyone wants something from you, so he keeps his circle a bit smaller these days. Mostly people he either works with now or the group of guy friends he's been close to since high school."

"Makes sense." I nodded. When Nora invited me to her brother's New Year's Eve party, I'd imagined a huge, glamorous bash, packed with every type of famous person imaginable. But walking around the main level of his house where most everyone had congregated in the large living room, I saw that there were only a couple dozen people here.

"Wanna see what kind of food he has in the kitchen?" Nora asked, her eyes sparkling as she glanced around the room.

"Sure." I smiled, my mouth already watering.

We made our way to the kitchen, and the moment we stepped inside, my eyes were drawn to a familiar face and broad shoulders standing by the kitchen island. He was loading up a plate with chicken wings and veggies, looking completely at ease.

"Looks like Miles got the night off after all," I murmured to Nora, nodding toward the famous quarterback she had a crush on.

Nora froze, her eyes widening as she stared at him.

And I couldn't help but grin. She'd been completely normal around him when we hung out here with him and Ky two summers ago. But apparently, one steamy dream and a few amazing football games later, she was suddenly starstruck.

"Come on," I said, nudging her lightly. "Let's go say hi."

We walked over to him, and when he saw us, Miles's face lit up. "Hey, ladies," he said, that easy smile of his lifting his lips, his voice as smooth as butter.

"Hi Miles," Nora said, her voice coming out more breathy than usual.

Yeah...she had it bad. Crushing on one of her brother's best friends.

"Nora and I were wondering if you'd be here tonight." I grinned as I grabbed a plate. "Does your coach know you skipped town for some fun?"

"Not exactly," he said, shooting us a flirtatious wink. And I instantly understood why he had millions of Instagram followers. The man was a walking dream. "And as long as no one rats me out and I'm at the airport on time tomorrow afternoon, he doesn't need to know."

Two other guys approached the island then, both with dark hair and nearly as tall as Miles. One of them slapped Miles on the back, whispering something in his ear that made Miles chuckle.

"Sorry, ladies," Miles said, clearing his throat. "Have you met my friends?"

I looked up at the guy on the left, and my heart skipped a beat. No way. It was the bartender from The Garden.

What was he doing here? Was he one of Ky's friends, or did he just happen to tag along with these guys?

"I know Bash, of course," Nora said with a bright smile, seeming to recognize the guy in the middle first.

"Good to see you again, Nora," Bash said with a grin. Then, glancing at me, he asked, "And who's your friend?"

"This is Lucy," Nora said, putting a hand on my shoulder blade. "My roommate and best friend."

"Nice to meet you, Lucy." Bash gave me a nod, and I was

caught off guard by how striking his eyes were—blue and clear behind the glasses he wore, standing out against his tanned skin and nearly black hair.

"And this is our friend Owen," Miles added, nodding toward the bartender.

"We met you at The Garden, right?" Nora asked Owen.

"Yeah," he said, his eyes flicking between Nora and me. "You two are friends with Theo, right?"

We both nodded.

"But you're also friends with Ky?" Owen asked, looking like he was confused at how we'd know both guys.

"You could say that." Nora smirked. "I mean, Ky and I fought all the time growing up, but well, he's actually my brother."

"Oh, really?" Owen's eyebrows shot up. "I didn't realize Ky had a sister."

"That's because he's ashamed of me," Nora said, but her smile gave away that she was just joking.

"And you're Nora's best friend?" Owen looked at me, his gaze lingering for a moment.

And man, if my body didn't have the exact same reaction to him as it had on Sunday...

Geez. Those eyes of his. They were amazing.

But even though I felt slightly jittery under his stare, I thankfully managed to say, "Yes." Then even added, "And how do you all know each other?" gesturing to the three guys.

"We all graduated high school together," Miles said with a casual shrug. "Well, everyone except Owen since he's old and graduated the year before us."

Which would probably make Owen a year younger than my brother, Theo. Twenty-eight or twenty-nine...

Dang. I knew I'd been hoping the next guy I dated would

be a bit more emotionally mature than Josh. But seven years was a lot older than I'd expected for some reason.

Not that Owen and I were dating—or would ever even go on a date.

He probably wasn't even interested.

But when we made eye contact again, I couldn't help but wonder what he thought about me. I was sure that after the whole Josh fiasco, the first impression I'd left him with on Sunday hadn't been the best.

Though...since I was so much younger than him, he probably hadn't really thought much about me at all. Our brief interactions probably hadn't crossed his mind after I drove away in my drunk ex-boyfriend's fancy car.

"So, are you guys staying here for the weekend?" Nora asked, looking between Miles, Bash, and Owen. "At Ky's house?"

"Nope," Miles said, shaking his head. "We're crashing at the Hastingses' beach house just down the street."

"Hastings?" My ears perked up. "Is that the same Hastings that donated a ton of money to the university?" I swear I'd seen their name on half the buildings around campus.

I didn't know too much about the family since I hadn't grown up in Eden Falls, but I was pretty sure I'd heard someone say something about them being the billionaires that owned half of the small town.

"That's them." Miles nodded. "Their son, Ian, went to school with us, too, and since he and Owen are practically brothers, he got their permission for us to stay at their place. We figured Ky would need the room for other friends staying over tonight."

"That's cool," I said, suddenly even more curious about Owen, who had seemed like a regular bartender just a few minutes ago. But if he was friends with all of these high-profile people—a football star, a pop star, and a billionaire—it made me wonder what kind of background he had.

Did he have a secret, high-profile job that he went to when he wasn't serving drinks at The Garden?

It sounded like he'd at least gone to the same fancy boarding school that Ky and all these other guys had gone to, so maybe it was just his parents that had the fancy jobs...

As the group went back to filling their plates, my attention was momentarily diverted as I thought whether it was worth it to try and stay with my nutrition plan tonight. I could definitely find a way to get in my protein and veggies with the variety of appetizers on the counter... But since it was New Year's Eve, it would be okay to have a little cheat day, wouldn't it?

Seeing that Nora seemed to be having similar thoughts, I started loading my plate with various cheeses, meats, crackers, and plenty of veggies to balance it out, along with a cup of a delicious-looking pineapple punch.

I was taking a sip when Owen stepped up beside me, his hand resting lightly on my shoulder. "Hey, just a heads-up," he said, his voice lowering. "I saw you drinking water at the club, so I'm not sure if you usually drink, but at one of Ky's parties a few summers ago, some guys spiked the pineapple punch pretty badly. Just wanted to give you a heads-up in case it's the same tonight."

"Oh..." I blinked, glancing at my cup and frowning before taking another sip. The drink tasted like pure, fruity sweetness. "I don't taste any alcohol," I said, studying the drink.

"That's the magic of the pineapple punch," he replied, his voice casual but knowing. "It's excellent at masking it."

"So, are you saying I shouldn't drink it?" I asked, surprised by his warning. Most guys at school seemed to be on a secret mission to get me really drunk at a party at least once, so it was abnormal to have this near stranger looking out for me.

"Well..." His eyes quickly scanned over me, and then he gave a slight, thoughtful pause before saying, "I guess as long as you're eating and you only have one cup, you should probably be fine. Two cups though, and you'll be blacking out."

"Yikes."

"I mean...that's only if it's been turned into the 'party juice,'" Owen said with a shrug. "Honestly, it could be fine. I just wanted to make sure you knew it probably wasn't regular pineapple juice."

"Thanks," I said, nodding appreciatively, though I was still unsure about the punch. I turned my attention to the bar and surveyed the selection of drinks. It was a little overwhelming, and I definitely didn't want to risk getting too tipsy tonight. I looked back at him. "Maybe I'll have something else..."

"What do you usually like?" he asked, leaning against the counter. "I can mix something up for you."

"Oh," I said, momentarily surprised by his offer. "I-I guess you're probably a lot better at that than I am since you do it for a living."

"Hazard of the job," he said with a wink.

Was that a flirty wink? I wondered as a flutter of butterflies flapped in my stomach.

Possibly.

But it probably didn't mean anything—probably just something he did with all the girls he served drinks to.

Likely got him better tips.

But he wasn't on the clock tonight, so hopefully, he wasn't pretending to flirt with me for tips.

I shook off the thought and bit my lip as I glanced back at the bottles, trying to focus on the drink choices instead. Then I spotted a bottle of white rum next to sparkling water, limes, and mint.

"Could you make me a mojito with all this?" I asked, gesturing to the ingredients.

"Of course," Owen said, moving with confidence as he started to mix my drink. And I couldn't help but admire how easily he worked, the way his hands effortlessly measured and poured, knowing the right amounts of everything from memory.

He handed me the drink a minute later, and when our fingers brushed, a quick jolt of electricity went up my arm. And when something sparked in his gaze, I wondered if he'd felt it, too.

But instead of searching his dark eyes like I wanted to, I lifted my glass to my lips. The cool, minty lime hit my tongue, refreshing and smooth.

"Is it okay?" he asked after I'd taken my sip.

"It's really good." I nodded. "You clearly know what you're doing."

"Thanks." He chuckled. "Glad my skills aren't too rusty."

"So, what are you having?" I asked, hoping to keep the conversation going just a little longer.

"If you're not planning to drink that pineapple punch," Owen said, grinning playfully, "I'll take it off your hands so it doesn't go to waste."

"Not one to throw out a good drink?" I asked, surprised. Most people in Ky's circle would have thought nothing of dumping a drink they didn't want.

People who had never had to go without didn't always value things the same way as those who had.

Though, the opposite could be true, too, I supposed. Super wealthy people didn't get that way by being wasteful.

Okay...I was definitely overthinking this.

But after dating a guy who always had everything handed

to him—who took everything for granted (including me)—it was hard not to be on guard for the same signs.

"If this punch has what I think it might have in it," he said, gesturing to the drink I'd set on the counter, "then the going rate for a cup that size would be about twenty dollars."

"Then by all means, don't let this liquid gold go to waste." I chuckled, handing it to him.

When he took the red plastic cup from me, I felt a flutter in my chest at the thought of him drinking from the same cup I'd used.

Sure, it was a small thing, but since we were near strangers, it felt somehow intimate to share a drink.

I watched as he put the drink to his lips and gulped when I realized he hadn't avoided the slight mark from my lipstick.

The fourteen-year-old version of me would have been over the moon about that fact since it was basically like he was kissing me, right?

"Can you tell if it's spiked?" I asked, pushing my weird thoughts away.

Did he have some sort of special palate as a bartender?

"Not yet," he said, his grin widening. "But give me about fifteen minutes, and we'll see."

I laughed, feeling strangely at ease with him, despite the way he was making my heart race.

"Shall we go join the others?" He picked up his plate and nodded toward the table in the dining area where Nora and the other guys were sitting with their food.

"Sure," I said, my cheeks warming.

I followed him to the table, my gaze running over the chairs, hoping to see two seats left by each other. But there weren't any.

"Here, I saved you a spot," Nora said when she saw me come up behind her, patting the chair next to her.

So after a quick glance at Owen, I set my food on the table and then slid onto the chair next to my friend.

4

———

OWEN

"YOU GUYS WANNA GET in the hot tub now?" I asked
Bash and Miles when people started going outside in their
swimsuits.

It was a little after eleven and the party had been fun so far,
lots of familiar faces that I'd seen at Ky's other parties, as well as
some fun new ones.

I'd only shared that brief moment with Lucy in the kitchen
—just enough time to fix her a drink and wonder how things
had gone with her boyfriend after she'd left The Garden. But
once we sat down at the table, Miles had taken over with his
entertaining stories, and then Ky came in to rally everyone for
the "Minute to Win It" games his backup dancers had
organized.

But Lucy seemed fine and friendly, and since her boyfriend
wasn't here, I figured that was a good sign.

"I'm getting in," Miles said. "Yesterday's practice destroyed
me, so the jets would actually feel amazing."

"I'm game," Bash said. "Getting out of the water will suck,
though, since it's like eight degrees out there."

"Yeah, it will." It had been a while since I'd been in a hot tub. Right after college, when Ian and I had lived in his family's pool house, it was a regular thing—either with girls we'd bring home or just the two of us kicking back and talking about life, the universe, whatever.

But two years ago, Ian and I had finally decided it was time to stop taking advantage of his parents' hospitality. So we moved out—Ian into the massive mansion he had built on the land his dad sold him (because as the son of a billionaire, my best friend was loaded.) And I found an apartment near Eden Falls University, which worked out perfectly when I was wrapping up my PhD, teaching chemistry at the local prep school, and working weekends at The Garden.

Yeah...the last few years had been intense, so it was about time that I wound down in a hot tub.

Not that I really imagined there would be much "winding down" tonight since everyone was pretty ramped up and in a fun partying mood.

But hey, hot tub parties in the snow with your friends were always a good time.

We grabbed our swimsuits from the backpacks we'd left near the door and took turns changing in one of the bathrooms upstairs.

While Miles was in the bathroom, Bash and I hung out in Ky's room, chatting as we waited. "Did you figure out who you're kissing at midnight yet?" Bash asked with a smirk before inspecting his reflection in the mirror.

"What?" I asked, caught off guard by his question.

"Your midnight kiss. You know, for New Year's?" He grinned, running his fingers through his dark hair and smoothing it back. "You can't tell me you're gonna break the tradition tonight."

"I guess I wasn't thinking about it," I said. "Ian was always the one in charge of that challenge." The one where he made each guy in our friend group pick a different girl at whatever New Year's Eve party we happened to be crashing that year to woo and then kiss when the clock struck twelve.

"Well, since he's all happy and engaged, I guess we'll have to continue it without him," Bash said. He turned to look at me. "So...who will it be? One of the dancers? Or possibly Nora's cute friend I caught you flirting with earlier?"

"You talking about Lucy?"

"Yeah, Lucy. She seems nice. Kind of has a surprising spunky side."

"Really?" I asked, surprised since I hadn't seen that side of her yet.

Bash nodded. "We were on the same team during the games tonight and she seemed fun."

Interesting.

Which, I would guess, was probably true. I'd just happened to meet her on what was probably a bad night.

"But she's cute," Bash said. "You should kiss her."

"She might have a boyfriend, though..." I said, taking off my watch and tossing it into my backpack.

"Oh..." Bash said. "I guess that's not surprising since girls like her are never single."

I nodded. "I mean, I'm not a hundred percent sure. When I met them at The Garden last week, Nora tried to get me to give Lucy my number...but then she left with a guy shortly after that, so..."

"So I guess you better figure that out before you kiss her." Bash chuckled.

"What about you?" I asked, giving Bash a sidelong glance. "You gonna try kissing anyone?"

"I don't know..." Bash shrugged as he studied himself in the mirror. He took his black-rimmed glasses off, then put them back on, as if trying to figure out which look he was going for. "I was kind of thinking about kissing Alessi."

"Really?" I raised an eyebrow. "You think it's a good idea to kiss an ex?"

"Probably not..." Bash chuckled. "But hearing her song everywhere I went this summer had me thinking about the time we dated. And I guess I wondered if she's been thinking about me, too."

Before I could say anything, Miles stepped out of the bathroom, saying, "You're planning to kiss Alessi tonight?" with a protective edge to his voice.

"I'm thinking about it," Bash said, looking back at Miles with a slight shrug. "Just curious if the spark is still there. You know, wondering if she's been thinking about me, too."

"Well, I've been trying to figure out my stepsister for years," Miles said with a sigh. "So, good luck on figuring that out."

The dynamic between Miles and Alessi had always been a puzzle to me. Their parents had gotten together right around the time Miles graduated from high school, and to be honest, I never really knew what to make of their relationship. Sometimes it felt like they hated each other, and other times they were best friends.

What I did know for sure, though, was that they both worked hard to keep their personal lives out of the spotlight. Miles with his football career, and Alessi with her singing career, which had exploded this past year when she opened for Ky on his European tour.

"You still trying to figure out if that one song is about you?" I asked Bash, recalling the conversation we had last summer at a party where he'd tried to convince us that Alessi's chart-topping hit was about him.

Bash shrugged. "I just can't think that it isn't."

"What lyrics are you talking about?" Miles asked, frowning.

"*Under the firework sky, your eyes meet mine, a secret spark ignites, but we're out of time,*" Bash said, mimicking the cadence Alessi used in her song.

"Because of the weekend you met, right?" Miles's face softened with recognition. "You think she's talking about Ian's infamous Fourth of July yacht party?"

Bash nodded, a small smile tugging at his lips. "Exactly."

"Well, I guess those lyrics could be about you." Miles raised an eyebrow. "But who really knows? My stepsister has had quite a few boyfriends through the years..."

"Should we head down to the hot tub and ask Alessi about her secret muse?" I suggested, intrigued, since I had my own theories. "Time to get to the bottom of this."

"Yeah, let's do it." Miles clapped Bash on the shoulder. "I've been curious about the meaning behind that song, too."

"Off to solve the mystery!" Bash raised his hand in the air. "And to kiss our fair maidens."

"Hear, hear!" Miles cheered.

And now we were just showing that we were all a little drunk.

When we got back down to the kitchen, I spotted Nora and Lucy talking and laughing at something on Nora's phone together.

"You girls planning on joining us in the hot tub?" Miles called out, flashing his usual grin. "Or are you too worried about making that freezing cold dash back inside?"

"Of course we're getting in the hot tub," Lucy replied with a mischievous glint in her eyes. "We were just waiting to see if you were brave enough to get in."

"You're doubting my bravery?" Miles bantered back. "Geez, Lucy. I thought we were buds."

Lucy rolled her eyes, a playful smirk on her lips. "We'll see you out there in a bit." And when she glanced briefly at me, something stirred in my chest.

Yeah, I really needed to find out if she was single before the clock struck midnight because a New Year's kiss with a cute girl like her was exactly what I needed to kick my goal of finding a girlfriend this year into gear.

"So, we were just talking about your new album," Miles said to his stepsister as we climbed into the end of the hot tub where she was sitting. The air was chilly, sharp enough that we could see our breath. But the moment we sank into the water, the cold outside seemed to fade away, replaced by the soothing heat. "And we came up with a few theories about where you drew inspiration for some of your songs."

"Oh, you did?" Alessi asked, her green eyes flicking between Miles, Bash, and me.

"Yeah..." Miles leaned forward, his signature smirk making an appearance—the one that usually meant he was about to stir things up. "And I've got to admit, the theories are pretty good."

"You think so?" Alessi pushed some of her dark hair off her neck, now damp from the steam of the hot tub. "W-what songs are you wondering about?"

"Mostly 'Under the Firework Sky,'" Miles said, meeting my gaze and then Bash's for a second before turning back to his stepsister. "That one's been stuck in our heads all night."

"Oh...that one..." Her eyes went wide for a moment before she schooled her expression. "W-what made you wonder about that one in particular? Is it everyone's favorite or something?"

"You already know it's my favorite," Miles said with a wink. Then with a bigger grin, he added, "And come to find out tonight that it also happens to be one of Bash's favorite songs, too."

"Oh really?" Alessi's gaze flicked to Bash. "I'm so glad you liked that one. It's really special to me."

"Was there any particular inspiration behind that song?" I asked, trying to get to the bottom of things.

"Oh, um..." Alessi hesitated.

"Was it because of Ian's summer yacht party?" Miles suggested. "About six years ago?"

Alessi's gaze shot to him, and...did she just glare at him for bringing that night up?

Did Miles know the truth already, then? And she didn't like him putting her on the spot like this in front of Bash?

"See? I told you guys," Bash said, assuming that he'd guessed the night that had been the inspiration for her song. "That's exactly what I was saying. Right?"

"What are you talking about?" Alessi asked.

Miles chuckled, clearly enjoying himself. "Bash thinks the song's about him."

"Ohhhh," Alessi said, her brow furrowing like she was only then connecting the dots. "That's...I guess that makes sense... We did start dating around that time, didn't we?"

"We were sitting next to each other during the fireworks, right?" Bash asked, like he was picturing that night right then. "Good times..."

"Yeah, it was a really good night," Alessi said, licking her lips, her gaze briefly darting to Miles. "Quite the memorable weekend, actually."

"So, is the song about Bash?" I leaned forward, not sure she'd actually confirmed Bash's theory yet. "Were *secret sparks igniting* during the firework show on the yacht?" I asked, paraphrasing her lyrics.

"Yes, sweet stepsister of mine," Miles said, resting his

muscular arm on the edge of the hot tub. "Was our buddy Bash the muse for that number one song of yours?"

"Uh..." Alessi's face turned a little paler.

"I get that musicians find inspiration from all kinds of places," Miles offered when she didn't say anything else. "So would it be more fair to say that multiple experiences might've inspired that song? Not just that magical night with our buddy Bash?"

"Y-y-y-yes..." Alessi said the word slowly, a sigh escaping her. "I mean, that party was definitely influential. I have some fond memories of it." She paused, glancing at Bash. "But I don't want you to think I'm, like, pining for you every time I sing that song on stage. I'm sure that would be pretty awkward for you, considering we only dated for like two months."

"I didn't think you were necessarily pining for me." Bash smiled, clearly pleased that he'd been at least somewhat right in his assumptions about the song. "But yeah, it's a great song. Totally deserves all the success that it's found."

"Thanks," she said, her gaze briefly flicking between all of us, but lingering on Miles for a beat longer. "It's been a crazy six months, that's for sure."

"I bet," Bash said. "But it's nice to know I left a small impression."

"I mean, who can forget their first summer fling before college?" she said, her usual confident smile returning.

"Apparently, not you." Bash winked. "But I'm sure it was quite thrilling to date a pre-med student going into his senior year at NYU." Bash was now in his last year of medical school, just about to start his residency.

"You know it." She chuckled. "Though, I'm pretty sure the fact that you were at NYU while I was at Eden Falls University made our relationship end that much quicker."

"Long distance tends to do that, doesn't it?" Bash shook his head. "If only you'd been a little more patient, though. Dr. Aarden is hooking me up with some of his connections in New Haven for my residency, so I'll only be twenty minutes away from Eden Falls next year."

"If only my eighteen-year-old self had known I'd only have to wait five years for the long-distance thing not to be an issue." Alessi laughed. "Oh the fun we could have had."

"It's okay." Bash shrugged. "We'll just have to see what happens next year." He winked.

I was about to ask Alessi if there were any other memorable moments that made it into her album when the back door opened and Lucy and Nora appeared in the doorway behind Ky, making my heart give an involuntary skip.

Both girls were bundled in bathrobes when they stepped outside, clearly more prepared than me for the cold dash back inside. When they approached us, it seemed like they were trying to figure out where to sit in the crowded hot tub. But then a couple of girls on the opposite end said they were just about to go inside and kindly offered up their spots.

"Thank you," Nora said, giving them a quick smile.

While we waited for the girls to climb out, Ky looked over at everyone and asked, "You guys want to play 'Never Have I Ever'?"

"Sure," Bash said.

"Yeah, that sounds fun," Alessi chimed in.

"You gonna get us something to drink? " Miles asked, shifting in the water. "Because once I get out of this hot tub, I'm not getting back in."

"Of course," Ky replied, looking at Nora and Lucy. "We're still dry. You two willing to help me get everyone's drinks?"

"Sure," Nora and Lucy said together.

"Probably just water for everyone at this point, right?" Ky glanced around at the group, who all nodded in agreement. It was getting late, and no one wanted to start the New Year with a hangover.

So with that, off they went to grab the cups.

By the time they got back, the other girls had exited the hot tub, and there was enough space for the seven of us left to get comfortable.

"Here's your cup," Lucy said, stepping up to the edge of the hot tub and handing me mine.

"Thanks," I said, taking it from her. Then, noticing she still needed to take off her robe before getting in with her water, I asked, "Want me to hold your drink while you climb in?"

"That would be great, thanks."

I took her cup in my other hand, trying not to stare as she took off her robe to reveal a bright pink bikini.

But even though I was trying to be a gentleman, I couldn't help but notice that the girl was ripped.

Dang. How did she get muscle definition like that? Did she lift weights for work? Was she a fitness instructor? Because abs like hers didn't just appear out of nowhere. She had to work out *a lot.*

When Nora climbed into the hot tub, I glanced at her, and to my surprise, she was just as toned.

Did they work out together, then? Maybe that was how they spent their free time.

Some people worked out for fun, I guess. I mean, just because I had to use lots of mind games to get myself to the university's weight room these days didn't mean it was the same for everyone.

"You can sit next to me if you want," Miles said to Nora as she was about to take the seat next to Alessi. "Bash was just saying he wanted the moon to his back for this game, so he's going to take the spot next to Alessi if you don't mind."

Had Bash actually said that? No, but it seemed like Miles

was actually trying to play matchmaker, setting Bash up next to the ex-girlfriend he'd been flirting with all night.

It was either that or Miles had decided to kiss Nora at midnight and needed her in the prime location for that to happen. I mean, with less than thirty minutes to go, the seating arrangements were pretty important if we were going to continue Ian's New Year's Eve challenge.

"Works for me," Nora said with a shrug, like it didn't matter where she sat before settling into the water beside Miles.

"And hey, Owen," Miles said glancing at me next. "If you scoot over just one seat, there'll be room for Lucy next to Nora. I know how inseparable these two are."

"Oh sure," I said, moving one seat to my right. "No problem."

And when Lucy slid into the now empty spot between Nora and me, I made a mental note to thank Miles later for helping us get the seating arrangements right.

Now all that was left was for me to figure out if Lucy was even single before making a move.

5

———

OWEN

"HERE'S YOUR DRINK," I said, handing Lucy her cup once she was settled in her seat.

"Thanks." She took it from me, our eyes briefly locking. And wow, she had really pretty eyes. Dark blue—at least out here with only the hot tub lights and the full moon above to light the night sky.

"Is it comfortable sitting like that?" I asked when I noticed she was actually sitting on her knees instead of her butt.

"It's all right," she said, glancing at me with a smile. "Kind of necessary when you're short and don't feel like sitting with your face in the water."

"I guess that's probably right," I said, chuckling lightly. "How tall are you?"

"Five-one."

"Nice," I said. A tiny but mighty little thing.

"You?"

"Just over six feet," I said. Then gesturing to the other guys in the hot tub, I added, "Basically a midget when I stand next to these guys."

"Six feet is not short at all." She giggled lightly. "But I get how you feel. When I'm with my gymnastics friends, I feel normal. But put me at a party like this and I feel like a little kid."

"You have a lot of gymnastics friends?" I raised my eyebrows, intrigued and suddenly understanding where that muscle tone must have come from. "Does that mean you're a gymnast?"

"Been doing it since I was three."

"You any good?"

"I'm all right." She chuckled. "At least I should be after doing it for most of my life."

"Dang," I said, impressed. "I'm guessing you did it competitively, then? Not just as a hobby?"

"You could say that."

"Did you do it in college?"

"Yeah..." She seemed to think for a moment before adding, "All four years."

"That must've been intense," I said. "Balancing school with training that hard all year."

"It was." She hesitated, like she was considering whether to say more, then shrugged and left it at that.

"Did you go to Eden Falls University?" I asked, wondering if she'd been there at the same time I'd been getting my PhD. Maybe we'd crossed paths before?

"I did..."

She probably knew Theo's sister then, since from what he'd told me before, it sounded like he had a sister who was on the team. Which could explain why she and Theo had been chatting at the club.

"Okay, guys," Ky shouted as he approached the hot tub with the last two drinks in his hands, his voice cutting through the conversation. "Who wants to start us off?"

"Start with the Never Have I Ever questions?" Nora asked, a playful grin already pulling at her lips.

"Yep," Ky said, stepping over the edge of the hot tub and sliding in between Miles and Alessi. "Everyone knows how to play, right?"

"One of us says something we've never done, and anyone who has done it takes a sip of their drink, right?" Bash clarified, looking around to make sure everyone was on the same page.

"Exactly," Ky said, his eyes gleaming with mischief.

"I'll start then," Bash said, his voice rising with confidence. He scanned the group, raising an eyebrow. "Never have I ever flirted with someone just to get a free drink."

"Oh, come on, Bash," Alessi groaned. "You know pretty much every woman has done that."

And true enough, Alessi, Lucy, and Nora all took a sip of their drinks. And then—not too surprisingly—Miles did too.

Everyone turned to look at him, waiting for an explanation. He shrugged casually, a slight smirk playing at the corner of his lips. "Alessi dared me to test a theory about her mom's cougar friend having a thing for me."

"And did she buy you a drink?" Ky asked, amused.

"Oh yeah," Miles said, his chest puffing out a little with pride. "Tried to take me home, too, but I told her I had an early football practice in the morning."

"She was devastated," Alessi explained. "Completely heartbroken."

"Only for a minute." Miles chuckled, waving the thought away. "Since one of my college teammates saw me leave the desperate housewife, and well...I think they're actually still together."

"Nice!" Ky laughed. Then he took his turn, saying, "Never have I ever gone skydiving."

To which only Bash took a drink for.

Miles was next to Ky, so he took his turn, saying, "Never have I ever shoplifted."

Which immediately made my muscles tense because yeah, I had to take a sip for that one.

"What?" Alessi's jaw dropped when she saw me taking my drink. "You're like the last person out of this group who I'd think would do that."

"I was quite the rebel when I was three." I chuckled awkwardly, feeling my face heat as I peeked to see Lucy looking at me with curious eyes. "Ran out of the grocery store with some yellow squash."

"Wait, really?" Ky asked, pulling his head back. "Did you, like, really love squash or something?"

"I don't think so," I said, holding my hands up. "Pretty sure I was just bored while my mom was shopping and thought they looked interesting. But don't worry, my mom caught me and made me give them back."

"So it wasn't even a successful mission," Ky said.

"I guess not," I said. "I guess it's good I never decided to go into a life of crime."

Not that I'd ever want to. Having one family member spending the last decade in prison was more than enough for my family.

"Anyone else successfully shoplift?" Miles asked, looking around the group.

"I stole lip gloss from the supermarket once," Lucy said, raising her hand. "But unlike Owen here, I never got caught."

"Oooh, such a rebel!" Nora chuckled, nudging her friend with her elbow.

"You know it," Lucy said before taking a sip of her drink. "But yeah, I did feel guilty enough about it that last year when I was doing self-checkout at the store, I scanned another lip gloss that I was buying two times instead of one so I could kind of pay back for the one I'd stolen."

Well, that was actually really sweet. Told me a lot about her character.

"Okay, it's your turn, Nora," Ky said when no one else fessed up to any shoplifting.

"Hmm..." Nora thought for a moment, tapping her chin.

"Done too many things, Nora?" Miles asked, a flirtatious tone in his voice. "Having a hard time thinking of anything you haven't done?"

"Har har," she said, rolling her eyes at him. Though from the way she blushed, I couldn't help but think she might actually like his teasing—*like pretty much every girl who talked to Miles.*

After a few more seconds, Nora said, "Never have I ever broken a bone."

Pretty much everyone took a sip for that one.

"How is that even possible with you being a gymnast?" Alessi asked. "Aren't regular injuries a part of the deal?"

"Oh, I've definitely sprained my ankle and torn muscles before," Nora said. "But no broken bones."

"Knock on wood," Lucy said. "You still have this coming season to get through."

Nora must still be in college if she still had a competition season coming up.

Which I guess would be a reason why the girls were hanging out with the college hockey team on Sunday...that was, if Lucy wasn't dating the hockey player who had started the fight.

Lucy had said she was done with college, right? So maybe she was a year older than Nora. So that would probably make Lucy around twenty-two or twenty-three.

Possibly six years younger than me.

Which was...quite a bit of an age gap.

Though, since I'd marked my dating range as five years younger than me on the Meet Your Match app, one year younger than that wasn't too bad.

Not that I was thinking about dating her. I didn't really know her.

"Oh right," Nora said, her eyes going wide as she looked behind her for some wood to knock on. There was a beam not too far behind the corner of the hot tub that Ky was in, so she quickly got up from her spot and bent over the edge to knock on it.

While she did that, I asked Lucy, "Did you have many injuries during your gymnastics career?"

"Oh yeah," she said easily. "I've torn my calf, shattered my toe, broke my arm once..."

"Not to mention the bruised ribs you had last spring," Nora added, plopping back down beside her.

"Oh yeah." Lucy laughed. "Gymnastics is fun," she said lightly—though her tone caught for a fraction of a second, a flicker of shadow passing behind her smile.

"Yikes," I said.

"What bones have you broken?" she asked.

"Just my arm," I offered. "Crashed my bike when I was a kid."

"Okay, Lucy, it's your turn," Ky interrupted our conversation when Nora had taken her seat again.

"Okay. Just a sec." She bit her lip for a moment, like she was trying to think of just the right thing to say. Then, with a mischievous look in her eyes, she glanced briefly at Nora before saying, "Never have I ever kissed someone to make someone else jealous."

"Oh geez, I wonder why you picked that one," Nora said

before making a face and throwing her head back to take a sip of her drink.

"Sorry." Lucy laughed. "All the other things coming to mind were too boring."

"It's okay, Nora," Miles said, nudging her with his elbow. "Alessi has done it, too." He shot Alessi a teasing look across the hot tub.

Alessi held up her cup and said, "Well, let's cheers to that then, sweet stepbrother, because we both know you love playing those jealousy games as much as I do."

"You got that right." He chuckled and they both took their sips at the same time.

Which was not surprising at all. Those two were always tangled up in one mess or another when it came to relationships.

It was my turn next, and I must have had Bash's midnight-kiss challenge in my mind mixing with my curiosity about Lucy's relationship status, because before I could think better of it, I was saying, "Never have I ever kissed someone who wasn't single."

A collective gasp sounded in the group. I must have hit a nerve because I caught a few members of the group glancing around like they were curious if anyone had kissed someone who was in a relationship with someone else...

And after a few strained seconds, Miles shook his head and said, "Fine. You got me."

"What?" Bash asked. "When was this?"

"In college. Just a girl I was hung up on." Miles shrugged. "But don't worry, karma kicked in real quick. Just when I was thinking she might be feeling the same thing as me, she pushed me away and told me it could never happen again. And then stopped hanging out with me for a couple of months."

"Dang," Bash said. And then, not so discreetly, took a sip of his own drink as well.

"Wait," Alessi asked, her jaw dropping. "You too?"

"It was in high school," Bash said. "And to be fair, I didn't know she had a boyfriend until after he punched me in the face."

Alessi chuckled. "Well, I guess that's okay. But Miles..." She tsked. "You should have known better."

He rolled his eyes and said, "Oh believe me, I know." It looked like he wanted to say more but seemed to have second thoughts. Instead, he skipped Alessi, Bash, and Ky's turns and said, "Never have I ever had a one-night stand." Then glancing across from him, he added under his breath, "Despite what the tabloids have been saying."

Miles had taken some heat from the entertainment news reel this past June when he'd been visiting Alessi on Ky's European tour in Vienna, only to be spotted going into a hotel with a mysterious blonde. No one had gotten a look at the girl's face, and he'd never addressed the rumors, so the chatter had died down a few weeks later.

But this past month, it all came up again when a girl on social media, looking for a minute in the spotlight, told her followers in a live video that she was the girl he'd been spotted with in June and claimed that they'd hooked up that night, stating: *Miles Hawthorne is just as impressive off the field as he is on.*

Yeah...I did not envy my friends who had to deal with the drama that came from their fame. *No, thank you.* Living a quiet life as a chemistry professor and weekend bartender was definitely more my speed.

But, at Miles's statement, curiosity rippled through the group as everyone wondered if anyone among us had their own one-night stands to confess.

And when everyone looked at Ky, expecting him to take a drink, given the number of groupies he had, he just held his hands up, saying, "Hey, believe it or not, I've been a good boy."

"That's impressive," I said, holding my cup toward Ky to cheer him.

"Why, thank you," Ky said, giving a little bow.

"Well, look at us," Bash said, a proud, fatherly smile on his face. "Just a bunch of wholesome folks."

"Only because Ian's not here." I chuckled, thinking of my best friend as I shot a glance around the hot tub, the steamy water swirling around us.

"But look at him now," Alessi said. "Apparently, even our favorite billionaire playboy can change his ways for the right girl."

"To Ian," I said, holding my cup for another toast.

"Yes," Bash said. "May we all be as lucky as him one day."

We all clinked our cups together, taking a drink in his honor.

It was a little strange not having him here tonight. Ian and I had been inseparable since we were kids, running wild through the neighborhood together. But now, with him engaged to Maddie and stepping into fatherhood with her nine-year-old son, I couldn't shake the feeling of being left behind.

He had exactly what I wanted: a beautiful woman to share his life with and an instant family.

And as much as Ian and his parents had included me in all their family gatherings after my own had fallen apart, it still wasn't the same as actually being part of a real family.

I still had my younger brother, Asher. But he was living in New York with his wife, and that didn't leave much room for the family moments I craved.

So with Ian all domesticated and spending most of his free

time with his future family, just having a girlfriend to share my weekends with would feel like hitting the jackpot.

We kept the game going, everyone shouting out their "Never Have I Evers" in a rush rather than taking turns.

When it was Lucy's turn, she scanned the group before saying, "Never have I ever had a secret crush on a friend's sibling."

Was she trying to play detective, seeing if any of us guys had ever secretly crushed on Nora? I knew Miles had been flirting with her all night, but I didn't think that counted as a crush.

But instead of any of the guys taking a sip, it was Nora who glared at Lucy before taking a drink of her own.

"I knew it," Lucy said, laughing.

Nora shot her a look. "You keep targeting me with your Never Have I Evers, and I might have to reconsider your best-friend status."

"Because you want to be my sister instead?" Lucy said, the cutest guilty smile lighting up her whole face.

"Ugh, you're the worst, you know that?" Nora covered her eyes with her hands, smiling despite herself.

"The worst and the best." Lucy chuckled, not looking sorry at all for revealing one of her friend's secrets.

"Whatever." Nora rolled her eyes. Then looking at everyone else in the hot tub, she held out a finger and said, "And none of you better tell her brother about this, okay? I just think he's cute and a good guy. Not anything serious."

"Who's your brother?" I leaned closer to Lucy since apparently, I was the only person here who didn't know. "Anyone I know?"

"Oh, it's Th—" Lucy started to say before Nora clamped her hand over Lucy's mouth, stopping her.

But before Lucy could break away from Nora's grip, Bash interrupted the temporary chaos by loudly asking, "Do stepsiblings count?" while looking between Miles and Alessi.

"Of course." Miles smirked, looking unfazed. "So you better drink up, buddy."

"The crush was in the past..." Bash turned to Alessi, his expression suddenly more serious. But with a hopeful look, he quickly added, "Unless you want it to be in the present, too?"

Alessi chuckled, shaking her head. "I guess we'll see where the night takes us, won't we?"

"I guess we will." Bash took a sip with a wink, clearly hoping his plans for a midnight kiss with his ex were still on track.

"Speaking of crushes," Nora said, bringing everyone's attention away from Bash and Alessi and the possibility of them reigniting their spark tonight. "Never have I ever had a crush on someone I know I shouldn't."

The group went immediately silent, only the steady hum of the hot tub's bubbling jets filling the air. And as I scanned the faces of my friends, there was a sudden heaviness on many of them.

Everyone was single, as far as I knew—my question over Lucy's status with the hockey player aside. But were there some forbidden crushes alive and well among us?

I remembered the short fling I'd had with Sloan, a colleague from when I'd been teaching at the boarding school before I got my job at the university. We'd done our best to keep it under wraps, sneaking around so the staff and students wouldn't discover our relationship.

But while the sneaking around had made it *feel* forbidden, looking back, it probably hadn't been that forbidden at all, as there were no rules against teachers dating each other.

And since I couldn't think of any other forbidden crushes, I just sat back, waiting to see if anyone else would fess up.

Did Lucy have any forbidden crushes?

But when I looked at her, she seemed to be watching everyone with the same curiosity I felt.

Then finally, after a long, heavy sigh, Ky took a sip.

"It's that girl Rachel, right?" Nora asked, looking at him knowingly.

"Yep," Ky said, emphasizing the "p" sound at the end like he wasn't interested in discussing it further.

Then, at the edges of my vision, I noticed Alessi and Miles both take a sip, their expressions suddenly solemn.

What?

I glanced at Miles, expecting him to make a joke like the ones he'd been making all night. But there was no humor in his dark eyes now.

Who had been his forbidden crush? Was it the girl he'd mentioned kissing earlier? The one who had a boyfriend?

Because that would fit this question.

But that happened in college, and he graduated four years ago. So if he was acting like this right now, this forbidden crush of his had to be more recent than that, right?

"Well, that got heavy real quick..." Ky muttered, glancing at Nora. "So thanks for that, sis."

"You're welcome," Nora said, seeming to feel a bit awkward for asking a question that probably turned out way more serious than she'd expected.

"Anyway," Ky said, making a smile lift his lips after whatever memories he'd just been reliving. "Speaking of sisters, I think it's about time I admitted that *never have I ever* chewed all the fingers off my baby dolls when I was younger."

"Are you serious?" Nora gasped, her jaw dropping as she glared at her brother.

"Pretty sure I am," Ky said with a playful smirk, clearly enjoying the sudden discomfort he'd caused.

"Okay," Nora said with a shrug. "But just remember that two can play this game, bro."

"It's all in good fun, right?" Ky laughed, unbothered.

"Whatever you say," she muttered, shaking her head before taking a sip of her drink.

Then, not missing a beat, Nora said, "Okay, I've got one," her eyes gleaming with mischief. "Never have I ever painted my bedroom walls with poop."

Lucy gasped, half-laughing, half-horrified. "Man, I would hope not."

"That's a very specific thing to say," I teased.

Nora smirked, her eyes locking in on Ky. "I think you forgot to take a drink."

Ky looked at her, narrowing his eyes, but he complied, taking a sip and muttering, "Not cool."

"I mean," Nora said, "I could always tell them about the time I walked in your room one night and found you—"

"Okay, okay, we'll call a truce," Ky cut her off quickly, hands raised in surrender. "And in case you're wondering, I was two and got very creative during naptime, all right? I promise it hasn't happened since then."

I couldn't help but smile at the playful exchange. Gotta love it when siblings hang out in the same friend group.

Is this what it would have been like if Callie, Asher, and I had gotten to hang out as adults? Would we have enjoyed spilling each other's secrets all for everyone's entertainment?

A sharp pang of grief hit my chest. How old would Callie be today?

She'd been just twelve when she died, so...twenty-two? Almost twenty-three?

Close to Nora and Lucy's age. Probably just finishing up college or getting her first real job.

"So..." Nora turned to look at her brother, raising a sculpted eyebrow. "Maybe we'll let some of our sibling secrets stay secret?"

"I guess." Ky rolled his eyes. "For now..."

6

———

LUCY

"YOU GUYS still want to keep playing out here or should we head back inside?" Ky asked after we'd been in the hot tub for about twenty-five minutes, playing the game. "It's getting pretty close to midnight."

"I'm good to stay out here a little longer," Miles said, glancing at his watch. "I'll need to head back to Ian's place shortly after midnight if I want any sleep before my drive back to Eden Falls, but it'll be fun to ring in the New Year with all of you out here."

"Sounds good to me," Bash said, glancing at Alessi who I'd noticed him checking out all night.

From what I'd gathered, it sounded like Bash and Alessi had dated briefly a few years ago—back when they were both in college. And while I didn't have any boyfriends that I was interested in reigniting any sparks with, these two were actually really cute together.

"I'm good to stay out here for a while," Nora said from beside me. Then looking over at me, she asked, "What about you?"

And even though I was feeling waterlogged from sitting in the hot tub for so long, I knew I'd already teased her enough tonight that I might as well help her stay close to Miles's side so she could at least have a chance of that hot-tub-kiss dream of hers coming true.

Maybe Miles was into kissing at the strike of twelve?

Though, if Ky was out here when the New Year arrived, Miles might not be the type to kiss his good friend's little sister right in front of his face.

Maybe I should get out and make up an excuse for why I needed Ky to join me inside?

"Are you still warm enough to stay out here?" Owen asked from the other side of me, his deep voice close to my ear.

And man, his voice was sexy. Deep. Smooth. Exuding a quiet confidence that I was finding I really liked.

Much better than the loud, macho chauvinism I was used to from Josh and his friends.

"I'm not sure..." I said, chewing on my lip as I debated whether staying next to a man I was undeniably attracted to was too selfish when I could be helping out my friend by distracting her brother.

"Maybe just a few more 'Never Have I Evers'?" he suggested, arching a dark eyebrow.

And when he looked at me with those dark-brown eyes that seemed to look right into my soul, I couldn't bring myself to leave.

"I'll stay out for a few more," I said, my heart racing as his lips curved into a smile, the kind that sent a flutter of anticipation straight to my stomach.

What was I anticipating? I wasn't sure.

But...I wouldn't mind *something* happening out here. Maybe something like the fantasy I'd entertained while watching him wipe down the bar last week.

I tried to be subtle as I checked him out, sneaking glances at the tattoo on his arm I'd only partially seen before, hoping no one would notice all the lingering glances I'd been giving him during the game.

And what I'd assumed was a simple bicep tattoo turned out to be so much more—two eagles, inked in bold, sweeping strokes, locked in a wild, intricate dance near a solar eclipse. The wings of the birds stretched across the sculpted curve of his shoulder and disappeared just beneath his collarbone, like they were protecting something sacred—or fighting to reach it. Feathers scattered like shrapnel, as if they'd been through hell but kept going anyway.

It was fierce. And beautiful. And I had a feeling that with all that depth, it also had to be meaningful to him.

Like maybe it wasn't just a piece of art but a piece of him, or possibly a tribute to something he'd lost or was still chasing.

And yeah...it was hot.

His well-defined muscles didn't hurt his overall appeal, either.

"Okay..." Ky said, biting his bottom lip. His gaze flickered toward the kitchen window behind him, checking on his friends inside. "I guess—"

"If you need to go back in, that's fine," Miles said. "We know we're not your only friends here...even if we are the coolest ones."

"You sure?" Ky asked, glancing between us. "I feel bad..."

"It's fine," Bash said, waving Ky's anxiety away. "We'll be good." He glanced at Nora and me, and as if thinking Ky thought he needed to stay here for Nora's and my emotional support, Bash added, "We're all buds now, right?"

"You two good with these hooligans?" Ky asked, looking at Nora and me.

"Hey," Alessi said, not liking being lumped into the "hooligans" category.

Ky chuckled. "I wasn't talking about you, Alessi."

"Good," she said.

Then Nora shrugged and said, "Yeah, we're good, Ky. You don't need to worry about Lucy and me. We're big girls."

"Okay." He nodded. Seemingly appeased, he pulled himself out of the water and climbed out, saying, "If you guys can put the cover on before you head inside, that would be amazing."

"Will do," Owen told him. I was glad the guys were planning on doing it because I had to put the hot tub cover back on one time in the winter before, and I'd be okay never having to do that again. Bolting inside once I was out of the water was way better than shivering like crazy in the freezing temperature.

Speaking of the cold weather, I was actually surprised at how comfortable it was out here. It was probably close to ten degrees tonight, but with the hot water covering everything from my neck down, and the steam rising to warm my face and ears, it actually wasn't so bad.

Plus, these jets were also working wonders for my sore muscles. Coach Chambers had given us a killer workout this morning as her end-of-the-year gift to us, and by the time Nora and I had arrived at the beach house, I'd already been feeling it.

"Okay, it looks like we only have about five minutes until New Year's now," Bash said, checking his watch. "Should we keep playing our game, or just hang out?"

"I think it would be fun to keep playing," Miles said. Then glancing over at Alessi, he added, "I mean, when else will I get the chance to find out about more of my stepsister's secrets?"

"Because I have so many." Alessi rolled her eyes but seemed to smile despite herself.

"You've always been a mystery to me," Miles said.

And Ky must've heard us decide to keep playing because just before opening the back door to head inside, he called out, "Never have I ever wanted to kiss someone currently in the hot tub."

"Well, no pressure with that one, guys." Owen chuckled awkwardly as Ky disappeared inside, conveniently avoiding the truth bomb he'd just dropped on all of us.

I watched as everyone looked around at the group in the hot tub. And then, one by one, we all took a sip of our drinks.

Interesting.

Dare I hope the person Owen was interested in kissing was me?

"So, I'm guessing you either broke up with that guy at the bar, or he wasn't your boyfriend to begin with?" Owen's voice dropped low against my ear after he set his cup back on the hot tub's ledge.

I gulped, a chill racing down my neck and spine from the sudden nearness of him. "We broke up last spring."

"Good to know." Owen's voice was steady, but when his shoulder brushed against mine in the water, my stomach swirled with a delicious heat that spread throughout my entire body.

And just that one touch made me hungry for more. I'd been careful so far not to let any part of me cross the invisible barrier between us, but maybe I shouldn't be so cautious? Maybe a few more brushes against his skin wouldn't be so bad.

I certainly wouldn't mind some physical touch from such a beautiful man, especially after so many months of barely any of it.

We did two more rounds of "Never Have I Ever," but with every passing second, as snow gently started falling all around us, something seemed to shift in the air—an electricity that made everything feel more charged.

"It's almost time, guys!" Miles said after glancing at his phone that he'd left along the edge of the hot tub. "Eleven fifty-nine p.m."

He quickly pulled the countdown clock up on his screen, setting it where we could all see it.

The seconds started ticking by, and with each second that got us closer to midnight, my heart seemed to race a little faster.

I shifted, trying to make myself comfortable, but my mind was racing. I had no idea what these guys usually did at their New Year's parties, but I was pretty sure it was customary to kiss someone at midnight, right?

And with everyone here being open to kissing *someone* in the hot tub, it seemed like the perfect opportunity to make that happen...

You know...as long as the person each of us was interested in kissing matched up with who they wanted to kiss, too.

I glanced over at Owen, watching him closely for a moment. His eyes were focused on the countdown clock, but there was something about the way he held himself, like he was feeling the same tension I was. Was he thinking about kissing someone? And could that someone possibly be me?

As the seconds ticked down, anticipation buzzed in my veins, my breathing becoming more shallow, as if the air was getting thicker.

I glanced at Owen again, and this time, when I did, his gaze flicked to mine, his eyes holding a question. That simple look only made my anticipation grow. *What's going to happen next?*

I bit down on my bottom lip, almost able to feel what those pouty lips of his would feel like if they grazed against mine. I'd never kissed a guy with lips like his before. They looked so soft, so inviting, and I was sure they could do all kinds of marvelous things to me.

His jaw was slightly clenched, his body still, but there was something in the way he watched the countdown that told me he was just as uncertain as I was.

Time kept moving, however, and before I knew it, the countdown was almost over.

"Ten...nine...eight..." Miles's voice broke into my thoughts, pulling me back to the moment. My heart pounded in my chest, and each second seemed to make the knots in my stomach tighten more.

"Seven...six...five..." I could feel my pulse racing with every number. "Four...three...two...one..."

And then, as we all shouted, "Happy New Year!" in unison, it felt like the world held its breath.

Bash was the first to kiss Alessi, followed quickly by Miles who turned to kiss Nora.

"Should we...?" Owen's quiet voice sounded close to me. He nodded toward the others, indicating that he was asking if I wanted to follow suit.

So I nodded, saying a breathy, "Yeah."

He leaned closer, his hand gently cupping my chin as he tilted my face up toward his. His lips brushed against mine in the next moment, soft, slow, and lingering as an instant crackle of electricity charged the moment.

And while his kiss was careful—the kind of kiss you'd expect from someone you just met—it also sparked a warm, delicious heat deep in my core that I hadn't felt in way too long.

When he pulled away a moment later—much too soon if I was honest—it was almost in slow motion, like he wanted to linger or come back for more.

His gaze flicked from my lips to my eyes as he held my gaze, something unspoken passing between us as I tried to steady my breath.

Holy heck, was it suddenly hard to breathe? Was the chlorine in the water finally getting to me?

More like the hottie in the water is stealing your breath with his kisses.

But man, if I didn't want to try that again... Kiss until I was drowning in him.

But before I could figure out a way to pull him back in for more, the sound of giddy laughter launched me back to reality.

Everyone around us started talking then, and the moment slipped away.

"Well, that was fun," Alessi's voice broke the spell. "But I think I'm ready to get out."

"Yeah, me too," Miles said. "Early morning and all."

And when they stood to leave, Bash followed along as well.

"You wanna head inside, too?" Nora asked me as everyone grabbed their towels and rushed inside.

I glanced over at Owen, noticing that he hadn't followed after his friends.

Was he planning to stay out here for a bit?

Because if he was, I was definitely not going anywhere yet.

"I was thinking I'd stay out here a bit longer," I said. "It just started snowing, and I've always wanted to sit in a hot tub in the snow."

Nora smiled at me, a knowing look in her eyes as she briefly glanced at Owen. "Okay, well, I'll head inside and take a shower then, so it'll be available when you come in."

"Thanks."

"Mind if I hang out here for a bit, too?" Owen asked as Nora stepped out of the water and pulled her robe around her.

"That would actually be nice," I said, a little thrill running through me at the thought of staying out here with him alone.

7

LUCY

"SO, how many days are you and Nora staying here?" Owen asked, his voice low and warm as we settled into the silence that followed everyone else heading inside.

"We're going back to Eden Falls on Sunday," I said, adjusting my position slightly to face him better. The snow was still falling in lazy flakes around us, like something out of a movie, but with the hot water gently bubbling around us, I didn't feel the cold.

"Nice," he said. "You get to soak up the whole weekend."

"What about you?" I asked. "Are you here the whole time, too?"

Because that would be...nice.

But he shook his head. "Just tonight. I'll probably sleep in a little tomorrow, but I need to get back to Eden Falls for my shift at The Garden tomorrow night."

"Your boss didn't give you New Year's Day off?" I asked, trying to mask my sudden disappointment. "Doesn't he know you have cool people to hang out with?"

"He actually does..." He chuckled—a low, throaty sound

that made my stomach flutter. "Since I am said boss—a manager, anyway. I set the schedule, but because I got tonight off, I figured I should let someone else have tomorrow night off with their family."

"That's actually really considerate," I said, liking that he seemed to care about his staff...but also kind of wishing he'd been a bit more selfish since it would have been fun to hang out with him tomorrow.

"Yeah. Though, if I'd known about *all* of the cool people Ky had invited here this weekend, I might have been inclined to be a little more selfish." He winked.

I blinked, a little startled that he'd just said exactly what I'd been thinking seconds ago. And then my heart fluttered in my chest because...he was hinting that he wanted to hang out with me more, right?

"Next time we'll have to ask Ky for his guest list," I said. "But it sounds like you help run The Garden then?"

"Yeah." He nodded. "I took on a lot of the responsibilities a couple years ago, when the owner had to step away for some family stuff."

Okay. So, he wasn't just hot and grounded, he was also responsible. The dangerous trifecta.

We lapsed into a brief silence, the kind that teetered between comfortable and uncertain. I didn't want him to get bored and head inside, so I searched for something—anything—to keep the conversation going. Then I glanced at him and said, "Oh, hey, I never asked. Did the pineapple punch end up being the fun kind?"

"It was definitely the fun kind." He grinned, amused.

"How many cups did you have?" I narrowed my eyes, wondering if he was drunker than he seemed and just better at hiding it than Josh had ever been.

"Just the one." He leaned back, resting one arm along the

ledge behind me. "Got a good buzz, but it's gone now." Then he asked, "And how did your mojito treat you?"

"It was perfect." I smiled. "Just enough to warm me up and make me giggly, but it wore off during the games. Which was just what I wanted since I don't like getting drunk"

"Me neither," he said.

"So you're more of the drug-dealing type than a druggie."

His brows knitted together. "What now?"

And I realized that that comparison probably sounded really bad since he hadn't been able to read my thoughts. So I rushed to say, "You know how people say you can either be a drug dealer or a druggie. But if you try mixing the two, you just end up really poor and high..."

"Yeah..."

"So since you're a bartender, you're just dealing alcohol instead of drugs."

Okay...that definitely sounded better in my head.

"Right..." But he thankfully seemed to understand my nonsensical logic because he added, "I'm a responsible supplier of questionable decisions."

"Exactly." I smiled, liking the way he'd worded it since I wouldn't mind making a few questionable decisions with him right now.

We fell into a brief silence as the snowfall thickened, swirling through the air like confetti from the sky. I lifted my arms from the warmth of the water to catch a few drifting flakes, but the sting of the cold made me laugh and draw back quickly and settle farther down into the warm water.

"Cold out there?" he asked, a glint of amusement sparking in his eyes.

"Freezing," I said, rubbing my arms. "And I just realized, with Miles and Bash already inside, I'm now morally obligated to help you put the hot tub cover back on."

"Oof." He winced. "Don't remind me about that part."

"Yeah, I think I'm gonna be regretting my decisions when I finally climb out."

"Better just stay here all night then, right?" He glanced at me.

"A little longer, at least."

We shared a quiet smile. Then he said, "Can I ask you something?"

"Sure," I said, my pulse jumping.

"When Nora asked if I'd give you my number at the bar...was that just her trying to make you feel uncomfortable? Or...was there some other reason behind it?"

My cheeks warmed despite the cold. "She might've been trying to help me out."

A slow smile curved across his face, his eyes crinkling at the corners—and wow. He was unfairly attractive when he smiled like that. Honestly, there should be laws about looking that good in a hot tub.

Not that I was complaining. Having Owen's full attention on me, even for just a few minutes, was definitely not something I minded.

"So," he said, tilting his head, "is it fair to guess that the person you were thinking about kissing in the hot tub...was me?"

"You're really putting me on the spot here, aren't you?" I gave him a mock scowl.

He chuckled. "Just wanted to make sure I didn't make an unwanted advance earlier."

"No," I said softly. "It was definitely not unwanted."

"So...it was me?"

I hesitated, then bit my lip to keep from grinning too hard.

"I'll take that as a yes," he said, his eyes gleaming. "And just so you know...you were the one I was thinking about, too."

"Good to know." A soft laugh escaped me.

He leaned in, just a little, and the space between us grew even more electric. "You know," he murmured, "you look really cute when you're trying not to smile."

I paused, letting the compliment settle in my chest. Then, after a beat, I tilted my head and took a chance, whispering, "And you've got a dangerously good jawline for someone trying to distract me."

His smile softened, fading just enough to let something darker flicker through his expression as his eyes dropped to my mouth.

"Well," he said, his voice lower now, "when you say things like that...it makes me think I might just have to kiss you again."

My heart stuttered. But I tried to play it cool, even as heat bloomed up my neck.

"I think I might be okay with that," I murmured, my voice feathering into the steam between us.

The grin that spread across his lips then was slow. Confident. *Devastating.*

He leaned in, brushing a strand of damp hair from my cheek before his fingers skimmed down, cradling my jaw. And when his lips met mine, it was soft—testing—like a secret passed between us. I exhaled against his mouth, chasing the kiss before it could slip away.

He deepened it instantly, the hand at my jaw tilting my face toward him as his other hand slid around my waist, pulling me closer. The water sloshed gently between us, but I barely noticed.

And man, the way he kissed... It was both exhilarating and grounding at the same time. Like he'd been waiting all night to do this, and he wasn't in any hurry to stop.

I slid my hands up his shoulders and around his neck, anchoring myself as his lips coaxed mine open, his tongue brushing against mine with the kind of slow, confident ease that made my stomach drop—like the split-second free-fall before sticking a blind landing off the balance beam.

And when he tugged on my hips gently, guiding me closer, I let him. He shifted both of us until I was straddling his lap with my knees, water rippling around us. And wow, if it didn't feel good to be that close to a man again... It had been ages.

My hands found his chest, solid and warm under the water, and as the kiss turned hotter—hungrier—I melted against him.

My hips tilted forward, instinctive and unintentional, and the quietest sound escaped the back of his throat.

Oops. Is that too close for someone you've only met twice?

But then his hands tightened at my waist, applying pressure to my lower back like he wanted to anchor me there.

And yeah...I didn't want to move.

This was so wild—probably insane.

I barely knew him.

But it felt *so* good.

And honestly? One of my New Year's resolutions had been to stop overthinking everything.

To live in the moment.

And there was no moment more alive than this—wrapped up in a sexy man's muscular arms with the snow falling around us and his mouth doing wicked things to mine.

Just as I was leaning in for more, lightning cracked overhead, lighting up the sky like a strobe light.

We both froze, lips parting, breath mingling in the steam.

Owen's eyes met mine, wide and a little dazed. Then he looked up at the sky. "We probably shouldn't be in the water during a lightning storm, huh?"

I let out a reluctant sigh, breathless and flushed. "You're probably right."

"Shame," he murmured, eyes dropping to my mouth again. "We were just getting to the good part."

"I know..." I whispered, his words fluttering through me like a spark before hitting low and hard, grounding me in heat and want.

Would it be too forward of me to suggest we continue this somewhere inside?

Because from the way he wasn't making any move to climb out, I got the feeling that he might just be okay continuing the moment—possibly even risk staying out here a bit longer. But then lightning flared again, closer this time, thunder cracking in its wake.

We groaned in unison, our limbs untangling with slow reluctance. The second we climbed out, the icy air slapped against my wet skin like a punishment.

"Oh my *gosh!*" I gasped, instantly shivering, my teeth chattering almost as fast as my heart was racing. "Putting the hot tub cover back on really is the ultimate mood killer."

Owen laughed, that deep, sexy chuckle that made my knees weak, even as I hopped from foot to foot. "Just hurry," he said, grabbing one end of the cover. "You've got muscles, we can do it fast."

"Fine," I grumbled with a dramatic eye roll but couldn't help laughing, too, as I grabbed my end. We slammed the cover into place in record time, then dashed toward the door, slipping and squealing like kids as our wet feet hit the icy deck.

I grabbed my robe from the chair I'd left it on and followed him inside, both of us breathless and laughing.

As we stepped into the warmth of the house, he paused just inside the door, water dripping down his chest, eyes still locked on mine.

"This was fun," he said, his smile softening in a way that made my heart flutter. "I hope I'll see you again soon."

I nodded, not trusting my voice just yet. "Me too."

8
____

OWEN

BASH and I pushed through the front door of Ky's beach house around ten thirty the next morning, the scent of cinnamon rolls hanging in the air. Laughter and clinking dishes echoed from the kitchen, warm and casual, like the afterglow of a really good party. But my nerves were anything but relaxed.

I hadn't slept much. My body was still humming with left-over adrenaline from last night—the games, the snow, that kiss. *Lucy.*

Dang, that kiss.

My mind replayed it more times than I cared to admit. The way she'd looked at me just before our lips met—eyes soft, curious, a little breathless. How she'd melted into me like her body already knew mine. The little sound she made when my hands slid around her waist and I pulled her in tight.

I'd been trying to tell myself, ever since waking up, that it had just been a fun moment. A midnight spark in a hot tub. Nothing more.

But moments like that didn't happen to me. Not like *that.*

Not in the last few years, at least.

And as much as I wanted to play it cool, act unfazed when I saw her again, the truth was I was wired. I wanted to know if she'd felt it, too. If she'd been lying in bed last night thinking about it the way I had.

If there was a chance that kiss wasn't the end of something...but the start.

Maybe we could talk before I left, sneak a walk on the beach or exchange numbers. Spring semester didn't start for another week, and for once, I actually had some free time.

So yeah, I was hopeful for the first time in a long time—probably way more than I should've been.

Bash and I stepped farther into the entryway, stomping snow from our boots and brushing it off our jackets. Just as I was about to call out and say hi, I heard voices from the kitchen.

Lucy and Nora and another girl—one of Ky's backup dancers?

"...and I saw you slumming it with the bartender in the hot tub last night," the backup dancer said, a teasing edge to her voice. "Your dad would absolutely freak if he knew you were kissing a guy like that. Like, come on, Lucy. He's cute, sure, but...he's a *bartender*."

I stopped mid-step, my body freezing as the words landed.

"I mean," the girl went on with a dramatic sigh, "that's, like, something you do to get through college. Not a forever job. He's, what—late twenties? That's just someone on the road to nowhere."

"You gonna correct them?" Bash's hand clapped onto my shoulder, a little too much sympathy in his eyes. "Let 'em know that *the bartender* has a PhD in chemistry?"

"Nah." I let out a low breath, staring down the hallway toward the kitchen. "If that's what they want to believe, let them."

I wasn't ashamed of bartending—honestly, I liked it. It gave me space to breathe, time to think, and more human interaction than any lab or lecture hall ever had. But standing here, hearing how inadequate I was in their eyes... Well, that stung.

"She's just one girl," Bash muttered, nudging me forward. "You can do better."

"Sure..." I said, though if he'd asked me how this "just a girl" had made me feel about eight hours ago, I would have said that who knows...maybe she could have been the one.

Crazier things had happened.

At least it had only been one night. Two kisses.

Better to find out how inadequate I was in these girls' minds now instead of weeks or months down the line.

Bash stepped into the kitchen first, and I followed right behind him. The second we crossed the threshold, all three girls turned toward us in unison.

And when they saw me, I knew the moment things clicked that their conversation had just been overheard because Nora's eyes widened. The backup dancer's face blanched. And Lucy, well—her cheeks were flushed pink, her hand flying up to her mouth.

"Oh my gosh," Lucy said, her voice thick with panic. "I didn't realize you were here. I'm so sorry you heard that."

"Heard that I'm beneath you?" I asked, keeping my tone neutral, my expression smooth. "Yeah...it's been noted."

Her blue eyes widened more. "No— I mean—" She fumbled for words, her voice rushing now. "I don't think that. I hope you know I don't think any less of you for being a bartender. It's honest work. And I'm sure you didn't fall into it because you're lazy or anything—"

She winced as the words left her mouth, clearly realizing she'd just said about four more insulting things than her friend had.

I gave her a tight, practiced smile—doing my best not to let anything show. "It's fine," I said, shrugging like it didn't matter. "Not everyone's on the same path. And bartending...it's a great way to meet people. I mean..." I looked right at Lucy, holding her gaze even though it felt like a slow twist in my gut. "That's how *we* met, right?"

"Right," she whispered.

I thought about making a joke. Playing the laid-back guy behind the bar. But I was suddenly off my game.

Hearing myself dismissed so easily by people who didn't really even know me just brought all my insecurities right back to the surface.

Sure, I was probably the most educated person in the room right now. But even with all my degrees and strong work ethic, they had somehow been able to sense that I was different.

Sure, I could be friends with famous singers who had huge beach houses. People whose problems were solved with phone calls and trust funds. I could go to their parties and play their games—sometimes even kiss the girl.

But I'd never actually *be* one of them.

"Hey, is Ky around?" I asked, tearing my gaze away from Lucy to look at Nora. "I wanted to thank him for the party before I head back home. Can't be late for my shift tonight."

"He's still sleeping," Nora said gently, clearly trying to ease the tension. "But I'll tell him you stopped by."

"Thanks."

I turned to Bash. "Should we head out?"

"Yeah," he said, shooting me a glance that said we'd debrief all this later.

I paused before walking out and looked at Lucy again. She still looked flustered, her mouth slightly open like she was trying to figure out what to say.

"I hope you guys enjoy your New Year's Day plans," I said.

Then I gave her a little smile. "And if you ever feel like slumming it again...I'm usually at The Garden on Saturday nights."

I didn't wait for her reply.

I just walked out.

I'd been hoping I wasn't the only one who'd felt that spark last night...but who knows, maybe I'd been wrong.

It certainly wouldn't be the first time.

9

———

LUCY

I SLID into an open seat near the back of the lecture hall in the university's science building, tugging my hoodie sleeves over my wrists as I pulled out my notebook. First day of spring semester. First class after my morning strength and conditioning workout. And it had to be chemistry—my sworn academic nemesis.

The room smelled faintly of dry-erase markers and old carpet. The giant whiteboard at the front had a few ghost-like equations from some other poor soul's chemistry class still half-visible. I stared at the blank page in my notebook, tapping the capped end of my pen against the corner.

Maybe this would be the year chemistry and I finally got along.

Unlikely.

I sighed and tucked a strand of hair behind my ear, glancing toward the door as another student walked in. Then another. Then—

My heart did a triple twisting double tuck in my chest.

Owen.

He was here. *In my chemistry class?*

Had he registered for classes after our conversation?

A smile burst across my face before I could stop it, and I lifted my hand in a wave. He looked up, caught sight of me, and a range of emotions seemed to pass over him—first shock, then confusion, then something else—*dread?*—before he settled on a polite smile.

Which, yeah, I guess I shouldn't be too surprised that he wasn't excited to see me after the way we'd left things at Ky's house.

Stupid Nicole saying stupid things.

And stupid me for panicking and just saying even more stupid things.

"Hey," I said once he made it to my row, sliding into the seat beside me to make room for him. "What are you doing here? I mean, not that I'm not glad to see you. I am. Really glad. I just...I didn't realize you were in college, too."

"I figured you'd be surprised to see me here after our last conversation," he said, sitting down and setting his leather bag on the floor beside him.

"Were you already signed up before New Year's, or did something we said make you decide to enroll last-minute?"

"Definitely already signed up." He huffed out a small laugh.

Really? Why hadn't he just told us then?

"You should've said something," I said. "Put Nicole in her place. She's so judgmental. I promise I'm not actually that close with her—just met each other at one of Ky's parties last year. We definitely don't share the same brain or opinions."

"That's okay," he said. "I get it." Then his gaze slid to mine. "I didn't realize you were a student. I thought you said you graduated..."

"Umm...about that..." I said, biting my lip as I tried to figure out a way to explain my little lie of omission. "You see, I guess I figured you were probably quite a few years older than me and when you assumed I was done with college, I decided to just let it go since I'm...actually not too far off. I'm a senior. So it's just a few months away. And well...I guess since I was already having such a good time with you, I didn't want the age gap to make you feel weird about talking to me..."

"Oh, so you're a senior?" he asked, a hint of relief in his voice. "This class is usually packed with freshmen and sopho-mores, so for a second I was worried I'd—" He glanced around, like he was suddenly aware of how loud his words might be. "Well...you know."

"Oh—" I laughed, understanding why he'd think that. "Yeah, I'm almost twenty-two." Which at least was better than being eighteen if he was worried he'd completely robbed the cradle.

"You're only twenty-one?" He groaned, blinking his eyes shut briefly.

Okay...so maybe the age gap was still an issue.

Which, I'd guess, was understandable. He was close to Theo's age. Six or seven years was a lot...

"So...what's your major?" I asked, hoping a change of topic might keep him from looking like he was going to be sick. "Did you decide on one yet?"

"Well, since being a mixologist is kind of like mixing chemi-cals..." He tilted his head. "I figured I'd give chemistry a try."

"That's cool. And I really do think it's awesome you're giving college a try. It's never too late." I grinned, trying not to be too obvious about how much I liked hearing that he actually did have some goals for the future. I mean, being a bartender was fine...but a degree was always good to have in your back pocket. "Maybe we can get on the professor's good side and score some extra credit points. I'm not exactly a science whiz."

"Let me guess," he said, glancing at me sideways. "You waited until your last semester to take this class?"

"Guilty," I said, wincing. "I was hoping the requirement would magically get cancelled or something."

He chuckled. "Well, I heard it's Professor Park's first year teaching here, so maybe holding out for the right professor will pay off."

"Hopefully," I muttered. "Though, with my luck, he'll be a cranky old guy with a superiority complex who can't grasp the concept that some people need extra help to understand chemistry."

"I think he's used to working with students who've had a rough time with the subject." Owen gave a small nod, something in his expression unreadable. "He used to teach high school students at the academy before EFU hired him this fall."

My brows pulled together. "You must've really researched our professor when picking this class."

"I usually like to know what I'm getting into," he said, checking his watch. "Oh, looks like it's about time for class to start."

And instead of pulling out a notebook or something to get ready for class like I expected, he grabbed his bag and stood.

Was he going to sit somewhere else then?

So much for hoping we could still be friends after that stupid blunder on New Year's morning.

"I hope you enjoy the class," he said, straightening his button-down. And then he stepped back into the aisle and started walking down the stairs toward the front of the room.

Maybe he just likes sitting in the front row, I told myself, hoping his reason for moving seats had nothing to do with me.

But instead of sitting at another desk, or turning down another row, he walked all the way to the floor and set his bag on the desk.

Wait.

What?

I blinked, sitting up straighter in my chair, every nerve in my body going on high alert as he stepped up to the podium with a printed sheet of notes in his hand.

No... He couldn't be...

He turned, scanned the room, and then looked right at me, the faintest smile tugging at his lips.

"Good afternoon," he said, his voice clear and steady. "I'm Professor Park. Welcome to Intro to Chemistry."

My jaw hit the desk.

He was—

No.

No, no, no.

My stomach dropped straight through the floor as the full weight of what I'd said...what I'd assumed—*what we'd done*—came crashing down around me.

Professor Park.

Owen.

The guy I made out with in a hot tub at midnight.

The same guy I'd just patronizingly congratulated on signing up for classes because I'd assumed he was "just a bartender" who'd slacked off for most of his twenties.

Oh.

My.

Gosh.

I was going to die. Literally combust in my chair from embarrassment. There would be no surviving this semester.

Because I'd kissed my chemistry professor.

Twice.

And then completely burned all the bridges the next day.

10

———

LUCY

WHEN CLASS ENDED, I stayed frozen in my seat long after everyone else had packed up and left, my thoughts spiraling in a thousand directions. When I finally stood and walked toward the front of the room, it felt like I was wading through molasses. My legs were heavy, my stomach twisting.

Owen—or rather, Professor Park—was gathering his notes from the podium, his brow furrowed in concentration.

"Hey," I said, a tentative smile on my face.

"Hey." He looked up, his eyes wary when they met mine.

Ok, so maybe he felt as uncomfortable as I did.

"Um..." I said, suddenly second-guessing my decision to talk to him instead of simply fleeing the room when class ended. But since I was already here, I forced myself to continue. "I just wanted to say...I'm sorry. For earlier. I didn't mean to assume you were a student. I just—after last weekend..."

"It's okay," he interrupted before I could say exactly what had happened between us last weekend. "I should've said something when I walked in here and saw you. I just...wasn't sure how to handle it. I haven't exactly been in a situation like this before."

"Yeah." I gave a small nod. "Me neither."

I promise I don't go around kissing all of my professors.

He tucked a loose paper into his folder and straightened. "Anyway, I hope you enjoy the semester. And...it's probably best if we keep what happened on New Year's Eve between us."

"Of course," I said quickly, even as something tugged at my chest. A small, annoying pang of disappointment.

"And obviously," he added, his jaw tightening slightly, "that was a one-time thing."

"Obviously," I echoed, my voice softer than I meant it to be.

But even as I said it, my gaze betrayed me—drifting to his lips, memory sparking like a match as I remembered what it had felt like to be in his arms in that hot tub, snow falling around us, his capable mouth on mine.

Nope. *Don't go there, Lucy.*

That kiss may have felt amazing at the time, but now that I knew better, it would do me good to stop remembering all the little details—like how safe I'd felt with him. Or how soft his lips had been.

And there we go again...

I blinked hard, forcing myself to focus, just in time to hear him say, "I'm glad you agree. Because I could get fired if anyone found out I kissed a student."

"Right." My stomach twisted. "I—I'm sorry. If I'd known you were my professor, I never would've..." I trailed off, cringing.

"No, I get it." He held up a hand, his tone gentler than before. "You didn't know. Neither of us did. So I can't really blame you for...putting my career at risk."

I'd put his career in danger.

Was that how he saw me now? Just a girl out to seduce her professor?

The shame hit hard, blooming across my cheeks.

It wasn't like I'd been trying to get him in trouble. At the time, I'd truly believed he was just a bartender and a friend of Ky's.

Was it really that wrong that I'd believed someone as smart, grounded, and kind as he'd seemed that night could be interested in me?

Apparently, it was. And now Owen wouldn't be able to see me as anything else. The moment was tainted, and now that we knew better, I was simply a complication he had to manage.

Well, if he thought things were messy now, he might as well know the full story.

"Sorry you feel like I put your career at risk," I said quietly. "I guess we should just be grateful Theo wasn't at the party."

His brows drew together. "What does Theo have to do with this?"

"He's my older brother..." I said, bracing for his reaction. "So if he'd been there and saw us...and happened to let it slip to our dad..." I gave a small shrug. "We'd be in much bigger trouble."

His expression shifted, blinking slowly like he wasn't sure he'd heard me right. "Wait—Theo's your brother?"

I nodded, offering a small, sheepish smile. "That's why I was talking to him at The Garden."

Owen's mouth opened slightly, realization washing over him in slow, dawning horror. Then, like he was solving the second layer of the puzzle, his jaw dropped, and he went pale as a ghost.

"So that means..." he said slowly, looking like someone had just pulled the rug out from under him. "Your dad is...President Archibald?"

"Yep," I said, the word falling like a weight between us. "That's my dad."

He ran a hand through his raven hair, exhaling slowly. "Which would make you..."

"Lucy Archibald," I said with a wince, the name feeling heavier now, like a steel door slamming shut between us. "I'm the university president's daughter."

His eyes met mine, and I could see it all clicking into place—how we'd been even more doomed from the start.

My dad had always made it very clear to me growing up: appearances mattered. Image mattered. The Archibald name came with expectations.

Kissing a bartender was one thing.

Falling for my professor?

That was full-on reckless behavior.

Owen stepped back slightly, like he needed more air between us. "Well...that definitely complicates things."

"Just a little," I said, trying to inject some humor into my voice, but my laugh cracked down the middle.

We stood there for a moment, the silence between us no longer charged, just...defeated.

We hadn't known. But now we did. And there was no going back.

"I should go," I said, my voice quiet. "I have another class."

"Yeah," he murmured. "Me too."

As I turned to leave, I caught one last glance of him—tall, composed, a mix of guilt and something else flickering in his eyes. Regret?

Well, whatever it was, it didn't matter.

Because whatever we'd started in that hot tub?

Could *never* happen again.

11

OWEN

THE REST of the day passed in a blur. I showed up to my next class. I taught. I answered questions. I even managed to explain molar mass conversions without anyone suspecting I was barely functioning on autopilot. But through it all, Lucy's face kept flashing through my mind—ping-ponging between that sexy smile she'd given me in the hot tub, snowflakes clinging to her lashes, and the way she'd looked this morning, stunned and wide-eyed in the back row like I'd just slapped her.

Yeah. Things were totally fine. Definitely not unraveling.

By the time I left campus, my head was pounding. I walked home, hoping the cold January air would give me a reset.

It didn't.

I unlocked the front door to my apartment and dropped my bag by the couch, shrugging off my coat as my eyes landed on the familiar stretch of exposed brick. The place had an industrial loft vibe—metal piping along the ceiling, newly installed laminate floors, and a fuzzy charcoal rug I'd scored during a winter sale that did its best to warm the space.

The leather couch was my one indulgence when I moved

in—deep brown, structured, just broken-in enough to feel like home. A flat-screen TV hung above a sleek black console across the room, though it mostly served as decoration when school was in session.

I tossed my coat over the arm of the couch and sank down with a sigh. There were a hundred things I *should* be doing, like prepping next week's labs, replying to Dr. Callahan's email about the upcoming research seminar, and finalizing next month's schedule for The Garden. But instead of doing any of that, I pulled out my phone and opened the text thread I had going with Bash and Miles.

> Me: Hey, don't tell anyone about what happened between me and Lucy on New Year's Eve, okay? Just found out she's in one of my classes. I promise I didn't know she was a student. She made it sound like she was done with college.

> Me: Also, her dad is President Archibald. So if this gets out, I'm definitely fired.

It took all of twenty seconds before Miles responded.

> Miles: Yikes. I didn't realize. I probably should have since I knew Theo was her brother, but I was so distracted that night I didn't put it together.

> Bash: Same. Crap. I had no idea. But don't worry—my lips are sealed.

> Me: Thanks. Seriously.

I tossed my phone on the coffee table and let out a long breath. My apartment was quiet, except for the occasional hum of the old fridge. I stood there for a moment, debating whether I should stress-eat, go for a run, or just hurl myself face-first into my mattress.

Instead, I sat down and opened my laptop. If I was really going to panic about this, I might as well be informed while I did it.

I typed: **"What happens if a university professor kisses a student?"**

Dozens of results popped up. Policy summaries. Forum threads. A few academic scandal exposés that made me feel like I was about to throw up.

I clicked through one that looked semi-reputable. The words blurred a little at the edges of my vision, but I forced myself to read:

> *"While romantic relationships between professors and students are not illegal in most states, they are generally prohibited under university policy— especially when a direct power dynamic exists. Even consensual relationships may be grounds for disciplinary action or termination..."*

Yeah. That tracked.

> *Professors are expected to maintain ethical boundaries. In cases where the relationship began before the class, disclosure is critical...*

Okay...so maybe I wasn't *completely* doomed.

Though somehow, *"We kissed in a hot tub before either of us knew the truth"* didn't sound like the kind of explanation the administration would appreciate.

Especially not when the girl in question was the university president's daughter.

I'd only met President Archibald twice—once at the funeral for Theo's wife a year and a half ago, and again at an open house he and his wife hosted at the president's mansion this past fall.

Both encounters had been brief, but the man had left an impression. He was sharp. Controlled. Not someone you'd want to disappoint...or piss off.

And though I'd hated hearing it at the time, I suddenly understood exactly why that girl at the beach house had said Lucy's dad would freak if he knew she'd been "slumming it" with a bartender. Because let's face it—the Archibalds weren't exactly known for dating or marrying outside their social class.

They came from old money. *Carefully curated* old money.

And even though Theo had struck out on his own during law school—working as a house dad at Eden Falls Academy to earn free room and board—he still ended up marrying Alisha Vanderbilt. An heiress from a family whose hotel empire had made them even more wealthy than the Hastings.

Yeah, suddenly everything I'd overheard on New Year's made sense.

"Rebellious Archibald Heiress Slums It with No-name Bartender During Wild Night Out." The exposé practically wrote itself. Just a reckless detour on Lucy's otherwise well-manicured path.

Something to try once before returning to the guys she was actually expected to end up with—ones who wore tailored suits, inherited legacies, and maybe had a drinking problem or two.

I leaned back in my chair and stared at the ceiling, letting the weight of it all settle. The job I'd busted my butt through grad school for? The career I'd just barely started to build? All of it could blow up if anyone found out what happened between us.

Sure, it was technically just a kiss. But I'd be lying if I said it hadn't meant something. If I said I hadn't let myself think, just for a second, that maybe Lucy could be more than just one night.

But that second was over now.

I closed my laptop, rested my head in my hands, and muttered to the empty apartment, "I'm so screwed."

12

LUCY

THE SHARP BOUNCE of my landing echoed through the gymnastics facility as I stumbled just barely out of bounds, my right foot slipping over the white tape line.

"Dang it," I muttered, hands on my hips as I tried to catch my breath. Most of the pass had been clean—solid even—but that stupid double layout was still giving me trouble. My feet felt just a little off every time, like my timing was a beat behind where it should be.

"You're getting closer," Nora called from across the floor, stretching her arms behind her back. "You've just got to trust the takeoff a little more. You're over-rotating on the second flip."

"Easier said than done," I grumbled, walking back toward her as I wiped sweat from my forehead with the back of my arm. "This routine was perfect in December. I don't know what my problem is this week."

"First home meet jitters?" she offered.

I shot her a look. "I don't get jitters."

"No?" She raised a brow. "Not even when your hot

professor turns out to be the guy you made out with in a hot tub?"

"Ugh." I groaned, flopping down onto a nearby mat. "Please don't remind me."

"Have you decided what you're gonna do about that, though?" Nora asked, sitting down beside me and pulling her knees to her chest. "Are you staying in Owen—uh, Professor Park's class?"

"I don't know..." I stared up at the high ceiling, the rafters crisscrossing like the tangled mess in my brain. "I've been going back and forth since yesterday. Trying to decide if it's going to be completely terrible trying to stay in his class."

"It has to be super awkward," Nora said.

"Understatement of the century," I said, shaking my head as I remembered my interaction with Ow—*Professor Park*—after class. "But I think I'll stop by the registration desk after this, just to see if there's another Intro to Chem section I can switch into. I doubt I'll be able to switch my lab with him, though, since it was already a miracle I managed to squeeze a three-hour block into my schedule with all my other required classes and practices."

"Oh yeah." Nora winced. "Lab times are the worst."

"Lucky for you, you were smart and took chemistry your freshman year."

"Truth."

If only I'd been so smart, then I wouldn't be in this predicament in the first place.

I sighed. "I just don't know how I'm supposed to pretend for an entire semester that I didn't memorize the exact sound he made when I was pressed up against him. Or act like he didn't look at me like I'd ruined his entire life when I told him who my dad was."

"Oh jeez," Nora said, her eyes going wide. "Exactly how far did you guys go in that hot tub? Because that sounds intense."

"We just made out," I hurried to say. "Nothing super crazy." I sighed again. "But yeah...it's probably better if I just find another class."

Nora nodded, but from the way she was watching me, I could tell she was waiting for another *but*.

Which, of course, the hopeless romantic in me *might* have been brainstorming ways we could still work.

You know, if he hadn't already slammed the door shut.

"And..." I exhaled, fully aware I was setting myself up for disappointment just thinking about it. "If there's even the tiniest chance that Owen's still remotely interested, then not being in his class would mean we wouldn't be breaking any rules if we *happened* to see each other at Theo's birthday party next month...and something happened again."

"Lucy," she scolded, though there was a twinkle of humor in her eyes. "Are you seriously already thinking about ways to get around this?"

"Maybe..." I said, my cheeks heating up. "I mean, it was a *really* good kiss."

"It must have been." She laughed. "If you're thinking up all this, he must be the best kisser in the world."

"Top five, at least," I said, laughing even though this situation wasn't really that funny. "And I know it's ridiculous and there's probably zero chance that he'll ever even talk to me again with how upset he seemed yesterday. But...I don't know. I guess I'm not quite ready to pretend it didn't mean anything just because it's suddenly inconvenient."

Was I being delusional? Probably.

But I'd already liked the bartender version of Owen before, so now that he was this super well-educated professor... That just made him even harder to resist.

Well...you know, if he could ever look at me like I wasn't trying to ruin his career, that is.

Before Nora could tell me I was completely off my rocker, Coach Chambers appeared behind us, arms crossed and a whistle around her neck.

"That double layout's not going to fix itself while you're off in dreamland, Archibald," she said, nodding toward the floor. "Run that last pass again. Make it clean this time, and you can call it a morning."

"Yes, Coach," I said, dragging myself to my feet.

I jogged back to the starting corner of the floor, took a deep breath, and sprinted forward, body coiling and springing into the air. The double layout came faster than I expected, and I twisted a little too much on the landing—but this time, I stuck it. Both feet even in bounds.

"Better." Coach nodded when I looked at her. "Watch your shoulder alignment, though. You're twisting your upper body too early on takeoff. Fix that, and you'll be golden."

"Got it," I said, my heart still racing as I stepped off the floor and made my way toward the locker room.

The registration office smelled faintly of printer ink and stress when I stepped up to the counter, gripping the strap of my backpack like it might help anchor me in this already rapidly spiraling semester.

"How can I help you?" a girl with a sleek ponytail and glasses asked when she noticed me.

"I was wondering if there are any other Intro to Chemistry classes open that would fit my schedule?" I said, forcing a polite smile. "I just had...a conflict come up that I didn't expect."

The conflict being my illicit, steamy make-out with the professor, I thought dryly.

The girl behind the desk nodded and started typing onto her computer. "Sure thing. Let me pull up your schedule along with the Intro to Chem sections. What's your name?"

"Lucy Archibald."

"And your student number?"

I listed off the nine-digit number, watching her fingers tap the keyboard as she typed it in.

"Okay, good news. We've got several sections with open seats," the girl at the desk said. "Are there certain days or times that work better for you?"

I hesitated, glancing down at the planner where I'd scribbled my schedule. Technically, I'd prefer the exact same time slot I already had, since I'd spent so much time getting my schedule just right last semester.

But saying that out loud might come across as...suspicious. Like I had a problem with the professor.

Which, okay, I did—but not for the reasons anyone would assume.

I swallowed, forcing a polite smile. "Can I just see which classes you have open?"

No need to raise any red flags.

"Sure." She gave me a quick smile and turned the screen slightly so I could see it better.

Rows of class times filled the monitor. I scanned the list, my stomach sinking with each line. Most of the available options overlapped with either my marketing courses or the hours I spent in the gym. One overlapped with the exact time I had a standing appointment with our team's physical therapist.

Maybe I could swap out my Marketing Strategy class on Mondays and Wednesdays? It wasn't ideal, but when I'd been registering, I was pretty sure I saw another section of that course taught later in the day—possibly at the same time as my current chemistry class.

"Can you click into that Monday and Wednesday section at eight?" I asked, pointing toward the one that might work.

She did. I leaned in to read the professor's name, and my stomach dropped.

Instructor: Park, Owen

Seriously?

Out of *all* the professors on this campus...

I bit my lip, trying to recover. "Um...could you scroll down to the later classes? Like afternoon?"

She nodded and kept scrolling, but my heart sank as I scanned each time block. The later options interfered with either my Advertising Psychology class, which only had a single section taught this semester, or with practice. And since Nora and I had worked hard to get our workout schedules lined up this year, screwing that up now—just because of a dumb kiss—felt like throwing away months of planning.

Even perfect routines can fall apart with one wrong step, my high school gymnastics coach's voice echoed in my head.

I sighed when my watch buzzed, vibrating with the reminder I'd set for my next class.

"Could you print those options out for me?" I asked. "I've got to get to class, but I'll look them over and see if I can figure something out later."

"Of course." She hit the print button and walked over to grab the pages.

I thanked her quickly, took the packet, and headed out of the building into the cold air, flipping through the options as I walked toward the business building. The wind caught one of the pages and nearly ripped it from my hands, but I grabbed it in time, skimming through the final page.

There was one section—Tuesdays and Thursdays at two. A tiny flare of hope sparked...until I remembered: my chem lab.

Thursdays from one to four. That time slot was already locked.

Perfect.

I shoved the pages into my bag as I walked by the snow-covered quad. Hopefully, I'd figure something out later. But if I couldn't...I'd just have to suck it up and go to Professor Park's class on Wednesday.

And hope to survive without spontaneously combusting in my seat.

13

______

OWEN

I GLANCED at the clock mounted on the back wall of the lecture hall Wednesday afternoon, doing one last scan of the rows in front of me.

12:59.

Still no sign of Lucy.

Good.

Maybe she dropped the class. Or switched sections.

It would be for the best.

Easier to keep my job, at least.

When the digital clock flipped to 1:00, I pushed my sleeves to my elbows and stepped toward the whiteboard. "Good afternoon, everyone," I said, projecting just enough to quiet the room. "Today we're diving into everyone's favorite topic: stoichiometry. Mole ratios. I know, I know...you've been dreaming about this since winter break."

A few students laughed. One guy in the second row raised a hand and deadpanned, "My favorite thing to dream about."

"That's the spirit." I gave him a dry smile. "But don't worry. By the end of the week, you'll be solving mole-to-mole conversions in your sleep." I uncapped my dry erase marker, and with a shrug, I added, "Or possibly having nightmares about them. It's a toss-up."

That earned a little more laughter. Not bad for day two.

Chairs creaked as students settled in and flipped open their notebooks. As pens started scratching against paper, I moved to the side of the board and began writing out the first reaction.

I had just started writing $\mathbf{2H_2 + O_2 \rightarrow 2H_2O}$—when the door at the back of the room creaked open again.

My grip on the marker paused. Just briefly.

And when I turned around, there she was.

Lucy Archibald.

Looking way too pretty as she slid into a seat near the back of the room.

She wore a red Eden Falls University Gymnastics hoodie and black leggings. Her hair was up in a loose, slightly messy bun with a few tendrils framing her face—the same hairdo she had when I kissed her in the hot tub.

Was that on purpose? An attempt to remind me of the moment that could never happen again?

No...probably not. Just because I'd been thinking about the possibility of running into her on campus the past two days didn't mean she'd been thinking about me.

In fact, from her cool, unsmiling expression, it would seem that she was as apathetic about being here as any student could be.

She wasn't smiling. Didn't give any sort of recognition. Just sat, tugged her sleeve down over her hand, and pulled out a pen.

I was just beginning to wonder if maybe I'd only imagined everything that happened between us on New Year's Eve.

Until our eyes met.

Something flickered across her expression—hesitation? Guilt? Longing?

No. Seeing any sort of longing or regret was definitely my own wishful thinking. I was reading too much into it.

Her face smoothed an instant later, and I forced myself to remember that there was absolutely nothing between us. She was just a student showing up for class. One of the many I had this semester.

I turned back to the board and forced my voice to stay steady.

"All right, quick refresher—stoichiometry is all about the math of chemical reactions. If we have two moles of hydrogen reacting with one mole of oxygen, how many moles of water do we get?"

A girl in the front row hesitated, then said, "Two?"

"Bingo. You just stoichiometrized. Welcome to greatness."

A few chuckles. I smiled faintly, but I felt it slip too fast.

I moved through the first example problem, writing the coefficients with extra care. But I couldn't help it. The moment I turned around to face the class again, my eyes darted back to Lucy's seat.

She was watching me.

Not intensely. Not obviously.

Just...watching. Head tilted slightly, pen poised but not moving.

Of course she's watching you. You're her teacher. Students are supposed to pay attention like that in class.

Stop trying to make this into something.

I cleared my throat and gestured to the whiteboard.

"So, if we wanted to go from grams of hydrogen to grams of water, what would be the first step?"

A guy with red hair in the front row raised his hand. "Convert grams to moles?"

"Yes." I nodded. "Gold star. Or, more accurately, a mole of gold, if you're lucky."

A few students looked completely clueless.

"That's about six hundred sextillion atoms of gold—give or take a few quadrillion." I added, "In case anyone's hoping to retire early."

Which was followed by a few groans.

Okay, rough crowd.

Which made sense. Most of these students were probably like Lucy and only taking this class for the required science credit.

I grabbed the eraser and wiped the board down, forcing myself to focus.

Just teach the dang class, Owen. Stop trying to be the fun professor.

I moved into the next example and kept talking, kept teaching, but every few minutes my eyes couldn't help but flick to the back of the room—like a reflex I couldn't resist.

Lucy was still there. Still watching.

And no matter how many jokes I cracked or equations I solved, the burn in my chest wouldn't fade.

The student I'd kissed—*in a freaking hot tub*—was staying in the class.

Which meant everything had just gotten a whole lot harder.

And if I wanted to make it through the semester with my job and my dignity still intact, I'd better shut down any feelings I'd let spark before I knew who she was.

Fast.

"So, how's the online dating thing going, anyway?" Ian leaned back on the couch and gave me a once-over, the kind only a smug, happily engaged man could pull off.

We were camped out in his living room after dinner—Maddie's homemade chicken enchiladas still sitting warmly in my stomach. Maddie had disappeared upstairs a few minutes ago, tucking in Grant for the night, leaving us with a few minutes of guy talk.

"You on your way to locking down a plus-one for the wedding?"

"For a wedding that's not till June?" I snorted. "Yeah...no. I definitely haven't found anyone I see myself with five months from now."

"I thought you had a few dates lined up, though?"

"I went on a couple of dates in December," I said, thinking of the girl I'd taken to dinner and the one I'd awkwardly escorted to her company's Christmas party. "But nothing came from them."

"Ah, dang." Ian scratched his jaw. "You been matching with anyone, at least? You said it's just a numbers game, right?"

"That's what I've been telling myself." I shrugged. "Sadly, though, it's easier said than done."

"Well, I guess you could always do what I did." Ian grinned. "Kiss a random girl at the club, then find out she's your assistant the next Monday. Worked for me."

It sure did. Lucky dog.

"Yeah..." I hesitated, then laughed under my breath and rubbed the back of my neck. "I, uh...actually did something like that already."

"What?" He furrowed his brow.

"Yeah, so, crazy story." I let out a humorless chuckle. "I kissed a girl at Ky's New Year's Eve party and well...when I showed up to teach my class on Monday, I discovered that the girl I'd kissed in a hot tub is actually a student."

"No way." His eyes went wide. "You're joking, right?"

"I wish I was."

"Dude."

"Oh, it gets better." I held up a finger. "Turns out she's Theo's sister."

Ian blinked. "Theo has a sister in college?"

"Yeah," I said. "She's actually on the gymnastics team."

"Nice," Ian said, looking like he was mentally running through every gymnast stereotype imaginable. "I never dated a gymnast..."

"Don't go there." I gave him a flat look. Since yeah...I'd been trying to keep my brain from going there myself.

"Hey, I'm a happily engaged man." He held up his hands, grinning. "I was just thinking of the perks for *you*, buddy."

"She's only twenty-one," I said. "And there's also the fun little complication that I could get fired for having a romantic relationship with a student. Not to mention the fact that her dad is President Archibald."

"Oh shoot." Ian's jaw dropped, like he was only just realizing how bad that could be for me.

"Exactly."

"If that gets out—"

"I'm screwed," I finished for him. "Career-ending levels of screwed."

"Dang." He let out a low whistle. "And I thought things were complicated when Maddie turned out to be my assistant. But at least my livelihood wasn't on the line."

"Yeah." I released a heavy sigh, feeling the stress of my situation all over again.

"But it was just a kiss, right? It's not like you did anything after that, did you?"

"We only kissed on New Year's Eve," I said. "We've only had two class sessions since I found out. But after the initial *oh-crap* conversation, we haven't interacted at all."

I remembered the way she'd come in late this afternoon and then was the first to leave. She clearly didn't want anything to do with me.

Which was...for the best.

Smart.

Prudent.

And yet...

Ian shook his head, still chuckling to himself. "I'm so glad I don't have to worry about any of that anymore."

"Yeah." I rolled my eyes. "Lucky you."

At that moment, Maddie walked into the room after coming back downstairs, her expression soft. "Why is Ian lucky?"

"Because I have you," Ian said smoothly, opening his arms like the smug, lovesick fiancé he was.

"Pretty sure I'm the lucky one," she said, plopping down beside him and kissing his cheek.

Ugh. This domesticated version of Ian was just so disgustingly...sweet.

I was so jealous.

"Anyway, just...don't tell anyone, okay?" I let out a heavy sigh and scrubbed a hand through my hair. "I just got this job, and I'd really hate to get fired right when I'm getting started."

The words hit harder than I meant them to. Because I wasn't exaggerating. I'd dreamed of this position. Fought for it. And now, with the dean hinting I could be promoted to a research professorship next year—if my grant came through—the idea of losing everything because of one stupid, perfect kiss... Yeah, it made my stomach twist.

"What are we not telling anyone?" Maddie asked, looking between Ian and me with a confused expression.

"Oh, just a little romantic mishap with a girl he didn't realize was a student," Ian said with a chuckle. "You know, fun stuff like that."

"Wait." Maddie's blue eyes lit up. "You kissed a student?"

"Yes." I groaned, dropping my head into my hands. "And no, I didn't know she was a student at the time."

"I'll tell you about it later," Ian said, shooting Maddie a grin, thankfully saving me from having to relive the story again. "She's actually Theo's little sister."

"Oh, I love Theo," Maddie said, smiling warmly.

Ian's jaw ticked as he looked down at her. "Well, he was still the inferior option."

"Relax." Maddie laughed and smacked his arm. "I'm just teasing."

Their banter made me smile, but the mention of Theo brought a sudden realization slamming into me.

Crap.

I'd completely forgotten about my conversation with Theo at The Garden a couple of weeks ago. The one where we'd floated the idea of a double date at the gymnastics meet this Saturday.

Yeah...that suddenly felt like a *terrible* idea.

I pulled out my phone and fired off a quick text.

> Me: Hey man, I totally spaced. I haven't found a date for Saturday after all. Gonna have to cancel our double date.

I hesitated, then added:

> Me: Sorry. First week of the semester is kicking my butt.

Sliding the phone back into my pocket, I pushed up from the couch. "I should probably head out. Thanks again for dinner. It was great."

Ian stood and clapped a hand on my shoulder. "Of course. Anytime."

Maddie gave me a warm smile as she got up, too. "It was great to see you again, Owen."

"You too." I grabbed my coat from the tree in the corner and shrugged it on. As I opened the front door, I paused. "And I'm sure this goes without saying, but if you could keep my kiss with Theo's sister just between us...that would be great."

"Of course," Maddie said immediately.

Ian grinned. "Theo who?"

Maddie playfully smacked his chest. "Stop."

They walked me to the porch, and I stepped out into the chilled night air, pulling my coat tighter around me. I hit the button on my keys to start my car, watching the headlights blink in the driveway.

As I climbed inside and waited for the heat to kick in, my phone buzzed.

> Theo: Oh no worries. I haven't gotten a date yet, either.

I relaxed slightly.

> Me: We'll have to try again some other time.

> Theo: Or we could still hang out at the meet. Just skip the double date part.

I considered that.

Honestly, it would be good to hang out with Theo more. We'd been casual friends for years, and now that Ian was all settled down with Maddie and Grant, having a solid buddy in town sounded like a win.

> Me: Sure, that would be great.

But then, Theo shot back another text.

> Theo: Great. My family usually sits in the seats beneath the donor box, so we can sit near them since they were already hoping to see Charlotte.

Oh. Crap.

I slumped back in my seat, staring at the dash as the windshield finally started to defrost.

Sitting with his parents? Watching Lucy perform?

While pretending I didn't already know what she tasted and felt like?

Yeah...that was definitely not a relaxing way to spend my Saturday evening.

But I'd already agreed.

It would be suspicious if I tried to back out now.

So instead, I closed my eyes, exhaled, and added one more thing to the growing list of reasons why that midnight kiss with Lucy Archibald had been a terrible, terrible idea.

14

———

LUCY

I TUGGED the sleeves of my red hoodie down over my hands and tried the chemistry lab door again.

Still locked.

I leaned back against the cinderblock wall, exhaling slowly and trying to shake off the nerves twisting up in my stomach. I wasn't normally anxious about school. Gymnastics meets? Sure. Big presentations? A little. But something about this chemistry lab had me way more jittery than I wanted to admit.

Probably because I'd never done one before.

Not in real life, anyway.

My entire high school experience had been online—out of necessity. There hadn't been time for traditional school between hours at the gym, traveling for meets, and competing at the elite level. So I'd done what any athlete with Olympic dreams and no life balance would do: I clicked my way through chemistry labs in a browser window while icing my ankle and watching floor routine replays on loop.

So, yeah. Hopefully, I wouldn't mix the wrong chemicals together and blow a hole through a lab table.

I glanced at my watch. Still fifteen minutes until the lab was supposed to start.

I'd rushed through lunch, thanks to the pit in my stomach, scarfing down half a protein bar and a handful of grapes before bolting over here early to scope out the lab room. Now I was just waiting...trying not to psych myself out more.

Not that I should have anything to be nervous about. Yesterday's class had gone fine. I'd slipped in late, stayed quiet, and bolted as soon as the lecture ended. Nothing weird happened.

Nothing aside from the fact that my heart had raced every time Owen looked in my direction.

Not that anyone noticed. I was chill. Collected. Totally unaffected.

Hopefully.

Okay, maybe I'd laughed just a little too hard at his dumb chemistry jokes. But seriously, he was funny. And that whole "hot nerd" vibe he had going? It was straight-up dangerous if I wanted to keep any forbidden crushes at bay.

Especially when I'd met him as a flirty, confident bartender with a chest tattoo and lips that made me forget my own name.

I sighed. *I really need to stop thinking about that night.*

Replaying those memories wasn't going to help them fade.

A pair of footsteps echoed up the stairwell and I straightened, tugging my hoodie back into place. But it was just another student passing by, probably on their way to some other lab.

I exhaled and pulled out my phone to scroll through Instagram. Maybe checking out a few puppy reels would distract me from the fact that I was slowly unraveling over freshman-level science.

But just as my finger swiped up the screen, a figure appeared in front of me.

I looked up—and there he was.

Owen.

Professor Park.

Looking unfairly good in a navy sweater and dark jeans, leather messenger bag slung over one shoulder, keycard already in hand.

Our eyes met and something caught in my chest—like I'd forgotten how to breathe for a second. He cleared his throat and glanced down, then said, "Hello, Lucy."

"Hi," I said, my voice a little too quiet, a little too breathless.

He stepped past me and tried the lab door. When it didn't budge, he tapped his keycard against the panel, the small light flashing green.

"How's your semester going so far?" he asked, his voice casual. Polished. Just a normal professor talking to a normal student.

"It's going all right," I said, matching his even tone.

Which was mostly true. But standing this close to him again—seeing the details I couldn't make out from the back row —was throwing me off.

I hadn't realized how striking his eyes were—warm brown, almost golden when the light hit them just right. Oval-shaped, with smooth lids that gave him a quietly intense look.

Yeah, he was definitely the hottest professor I'd ever had.

Way too attractive for my own good.

"I'm glad it's going okay," he said, opening the lab door and stepping aside so I could enter first. "I know you mentioned chemistry wasn't your favorite. Are you feeling like you're catching on?"

"Uh huh." I nodded as I entered the room, glancing around. "So far it's been good. You're a good teacher."

"Oh. Thanks." His cheeks colored slightly, and he glanced down like he was embarrassed.

Ugh. He was cute.

Dangerously so...

He walked ahead and flipped on the lights, motioning toward the long black tables set up around the room. "You can sit wherever you like."

I nodded and made my way to a table near the windows, dropping my bag onto the stool beside it. As I started unpacking the gear I'd bought from the supplies list online—goggles, gloves, a lab notebook—I scanned the rest of the room.

A few students had trickled in behind me, most of them familiar faces from my lecture hour, though there were a couple I didn't recognize. Probably from one of Owen's other intro sections.

I sat down and glanced around, wondering if I was supposed to pick a lab partner. Most of the students were already chatting in pairs or settling into their usual cliques.

No one sat next to me.

I bit the inside of my cheek. Maybe I needed to move and find someone to pair up with.

But then, a few minutes before one, Brody—the hockey player Josh had tried to fight at The Garden—strolled in, wearing a beanie and a crooked smile. His gaze swept the room until it landed on me.

"Hey, Archibald." He grinned. "Want to be lab buddies?"

I blinked then gave a half-smile. "Sure."

"Sweet." He dropped his bag on the stool beside mine. "We can be the old farts in this class together."

I laughed. "Seniors unite."

"You know it." He held his hand out for a fist bump.

Okay. So maybe lab wasn't going to be a total disaster.

At least I wouldn't be blowing things up alone.

"This station here is for waste disposal," Owen said, gesturing to the back counter as he gave us a quick tour of the lab. "Label all your beakers, wear your safety gear, and please, for the love of science, don't mix anything without reading the directions."

A few students laughed quietly, and he cracked a smile, glancing around the room before continuing. "Today's a basic intro to lab safety, along with a simple reaction to get you comfortable working with your partner. The procedures are printed out at each station. If you need help, just raise your hand—there's no need to light anything on fire to get my attention."

My eyes flicked up to the front of the room, just in time to catch the smallest smile on his face before he looked away.

He was acting in a totally appropriate way.

Completely professional.

But even though I knew I shouldn't, my mind wanted to think that all his jokes and little smiles were just for me.

"All right, let's do this," Brody said, rolling up the sleeves of his hoodie as he plopped onto the stool beside me and scanned the laminated procedure sheet. "Ready to get nerdy, Archibald?"

"As long as we don't blow anything up," I said, pulling on my goggles. "Then I guess I'm ready."

"Don't worry." He grinned. "I got a B-plus in high school chem, so I'm basically a pro."

"Oh wow. Glad I partnered with a chemistry genius."

"You're welcome," he said, grabbing the first beaker and reading the label. "But fair warning—I'm more of a hands-on learner."

I raised a brow. "That supposed to be a pick-up line?"

"Maybe." He smirked. "Did it work?"

I rolled my eyes but couldn't help the laugh that slipped out.

We worked through the first few steps, measuring out the solutions and carefully combining them in the beaker. It fizzed a little—nothing dramatic—and Brody leaned in, peering at the reaction.

"Smells like high school all over again," he muttered.

"Wouldn't know," I said, adjusting the burner with a careful turn. "I did online high school."

Brody glanced over, eyebrows raised. "Seriously?"

"Yeah. Full-time gymnastics didn't exactly leave room for AP Bio and Friday night pep rallies."

"Ah, right." He leaned back on his stool, nodding like it all clicked now. "That makes sense." After a beat, he asked, "Hey, were you at the hockey game on Sunday?"

"Nope." I shook my head. "We had a meet at Penn State that afternoon."

"Oh yeah, that's right. How'd it go?"

I twisted the cap off a graduated cylinder and started measuring. "Pretty close. We only lost by half a point. I placed third in the all-around, though."

"Wow—third?" He whistled. "That's freaking impressive."

I felt my cheeks warm slightly, but I waved him off. "It was all right, I guess."

If I'd stuck the landing on my second tumbling pass—and managed to keep both feet in bounds—I might've placed first.

Still, third wasn't bad. A solid start to the season. Hopefully, I'd only improve from here.

"Your turn to test the pH." Brody nudged me with his elbow when the solution was ready, handing over a test strip. "Let's see if I managed to make this reaction acidic enough to melt the table."

"Ok..." I said, taking the test strip from his fingers.

I double-checked the instructions on the lab sheet before dipping it into the solution, trying not to let my nerves show.

Out of the corner of my eye, I caught movement—Owen was leaning over another group's table, adjusting the flame on their Bunsen burner, sleeves pushed up to his elbows.

And wow. His forearms were...just as distracting as they'd been that first night at The Garden.

Lean muscle. Just the right amount of arm hair. A few well-defined veins that shifted when he moved.

I suddenly understood why Nora always said men's forearms were the most underrated body part in society.

And apparently, I'd been staring too long because his eyes flicked up to mine. Just for a second. A quick, unintentional glance.

But it was enough to make my breath hitch.

Lab sheet. pH test.

I turned my attention firmly back to the table, pretending my heart wasn't pounding for completely unnecessary reasons.

Focus.

As the color on the test strip darkened, I glanced sideways at Brody. "Hey...are things chill with you and Josh?"

"They've been all right." He looked up from writing in our lab notebook. "No more fights, if that's what you mean."

"That's good." I placed the strip onto a paper towel to dry. I hadn't run into Josh yet this semester or heard from him. Hopefully, that meant things were going okay. Hopefully, he was handling the pressure of being team captain better than he'd handled everything last year.

"What was that fight about, anyway?" I asked, curiosity getting the better of me.

"Ah, just something dumb." Brody rolled a shoulder. "I was giving him a hard time about something, and he didn't take it well."

I thought about what Nora had told me. That Brody said

their fight started because he'd teased Josh about trying to ask me out.

Which...I still didn't know how I felt about that. Brody was cute, objectively. Dirty-blond hair. Blue eyes. A little scruff on his jaw. Nice face.

Charming in a way most athletes were.

But hockey players weren't exactly known for their chill reputations.

And even if he had been serious in considering asking me out, I wasn't sure what I would've said. I didn't know him well enough to know if his flirting was just for fun or something more.

Brody cleared his throat. "How are things with you and Josh, anyway? Haven't seen you hanging out as much."

"We're okay," I said, keeping my eyes on the test strip.

He paused, then asked gently, "Mind if I ask why you broke up?"

I hesitated, unsure how to answer. There were so many reasons. Some obvious, some buried under years of pretending things were fine when they weren't.

Before I could speak, movement caught my attention again.

Owen was back at his desk now, flipping through a folder—but there was a stillness to his movements that made me wonder if he'd heard the question.

If he was...listening.

My eyes flicked to him again.

And just as quickly, he looked down, suddenly far too interested in the papers on his desk.

My heart gave a traitorous little flutter.

I turned back to Brody, tucking a strand of hair behind my ear. "It just wasn't working anymore."

"Fair enough." He nodded, like he wasn't going to press me on it.

Which I appreciated. I didn't really have the mental band-width for unpacking my relationship trauma mid-lab, especially with Owen standing a few feet away.

"Anyway," he said, lightening the tone, "looks like we didn't melt anything, so I'd call that a win."

I smiled. "First lab survived."

"Barely."

We clinked our plastic test tubes together like champagne glasses.

Okay. Maybe this whole lab thing wouldn't be so bad after all.

15

OWEN

BY THE TIME I stepped out of the university's weight room, my shirt clung to my back and my arms felt like overcooked spaghetti. Lifting with another professor buddy a few times a week kept me sane—bench, deadlifts, rows. But now that the hard work was over with, I needed food.

And caffeine.

Preferably both at once.

And since The Brew was just a block away, I made a quick detour, figuring I'd grab something before heading home to shower.

The coffee shop was bustling like it always was on Saturdays. Students with laptops. Locals reading the paper. Acoustic indie covers playing just loud enough to fill the space but not drown out conversations.

I stepped up to the counter and ordered a hot mocha and a bacon-and-egg-white bagel sandwich, then made my way to a corner table while the barista filled my order.

My phone buzzed as I sat.

Theo: Still good for tonight?

I stared at the message a beat too long, my thumb hovering over the screen.

This could be my out.

I could say I wasn't feeling great. Blame a pile of ungraded labs.

Bow out before I had to spend my Saturday night sitting next to Lucy's parents...watching her compete in a leotard that would absolutely remind me of how it felt to have her in my arms in a bathing suit.

Such a tempting idea.

Really tempting.

But...I bit my lip as I reconsidered. Thursday's lab had gone fine. No slip-ups or anything unprofessional.

Even the short moment before class—when it was just the two of us—had been good. Normal. Above board. Like any conversation I might've had with a regular student.

So really, I should be fine watching her and her team do their routines tonight. I would simply be a professor supporting my students—showing school spirit while also hanging out with a friend.

So I texted back:

Me: Planning on it.

"Owen," the barista called my name. I looked up and watched her set my drink and breakfast sandwich on the counter.

I walked up to the counter and grabbed my order, thanking her before heading back to my corner table. As I took the first sip of my drink, I picked up my phone and tapped open my browser.

I hadn't meant to look her up. I really hadn't. But ever since I'd overheard her tell Brody that she'd done online high school because of her rigorous gymnastics training schedule, I'd been curious to learn more.

I typed *Eden Falls University Women's Gymnastics* and clicked onto the team page. A photo of Lucy in mid-vault popped up first—ponytail flying, expression fierce.

I clicked the roster tab and saw various gymnast headshots populate my phone's screen. Lucy's headshot was first since they were listed in alphabetical order by last name. Her hair was down and curled and she wore what looked like a black warmup top. Beneath her photo were a few stats.

Lucy Archibald
    Height: 5'1
    Class: Senior
    Position: All-Around
    High School: Elevate Online Academy
    Hometown: Eden Falls, Connecticut
    Major: Marketing

I clicked on her photo to view her full bio and skimmed over some of her stats. I didn't know a ton about gymnastics or what the various numbers meant, but it mentioned a few of her career highs—vault 9.8875, uneven bars 9.9375, beam 9.9675, and floor 9.9500.

They all seemed like pretty impressive numbers to me since I was pretty sure the highest score you could get in gymnastics was a 10.

When I overheard Lucy telling Brody that she'd taken third place at her meet last weekend, she sounded disappointed. Which I'd thought was a bit strange since third place was pretty great in my book.

But maybe, with career high scores like that, she was used to winning? Or at least getting second place.

I continued scrolling down the page, reading that before coming to Eden Falls University, she'd been a level 10 gymnast from Prestige Gymnastics in New Haven under coaches Jamie and Arnold Grimwald.

Lucy was on the national team for three years with multiple regional and national medals.

Okay, so...wow.

She wasn't just good. She was exceptional.

I continued down to the "Fun Facts" section.

 **Favorite Skill**: Front layout on beam

Favorite Food: My mom's lasagna soup

Favorite Musical Artist: Incognito

Favorite Movie/TV Show: The Notebook, Modern Family

Favorite Quote: "Hard now, easy later."

Hobbies: Makeup, movies, dancing

Favorite College Memory: "The night of the rock!"

Advice to Future Gymnasts: *Do it for yourself, never give up, and have fun while doing it.*

I smiled at that last line, then clicked open one of the attached articles—an interview from her junior year. She talked about discipline, resilience, and how she balanced school, training, friendships, and dating.

She sounded mature. Grounded.

Not exactly the type of girl who'd kiss a random stranger in a hot tub.

And maybe that was what was messing with me. That girl —the flirty, confident one—she was real. But so was this version.

A sudden gust of cold air swept in as the front door opened. I looked up, still chewing the corner of my bagel sandwich, and nearly choked.

Because the girl I'd just been researching...had just walked into The Brew.

Along with her friend Nora and another girl I didn't recognize.

Crap!

I quickly minimized the browser tab and set my phone face down on the table.

Caught like a kid with his hand in the cookie jar.

Had she seen my phone screen as she passed the windows?

No, probably not. She was laughing with her friends, like she had no idea I was even here.

Not that it was illegal to look up my students' public bios. But still. It felt...weird. Invasive.

She turned her head in my direction as she tucked some loose hair behind her ear.

A second later, our eyes met.

Her eyes widened briefly, like she hadn't expected to see me here.

And not knowing what else to do, I gave her a small nod— cool, casual. Like I hadn't just been low-key reading her gymnastics résumé like it was a love letter.

She nodded back—polite, unreadable—and turned back to the counter with her friends.

No smile. No double take. Just another day in Eden Falls.

Which was exactly how it should be.

She was my student.

Not my friend.

Not the girl I kissed in a hot tub.

Not the one I'd been thinking about way too much for someone who should've moved on by now.

Just a student.

I stared down at The Brews logo that was stamped on the cardboard sleeve of my coffee cup and tried to shake my paranoia away.

I needed to get Lucy out of my head. Needed to find someone else to occupy my mind.

So, doing that the best way I knew how, I pulled up the Meet Your Match app on my phone and started swiping through the various women who popped up.

Hopefully, a few dates with other interesting women would help me stop thinking so much about the one who was completely off-limits.

The energy inside the EFU arena hit me the moment I walked through the doors—upbeat pop music pulsing through the speakers, the buzz of conversation echoing off the high ceiling, a low hum of anticipation beneath it all.

There were still fifteen minutes until the meet officially started, but the place was already filling up. Students, families, faculty. Even a few little kids in sparkly leotards running around near the bottom rows.

I glanced toward the competition floor, scanning past the balance beam and uneven bars until my eyes snagged on the red leotard near the vault runway.

Lucy.

She was talking with her coach, head tilted slightly, hands on her hips, her expression focused like she was getting some sort of feedback.

Her bleached-blonde hair was parted cleanly down the

middle, two tight French braids slicked back and twisted into a bun at the crown of her head. A light dusting of chalk clung to her thighs, probably from brushing against the bars or beam mid-warmup—evidence that she'd already been hard at work.

And despite all the reasons I'd been dreading tonight—sitting near her parents, praying they didn't pick up on the fact that their daughter's professor had a not-so-mini crush—I found myself suddenly, stupidly eager to see the expertise I'd read about in her bio in action.

I just had to make sure that if I looked impressed, it came across as academic. Respect for her athleticism. Her power. Her technique.

Not because I was fighting off memories of what it felt like to hold her in a hot tub.

Her gaze drifted toward the stands and for a split second, I could've sworn we locked eyes.

My heart thudded. Hard.

But then, she turned back to her coach, rubbing her shoulder absently while listening to whatever correction she was given, like nothing had just happened.

Okay. Maybe she hadn't seen me.

Or maybe she had and was doing exactly what we were both supposed to be doing.

Acting like none of it meant anything.

I blew out a slow breath.

Chill. Relax. Be cool.

You can do this.

After matching with a few girls this morning and messaging back and forth with one of them, I'd spent the rest of the afternoon inputting grades and doing my best not to think about tonight.

But ever since spotting Lucy at the coffee shop, I'd been wound tight.

And seeing her now—poised and focused—wasn't exactly helping.

Yeah, I needed to line up an actual date. Fast.

So before heading down to meet Theo, I pulled up the thread I'd started with MaryAnn—the kindergarten teacher who seemed funny, smart, normal—and typed out a message.

> Me: Hey, this might be jumping the gun a little, but would you be up for grabbing dinner sometime soon? My buddy just opened a Thai place downtown. I've been meaning to check it out and would love some company.

I hit *send*, then switched over to my texts to double-check where Theo said he was sitting.

> Theo: We're sitting in section D, about halfway up. See you soon.

I scanned the stands, eyes skimming over clusters of students and families until I spotted Theo. His brown hair looked unruly, like he'd let his three-year-old daughter run her brush through it again. And perched neatly in his lap was Charlotte, her curls pulled into their signature pigtails, the only style Theo ever seemed to manage. She was wearing a tiny red leotard that looked suspiciously like a miniature version of the team's uniform.

Of course she was.

I smiled despite myself.

I jogged down the cement steps, the echo of my shoes bouncing faintly off the walls as I made my way toward them. Theo spotted me and lifted a hand in greeting.

"Hey, man," he said as I reached them. "Grab that seat." He nodded to the chair on his left. "These two on the aisle are for my parents. Mom should be here soon, but Dad's doing his usual thing—making the rounds, chatting up the donor box, maybe leading a cheer in the student section. You know. Presidential duties."

"Right," I said, exhaling as I sank into the seat.

Dare I hope the presidential duties took up a good chunk of the meet? Because, yeah, if I only had to pretend I wasn't hyper-aware of the fact that I'd kissed his daughter two weeks ago for part of the night, that would be great.

Still, as I glanced back toward the floor and caught another glimpse of Lucy prepping at the vault runway, that small comfort didn't do much to quiet the thud in my chest.

This was going to be a long night.

And I was already in way over my head.

16

LUCY

I STOOD at the edge of the mat, waiting for my turn on bars, the familiar buzz of chalk and adrenaline running through my veins. The uneven bars weren't my favorite event—floor and beam were where I shined—but my routine tonight had one of the higher difficulty scores. Second highest of anyone competing, actually. So even if it wasn't perfect, I still had a shot at the all-around.

Vault had gone well. Not my career best, but I'd scored a 9.85, which was good enough to put me in first on our team for now, with Nora trailing just a tenth behind.

But it was still anyone's game.

My gaze drifted toward the stands, as it always did between events—out of habit, out of nerves, maybe just to ground myself.

Not that I was scanning the crowd for the new addition sitting with my family or anything...

Why had Owen come, anyway?

Did he usually come to the gymnastics meets?

Had Theo just randomly invited him?

I had no idea. But seeing him walk in before the meet started had definitely been startling.

Not in a bad way necessarily, but my pulse had definitely picked up.

Though, interesting as that was, it actually hadn't been my biggest surprise of the night.

No, that honor belonged to the moment I'd seen Josh take a seat in the student section. With a girl.

His arm was draped casually around her shoulders, the way he'd always done with me. And judging by the way she'd leaned into him, smiling up like she'd known him forever...it probably wasn't their first date, either.

The sting had come fast, sharp and unexpected.

Because even though we'd broken up months ago, even though we weren't right for each other... Even though I'd told myself I didn't care anymore... Apparently, some part of me still did.

I blew out a deep breath and swung my arms forward and back, trying to shake off the tightness curling in my chest. *Not now*. I could analyze my feelings about Josh and his date another time. I needed to be here—focused, present. Not living in my head while my hands were flying between a pair of metal bars.

Still...why bring her *here*? To my gymnastics meet?

He knew I'd be competing. Knew how much I needed my head clear for nights like this.

Was he trying to get under my skin? Trying to show off how fine he was, how easy it'd been to move on after I'd pushed away his drunken attempt at a kiss the night I drove him home from The Garden?

Whatever. Let him have his petty moment.

He wasn't the one about to fly through the air in front of a packed crowd.

Nora wrapped up her routine with a clean dismount, a small hop on the landing but otherwise solid. The gym erupted with applause, and I let out a long, steadying breath.

Almost time to go.

The assistant coach and one of my teammates stepped in to adjust the bars for my height while I did a few quick shoulder rolls and shook out my hands. I closed my eyes and drew in another deep breath, visualizing myself in the gym and the hundreds of times I'd run this routine. I could do it blindfolded.

The judges gave me the signal, and I stepped forward.

Here we go.

I launched off the springboard, catching the low bar with both hands as my body swung into motion—a rhythm I knew by heart. The sting of chalk in my nose. The clink of metal. My breath syncing with every kip, every cast.

Then the moment came—the transition from low to high. The hardest part of the routine, where I had to time my grip just right.

My fingers caught the bar, but barely. For half a second, my heart lodged in my throat.

But my grip held. I adjusted mid-air, used the momentum to swing through and keep going, hitting the rest of my sequence cleanly.

I took another breath, centering myself for the dismount.

One long swing around...then another...and on the third, I released—twisting through a double layout, my body tightening with every rotation.

My feet hit the mat with a sharp, satisfying thud.

No step. No wobble.

Just—stuck it.

The crowd erupted.

A rush of adrenaline surged through me as I threw my arms

into my final pose, my grin stretching wide. I couldn't help it. I'd nailed it.

"You crushed it!" Nora called, the first of my teammates to reach me before I was completely swarmed—girls hugging, shrieking, enveloping me in a tangle of red and black leotards and chalk-covered hands.

"Stick queen!" Mayci said.

"That transition was *chef's kiss*," another girl called.

Laughing, I hugged them back, trading high-fives as I made my way off the mat, my limbs buzzing with post-routine energy.

Across the arena, the announcer's voice cut in. "Up next on vault for Minnesota is..."

I slowed as I reached the sideline, letting my breathing steady, and looked toward the stands.

Mom was easy to spot—both hands clamped to her mouth before she gave me an enthusiastic thumbs-up, her eyes shining.

Dad was seated now, too, Charlotte bouncing on his knees in her tiny red leotard. When he noticed me looking, he helped her wave and clap.

I glanced at Theo next. He was seated by my dad with that proud, older brother smile and a hand cupped around his mouth as he mouthed, *That was awesome.*

I smiled, lifting my fingers in a quick wave.

And that was when I snuck a glance at Owen.

He wasn't cheering. He didn't mouth anything or throw me a grin like Theo did.

But he was watching.

Or at least, he *had* been. Our eyes met for the briefest flicker of a second before he quickly looked away, glancing toward my parents like he was making sure no one had noticed.

Like making eye contact with me in front of them was some kind of crime.

Which, to be fair, it kind of felt like it was.

I bit the inside of my cheek to keep from laughing. What was he thinking right now? Did he even know?

"Nice work out there," came a voice behind me.

I turned to see Coach Brent jogging toward me, clipboard in hand and that easygoing grin he always wore. He'd only been with our program for a few months, but he'd already proven to be the perfect counterbalance to Coach Chambers' no-nonsense intensity.

"That Jaeger was masterful. You had the whole arena holding their breath."

"Thanks," I said, pushing a loose wisp of hair back toward my bun. "I was worried I'd missed the high bar for a second."

"You corrected quick," he said, nodding. "Excellent recovery."

I smiled, my shoulders relaxing just a little more. Compliments from Brent always felt earned.

Just then, the judges flipped their score cards and the announcer read them out loud: "We have a 9.9275 for Lucy Archibald on the bars!"

The Eden Falls crowd erupted behind me—students, alumni, parents, and even a few little girls in leotards shrieking like it was the Olympics.

I let the cheer wash over me and clapped with my team, letting myself enjoy it for a heartbeat longer. Then I stepped away, grabbing my water bottle and towel from my chair as I sat and let the rush of it all settle in my chest.

Two events down. Two to go.

After the meet, I barely had time to catch my breath before my family found me on the floor. My mom reached me first with her arms outstretched, Charlotte clinging to her hip like a koala in sparkly sneakers.

"Congrats on taking first on beam!" Mom said, pulling me into a hug with her free arm.

"Thanks." I smiled and hugged her back, even as my brain filled in the parts she didn't mention, like how I'd placed second on both floor and bars. Solid scores. But not quite enough.

Which meant second place overall in the all-around.

So close.

But not quite good enough since a girl from Minnesota had edged me out by one-tenth of a point.

One-tenth.

Ugh.

Theo appeared at my side then, wearing his usual lopsided grin. "You crushed it tonight," he said, pulling me into a quick side hug. "That beam routine was insane. I don't think you blinked once."

"Thanks."

Was my family purposely only talking about the beam? It was definitely my most impressive event tonight—I'd gotten a near perfect score of 9.9325...but I had other great moments, too.

It's probably just all in your head, I told myself. *It's not that deep.*

Well...with my mom and Theo, it wasn't. My dad on the other hand... I guess I was still bracing myself for his critique.

Theo shifted his stance, stepping aside slightly to make room for someone behind him.

Owen.

Our eyes met for a split second before he looked over at Theo, clearly waiting for an introduction.

"Oh, right," Theo said, catching the cue. "I don't think I've ever officially introduced you two. This is my friend Owen. I invited him to the meet tonight." Then, turning to Owen and gesturing toward me, he added, "And Owen, this is my very talented little sister, Lucy."

I let myself take in Owen more fully, and when our eyes met again, there was something in the slight tug of his smile, the flicker of hesitation just beneath it, that made my stomach tighten.

"You guys actually met at The Garden a few weeks ago," Theo continued. "But Owen and I didn't realize you were one of his students until tonight, when I pointed you out during warmups and he recognized you from one of his classes this week."

"Oh yeah," I said, turning toward Owen, forcing my pulse to chill out and my expression to stay casual. "I'm in your Monday and Wednesday lecture. And your Thursday lab. I kept trying to figure out why you looked so familiar when I walked into class. I didn't realize you were also the bartender."

His mouth curved slightly at my innocent act, but before he could respond, my dad—who'd apparently been eavesdropping—cut in.

"You're one of Lucy's professors?"

"Uh, yes sir." Owen straightened slightly. "I guess so." His voice stayed calm, but I caught the flicker of unease in his eyes. "This week's been a blur. So many new students—I'm still matching names to faces."

Right. Just another student.

Which was exactly what I was supposed to be.

Still, I hated how that small comment seemed to erase the moment we'd shared at Ky's party.

It had meant something to me, at least.

And hearing it brushed off like it was forgettable? That stung a little.

But then, he looked back at me, and with a smile that was warm and genuine, he said, "You were incredible tonight, by the way. Seriously. I could tell how much work and training went into that. Super impressive. Awe-inspiring, honestly."

My chest warmed instantly, my disappointment melting under the soft glow of his praise. Compliments always felt good. But from him? It was like getting a gold medal in a private category no one else knew existed.

"You did great out there," Dad said next, giving me a brief one-armed hug. "Beam was flawless. And that first tumbling pass on floor—nailed it."

I smiled again, bracing myself.

"But that second pass...little rough on the landing."

And there it was.

I nodded slowly, biting the inside of my cheek. "Yeah..."

"But hey," he added, in that way he always did when he tried to soften a critique with encouragement, "it's the first home meet. You've got time to clean it up before nationals. I really think this could be your year."

The pressure hit like a wave.

Because while I loved this sport—loved performing, loved flying through the air, chasing the perfect routine—sometimes it was hard to always love something that constantly demanded perfection.

Owen must've picked up on the shift in my expression because his voice cut through the noise, quiet and curious, "You've been to the national championship before? That's amazing."

I glanced over at him. His eyes were steady on mine, his tone sincere.

"Yes," I said softly. "Last year."

"She made it all the way to the finals," my dad added, his arm tightening across my shoulders. "Probably could've won the whole thing, but she missed her hand on the high bar transition and had to add an extra swing. Ended up placing fourth in the all-around."

I heard it—the subtle note of disappointment in my dad's voice—and felt that familiar pinch in my chest. Archibalds were winners. That was the unspoken rule. Fourth place didn't exactly qualify.

Most people would've been thrilled with how far I'd gone. I knew that. But in his eyes, after *barely* missing out on the Olympic team when I was sixteen, it wasn't enough.

But the truth was...the fact that I'd even competed at nationals last year at all had been kind of a miracle.

No one knew that, though. Not the judges. Not my teammates. Not even my parents.

Because two weeks before the championship, I'd ended up in the hospital.

Bruised ribs. From a bad dismount—at least that was what I'd told the doctor when they'd taken my x-ray.

Only...it wasn't a hard landing on the bars that had nearly cracked my ribs. The damage had come from a fight.

With Josh.

Just thinking about it made me flinch inwardly, like my body was still bracing for impact. I hated that memory. Hated that I'd ever been in that kind of situation. That I'd stayed. That I'd let myself believe it would get better.

He was just stressed. Once his coach and professors stopped breathing down his neck about getting his grades up, he'd be better.

At least, that was what I'd stupidly told myself.

No one would've guessed—not me, not my friends—that I would be the girl with a boyfriend who pushed her around.

But when you love someone, and they swear they didn't

mean it...that they're sorry...that it'll never happen again...you want to believe them.

And I did.

A few too many times.

But I'd gotten out.

Eventually, I stopped listening to the apologies. The excuses. The promises.

I packed up what little self-worth I had and left the apartment that I'd delusionally believed could be a sanctuary for us. If we could just shut out the rest of the world, surely that would fix us.

My heart might have gotten bruised. My trust definitely had cracks. But I was healing. Slowly.

The emotional scars didn't ache quite as often, and the physical ones—those deep-purple bruises I'd covered with makeup and long sleeves—had faded months ago.

My gaze drifted toward the student section, back to the row where I'd spotted Josh earlier. He was still there, leaning in close to the girl next to him, his arm slung casually behind her shoulders.

Was she his girlfriend? A date? Just someone he was trying to impress?

Should I warn her?

Tell her the truth about who he'd been with me?

Or maybe he'd changed. Maybe he'd grown. Maybe I'd been the one who triggered it, and she'd never have to learn what it felt like to flinch when someone raised their voice.

I didn't know.

But I knew this much—it wasn't my job to save him anymore.

Saving myself had been hard enough.

17

LUCY

THE WIND CUT sideways across the parking lot, sharp and biting as I left the gymnastics facility on Tuesday evening, gym bag bumping against my hip. My hood was halfway up, hands stuffed into the sleeves of my puffer coat, but the cold still found its way in anyway.

I typically walked to campus early in the mornings since the scholarship housing I lived in with Nora wasn't too far away and parking on campus was always a nightmare, but freezing cold nights like tonight definitely made me regret that choice.

"Hey, Lucy!" a deep voice called, startling me. "Is that you?"

I slowed, glancing over my shoulder, hoping it was someone I knew instead of a stranger. Then I saw Brody by his white Jetta, tossing his duffel bag into the backseat like he'd just finished practice, too. He jogged toward me, his familiar grin already tugging at his mouth.

"Where're you headed?" he asked, falling into step beside me.

"Dining hall," I said, adjusting the strap of my gym bag on my shoulder. "I was gonna grab something quick before heading to the library. I've got a few assignments to catch up on."

"Same," he said, tugging his cap lower over his eyes. "Well, for the grabbing dinner then doing homework part. I was actually headed to that new Thai place next to The Brew." He pushed his hands in his pockets, the yellow light from the lamps above us highlighting his cheekbones. "Since you were planning to eat anyway, wanna join me?"

I hesitated.

Brody was fun. Cute too. And the girls on the team had been raving all week about the Pho at the new restaurant.

Plus...after seeing Josh with another girl at my meet, it was only fair I hang out with someone from his hockey team. Right?

"Yeah, sure," I said, shrugging. "I'm just getting out of practice, though, so I might look a little crusty."

"You look great," Brody said immediately, his eyes warm and sincere. "You always do."

I rolled my eyes, but a smile tugged at my lips anyway. "Okay, fine. Let's go. I could use something warm."

We climbed into his car, and he drove us toward the new Thai-Vietnamese fusion place next to The Brew. If the weather hadn't been so miserable, we probably would've walked since it was only two blocks away. But with the wind chill creeping through every seam of my coat, I was grateful for the blast of heat from his car's vents.

When Brody opened the restaurant door for me a couple of minutes later, a wave of fragrant warmth rolled out—ginger, spice, and something rich that made my stomach tighten with hunger. Inside, the space felt cozy and inviting. Soft lighting. Polished wood floors. A low hum of conversation and clinking dishes. The tables were small, dressed with vases of fake flowers that looked surprisingly real.

It was busy but not packed. Which was nice since I was starving and didn't want to wait long to be seated or get my food.

"Sit wherever you like," the hostess said from behind the counter, her hands full with takeout orders.

We grabbed a table near the front window, and I took in more of our surroundings as I sank into the chair.

The waitress appeared a moment later with two glasses of water and handed us menus with a friendly smile before disappearing again.

"Know what you're getting?" Brody asked, glancing up from his menu a minute later. "Anything sounding particularly good?"

"I can't decide," I said, chewing on my bottom lip. "It's between the Pad Thai and the Pho."

"Solid picks," he said, nodding. "I'm definitely getting the Pad Thai."

"Okay, cool." I looked over the Pho section again. "Then maybe I'll try the Pho. That way we can tell each other if what we got was good and know what to order next time."

"Oh?" He raised an eyebrow, his grin crooked. "So you're already planning on eating with me again?"

"I wasn't trying to say that exactly..." I laughed, trying to brush it off. "But I guess we'll just have to see how this dinner goes."

"Well..." He leaned forward on his elbows. "It's already going great from where I'm sitting."

A flirty grin curved across his mouth, and despite myself, I felt heat crawl up my neck.

"You're just saying that because you haven't seen me with

chopsticks yet." I gave him a playful look. "It's about to get real awkward real fast."

We were still laughing when the front door opened, and I looked up on instinct.

And instantly regretted it.

Because Owen was just walking in.

With a girl.

Pretty. Brunette. Wearing a cropped cream sweater and jeans that hugged her like they were made for her. She laughed at something he said as he held the door, and he smiled back— his real smile. The one that softened his entire face and made it hard to look away.

My face flushed instantly.

What was it with this week and seeing guys I'd kissed with other women?

First Josh...now Owen?

I forced my gaze back to my menu, pretending to read it like it hadn't just gone blurry. Ugh.

It's not like you have a claim on Owen, I tried to tell myself to keep my sudden disappointment at bay. *He's your professor. Practically a stranger in real life.*

Still...the ache in my stomach said otherwise.

"You okay?" Brody asked, tilting his head.

I blinked and nodded quickly. "Just a little tired."

"Same," he said easily. "So, Pho it is?"

"With beef," I said, grateful for the redirection. "And I'll do the number one spice level. I usually like a two, but I want to see where their heat scale starts first."

"Smart," he said, grinning. "Gotta ease into that fire."

The waitress came over, pen ready, and we placed our orders.

Once she left, I did my best to focus on Brody as he told me about a fight that broke out between a couple of guys on the team during practice that afternoon, but every few seconds, I found myself glancing over at where Owen and his date were sitting.

Was this their first date?

Had they gone out before?

Were they already boyfriend and girlfriend?

The way my stomach turned at that last thought told me I really didn't like that particular idea.

I sipped my water, trying to cool the inexplicable heat rising in my chest, but it didn't quiet the swirl of questions in my head.

Why did I care who Owen ate his meals with?

He was my professor. Off-limits. An impossible idea.

Still, when I risked one more glance—just in time to see him leaning in to say something that made her laugh—something hollow cracked open inside me.

I pressed my lips together and forced myself to look away for good.

Because even if it made no sense to care who Owen might be spending his down time with...I apparently cared, anyway.

Which was just really, really stupid.

I lifted the spoon to my lips and took another sip of the Pho, leaning over the bowl a little more this time. The warmth hit my tongue first—rich, salty, comforting—and then came the kick of spice, just enough to make my nose tingle.

It was exactly what I'd been craving.

But just as I went in for another bite, I heard Owen's deep chuckle, low and unmistakable, drifting across the restaurant like some cruel cosmic reminder. He was laughing at something his date must've said, and the sound of it—so easy, so real—sent a sharp twist through my chest.

My hand slipped.

The spoon clattered back into the bowl, and a rogue splash of broth shot up and hit me square in the eye.

"Ahh!" I yelped, jerking back as the burn seared across my right eyeball.

"What happened?" Brody looked up, wide-eyed, halfway through a bite of Pad Thai. "Are you okay?"

I blinked rapidly, my eye watering like crazy as I grabbed the edge of the table. "I just got some of the spicy broth in my eye."

"Oh man." He winced. "Maybe use water? Try dabbing it out?"

"Okay..." I muttered, grabbing my napkin and dipping it quickly into my glass. I pressed the cool damp cloth to the corner of my eye, blinking hard, hoping it would flush out whatever chili-laced demon had launched itself into my face.

But it didn't help.

If anything, it made it worse.

"Crap." Brody leaned across the table slightly, brows pinched. "Do you need help? What can I do?"

"I don't know..." I whispered back, laughing and wincing at the same time. "But if I don't fix this soon it really might burn a hole in my eye. Do you think it can cause damage?"

Without waiting for an answer, I scrambled out of my seat and made a beeline for the bathroom, barely registering the way I passed Owen's table in my panicked haze.

Of course.

Because why wouldn't I run out of a dinner with another guy right as Owen was glancing up, catching my eye like I was fleeing an awkward first-date disaster? His expression flickered as our eyes met—concern? Confusion? Definitely suspicion.

But really, I didn't have time to figure that out because I needed to get the stinging to stop.

I barreled into the bathroom, shoved the door open, and made a beeline for the sink. Cold water. Rinse. Blink. Repeat. I tilted my head sideways and let the water run into the corner of my eye. Then creating a little pool of water in my cupped hand, I put my eye in the water and blinked furiously to move the water gently around.

It took a minute and a few more handfuls of water, but the burning eventually dulled.

Finally. I exhaled slowly, bracing my hands on the edge of the sink. When I looked at my reflection in the mirror, the girl looking back at me was frazzled, pink-eyed, and mildly tragic.

So much for Brody saying I looked good all the time.

The right side of my eyeliner had all but vanished, the lashes were bare, and the skin under my eye was definitely blotchy. *Awesome.*

Still, there wasn't much I could do now except hold my head high and return to dinner like I hadn't just staged a dramatic chili-oil-related exit.

I opened the bathroom door, ready to make a quiet return to the table, but stopped short when I saw a guy with dark hair and broad shoulders right outside the door.

Owen.

"Hey. Everything okay?" His brow furrowed with quiet concern when he saw me, taking a step closer.

"Oh—yeah." I blinked at him. "Yeah, I'm fine."

"You looked like you were running out of there pretty fast," he said, his voice low. "Did your date say something? Or do something?"

My heart gave a strange little stutter. "What? No!" I shook my head quickly, cheeks warming. "Nothing like that. I swear. It was totally my fault."

Not like I could tell him it was his distracting laugh's fault.

His eyebrows rose, not convinced.

"I dropped my spoon in my Pho and got some of the broth in my eye," I explained. "Which, in case you were wondering, burns like lava. So yeah, I was just trying to flush it out."

Owen blinked, then huffed a quiet laugh and rubbed the back of his neck. "Oh. Okay. Good. I mean, not good that you got broth in your eye but...I'm glad that guy didn't do anything. He's your lab partner, right?"

"Yeah. Brody," I said. "And he was only trying to help." I paused. "Probably thinks I'm an actual hazard to myself now, but still."

Owen gave a small smile, and for a second his gaze dipped, like he was checking for visible damage. "So, you're okay now?"

"Yeah." I nodded. "I mean, I'm sure my eye's a little red and my makeup looks tragic, but I'll survive."

I followed his gaze as it flicked briefly over his shoulder toward the dining area. His date was still seated at their table, facing away from us.

"Your date is probably wondering why you ran after me," I said, not quite able to keep the awkward edge out of my voice.

"It's fine," he said easily. "I told her you're my friend's little sister and I wanted to make sure you were okay."

"You didn't tell her I'm your student?" I tilted my head.

"Not exactly..."

"Right." I nodded knowingly. "Because there are just *so* many students, it's hard to remember everyone." Okay, I'd tried to say it as a joke...but it came out more like I was butthurt over what he'd told my dad after my meet.

Great.

"Would you rather I told your dad I kissed you in the Hamptons, then?" he asked. "And that I can't stop picturing it every time I see you in class?"

My heart stopped.

I froze, completely stunned.

Had I just heard him right? Was that a Freudian slip?

Or had that spicy broth gotten to my brain somehow and was causing it to short-circuit?

Owen's eyes widened like he just realized what he'd said. "Wow. Sorry." He groaned, dragging a hand down his face. "That sounded...really bad. I didn't mean it like—" He broke off, clearly scrambling. "That was inappropriate. I shouldn't have said that."

But despite the sudden awkwardness, something in my chest fluttered.

Because as shocking and probably inappropriate as that comment was...it felt nice to hear it.

Especially after seeing him sit across from his beautiful date tonight.

"It's okay," I said.

"Really?" He glanced back at me, clearly unsure if I meant it.

"Yeah." I nodded. "I mean, I probably would've said the same thing."

"That you think about that kiss every time we bump into each other?" His brows lifted slightly.

"No," I said quickly. "I mean, yes. I mean—" I groaned and covered my face with one hand. "I mean, it was good you told my dad you only vaguely recognized me from your class. Kept things less suspicious. Professional."

"Exactly." Owen gave a small, awkward laugh. "That's what I thought."

We hovered there for a beat, like neither of us really wanted to go back to our tables, even though we both probably should.

After a moment, Owen cleared his throat and shifted his weight. "Well...I better get back to my date."

"Yeah. Me too," I said, offering a small smile. "Thanks for checking on me."

He nodded. "Anytime."

I turned and made my way back toward our table, making a concerted effort to resist glancing over my shoulder once more to watch Owen.

"Feel better?" Brody looked up as I sat down, his eyes flicking toward the bathroom hallway. "Wait...is that Professor Park?"

I followed his gaze, catching the back of Owen's head as he sat down across from his date again.

"Oh. Yeah." I shrugged, working hard to sound casual—like I wasn't the least bit flustered from the hallway detour. "I guess it is."

I could've said Owen had stopped me outside the bathroom. That he'd only followed me out to make sure I was okay.

But I didn't.

Saying it out loud would've made it feel like more than it was.

And the last thing I needed was to start reading into my professor's concern.

18
———

OWEN

I PULLED my apartment door shut behind me on Thursday morning, locking it with the keypad. It was mid-January in Connecticut, which meant the air felt like punishment and the sun was mostly for decoration. My breath fogged in front of me as I adjusted the strap of my satchel across my chest and started down the stairs from my second-floor apartment, squinting against the sharp gusts of wind that whipped across the parking lot.

Then I saw her.

Lucy.

She was walking past my building, bundled in the puffy white coat she'd worn the first night I met her. Her hood was up with her long blonde ponytail draped over one shoulder, head slightly bowed against the wind.

I froze mid-step.

I could duck back inside, pretend I forgot something, and avoid that awkward shuffle where we both had to decide whether to walk together or politely ignore each other—something I should probably do if I wanted to avoid any slip-ups like the one I had when I bumped into her Tuesday night.

But then, she looked up.

Saw me.

And smiled.

It was casual. Innocent. Just a girl acknowledging her professor on the sidewalk.

At least, that was what it was probably supposed to be.

So naturally...I read way too much into it.

And instead of heading back inside like a sane person, I made my way down the steps and toward the sidewalk so I could meet up with her just as she was passing by.

"Hey," I said, boots crunching on the salted pavement.

She pulled one earbud out and glanced over at me. "Morning."

"Heading to campus?"

She nodded. "Just heading to the dining hall to grab something to eat before class."

"Nice," I said, matching her pace. "How's the semester going so far?"

"Pretty good," she said, tugging her coat tighter. "I only have twelve credits this semester, so it's been a dream compared to last semester."

"Do you usually take more?"

"Usually," she said. "But I only needed a few more classes to graduate. Which is good since competition season always kicks my butt."

"I bet." I chuckled softly. "You've got a full-time job just keeping your body from falling apart."

"Pretty much." She gave a little laugh. "Most of my classes are fine, though."

"Even your chemistry classes?" I arched an eyebrow, trying to sound casual as I inquired about the classes she had with me.

"I mean, I had a bit of a rough start." She glanced over at me, her expression teasing. "Totally insulted the professor. So that wasn't great."

"I'm sure it was an honest mistake," I said, thinking back to that first class when she'd assumed I was a non-traditional student, wide-eyed and taking a crack at college for the first time.

"Maybe." She shrugged, a playful smirk tugging at her lips. "But I'm a little worried he's gonna be extra hard on me."

"Why's that?" I furrowed my brow. Had I done something to make her think I was upset with her?

Sure, I'd been surprised when I saw her in my class. Might've freaked out a bit when she mentioned her dad was President Archibald.

But I didn't think I'd treated her any differently since that first day.

If anything, I'd probably been too nice.

At least in my head I had.

Hopefully, she hadn't noticed the way I'd stared at her as she twisted her hair into that messy bun during last week's lab, or how I secretly wished she'd sit in the front row of the lecture hall instead of the back just so I could actually see her face when she smiled.

"Oh, you know." She glanced over at me, blue eyes dancing with mischief. "I just figured my chemistry professor might be a little tougher on me...just so no one suspects that I tried to seduce him into giving me an A before the semester even started."

I stumbled slightly on a patch of ice, catching myself just in time.

Smooth. Real smooth.

"Too soon?" She laughed, clearly amused by my lack of

coordination—or maybe by how hard I was trying to play it cool.

"Yeah, maybe," I said, dragging a hand up to tug at the collar of my coat, trying not to smile.

Trying harder not to think about the truth behind the joke.

We walked in silence for a few seconds, the wind howling softly between us.

Then I said, "Also...in case you were wondering, I'm slightly terrified of your dad."

"What?" Lucy shot me a skeptical look. "My dad is scary? That's crazy talk. He's like...the biggest softy I've ever met."

I gave her a long, pointed look.

"Okay, fine." She huffed a laugh. "So maybe my cute niece is the only one who brings out that side of him."

"Yeah." I shoved my hands deeper into my coat pockets. "When he sat by us at the meet, I about had a heart attack. I was convinced he'd somehow pick up on...something. Like if I so much as glanced your way, he'd know."

She gave me a sideways glance, cheeks pink from the wind —or maybe from the memory of the meet. "Well, did you like it? What you said afterward was really nice. But do you actu- ally like watching gymnastics?"

"It was really cool," I said honestly. "I've watched a little. The Olympics, a few meets back at Yale...but that was my first in a while."

"Yale?" Her brow lifted. "The *bartender* went to Yale?"

I chuckled under my breath. "Yeah. Full-ride scholarship too."

"Geez." She shook her head with a sheepish grin. "How embarrassing for Nicole and me to assume you'd never even been to college."

I shrugged it off and pivoted the conversation. "You got a scholarship here, though, didn't you?"

"For gymnastics," she said. "Academics were okay. But spending so much time in the gym and barely scraping by with my online classes...let's just say, academics weren't exactly my forte. Which I'm sure you already know if you've graded my test from yesterday."

"You didn't do too bad," I said, glancing at her. "A B's pretty solid."

She let out a sigh. "Tell that to my dad."

"Is he pretty tough, then?" I asked, remembering the way he'd critiqued her routine. Not harsh but definitely exacting. Focused.

We stopped at the intersection, and I hit the crosswalk button. A few cars whooshed past, tires hissing against damp pavement.

"I don't know how much Theo's told you about growing up," she said, checking for traffic. "But Archibalds don't get B's."

"So he expects a lot."

"Yep." She gave a small nod. "But it pushes me to do my best. To work hard. So I guess I can't be too upset."

I looked at her, noticing the tight line of her shoulders, the fatigue behind her eyes. It wasn't hard to recognize the signs of burnout when you'd lived through it yourself—and I'd bet she was closer to the edge than she wanted to admit.

She must've noticed me watching too closely because she cleared her throat and glanced away.

"Anyway," she said quickly, "Theo's turning thirty in a few weeks. I was thinking of planning a surprise party and inviting a bunch of his friends."

"That sounds fun."

"I thought so." Her smile returned. "And since you two seem to be buddies, I had this idea that maybe you could take him out for dinner or drinks that night. I'll offer to babysit

Charlotte as an excuse to get in, and while you're out, Nora and I can decorate and get everything set up. Then when you bring him back—bam! Surprise party."

I smiled. "That's actually a pretty genius plan."

"Thanks. So...would you be up for that?"

"What day were you thinking?"

"February twelfth."

I pulled out my phone and swiped to my calendar, scanning through the second week of February. "Looks like it's a Saturday," I said. "I sometimes work at The Garden on weekends, but I haven't made the schedule for that one yet. I'll just swap and work Friday instead."

"Thanks," she said, her breath puffing visibly in the cold air. "That would be amazing."

We were almost to the intersection where I'd need to veer right for the science building. She was headed to the dining hall in the student center. Our impromptu walk was coming to an end, but she slowed slightly, like something else had occurred to her.

"Hey...do you happen to have the numbers for Theo's friends?" she asked. "Maybe Miles and Bash? Anyone else you think he'd want there? I was hoping to text out the invites soon, but I don't want to be suspicious and ask Theo for a 'friend list.'"

I nodded. "I can send those to you. I should have a handful of numbers at least."

"Perfect."

We both paused at the edge of the sidewalk, a little awkwardly, realizing at the same time what that meant.

"I, uh, I guess I'll need your number to do that," I said, glancing around instinctively as I pulled out my phone again.

No one seemed to be paying attention—just a stream of

students rushing past us, bundled in coats, backpacks bouncing as they crossed toward their respective buildings.

"Oh, right. Of course," she said, fishing out her own phone.

"So...what's your number?" I asked, thumb poised to enter it.

She gave it to me, and I typed it in, then fired off a quick message:

Me: This is Theo's bartender friend.

Her phone buzzed a second later, and she looked down at the screen, a tiny smile tugging at the corner of her lips.

I saved her contact info under the safest thing I could think of: *Theo's sister*.

She peeked at my screen as I tapped it in. "Nervous one of the other professors will see your phone in the faculty lounge?"

"I might be slightly paranoid," I admitted, pocketing it again.

She gave me a knowing smile but didn't press it.

I glanced to the right, toward the science building. "Well, I gotta go this way."

"And I'm headed this way." She nodded, motioning to the left.

"I guess I'll see you in the lab this afternoon."

"Yep." Her smile tilted playfully. "Can't wait."

I watched her go for a beat, wondering if that had been sarcasm because chemistry definitely wasn't her favorite subject. But who knows, maybe there was a part of her that looked forward to it for the new reasons I did.

I sat at my desk near the back of the lab, pretending to review quizzes while doing a truly pathetic job of not watching Lucy Archibald.

She was packing up her station with Brody, chatting easily as they wiped down their workspace. I'd only had to step in once—when their thermometer wasn't fully submerged in the calorimeter during the enthalpy change experiment. Brody had caught it halfway through my explanation, fixed the issue without fuss, and double-checked the measurements like he'd been born holding a pipette.

Which...made him a really solid lab partner for Lucy.

Almost too solid, though...

Sure, Lucy deserved someone competent. But did it have to be a star athlete who made her laugh like that?

A six-foot-four golden boy who leaned in close enough to look like he'd be happy to help with more than her chemistry homework.

Okay, so maybe that was exactly the kind of academic partnership I should be encouraging.

If only it didn't cause a hollow thud in my chest every time I watched them work together.

They finished packing up along with the rest of the class. Lucy shrugged on her coat. And when they walked to the door, Brody held it open for her.

"Thanks," I heard her tell him, her voice cheerful.

And then, they were gone, headed to whatever plans they had next.

I stared after them a beat longer than I should have.

That was the last class I'd have with her until Monday. Where I would just teach her from the front of the class and make a few stupid jokes with the hope that I might hear her cute laugh from the back of the room.

I sighed as I slid various class data sheets into my satchel. I really needed to stop letting Lucy take up so much of my brain space.

"See you next week, Professor Park," one of my students called on his way out the door.

"Have a great night," I said.

The rest of the students filed out shortly after that, and then it was just me.

Time to head to my office and see if any students will drop by for office hours. It wasn't super likely since we were only two weeks into the semester, but I needed to be there just in case.

I was just walking toward the door, hand lifting to flip off the lights when suddenly, a flash of blonde hair appeared in front of me.

"Oh! Hey, Lucy—" I startled, taking a quick step backward.

For a moment, I wondered if I'd conjured her out of pure wishful thinking.

But then she said, "Oh good, you're still here." Her breath came quick. "I-I think I left my phone in here somewhere."

"Uh...okay." I stepped back to let her inside. "Yeah. Come in."

She headed straight for the station she and Brody had been at earlier, eyes scanning the countertop. But when she didn't see anything, she crouched down and picked something up from beneath her stool. "Got it," she said, holding her phone up. "Must've fallen out of my coat or something. Thanks."

"No problem." I cleared my throat as we started toward the door again. "You have any more classes today?" I decided to ask, forcing a casual tone.

"Nope," she said, falling into step beside me like it was the most natural thing in the world. "This is my last class today. What about you?"

"I just have office hours."

"Oh, cool." She looked ahead like she was making a mental note. "Have you had many students come in for help yet?"

"Not yet. But we're only two weeks in. I'm sure the panic will set in soon enough."

"Oh, I bet," she said, smiling. "Pretty sure I'll be one of those panicked students."

I glanced sideways at her. "It looked like you and Brody had a pretty good handle on today's lab."

"It went okay." She shrugged. "Mostly thanks to Brody."

"You two seem to work well together." I hesitated before adding, "Do you know each other outside of class?"

"A little," she said. "He's on the hockey team with my ex." She looked up at me as if remembering something. "Actually... he's the guy Josh punched at The Garden that first night we met."

"Oh." My brows lifted. "That's...interesting."

I'd never really gotten much of an explanation about where things were with the guy she'd driven home. But she was calling him her ex, so maybe her spending time with him that night was just an oddity.

Especially if she was friendly with the guy he'd been in a fight with—having dinner in restaurants with him, too.

Which made me curious. And even though I knew it was none of my business and that I probably shouldn't ask, I found myself saying, "That dinner at the restaurant with Brody, was that a date?"

"Oh, that." She slowed half a step, then gave me a sideways glance. "I don't really know what it was. Just dinner...?"

"Nice," I said, hoping it wasn't completely obvious how relieved I was by that answer. Because I *really* shouldn't care whether they'd been on a date or not.

"Your date was cute, by the way," she said, something in her tone I couldn't interpret. "You two serious? Boyfriend-girl-friend perhaps?"

"Not quite." I chuckled awkwardly. "It was a first date."

"Oh..." Her voice trailed, her expression unreadable. "Well, it looked like you were having a good time together."

She'd been paying attention?

Not that I should care.

"Yeah, it was fine." I cleared my throat. "Uh, I mean, we had a good dinner."

At least the first part had gone well...right up until the point when I'd seen Lucy and suddenly became distracted.

Silence settled between us for a moment as we took the turn to where my office was.

"Well, this is my office." I cleared my throat again and nodded toward the door ahead. I pulled out my keycard and swiped it, hearing the lock click open.

"Ooh." She leaned forward for a peek as I pushed the door open. "Looks nice. Very...chemistry professor-like."

She must have been referring to the periodic table art on the wall, which was a parting gift from the faculty at Eden Falls Academy when I left my position there to come here.

"I guess." I dropped my bag beside the desk, glancing over my shoulder. "All it's missing is a leather armchair."

She lingered just inside the doorway as I sat on the edge of my desk. After taking in more of my office, she smiled, saying, "So this is where the chemistry happens."

I was not proud of where my brain went next. A scene from some steamy student-teacher film came to mind—her walking in, clicking the door shut. Me pulling her into a kiss that had nothing to do with lab reports or energy equations.

I flinched and pushed the thought away. I definitely didn't need to be picturing something like that.

Especially not when the girl I'd very much like to do that with was standing just a couple feet away.

I cleared my throat, hoping the sound would scrub the images from my head. "Uh, yeah. I pretty much just log students' grades in here and answer questions."

"Of course," she said, but the flush in her cheeks made me wonder if her brain had gone somewhere similar to mine. Her walking in, shutting the door behind her, me pinning her against it, kissing her until—

Nope. Not going there.

I opened my mouth to say something—anything to steer the conversation into safer territory—when I heard footsteps in the hallway. And then a voice.

Dean Harris.

He was chatting with someone just outside. I stiffened, pulse spiking. Maybe he'd just keep walking.

Please keep walking.

"Have a good evening, Professor Marks," the Dean said, and I winced.

Great.

I shot a quick look at Lucy, who was still standing near my desk, utterly unaware of the panic crashing through my chest.

I needed this to look aboveboard.

Like an actual office-hours interaction.

"So basically," I said suddenly, loud enough to carry, "you're measuring the enthalpy change, which is just a fancy way of saying how much heat is released or absorbed during the reaction."

Lucy blinked at me, obviously confused why I was suddenly talking science nerd. So I gave her a barely-there nod toward the door, hoping she'd understand we were on display.

Her eyes widened slightly in understanding.

"Yes," she said, recovering smoothly. "Thank you. I think I'll be able to complete the assignment now."

"Perfect," I said, just as Dean Harris appeared in the doorway. "And of course, if you have any questions over the weekend, feel free to email me."

Dean Harris stepped up beside her. "Miss Archibald?"

Lucy turned, smiling politely. "Hi."

"I didn't recognize you for a second," the Dean said. "Are you taking a class from Professor Park?"

"Yes." She nodded. "Intro to Chemistry. He was just helping me with an assignment."

"Perfect." Dean Harris beamed. "Professor Park is an excellent teacher. You're lucky to have him."

"He's been very helpful so far." Lucy shot me a quick glance, her lips twitching like she was trying not to smile too hard. "Thanks again, Professor Park. I'll see you in class next week."

"Yes." I cleared my throat, trying to keep my voice neutral. "Have a good weekend. Good luck on your meet in Michigan."

She paused, giving me a slightly puzzled look.

Right. Because she'd never told me where she was competing this weekend.

Because I'd done that little bit of research on my own.

Which meant I'd just outed myself for looking up her schedule.

Fantastic.

19

———

LUCY

WHEN I GOT BACK to my apartment, it was quiet. Peacefully, gloriously quiet.

Nora had mentioned she had a study group tonight, so I wasn't surprised. Still, the silence felt like a small gift after a day that had pulled me in seven different directions. I dropped my bag by the door, kicked off my shoes, and flopped onto the couch to scroll through my phone for a minute.

When my screen lit up, I was surprised to see a message from **"Theo's friend."**

Eek! My stomach did a back tuck at the sight of the nickname I'd given Owen when I added him to my contacts.

I swiped up to read the message.

> Theo's friend: Hey, sorry for getting weird when Dean Harris showed up. I'm clearly great at panicking around people who can fire me.

I laughed softly, shaking my head as the image replayed in

my mind—Owen standing in his office, suddenly flustered and talking about some chemistry concept that was over my head.

It was kind of cute.

Okay, really cute.

And honestly? Totally understandable. Dean Harris definitely had that whole "stern but fair" energy that could make anyone sweat.

Which is probably why he and my dad get along so well.

I typed out a quick response.

> Me: It's totally fine. I get it.

I hovered for a second, debating whether to add something else—something flirty, maybe. A little joke. A wink.

But no...

Better to keep it appropriate.

So I just hit *send*.

Then...waited.

My phone stayed in my hand, thumb hovering like maybe he'd respond immediately.

The message shifted from *delivered* to *read*, but no dots.

No typing bubble.

I stared for another second—okay, maybe twenty seconds—then sighed and put my phone back in my pocket.

Guess that was it.

So I padded to my room to change into something cozy and oversized.

I shed my jeans quickly, grabbed my favorite fleece pajama pants—the thick pink ones with tiny, faded stars—and tugged them on. Then came the oversized red EFU Gymnastics hoodie that had survived more late-night cramming sessions and post-practice naps than I could count.

I was just pulling it over my head when my phone buzzed from where I'd dropped my jeans on the floor.

Dare I hope it's him?

My heart did a hopeful little leap as I retrieved my phone and checked the screen.

It *was* him.

But the smile that had started to bloom on my lips dimmed slightly when I opened the message and saw it was all business. Like he'd just handed me a clipboard and walked away.

> Theo's friend: Sorry I didn't have a chance to send these over until now. But here are the phone numbers I have for a few of Theo's friends.

A second later, my screen filled with contact cards. Sloan. Jennifer. Miles. Bash. Rosalyn. Freddy. Ian. Evan.

Looks like my brother has more friends than I thought.

I waited a beat to see if anything else would come through, but nothing did. So I sent a quick response.

> Me: Thank you so much for these. I'll send out the invites soon.

> Theo's friend: No problem.

And just like that, the conversation was over.

Apparently.

I stared at the screen, trying to think of an excuse to keep talking.

Should I ask him something about the chemistry assignment he'd given us? (The one that I'd already finished last night.)

Though...that would probably only reinforce the whole

student/professor thing, which I really didn't want to do right now.

Maybe I could thank him again for helping with Theo's party?

Though...that would just be redundant, and he'd probably only respond with a "you're welcome" text or something impersonal like that.

What I really wanted to ask was how he'd known I'd be in Michigan this weekend. Because I was pretty sure I hadn't mentioned anything about it.

But no. I probably shouldn't go there either. We'd exchanged numbers for Theo's party, and now that he'd given me those contacts, the only reason I had for texting him was technically fulfilled.

Which meant I should probably move on with my evening and get myself something to eat.

Normally, I'd grab something quick from the dining hall before coming home. But it had been such a chilly day that I'd just wanted to get home and cozy as soon as possible.

Of course, that meant I still had to figure out dinner.

I considered ordering in—but when I spotted a packet of my favorite ramen in the cupboard, I smiled.

Not exactly meal plan approved, but sometimes perfection was for the birds.

I got a pot boiling, cooked the noodles, cracked in two eggs for protein, and stirred everything together. It wasn't gourmet, but it would do.

Just as I was pouring the steaming broth into a bowl, my phone buzzed again.

Another message from Owen?

I wiped my hands and reached for it, only to see Nora's name.

Nora: Hey, I know I said we'd watch a movie tonight, but my study group invited me to hang out, so I'm gonna do that instead, if that's okay.

Me: No worries. Have fun.

We'd spent so much time together in the gym already today, I wasn't bothered. Especially since she'd mentioned there was a cute guy in her study group she was hoping would ask her out.

Hopefully, there'd be sparks.

With my ramen in hand, I curled up on the couch, pulled a cozy blanket across my lap, and flicked the TV on.

I never had time to watch anything, but the newest season of *Finding Your Soulmate* had just started airing, so I pulled it up and hit *play*.

Nothing like watching a good reality TV trainwreck to distract me from the fact that my own love life was just as derailed.

I settled into the cushions, took a bite of noodles, and had just started sinking into the show when my phone buzzed again.

Nora?

I glanced down, but it wasn't Nora at all.

Theo's friend: Hey, I know this is probably me just digging my grave even more. But I hope you aren't weirded out that I knew about your meet in Michigan this weekend. I was just

I stared at the message, the rest of it cut off.

Was just what?

Looking? Curious? *Secretly obsessed?*

Okay, probably not that. But still—

I bit my lip and waited.

Please send the next part. Please don't leave me hanging.

> Theo's friend: Uh, sorry. Hit send before I meant to.

> Theo's friend: What I meant to say is that I was curious if there was a gymnastics meet here this week because I was thinking about going. And I saw that it was away. In Michigan.

I bit back a smile, my thumb hovering over the keyboard.

So he'd wanted to come watch again?

That was...unexpected. Sweet.

Maybe even a little reckless, considering everything.

I stared at the blinking cursor in our message thread for a full ten seconds, then typed:

> Me: Any reason you're suddenly interested in the sport? ••

Dare I hope it might have something to do with me?

My finger hovered over the *send* button.

Was that too much?

I could just delete it. Ask something normal. Neutral.

But...he'd started this text thread. And if he was testing the waters, maybe I could dip a toe in, too.

Just a toe, I reminded myself.

I hit *Send.*

The conversation dots appeared instantly.

And just like that, my heart was doing its usual traitorous thing—leaping into the air like it had just nailed a perfect routine.

> Theo's friend: It's a fun sport to watch. Very...
> interesting.

I blinked, rereading that last line. Paying probably too much attention to those three dots.

He was flirting with me, right?

Hinting that he liked watching me perform...

I mean, it wasn't as out there and obvious as what he'd said at the restaurant—when he'd mentioned that he imagined our hot tub kiss every time he saw me in class.

But...this was still something. Wasn't it?

Trying to keep it breezy, I texted:

> Me: Glad you like it. It's my favorite sport to
> watch. Compete in too. 😉

His reply came quickly.

> Theo's friend: I had a hunch it might be. Since
> you're...pretty impressive at it. Definitely
> great to watch.

There were those three dots again.

And he thought I was impressive?

My cheeks flushed. I had to set my ramen on the end table before I accidentally spilled it all over myself. I sat up straighter, fingers tingling as I typed:

> Me: Thanks. I could probably say the same
> about how you teach chemistry... Dragging
> myself to class hasn't been nearly as hard as
> I thought it might be this semester...

I stared at the message after hitting *Send*.

Was that too much? Putting those three dots in my text like he had?

Too obvious?

But then, another message pushed through.

> Theo's friend: If you like class that much,
> maybe you should sit on the front row next
> time. Easier to see from up there…

A laugh bubbled out of me before I could stop it.

Professor Park was letting his flirty side out.

And I was definitely not mad about it.

Two nights later, after dinner with the team in Kalamazoo, Michigan, I curled up on my hotel bed with my laptop open, a half-eaten protein bar next to me, and my marketing strategy notes spread out like a sad little fan.

The TV was playing a 90s sitcom in the background, and Nora and Mayci were on the other bed talking stats on Michigan's top vaulters.

I should've been listening to their conversation. Or at least focusing on my notes.

But instead, I glanced at my phone.

Then checked it again.

Because yes, I might have been hoping for another message from Owen. Since yeah…we'd been texting off and on since Thursday night.

As if he'd read my mind, my screen lit up.

> Theo's friend: What are you up to tonight?

I hesitated only a second before snapping a photo of the mess beside me—highlighters, laptop, and the corner of my pajama-clad leg. Nothing scandalous. Just the plaid flannel pants I'd borrowed from Theo over Christmas break and never returned.

> Me: Living the glamorous life. Homework and hotel TV.

I probably shouldn't be sending photos to my professor...
But it was innocent enough. Right?
A second later, a message came through.

> Theo's friend: Those pajamas look dangerously comfy.

I smiled, biting my lip. Liking that he was getting more risky with his texts. Pushing the boundaries between professional and flirty a little more.

> Me: They are. Might wear them to my meet tomorrow.

> Me: You doing anything fun tonight?

Please don't say you're on another date with that girl.
A beat passed and then he sent a photo, too. The dim glow of overhead lights and the soft blur of liquor bottles.
The Garden's bar.

> Theo's friend: Just working.

> Me: You work too much. You should make time for more fun.

> Theo's friend: I could say the same about you.

Touché.

I stared at the photo a second longer, his viewpoint still glowing.

Then, before I could talk myself out of it, I typed:

> Me: Too bad you couldn't make it to the away meet. Word on the street there's a hot tub at my hotel.

Okay. That was probably a little too much. Definitely riding the edge.

But I couldn't help it. He'd been flirty in our texts. So I was just matching his energy.

That was allowed, right?

Plus, he was seven hundred miles away. It wasn't like we could even act on it.

I was just...painting a picture.

His reply came a moment later.

> Theo's friend: Wouldn't mind a redo of the last time I was in a hot tub.

A warm flush rolled through me, curling low in my stomach.

Okay, so *now* we were officially playing with fire.

But when you had the kind of chemistry we did—no pun intended—was it really a surprise that we'd still be thinking about it?

Even if we couldn't actually *act* on it?

> Me: It was quite fun.

> Theo's friend: Especially the part where everyone else was gone.

My stomach dipped at the memory of that moment. The way the world had gone quiet. The heat of his hands, the steady strength in his arms, the way he'd looked at me like he already knew and accepted everything about me.

Was there any chance of that happening again?

I stared at the screen for a long second, then typed:

> Me: Too bad you're my professor now.

> Theo's friend: Too bad your dad could fire me and get me blacklisted.

Yeah...my dad definitely had the power to do that. Which was not a fun reminder to have when I'd been having so much fun not thinking about it.

I blinked down at my screen, something hollow opening just under my ribs as I asked something I hadn't realized I'd been wondering until now.

> Me: Is your dad as strict as mine?

A minute passed.

Nothing.

Maybe he'd gotten distracted, pouring someone a drink. Maybe someone had flagged him down across the bar.

Or maybe he just didn't want to answer that one.

I picked up my laptop again, trying to focus on my assignment and the murmured conversation Nora and Mayci were having across the room about the Michigan beam lineup.

But then, my phone buzzed again.

Theo's friend: He wasn't too strict. Lost his temper from time to time, but now that I'm older I can see that was mostly just his stress taking over. There was a lot going on back then. My mom was checked out at times so he was raising three kids on his own at some points.

I blinked, something in my chest softening as I read it again.

I hadn't expected that answer. He'd seemed so perfect and grounded, like he'd grown up in a house with matching holiday pajamas and French toast Sundays.

Me: Has he chilled out since then?

My dad definitely had, once Theo and I moved out.

Apparently, parenting was stressful for everyone.

And his mom had been checked out?

Owen's response didn't come in immediately. But then he said:

Theo's friend: He actually passed. Almost ten years ago.

I stared at his message, the words sinking in slow.

He actually passed. Almost ten years ago.

I sat back a little, fingers still on the phone, but no words coming right away.

I hadn't expected him to say that.

And now that he had, I realized I didn't know anything about his family. Nothing about where he came from.

Nothing about his loss.

I exhaled slowly, trying to think of what to say. Something that wouldn't sound stiff or awkward. Something that wouldn't feel like I was tiptoeing around grief like it was a puddle on the sidewalk.

Something Theo might have needed to hear after Alisha died.

Finally, I typed:

> Me: I'm really sorry, Owen. That must've been so hard.

I stared at the blinking cursor for a second longer.
Then added:

> Me: He must've been a really great person. Raising someone like you.

I sent the message, my stomach tight.
And waited.
The screen stayed still. No dots. No reply.
Maybe I'd said the wrong thing. Maybe he didn't want sympathy. Maybe I should've kept it lighter—just said *I'm sorry* and left it at that.

I stared at my phone, thumb brushing against the edge of the case as I tried listening to Mayci and Nora, but my brain was only half there.

He said his dad had passed about ten years ago. So...with Owen being twenty-eight or twenty-nine, that meant he'd lost his dad when he was probably just starting college.

Younger than me.

Maybe his mom had checked back in when his dad died. Hopefully, he and his siblings were able to rely on each other.

Was Owen the oldest? Youngest?

Or in the middle?

It would definitely affect any responsibility he would feel like he'd need to take on if he had younger siblings at that time.

I wanted to ask him those things, but since I still had no response, I didn't want to overload him with messages.

Hopefully, he just got busy serving drinks.

Hopefully, we could talk some more soon.

20

OWEN

LIGHT WAS ALREADY SLIPPING through the blinds in my small bedroom when I woke on Sunday morning, cutting across the comforter in long, lazy lines. My head sank deeper into the pillow as I stretched one arm across the mattress, still half-asleep.

After giving my body a few minutes to decide whether it wanted to drift back to sleep, I rolled onto my back and reached for my phone on the nightstand.

Notifications filled the screen—group-chat updates from Bash, Ky, and Miles; a few emails; a reminder about a meeting with Dean Harris on Monday—and then one that made my stomach twist a little.

Lucy.

Right. Our conversation from last night.

I scrolled up, trying to remember where I'd left things...and immediately winced.

She'd replied to my text about my dad. Twice.

And I'd just left her on *Read.*

Not because I meant to. Not because I didn't care. Just...

The Garden got slammed after that big birthday group walked in, and by the time I remembered to check my phone again, it was well past two. Too late to reply without seeming like a total creep.

Still, a pit of guilt settled in my stomach as I opened our thread again.

Her messages were sweet. Gentle. Exactly the kind of responses I didn't know I needed until I read them.

But then I scrolled a little farther up and saw the other part of our conversation. The part where the late-night version of me—the looser, more open, bartender me—was behind the wheel.

Yeah...in the light of day, those messages suddenly felt reckless.

And I probably shouldn't have said half the things I'd said.

Not because I didn't mean them.

Just...because I knew better. She was my student.

And this was complicated.

Even so, I found myself tapping out a reply.

> Me: Hey, sorry for leaving you on read last night. Got slammed at The Garden and didn't get back to my phone. But thank you—I really appreciate it.

Then I decided to add another text.

> Me: It was definitely hard at first and everything was kind of a mess. It's a long story that I don't really want to get into over text since it's...a lot. But you're sweet. And I'm okay now.

I hit *Send* and stared up at the ceiling, letting the reminders of those hard times settle. I hadn't talked about my family with anyone new in a long time.

A few seconds passed before my phone buzzed again.

> Theo's sister: Glad I didn't offend you or anything. I'm not always the best with my words. (Or texts in this case.)

That made me smile.

> Me: You're just great. And from where I'm sitting, your texting abilities are perfect.

I'd had fun chatting, at least.

Even though I probably shouldn't be doing it...

But the line between *appropriate* and *not* had been severely blurred from the beginning.

She'd started as just a cute girl at the bar. Then a fun girl at Ky's party.

In any other universe, I would've asked her out by now. Taken her to dinner. Maybe kissed her under something other than string lights and poor judgment.

It wasn't her fault she'd walked into my classroom a week later.

My phone buzzed again.

> Theo's sister: I'm glad you've enjoyed it. I've liked texting with you too.

My heart gave a soft thud.

We were being good. So careful.

Tiptoeing around this undeniable pull that didn't feel like nothing.

I typed back.

Me: What time's your meet today? You already at the arena?

Theo's sister: It doesn't start until 1:00, but we're just about to leave the hotel and head over.

Me: Cool. Well…good luck. I hope you have a great meet.

Theo's sister: Thanks 😊

I stared at that emoji longer than I probably should have. And then closed my eyes, wondering how much longer we could play this game without someone getting burned.

21

———

LUCY

I PULLED my backpack over my coat, my body heavy with that bone-deep kind of exhaustion that makes you question every life choice you've ever made—including taking a marketing class with a professor who clearly hated joy.

Yeah, the honeymoon phase of the semester was officially over. Two weeks in and things were getting serious.

I'd been holed up in the same corner of the library for hours, and even though it was only Tuesday, it already felt like I was dragging myself through the last leg of finals week.

But after traveling all day Saturday and Sunday for our Michigan meet, it wasn't like I'd had a real weekend.

I'd stayed way later than planned tonight, determined to finish my marketing project before the deadline. I'd meant to do it over the weekend, but between the meet, the flight, and the general chaos of competing, it hadn't exactly happened.

At least it was done now, submitted with a few hours to spare. Now all I wanted was to get home, face-plant into my pillow, and sleep.

Silly me for believing that taking twelve credits this

semester would mean less homework. Apparently, Professor Walker was serious about her belief that we should have three hours of homework for every single hour we spent in her class.

Yeah. She wasn't exactly winning the title of favorite professor right now.

And it wasn't just because someone else had already accidentally claimed that spot. A certain professor with a ridiculously nice smile and a habit of making chemistry feel way more appealing than it had any right to be.

Speaking of Professor Heartthrob...had he texted me?

I reached for my phone in my back pocket before remembering I'd shoved it deep into the bottom of my backpack hours ago to keep myself from checking it.

Because, yeah, texting my very off-limits professor was definitely more fun than finishing a project that felt like pulling teeth.

I made my way down the steps to the main level of the library. When I stepped outside, the night air hit me—crisp, still, and a little eerie in the way late nights tend to be. The kind of quiet where every sound feels louder, and every shadow makes you wonder who or what might be watching.

It was fine, though. I lived just a few blocks off campus. I'd walked this route a hundred times. I didn't need to ask Nora to come meet me.

But as I crossed the library parking lot, I started to feel it. That instinct that makes you wish you weren't walking alone.

I wrapped my arms tighter around myself and picked up the pace a little.

I'll be home in ten minutes or less. No need to worry.

Bright lights switched on and the roar of a car engine sounded from a few yards in front of me.

It's just someone leaving the school.

But when I started walking past it, instead of pulling out

onto the road quickly and going its merry way, the car crept forward slowly.

My heart thudded once as I glanced over my shoulder and my brain immediately started spinning worst-case scenarios.

Had the person in the car been waiting for me?

Was someone going to jump out and grab me?

But then, the driver suddenly floored it, making the tires squeal on the road as it sped forward and disappeared.

I let out a quiet breath.

Only a few blocks left. I could do this.

I was just trying to talk myself out of being paranoid when I spotted a figure coming from the PE building—tall, dressed in dark clothes, and heading the same direction I was.

Okay. It was probably someone who worked in the equipment cage. Or a student finishing a late-night pickup game.

Totally normal.

Still, my gut tensed.

He was big. Well over six feet—probably close to the same size as Josh.

Too big for me to take on.

I kept walking. Tried to look casual. Normal. Not like someone silently rehearsing every self-defense tip she'd ever heard on TikTok.

But when I heard footsteps closer than they'd been before and just a little too in sync with my own, I couldn't ignore it anymore.

Was he closer?

I didn't want to turn around again. Didn't want to draw attention to myself, or my fear, if this was nothing. But...what if it wasn't?

I glanced back.

He was behind me.

And yeah. Definitely closer than before.

He could just be headed the same way, I told myself. If he was an athlete, he probably lived in the same dorms. He could—

He picked up his pace.

Nope. No. My stomach dropped.

I sped up, practically speed-walking now, my heart thudding louder with every step. Everything felt tight—my chest, my throat, my limbs still sore from training.

Come on, Lucy. Don't freak out yet. Just find somewhere, anywhere you can duck into.

Except everything nearby was dark. Closed. Was there an emergency button somewhere?

I scanned the street like my life depended on it. And then I saw it.

Owen's apartment.

Or at least the one I'd seen him leave last week.

I was pretty sure he'd come down from the second-floor unit, the one with the faint porch light still on.

Maybe I could hide out there for a bit? Just until this guy passed by?

If I crossed the street now, and the guy behind me didn't follow, then I could just continue home. No need for a detour. But if he did stop…

Well, hopefully Owen was home and would be okay with a visitor.

I sprinted across the street. Cut straight for the steps. Risked one more glance over my shoulder.

And there he was.

Jogging across the street.

Straight toward me.

No.

Nope. Not waiting to see if this was some harmless misunderstanding.

I ran.

Boots slamming against the concrete as I bolted toward the stairwell, heart pounding. I took the stairs two at a time, adrenaline giving me wings—until my foot slipped on a patch of ice.

My leg shot out. I slammed my shin against the metal stair with a sharp cry, "Oww—" Pain was instantly shooting down the front of my leg.

But I couldn't stop.

I scrambled up the rest of the stairs, one hand gripping the rail as I reached the landing, praying I'd picked the right door, praying Owen was home.

I knocked frantically.

Come on, Owen. Please be around. Please don't be in the shower or something.

My heart thumped in my ears, and I risked a glance over my shoulder.

Hey, wait— Was he gone?

The street looked empty now, nothing but the dim orange glow of the lamplight.

But then, movement.

A shadow shifting behind the tree near the curb.

My stomach twisted and I knocked again, even harder.

Please, Owen. Please be home.

The door opened.

Owen stood there in sweatpants and a hoodie, his hair tousled like he'd just pulled himself off the couch. His expression went from startled to alarmed in half a second when he saw me.

"Lucy?" he asked, stepping forward. "What—what's wrong? Are you okay?"

"Can I come in?" My voice came out rushed, breathless. "Someone was following me."

"What?" His whole body went stiff. He glanced past me

toward the street, scanning the sidewalk, his expression fierce. But from here, the shadows gave nothing away.

"Of course. Come in." He stepped aside immediately, hand on the door to hold it open. I slipped past him, my body still shaking as I crossed the threshold.

"Can you lock it?" I blurted. And he did, twisting the deadbolt and then checking it again.

Only once it clicked into place did I finally let out the breath I'd been holding.

And then—without saying a word—he pulled me into his arms.

I hadn't even realized I needed his embrace until I was folded against the steady warmth of Owen's chest, his arms wrapping around me like a shield.

"It's okay, Lucy," he murmured, low and reassuring, his hand gliding gently over my hair. "You're safe now. I've got you. You're okay."

The words sank into me, dissolving some of the cold terror still locked in my bones. I didn't even care that my cheeks were probably freezing against his chest. I just stood there, letting him hold me, letting the panic slowly ebb away.

After a minute—or maybe longer, I wasn't sure—he pulled back just slightly, his hands coming to either side of my face, his brow furrowed as he scanned me like he was looking for bruises.

"Are you hurt?" he asked, voice gentle but urgent. "Did anything happen?"

That was when I felt the dull ache throbbing in my leg again.

"Just my shin," I said, finally catching my breath. "I slipped on the stairs on the way up. Banged it pretty hard."

"Let me see," he said immediately. "We'll check it out. Get you some ice."

I nodded, and he was already on the move, heading toward the little industrial-style kitchen behind us.

I slipped off my coat and backpack and followed him, my legs still a little wobbly. He pulled open the freezer and grabbed a Ziploc bag, then filled it with ice and wrapped it in a kitchen towel.

"Hop up here," he said, nodding toward the counter.

I did as I was told, pulling myself up and settling on the edge while he walked over with the makeshift ice pack.

"Which leg?" he asked, his gaze meeting mine.

"This one." I reached down and touched my right shin.

"Let's take a look-see," he said, his voice softening just enough to make me smile, even as I winced.

I glanced down, trying to angle my leg and pull up the cuff of my jeans without making it worse.

"Here, I'll take that." He held out his hand for the ice pack, which I gratefully handed over before tugging up the denim to reveal a growing bump and a darkening bruise.

"Oof," he said quietly, kneeling slightly to get a better look. "That's gonna be nasty. Is it pretty tender?" He reached forward and touched it, just barely, his fingers brushing the bruised skin with featherlight care.

"Yeah." I sucked in a breath through clenched teeth. "Pretty tender."

"Sorry." He immediately drew his hand back, eyes flashing with concern. "I probably shouldn't have touched it."

"It's okay," I said quickly, since I'd been wishing for weeks that he'd touch me.

He handed me the wrapped ice again. "Better leave this on for twenty minutes."

"Oh, I know the drill." I let out a laugh.

"Right. Gymnast." He raised an eyebrow. "You're probably a pro at this kind of thing."

"Basically," I said, holding the pack in place.

Then I realized how close we were—only a foot apart. If that.

And suddenly, the kitchen felt smaller. Warmer. Charged in a way that made my pulse thrum in my ears.

Owen's gaze found mine, locked on for a beat. And then—just barely—his eyes flicked down to my mouth.

My breath caught.

Because I looked, too. Stupid, impulsive, reckless—I didn't care. My eyes dropped to his lips before I could stop myself, remembering exactly how they'd felt on mine.

That first press of his mouth in the hot tub. The slow exploration that had followed. The way his hands had curled around my waist like he didn't want to let go.

My stomach flipped. Heat pooled low in my body.

This close, I could smell him—warm and woodsy and familiar in a way that made something ache in my chest.

The ache that reminded me how much I wanted him. That I hadn't stopped thinking about that night, and judging by the way his jaw tightened, the way his chest rose just a little deeper than normal...he hadn't either.

The air between us stretched thin, electric.

I should look away. Say something to break the spell.

But I didn't.

I stayed right there, watching him. Letting the moment linger longer than it should.

His hand twitched at his side like he almost reached for me. And for a second, I actually thought he would. That maybe he'd pull me in again. Maybe this time, he wouldn't stop himself.

I held my breath.

But then he blinked, hard—like he was dragging himself out

of a trance. He cleared his throat, took a quick step back, and shoved a hand through his hair.

"I, uh...I'll grab you some water," he said, his voice rougher now. "Maybe some pain medicine?"

"Just water's great," I said, still trying to gain control of my breathing.

He turned toward the cupboard, but I could still feel the heat of him. The pull of what almost happened...and what couldn't.

Not really.

22

———

OWEN

LUCY and I ended up on the couch in my living room, a comedy mockumentary playing in the background as she balanced the ice pack on her shin.

I'd let her choose what we watched, hoping it would help calm her nerves after her scare. But even though she'd said the show was one of her favorites, I wasn't actually paying attention. Not to the TV, anyway.

We sat close—but not too close—Lucy's legs curled up on the cushion, the faint sound of her breathing helping my pulse settle after everything that had just happened.

"I can drive you home after this, if you want," I said, glancing at her out of the corner of my eye. "No pressure. Just... whenever you're ready."

She nodded, eyes still on the screen, but she didn't say anything. And not five minutes later, her head dipped back into the cushion.

By the ten-minute mark, she was out—completely asleep.

I turned the volume down and angled toward her, taking her in for a second. Her lips were parted slightly. One hand tucked under her cheek, the other still loosely holding the ice pack against her shin like she hadn't quite wanted to give up on being responsible—even in sleep.

She must be completely worn out.

Between the travel, school, practice, and whatever emotional toll tonight had taken...no wonder she crashed.

Carefully, I slipped the ice pack out of her grip, then grabbed the throw blanket from the back of the couch and draped it over her. She didn't stir. Just shifted a little, nestling deeper into the cushions with a soft exhale.

I sat there for another moment, watching her.

Gosh, she was beautiful.

Not just in the obvious, knockout kind of way. Though, yeah, her features were ridiculous. The kind that made your brain short-circuit the first time you laid eyes on her.

But it was more than that. It was how she cared so deeply. How she pushed herself even when she was running on empty. How she'd come here tonight, scared but brave enough to knock on my door anyway.

I reached out, brushed a strand of hair from her forehead. My fingers barely touched her skin, but I felt it like a jolt.

Yeah. I was completely screwed.

I hadn't even kissed her since New Year's. But somehow, this felt more intimate than that ever did.

Which was unsettling.

I should've stopped this weeks ago.

Should've drawn a clear, hard line and never let myself cross it.

But it was impossible when she made me feel like I was someone she could trust.

Someone she...wanted.

I swallowed hard, my hand falling back to my lap as I leaned into the cushions beside her with a sigh.

I was a goner before I even had a chance.

And I knew better.

Knew how this story went.

Still...I let myself look at her one last time, let the quiet settle over me. Then, forcing myself to move, I stood, stretching the stiffness from my back and reminding myself I had an early alarm.

Maybe tomorrow morning I'd have a clearer head.

Maybe I could find the dang boundaries again—the ones I kept knocking over like a fool every time she was near.

But tonight?

Tonight I was letting her sleep.

23

———

LUCY

I BLINKED awake to soft morning light filtering through a window that didn't belong to me.

For a second, I didn't move—just stared up at the ceiling, my brain slowly trying to piece together where I was and why everything smelled like clean laundry and faint cologne instead of the vanilla diffuser in my dorm.

Then I heard the low hum of a fridge and felt the weight of the throw blanket draped over me.

Right. Owen's couch.

And then, the rest hit me all at once.

The dark walk. The man following me. The stairs. The fall. Owen opening the door like a real-life superhero. Wrapping me in his arms. Icing my leg. Standing way too close.

And me...falling asleep on his couch.

Oh gosh.

I sat up slowly, glancing around, and pushed a hand through my hair that I was ninety percent sure looked like a bird had nested in it overnight.

My stomach twisted. What must he think?

I wasn't even supposed to be here. I hadn't planned to stay.

And now I was just...casually waking up in my professor's apartment like it was normal or something?

I reached for my phone and saw a string of missed texts from Nora.

> Nora: Where are you??

> Nora: Are you okay??

> Nora: I'm trying not to freak out, but you said you'd be home by ten and it's LITERALLY one a.m.

> Nora: Checked your location. Looks like you're somewhere near campus??

> Nora: Soooo either you're fine and had a long night with a hot guy or you've been kidnapped. Text me either way pls.

Oh no.

I winced and quickly typed a reply:

> Me: So sorry. I'm fine. I fell asleep. I'll explain when I get home...

I didn't dare say more. The last thing I needed was some nosy teammate seeing Nora's phone and realizing I'd spent the night at the apartment of a man whom I was only ever supposed to see at the front of my college chemistry classroom.

My eyes darted to the window. It was 7:05. Early enough that hopefully not too many students would be walking past yet.

I needed to get out of here before anyone saw me. Before this whole situation became something I couldn't explain.

I was still calculating my exit plan when Owen's bedroom door creaked open. I turned quickly, heart jerking like I'd been caught doing something wrong.

He stepped out wearing a worn gray T-shirt and the same sweats he had on last night, his hair slightly mussed like he'd just woken up.

He blinked at me, his expression somewhere between surprise and a kind of awkward tension. "Uh, good morning."

"Morning," I said, my voice scratchy with sleep and way too much self-awareness.

"I was just about to make some breakfast—eggs, toast." He looked around awkwardly, like he wasn't sure what the protocol was for accidental overnight guests who were also your students. He cleared his throat. "You want some?"

"That's really nice," I said quickly, standing and brushing imaginary lint off my jeans, "but I should go. I promise I didn't mean to sleep here. I really wasn't...trying to stay over."

"It's okay." His brows pulled together. "You were exhausted. Had a scare. It was...fine. No problem."

"Okay..." I shifted my weight like I was auditioning for Most Awkward Exit Ever. "Again, I promise it wasn't on purpose."

"Don't worry about it," he said gently, stepping toward the fridge and pulling out things. "I'm glad you felt like you could come here. I know things have been...complicated, but I want you to be safe."

Something in my chest gave a little tug at that. "Thanks."

I looked around, like maybe the couch or the blanket could give me a clue on what to do next. A huge part of me didn't want to leave. *Even if I know I should.*

"You sure you don't want anything to eat before you head out?" He nodded toward the counter where eggs, sourdough bread, and half an avocado were now laid out like the world's most wholesome trap.

Tempting. Stupidly tempting.

But no. I couldn't stay. Not when he looked that good in gray sweats, with his sleepy eyes and that soft, scruffy jaw that had absolutely no right to make my pulse spike.

And I definitely couldn't stay in the same clothes I'd worn yesterday with mascara probably smudged halfway down my face.

"I probably look terrible right now," I muttered under my breath.

"You look just fine," he said.

Which meant he'd totally heard me.

Oh well. At least I looked *fine*.

"Thanks," I said, forcing myself to take a step back. "But I should go. I still need to shower and get ready before class."

He nodded slowly. "Okay. Well...I guess I'll see you later on, then."

"In chemistry," I said, my voice faint as I grabbed my backpack. "Have a good day."

"You too."

I walked to the door, my hand hesitating on the knob before finally turning it. Then I cracked it open just an inch and peeked outside.

No one in sight.

Good.

Slipping out quickly, I pulled the door shut behind me and hurried down the steps, my pulse only calming once I'd made it half a block away—far enough from Owen's apartment that hopefully, no one would connect the dots.

Still, as I walked toward my place in the early morning quiet, I couldn't help but feel like the dots were already connecting inside me.

And that...well, that was the most dangerous part of all.

Nora and I were sitting side by side on the mats in the gym an hour later, reaching for our toes in a slow hamstring stretch, the smell of chalk and sweat already in the air.

"So..." Nora leaned over and bumped her shoulder into mine. "Where were you last night?"

I paused. Not sure if I actually dared tell her.

When I'd gotten home this morning, there had been no time to talk. I had to quickly shower, switch out my backpack for my Wednesday classes, give my phone a quick charge, and then rush out the door with Nora, practically running the whole way and promising that I'd explain everything once we were here.

But...could I actually trust her?

I mean, not that anything bad or super forbidden had happened. I'd simply fallen asleep at my professor's house on accident.

But...most students didn't know where their professors lived. Or had casual text sessions with them on the weekends.

"You said you'd tell me when we got here," Nora said, prodding me. "Come on, Lucy. The only times you ever haven't come home were when you stayed with Josh. So, were you with another guy?"

I bit my lip and drew in a deep breath before saying, "Yeah... I mean...not in the way that you're probably thinking. But I did stay at someone's house last night."

"Who is it?" Nora asked, her eyes wide with intrigue. "Anyone I know? Brody, perhaps?"

"No, definitely not Brody," I hurried to say. "We're only friends."

Though…technically, Owen and I were only friends, too… If that was the right word for it.

Acquaintances, maybe?

We certainly weren't dating or anything like that.

"So?" Nora prodded.

"Okay," I exhaled, knowing she wasn't going to back off until I gave her something. "But you have to promise you won't tell anyone."

"Ooh, so it's one of *those* secrets?" Nora sat up straighter, instantly intrigued. "Then I won't tell a soul. Cross my heart." She held up her hand like she was swearing an oath, then made an exaggerated zipping motion across her lips.

I hesitated again. Because once I said it, there was no taking it back. Once someone else knew about it, it would be more real.

But knowing it was too much of a secret to keep all to myself, I folded forward, staring down at my toes so I wouldn't have to look at her as I whispered, "I was at Owen's apartment last night."

"Owen…" Nora froze, repeating his name slowly. "As in… New Year's Eve Owen?"

I nodded, still not looking at her.

And then, in a stage whisper laced with shock and glee, she said, "As in, you *slept* at your professor's house?"

"*Shhhhh!*" I hissed, jerking my head upright and scanning the gym to make sure no one—especially Coach Chambers— was in earshot.

A few of the other girls were stretching across the floor, but no one seemed to be paying attention.

Still, I scooted a little closer to Nora and lowered my voice. "You're making it sound like I slept *with* him. I didn't. I just… crashed on his couch. Nothing happened."

"Nothing happened?" she asked, a hint of disappointment in her tone. "Not even a little kiss?"

"No!" I said, probably a little too quickly. "Of course not!"

She gave me a look. "Well, that's too bad."

I opened my mouth to say something, then closed it again. Because...was it?

I mean, of course it was better that nothing had happened. Safer. Smarter.

But there was a traitorous part of me that couldn't help thinking that a kiss of comfort would have been nice.

Except those didn't exist. Kisses of comfort weren't a thing. Were they?

Comfort *hugs*, on the other hand... I knew firsthand that those were totally a thing since I had definitely gotten one of those.

And it had been perfect.

The way Owen had pulled me in like he didn't even have to think about it. The way his voice had gone all low and steady while he told me I was safe.

The way I had believed him.

Which wasn't something that happened with many guys. Definitely not with Josh. With him, I always had to convince myself that everything was okay, even when it clearly wasn't.

But with Owen...every time I was remotely near him he had a way of quieting everything else going on in my head.

"Hellooo," Nora sing-songed beside me, cutting through my thoughts. "Earth to Lucy."

"Sorry," I said, bringing myself back to the present.

"So," Nora continued, "do you have class with Professor McDreamy today?"

"Yeah." I sighed, pushing my hair out of my face. "First thing after lunch."

"Think he'll look at you differently now?" She grinned as

she wiggled her eyebrows. "I mean, you *have* seen him in pajamas."

Not to mention shirtless in swim trunks, I thought, my mind conjuring up the memory of his tattoo with the two eagles.

"I don't know." I tried to laugh, but my nerves fluttered. "I always look forward to seeing him." *Even if chemistry and I are in a very toxic relationship.* "But now...I just hope he doesn't think I made the whole thing up about the guy following me."

"Wait—" Nora gasped. "A guy was following you last night?"

"Yeah," I said, then explained more about that scary moment. "Anyway, I just hope Owen didn't think my showing up was some sort of... I don't know, tactic."

"Tactic?" Nora tilted her head to the side, confused.

"Like...maybe he thinks I was trying to seduce him for an A or something." I buried my face in my hands.

Ugh. I never should've made that joke last week.

Nora laughed under her breath. "Well, for what it's worth, if I were a guy and you showed up at my place looking like a damsel in distress, the last thing I'd be thinking about is your GPA."

I gave her a look.

She laughed. "I'm sure everything will be fine. In fact, he's probably counting down the minutes until he sees you in class today."

Which was something I *really* shouldn't be excited about.

24

———

OWEN

I LEANED against the edge of the podium and let my gaze scan the room while the students worked on the short quiz I'd handed out. Most heads were bent over their papers. A few were staring at the front of the class like they were already done and ready to turn theirs in.

And then my eyes found Lucy.

Sitting in her usual spot in the back row.

Which was probably a good thing.

I'd teased her last week about moving up to the front so she could see better—just because I'd wanted a better view of her myself. But today, I was grateful for the distance. The last thing I needed was her sitting close while every part of me was still on edge from this morning and last night.

Because I hadn't been able to stop thinking about it.

About her.

About what she said about someone following her.

I rubbed the back of my neck and glanced down at the watch on my wrist. Three minutes left.

I should've been prepping for tomorrow's lab. But instead,

my mind wandered back to that moment she'd shown up at my apartment. Breathless. Scared to death.

Had someone actually been stalking her?

Or had it just been bad timing? A stranger walking in the same direction? An unfortunate coincidence?

I wanted to believe it was the latter. That the guy she'd seen hadn't meant to cause any harm. That he'd just left a building and headed the same way she was going.

That he might even live in my same building.

But the truth was...creeps existed. The university had emergency call posts for a reason.

And Lucy... She was tiny.

She'd told me she was five one, right? Maybe a hundred pounds soaking wet. And sure, I knew she was strong—she was an elite-level gymnast, after all.

But to someone looking for a target? She'd look like easy prey.

My jaw clenched as I imagined what could've happened if she hadn't known where I lived. If she hadn't recognized my building from the week before. If I hadn't been home.

If she'd been hurt.

My stomach twisted.

No. I couldn't let my mind go there.

Couldn't picture her as some unsolved case on a crime show, the kind that started with "She was a promising college gymnast" and ended with too much blood and too little justice.

Even if that guy on the sidewalk had been harmless, it still wasn't safe for her to be walking alone like that. Not that late.

Did she usually study that late? Walk home from the library in the dark?

Heck, even six o'clock was dark in winter. The cold and ice making everything feel worse—lonelier, more vulnerable.

I checked the time again.

"Two minutes left," I called out. "If you're already finished, you can go ahead and turn in your quiz. Otherwise, wrap it up and I'll see you next time."

A few students started writing faster.

Lucy's head was still bent, her teeth lightly tugging on her bottom lip as she finished the last of her answers.

I shouldn't have said anything. I really shouldn't have. But the words left my mouth before I could stop them.

"And Miss Archibald—" My voice was smooth, professional, though my pulse kicked up half a beat. "Could you see me after class? I have something to discuss with you."

Her head snapped up, eyes wide, a flicker of nerves dancing across her face.

I offered the smallest smile, hoping to wordlessly say, *You're not in trouble.*

And she seemed to relax.

Barely.

When she finally stood and handed in her paper, I packed up my notes and laptop, keeping an eye on the door.

Students from the next class were already trickling in.

And since I didn't want to call extra attention to our conversation, I caught her eye and gave a small nod toward the door. "Actually...can we chat in the hall?"

"Sure," she said quietly, falling into step beside me.

We walked a short distance down the hall until we reached a quiet stretch near a row of closed office doors. No one lingered nearby. Just the low hum of conversation from students back in the classroom and the occasional squeak of sneakers against linoleum.

"Is something wrong?" She looked up at me, concern flickering in her eyes.

"No." I shook my head quickly. "Nothing like that."

I met her gaze then—those clear, steady, impossible-to-look-away-from eyes—and added, "I know you were in a rush this morning, but...I just wanted to make sure you're doing okay. After everything."

She hesitated, like she was weighing her answer.

Then she nodded slowly. "I was a little shaken up last night. And this morning I kind of panicked when I realized I'd fallen asleep at your place. But...I'm okay now."

"That's good." Relief tugged through my chest. "Did you, uh...tell anyone about it? Your dad, maybe?"

"Oh, no. I didn't tell him," she said quickly, almost too quickly. "Just Nora."

And that was when I realized what she thought I meant. That I was worried about *me*. My job. My reputation. That I was afraid she'd reported spending the night at my place to the university president.

Crap.

"I mean..." I shifted my stance, my voice softening. "I'd understand if you did. Of course, I'd like to be left out of it, for obvious reasons, but if telling him about the guy who was following you would help keep you safe, then I'm all for that. Honestly."

"Oh. Okay, yeah," she said, her shoulders relaxing a little. "I guess I just feel kind of silly making a big deal out of it when...nothing actually happened. It makes it hard to know if I was ever actually in danger."

"I get that," I said, though the truth was, I wasn't totally sure I *did*. Not in the way she meant. I'd never had to think twice about walking alone at night. Not really. The only time I'd been even remotely nervous like that was when I'd gotten lost in a sketchy part of Manhattan while visiting my brother and his wife.

But Lucy?

She was small. And no matter how strong she was—which I was sure she *was*, based on what I'd seen of her training and the ridiculous control she had over her body in motion—she probably still looked like an easy target to someone with wrong intentions.

I cleared my throat, pulling myself back to the reason I'd asked her out here in the first place. I had another class starting soon, and I was sure she had somewhere to be, too.

"Do you usually walk home alone in the dark?"

"Sometimes." She glanced down, like she didn't love the question.

"Really?" I frowned. "Like regularly?"

She nodded. "I have a study group I meet with a couple nights a week. With other students in my major."

"Do any of them live near you?" Would any of them be up to being her walking buddy on those nights?

"I don't think so." She scrunched her nose, thinking. "No one's ever walked the same direction as me after study group. Not that I remember, anyway."

Well...that wasn't good.

It was great she had classmates to study with. But walking home in the dark? Alone? Especially now?

I pressed my tongue to the roof of my mouth, debating.

"What days do you usually meet?"

"Monday and Wednesday," she said. "We usually wrap up around six thirty."

Of course—after the sun had already set this time of year.

I nodded slowly, doing the mental math. That would usually line up with the time I was still in my office, finishing up grading or prepping for the next day.

I took a breath. "Would it help if I walked you home? I

mean...I'm usually working in my office until around then, anyway. It's no trouble to meet you."

She blinked. "You'd walk me home?"

"Only if you want," I said. "I just—after last night—it doesn't feel right knowing you might be out there alone."

She hesitated, eyebrows knitting. "Wouldn't that look... sketchy? Us walking together a couple nights a week?"

Probably.

But I shrugged. "We'd just be walking." Then lowering my voice, I added. "It's not like I'd be holding your hand or kissing you or anything."

The words were out before I could stop them.

Her eyes went wide. And then pink bloomed high on her cheeks.

Which...yeah. I felt that heat slide up my neck, too.

Because *I* remembered last night. The way she'd looked in my kitchen in that oversized sweatshirt. Her hair in her signature messy bun, her mouth slightly parted.

The way I'd almost leaned in before coming to my senses.

She bit her lip, which made me wonder if she was picturing that moment, too. Then she said, "I guess that could be okay. I mean...you're friends with Theo. If someone said something, you could just say you were looking out for your friend's little sister."

"Right," I said, grasping onto that reason. "So, if you just text me when you're leaving and where you'll be, I can meet you."

She looked like she was trying to decide if this was overkill.

"I don't want to pressure you," I added. "If you think I'm being overprotective, I get it. I just—"

"No, it's fine," she said, cutting me off. "I was really scared last night. Honestly, I get scared a lot when I'm walking alone. So this...might be nice."

"Okay. Good." I let out a slow breath.

"So, if you're really up to it..." she said, biting her lip, "I'm meeting with my study group in the student center lounge tonight. The one across from the dining hall. So, I can let you know when I'm done."

"Perfect," I said. "Just text me when you're heading out and I'll be there."

25

———

LUCY

OWEN WAS LEANING against the wall just outside the dining hall, hunched over his phone when I walked up.

"Hey," he said, smiling slightly when he saw me. "Did you already eat?"

"Not yet," I said, tightening my grip on the straps of my backpack.

"Do you usually eat here?" He nodded toward the dining hall that was currently bustling with students. "Because I can wait while you grab something if you're hungry."

I glanced past him, toward the glass doors and the line that had formed inside.

And that was when I saw Josh. Standing in line, laughing about something with the girl next to him.

The same girl he'd been with at the meet.

Only now they were holding hands. Fingers laced. Shoulders touching like they were perfectly in sync.

His new girlfriend, apparently.

My stomach knotted, appetite vanishing on the spot.

"I'm good," I said, taking a half-step back. "I can just whip something up at home."

"Okay." Owen followed my gaze, his brow furrowing for a beat before he nodded. "Or...I was thinking of grabbing some takeout. You can join me if you like."

Really? I looked up at him, surprised.

Were we really not playing by our unspoken rules now? Had me showing up at his place changed things?

Or I'd guess, more likely, the flirty texts we'd been sending probably started that shift.

"That would actually be great," I said before he could take the offer away.

"Perfect." He smiled. "My car's just parked at my place."

We walked quickly in the direction of his building, keeping our heads down. Campus wasn't packed, and with it being dark already, I doubted anyone noticed us walking together.

Still, I felt amped up, a little breathless. Like being near him in public—even casually—was somehow both exhilarating and dangerous.

His car turned out to be a white sedan, probably about ten years old or so. He unlocked it with a beep and opened the passenger door for me before slipping into the driver's seat.

"Do you like The Italian Amigos?" He turned to me once we were inside and out of view. "That Italian–Mexican place on Main?"

"Love it," I said, smiling. "Best breadsticks in town."

"I'll call in our order, then." He pulled out his phone. "My brother used to work there when I was teaching at the Academy, so I practically memorized the menu from all the times I stopped by to see him."

"Oh cool," I said, sitting up a little straighter, my curiosity instantly piqued since I was hungry for any details about his family. "So, your brother's younger than you?"

"Five years." He nodded, scrolling through his contacts. "He lives in New York now with his wife."

"Oh, that's awesome," I said, warmth blooming in my chest. "I love New York. I've actually been thinking about sneaking away to Manhattan during spring break. Maybe try to catch a Broadway show or something."

"Wait—seriously?" He looked up, brows raised.

"Yeah." I tilted my head, not sure why that surprised him. "I mean, I haven't made actual plans yet, since who knows if Coach will even give us a break from training—but Alisha's sister, Theo's sister-in-law—said I could stay at their family's hotel if I ever came to visit."

"That's so funny," he said, smiling like we'd just stumbled onto some strange inside joke. "Because that's literally what I've been planning to do for spring break."

I blinked. "For real?"

"Yes, for real," he said with a laugh. "My brother and his wife are starring in *Beauty and the Beast* right now. They're almost at the end of their run, so I wanted to see the show one more time. I mean, it's not every day your brother and sister-in-law are Belle and the Beast on Broadway."

"No way." My jaw dropped. "You're related to *Asher Park* and *Elyse Cohen*?"

"Yep." He chuckled, nodding. "That's my little bro and his wife."

"Oh my gosh," I said, laughing now. "I've totally seen their reels on Instagram. They're incredible. Like, next level. I didn't know they were *your* family."

"Well, they are." He grinned, the kind of smile that softened every edge of his face. Genuine. Warm. Like just talking about his brother made something inside him relax. "Anyway, you never know when he'll get a shot like this again. So, I gotta soak it all up while I can." He paused, his voice dipping just slightly. "It's just...it's really awesome to see him having so much success after everything."

My breath caught on the unspoken weight of those last two words: *After everything.*

What did that mean?

Was he talking about after their dad passed? He'd said he was five years older than his brother, which meant that if their dad died when Owen was eighteen, then Asher might have still been in middle school. Young enough that Owen might have felt like he needed to step into a bit of a fatherly role.

Which would have been a lot of pressure. Especially since that would have also been the age he would have been in college. At Yale.

Chasing after dreams of his own.

And suddenly, I was seeing him in a new light.

Knowing these little details—these hints of a life before we met—made Owen feel more real.

He wasn't just the professor I'd accidentally kissed on New Year's Eve.

Not just the guy from the bar who made my heart race on sight.

He was so much more.

"Anyway," he said, his tone easy—like he had no clue my brain was currently spinning in circles over everything I was learning about him and everything I still wanted to know. "Do you know what you want from The Italian Amigos? Or do you want to scroll through the menu?"

He tilted his phone toward me, the glow of the screen casting soft light between us as I leaned in, acutely aware of how close we suddenly were.

"I'm definitely in the mood for something Italian tonight," I said, tapping that section of the digital menu.

Though, if I was being honest, part of me was tempted by something with a little more Korean flair—him, specifically.

I remembered watching an interview clip where his brother—Broadway's Asher Park—mentioned being half Korean. I'd gone down a whole rabbit hole over the summer, obsessing over his performances and, okay, maybe learning more about him than was entirely casual.

Since Asher was still in his early twenties, I'd initially assumed he was single. And the hopeless romantic in me—the one who'd just broken up with Josh and dreamed of finding a kind guy who wasn't a hot-tempered jock—had totally daydreamed about meeting him someday and falling in love. Especially after Theo's sister-in-law Bailee once mentioned she knew him from high school.

But then, I found out he was married to his co-star Elyse Cohen, and...well, that fantasy fizzled fast.

Now, though? Knowing he had a brother—an older, arguably even hotter brother with those same soulful brown eyes?

Yeah...a new crush was very much alive.

Owen scrolled a little further, and when a dish popped up that looked good, I pointed. "I'll get that—the rigatoni carbonara with blackened chicken."

"That actually sounds really good," he said with a nod. "I'll get the same."

He placed the order, his fingers moving with the kind of practiced ease that told me he really had been a regular at the place when his brother had worked there.

When we pulled up in front of the restaurant a few minutes later, I instinctively reached for my seatbelt and the door handle. But Owen stopped me with a quick glance and a quiet, "I'll get it. You can just wait here."

I paused, hand halfway to the latch. "Don't want to be caught grabbing food with a student?"

"Probably shouldn't risk it." He let out a low chuckle. "But also, it's cold out. No need for both of us to freeze."

My heart did a small, traitorous flutter.

Chivalry, it turned out, looked very good on him.

While he headed inside, I glanced around the car, curious.

It was clean like his apartment, which I'd seen was tidy in that not-too-fussy, not-trying-too-hard way.

The backseat only had two things: his worn leather school bag and my backpack, which I'd dropped there when I got in.

No crumpled fast-food bags. No receipts scattered on the floor. No gym gear or stray papers or whatever else usually accumulated in mine.

Tidy and understated.

Like him.

It was probably a stupid thing to find attractive. But I liked it. Probably more than I should.

And before I could stop myself, I was imagining what it might be like to ride in this car more often. To be the reason there was an extra coffee cup in the cupholder. To know which station he listened to without having to ask. To have this—whatever *this* was—not feel secret or complicated or borrowed.

The driver's side door opened, and Owen slid in with the takeout bag in his hand.

He glanced around like he was weighing his options. "Eating in the car probably isn't ideal, is it?" he asked, biting his lip as he looked over at me. "Puffy coats and greasy pasta don't really mix..."

"I guess not..." I said hesitantly, trying to think of a solution that didn't involve him just driving me home and calling it a night.

Because now that we were alone, I didn't want the night to

end. Not yet. Not when it finally felt like I was actually learning real things about him.

Plus, we were just...talking. Getting to know each other. Laughing a little.

There shouldn't be anything wrong about that.

Okay, *technically*, it probably wasn't the wisest choice. But it wasn't like I was about to throw myself across the console and make out with him. No matter how sharp his jawline looked in the dim lighting. Or how his forearms flexed when he adjusted the gear shift.

Or how his voice somehow made my brain short-circuit on a regular basis.

I cleared my throat. "I mean this in the most appropriate and completely platonic way possible...but what would you think about taking this back to your place?"

"Huh?" He looked over, eyebrows raised slightly.

"I just—" I hesitated, not sure I should be this open with him. But since I was apparently throwing caution to the wind tonight, I said, "I like hanging out with you. And...I don't really want to say goodbye quite yet."

His expression softened, and the look he gave me made me think that maybe he, too, wasn't ready for the night to end just yet.

"And," I added, a grin tugging at my lips, "if anyone sees us, we can just say we're planning my brother's surprise birthday party."

That made him perk up. "Oh yeah. That's a good cover. I mean, you *do* still have stuff to plan for that, right?"

"Pretty sure the only thing I've done so far is pick the date and time and text his friends about it." I laughed, then exhaled. "Honestly, I'm kind of overwhelmed. I want it to be amazing for him, but I've never actually thrown a surprise party before."

"Then that's what we'll do," he said, settling back into his seat, like the decision had been made. "Just two people planning an epic party over dinner."

"Epic might be a bit ambitious." I chuckled, raising an eyebrow. "I'm not exactly the world's most experienced party planner."

"Okay, fine." He smiled, pulling out of the parking spot. "Two friends planning an *adequate* birthday party."

"Exactly." I laughed, warmth spreading in my chest as we pulled onto the street.

26

———

OWEN

I UNLOCKED the door to my apartment and pushed it open, feeling a flicker of nerves kick in as I stepped aside to let Lucy in.

The last time I had a girl over was—well, technically last night. But aside from Lucy knocking on my door?

It'd been a while.

I racked my brain as I flicked on the lights to the living room and kitchen, casting everything in a warm glow. No ex-girlfriend memories here. No shoes by the door that weren't mine. No hair ties forgotten on the bathroom counter.

Since moving in two years ago, this place had only belonged to me.

Which probably said a lot about my dating life lately. Or lack thereof.

I glanced at Lucy as she stepped inside, her eyes scanning the space. She didn't seem nervous, which was good.

One of us had to hold it together.

"When you left this morning," I said, trying to keep my

tone light, "did you ever imagine you'd be back here again so soon?"

"I promise I didn't." She smiled, and something in my chest tightened. The way her eyes lit up when she looked at me—yeah, that was going to be a problem.

"Well..." I ran a hand across the back of my neck. "Even if you did, I don't think I'd be mad about it."

She smiled again, soft, a little shy, and I swore I felt the air shift between us.

I cleared my throat. "Can I take your coat?"

"Oh, sure." She slid her backpack from her shoulders and started to shrug out of her coat, and I stepped in to help.

Just to be polite.

Trying to be a good host.

Not because I wanted an excuse to get close to her.

Okay, so maybe it was exactly that.

I carefully draped her coat over the back of the couch, allowing myself a second to breathe, then turned around to find her taking a seat at the table. Her blouse hugged her in just the right way, her jeans rolled casually at the ankles, her hair pulled into a messy bun that somehow made her look even more gorgeous.

And then, she let it down.

Right there at my kitchen table, she untwisted the tie from her hair and shook it loose, and I had to look away for a second just to keep my thoughts in check.

What the heck was I doing?

I was having dinner with a student. Alone.

In my apartment.

My heart thudded hard in my chest—not just because of how she looked, but because this felt like sneaking around, even if we were just sitting down to a meal.

Just planning her brother and my friend's birthday party.

That was all this was, right? Two friends just spending a little time together.

I walked to the fridge, pulling it open, more for something to do than for any real reason. "Would you like something to drink?" I asked over my shoulder. "I've got...water. And...uh..." I squinted at the mostly empty shelves. "Ice water."

"Ooh, fancy." She laughed, and the sound cut right through my nerves. "I'll take the ice water, please."

"Coming right up," I said, grabbing two glasses from the cupboard and filling them quickly.

I brought the glasses to the table and sat across from her, still trying to remind myself that this was fine.

Just friends. Just food. Just planning a party.

We opened the boxes of takeout, and the smell hit instantly—rich, savory pasta and that hint of spice from the blackened chicken.

"This smells amazing," she said, already stabbing her fork into the rigatoni.

"Right? I don't think I've ever had a bad meal from this place."

We dug in, and for a moment, the only sound was the quiet clink of silverware and the low hum of the heater kicking on.

"So..." I looked up at her between bites, still trying to play it cool. "Has your family always lived in Eden Falls?"

"Nope." She shook her head. "I actually grew up in New Haven."

"Really?"

"Yeah. My dad used to work for my grandpa's company there when I was little." She paused to take another bite, then added, "But then, there was some drama with my dad and uncle about what they wanted to do with the company when my grandpa died. So my dad ended up leaving. When he found out the job at Eden

Falls University was open, he applied. It was kind of a perfect fit, since the stuff he'd been doing at the company translated well into the responsibilities of being a university president."

"Huh." I blinked. "So it wasn't that big of a move."

"Nope." She smiled. "Just twenty minutes away."

"How old were you when you guys moved here?" I asked, leaning back slightly in my chair.

"Sixteen," she said.

"Oof." I winced. "That's a tough age to start over."

"Tell me about it." She gave a soft laugh. "I might've thrown a bit of a fit when my parents told me we were moving. I didn't want to leave my gymnastics club. My friends, my coaches—everything I'd worked for was there. But my parents made a deal with me and said I could keep training in New Haven, so...it ended up working out."

"That's good," I said. "I'm sure you had a strong bond with your coaches. It would've been a terrible time to start over, especially since you were joining the national team."

Her fork paused mid-air.

She blinked at me. "Wait...how did you know I was on the national team back then?"

Crap.

My stomach dropped.

Think, Owen. Think.

"Did Theo tell you?" she asked.

If only that were the case.

I tugged lightly on my collar, suddenly very aware of how warm the room felt. "Uh...please don't take this the wrong way," I started, feeling about as smooth as a bumper car, "but I might've looked at your bio before the meet I went to. Just to... you know, get a sense of your background."

"Mm-hmm." Her smile came slow but sure, curving in a

way that made me think she saw right through me. "Just some casual research."

I coughed out a laugh, embarrassed. "Strictly for educational purposes."

"Right," she said, eyebrows raised.

But she didn't seem mad. In fact, she seemed...pleased. Her cheeks pinked a little as she looked down at her plate.

"But anyway," she said after a beat, voice quieter now, "I was on the national team when I was sixteen. Hoped I'd make the Olympic team, but...didn't quite get there."

"You almost went to the Olympics?" I sat back, kind of stunned.

She shrugged, not meeting my gaze. "*Almost* being the key word."

"Now you're just being humble. That's incredible, Lucy. Seriously."

Her eyes flicked up to mine, cheeks flushing deeper, and I caught a glimpse of something raw there like she was still holding onto some disappointment.

Which made me wonder if her recent frustration with anything short of first place wasn't just about the present but about what she'd missed. Like she was still chasing something she didn't quite catch at sixteen.

But making the Olympic team? There were, what, five girls in the whole country who could manage that? Only five girls, every four years.

It was an insane standard to measure your worth against.

And yet...I had a feeling she did.

Deciding to change the subject, I asked, "Did you apply to any other universities, or was Eden Falls always the plan?"

"I applied to a few." She nodded after swallowing her bite. "Southern Utah—which is about the same size as here and has a great program. Then also University of California and LSU."

I raised my brows. "Impressive lineup."

"Says the guy who went to Yale." She gave me a small smile. "In the end...I chose here."

"What made you pick Eden Falls?"

"Honestly?" She hesitated, stabbing a piece of chicken. "Mostly because I wanted to stay closer to home. I might have a bit of separation anxiety." She gave a sheepish shrug. "The idea of going months without seeing my family? I just didn't think I could do it."

"There's something to be said for having family close by," I said, and didn't miss the subtle ache that came with those words.

What I would have given to be able to call my dad whenever I needed advice. Or text my sister when I had good news. At least I had Asher. And Ian. And Evan, Miles...that whole ragtag group of brothers-by-choice.

"What about you?" Lucy tilted her head. "Where are you from?"

"I grew up here, actually," I said. "My dad had a good job, so we lived in a nice neighborhood. Not sure if you know where the Hastings place is, but we were just a couple of houses down from them. Made it pretty easy for Ian and me to pal around all the time."

"That's fun," she said with a wistful little smile. "I've always wanted friends in my neighborhood. Not that I would've had much time to hang out with them since most days I went straight from school to the gym."

"Sounds intense."

"It was," she admitted, her shoulders dipping just a bit. But then she perked up, like she'd caught herself. "Good thing I love it."

Though, loving something didn't mean it was always easy. Especially when it started to feel more like work than joy.

"Have you lived in Eden Falls most of your life?" she asked, shifting the focus back to me.

"I lived here until college," I said. "Left for my bachelor's, then came back to teach at the Academy for Asher's senior year. So...all but four years, I've been here."

"Does that mean your family still lives here?"

I paused.

There it was—the part of every conversation that took a sharp left turn.

The moment when everything got real. Where small talk ended and the air got heavier. I usually tried to avoid it, but with her...I didn't want to hide. Even by omission.

"Uh, no," I said, keeping my voice steady. "It's just me here. I already told you that my brother Asher lives in New York now. And my dad and sister...they died in a car accident."

Her eyes widened, and she gasped, covering her mouth. "I didn't realize you lost a sister, too." And when her eyes met mine again, I didn't see pity—just this quiet kind of heartbreak. Like she'd felt loss, too. Like she knew.

I nodded once, feeling the usual tightness wrap around my lungs.

I probably should've said more about that—about Callie. But the rest was right there, too, heavy and waiting.

So plowing through, I added, "And then, my mom, of course, is in prison."

"Oh—" Lucy's lips parted slightly, like she wasn't sure she'd heard me right.

I didn't look at her as my cheeks burned. Just stared down at the untouched bite of pasta on my fork and waited for the silence to stretch or break.

"That's..." she began, then stopped, her voice softer when she finally added, "I'm really sorry, Owen. That's...a lot."

27

OWEN

"YEAH," I said quietly. "It is a lot."

Lucy watched me carefully, like she was trying to thread the needle between asking and overstepping. Then, gently, "Has your mom been in prison a long time?"

I gave a slow nod. "Almost ten years."

Her eyes searched mine, piecing things together. "So...ever since your dad and sister passed?"

"Just after that..." I dragged in a breath, steeling myself. I'd told the story before, but even though almost a decade had passed, my chest somehow still felt like it was splintering open.

I kept my eyes on the table as I spoke. "She was convicted of two counts of vehicular manslaughter. For my dad and my little sister Callie."

Lucy's hand stilled on her fork. Her lips parted like she wanted to say something but couldn't quite find the words.

"She was high at the time," I said, not waiting for her to fill the silence. "She'd had an addiction since I was a kid. Painkillers at first, then other stuff. When I was young, everything looked picture-perfect from the outside—nice house, good schools, plenty of money. But behind closed doors…" I swallowed hard. "Behind closed doors my mom was checked out. Sneaking pills."

Lucy let out a soft breath, eyes wide and sad.

"She overdosed when I was thirteen. That's when she finally got help. Got clean. Or at least she was clean for a while." I shook my head. "And things were good again. She was present. Sober. Trying."

I ran a hand down my face, the old ache stirring again.

"But a few years later, when I was at Yale…she relapsed without any of us knowing. At least…not until it was too late."

"That must've been so hard." Lucy's brows pulled together, pain flashing across her face as she whispered, "Watching your mom go through something like that. Feeling like you couldn't help her. Like you were helpless."

"Yeah," I said, my throat tightening. "Exactly that."

I stared at my plate, not really seeing it anymore.

"There were nights when my dad was on a work trip that I'd just sit by her bed," I admitted, my voice lower now, rougher, "and watch her sleep. I just…wanted to make sure she was still breathing. I'd sit there and count her breaths and tell myself that if she made it through the night, maybe tomorrow would be better."

Lucy didn't speak. She just let the silence hold what I couldn't.

"I wasn't there when it happened," I added quietly. "The accident. I was in New Haven, at school. Trying to stay on top of classes, praying everything was okay back home. And then one night, it wasn't."

The guilt—old and familiar—settled across my shoulders again. "I should've known she was slipping," I murmured. "I should've noticed. Visited more. Checked in."

"But you were a college kid," she said, her voice thick with emotion. "Trying to build a future. That wasn't your job to manage."

I looked up, and for a second, her gaze locked with mine. There was something in it—compassion, understanding, maybe even something like admiration—that eased the rawest edge of my shame.

I hadn't realized how much I'd needed her to say those exact words.

"What happened to your brother after the accident? He was still pretty young, right?" She tilted her head slightly. "Did he go into foster care? Since you were still in college and so young yourself?"

"He was in foster care for a little while." I sat back, dragging a hand across the back of my neck. "Everything was just... chaotic. But once my mom was sentenced, I applied for guardianship."

"How old were you?"

"Nineteen."

"Geez." Her eyebrows lifted. "That's two years younger than me."

"I know," I added with a dry chuckle. "It was insane. But Asher ended up getting a scholarship to Eden Falls Academy—with room and board—which was honestly a lifesaver. I don't think I could've held it all together otherwise. The teachers and staff were incredible. Theo was actually one of the house dads back then. And he kept me in the loop when I couldn't be there myself."

Lucy leaned forward slightly. "Do you think that's why Theo was considering going into family law for a while?"

"I think so," I said, then smirked. "At least until he realized the big bucks were in corporate law."

She laughed. "Well, he did have Alisha Vanderbilt to impress."

Her voice dipped a little at the end, and I caught the subtle flicker of sadness that crossed her face. Alisha, Theo's late wife. Another loss from a car accident that neither of us wanted to talk about but couldn't quite forget.

Our eyes met, and for a second, it felt like the room went still.

Then—quietly, deliberately—Lucy reached across the table and covered my hand with hers.

Comfort wasn't something I was used to receiving. But in that moment, I let myself take it. Let her hand rest over mine, steady and sure.

We sat like that for a beat. Two people who knew what it was like to lose someone in a blink. Who understood the kind of grief that never fully lets go, no matter how much time passes or how well you learn to carry it.

"Anyway..." I cleared my throat, trying to find my footing again. "Sorry for being a total mood killer. This was supposed to be a lighthearted, party-planning dinner."

"No, it's..." She smiled gently. "I appreciate you telling me. I'm sure that's not easy to talk about."

"It's not," I admitted. "But that's just...life, I guess."

"That it is," she murmured, her eyes dropping for a second. And I wondered, briefly, if she had things tucked away, too. Things that hurt too much to say out loud.

She glanced up again. "How long is your mom's sentence for?"

"Ten years."

"So...does that mean she'll be getting out soon?"

"Yeah." I bit the inside of my cheek. "I got an update recently. Looks like she'll be released in August." I exhaled slowly. "And I honestly don't know what to do with that."

She stayed quiet, watching me carefully.

"She's still my mom. And I love her. Sometimes I even miss

her. But I've been angry for so long for what she did. What she took from me and Asher. From Callie and Dad. The birthdays we never had. The memories we never made. There's just this... ache. And it hasn't gone away."

I ran a hand through my hair, suddenly feeling exposed.

I was probably saying too much.

Unloading on Lucy when she hadn't asked for any of this.

But once I started, I couldn't seem to stop.

"She's apologized," I said, my voice quieter now. "Over and over. Cried. Screamed. Begged. And I know she regrets it—I do. She's heartbroken, too. She'll carry the guilt for the rest of her life. But now that I'm finally starting to find my footing again—finally breathing again—I don't know if I have it in me to help her start over."

"You shouldn't have to," Lucy said, her voice steady.

I looked at her, caught off guard. I hadn't expected her to say that.

"I know it's kind of expected," she went on with a small shrug, "that family drops everything when someone needs them. But if it's not something you can handle, you shouldn't feel bad about that. You're allowed to protect your peace, too. You're only human. And from the sounds of it, you've already carried a lot."

I met her gaze again, and somehow, her eyes were even softer than before.

She gave my hand a gentle squeeze.

And in that simple touch, I felt something loosen in my chest. Like she understood. Not just what I was saying, but the weight of it all. Completely.

"I guess I've still got several months to figure out what I'm going to do with that," I said. "And who knows, maybe my mom can stay with her sister while she figures out her next steps. My aunt Vivian helped Asher out a lot when things got rough his junior year of high school. Maybe she'll be willing to step in again—fill in the gaps that Asher and I can't."

"Might be worth looking into," Lucy said. "Even just having a few options to offer your mom could make the transition a little easier on all of you."

I nodded slowly, my thumb brushing over the side of her hand. "Thanks for being so cool about this. I didn't really know what to expect when I dropped the whole 'my mom's in prison for manslaughter' thing. But somehow you made it feel easy. Which is probably crazy, since we barely know each other."

"I'm glad you felt safe sharing it with me," she said softly. "I know how difficult it is to talk about the hard stuff. I'm not exactly great at it myself."

And there it was again—that flicker in her eyes. A shadow of something tucked away. Quiet. Private.

The kind of pain you learned to live with but didn't talk about.

And I couldn't help wondering...what was Lucy not saying?

28

——

LUCY

"WELL..." Owen glanced across the table at me when we were done eating, his smile a little crooked in that way I was starting to love. "We still never got around to talking about that party-planning thing, did we?"

"Oh. Right." I let out a small laugh. "Guess we didn't."

But that was okay. The party planning was just our backup excuse for having dinner together anyway.

I appreciated him letting me in tonight, though. That he'd trusted me with those hard parts of his story.

It couldn't have been easy. But then, it sounded like Owen was used to hard things.

Losing his dad and sister in the same moment.

Watching his mom disappear into addiction.

Taking care of his younger brother after everything fell apart.

Carrying more fear and responsibility than any kid should ever have to.

I could just picture a twelve-year-old Owen sitting by his

mom's bed, counting her breaths, just hoping she'd still be alive in the morning.

How did you even survive that kind of reality? Living in constant fear yet being helpless to actually fix anything, never knowing if one day everything would finally fall apart?

Which...it had.

A couple of times.

His mom had overdosed at least once. And then, just when they thought things were going okay and the nightmare was behind them, she relapsed, and two people he loved were gone in an instant because of it.

It was a miracle that Owen turned out as well as he had.

And the fact that he was sitting here now—calm, kind, and offering to help me plan a party when he had so much on his own plate—spoke volumes about the kind of man he was.

The kind of man any woman would be so lucky to have.

"I know you've got a lot going on," he said, gently pulling me back to the moment. "Meets every weekend, right?"

"Right." I nodded, tucking a piece of hair behind my ear. "But this weekend's a home meet, at least. So no traveling."

"That's good," he said, his voice warm, steady. He leaned forward, resting his elbows on the table. "So...what were you thinking for this party? Cake and ice cream? Appetizers? Drinks?"

"Um...all of the above? Plus decorations," I said, feeling slightly anxious thinking about it all. "But with just over two weeks left, I'm not sure I'll have enough time to pull it all off."

"Which is why I'm here to help," he said. "Do you have a budget you're working with?"

"I've talked to my mom about it." I shifted in my chair, suddenly hyperaware of how young that probably made me sound. "She said she'll cover it...since I don't exactly have a job right now."

"Gymnastics and school are your job." He tilted his head slightly, raising an eyebrow.

"I guess... I think I'm just a little self-conscious. Like, weren't you teaching at the prep school while getting your master's and PhD...and bartending on weekends? Meanwhile, I can barely juggle my classes and training."

"You are not lazy, Lucy," he said, voice steady and sure. "And in case you haven't realized it...you've been impressing me since the moment we met."

Our eyes caught, holding for a second too long. Just long enough to feel like he'd stepped across some invisible line with his admission.

He cleared his throat. "Impressing me with your excellent work ethic in the chemistry lab, of course."

"Of course," I echoed, unable to stop the grin that tugged at my lips. I liked that he seemed a little flustered by his own words.

"So," he said, nudging the conversation forward with a small smile, "what are you thinking for the appetizers? Are you planning to make everything yourself, or...?"

"I'm not sure how much the food will cost yet," I admitted. "But I was thinking it might be easier to have it catered. I just don't think I'll have time to cook or bake or even shop for everything."

"Well," he said, eyes twinkling, "not to create a conflict of interest, but The Garden caters parties. I could hook you up if you wanted. You'd just need to handle the cake." He smirked and added, "And I also happen to know a great contact for that. The owner of the bakery next door is a friend."

I arched a brow. "So basically, if this whole professor gig doesn't work out, you could go into event planning?"

"I don't know about that." He laughed. "But I do have some connections, if you want me to reach out."

"Honestly? That would be amazing." I hesitated, wondering if he was too good to be true. "If you really don't mind helping with this stuff, that is..."

"It's no problem." He leaned back. "We've got a few catering packages at The Garden that make it easy. I can show you. But no pressure if you want to go with someone else. There are plenty of great places in town."

"Oh no, that sounds perfect. I already know Theo likes the food and drinks at The Garden."

We migrated to the couch with our water glasses in hand. He pulled out his phone and scooted close enough that we could both see the screen, and I tried really hard not to notice how good he smelled. Clean and woodsy, with something warmer beneath it. The kind of scent that made you want to press your cheek to his chest and forget the world for a while.

I almost leaned in closer to breathe him in better. Almost.

But I didn't. Because he was still my professor.

Even if those lines were getting very, very blurry.

He clicked through a few images, describing each option. I nodded along, pretending to focus, but every time his arm brushed mine, my thoughts scattered. I caught him glancing at me once, and for a second, when our faces got close, I couldn't help but wonder if he was feeling the same things I was.

Did he like this closeness, too?

Was he having just as hard of a time breathing as me?

I looked back at the phone and focused on choosing the package that had the things I thought Theo might like.

"I think this one will work for Theo's party," I said, pointing to the option I liked best.

"Great," he said. "Then I guess we just need a headcount. I can have everything delivered once I'm out with Theo."

"Did you already set something up with him?"

"Not yet," he said. "It's just over two weeks away. I figured that might be a little too early—didn't want to make him suspicious."

"Right," I agreed. "If we make it too official, he'll smell a surprise coming."

"But I also don't want him to make other plans or go out of town," Owen added. "So I'll probably text him tomorrow. Just need to figure out what we're doing."

"Are you the type of friends who go to dinner together?"

"Uh, we haven't done that yet." He gave a little shrug. "Mostly just see each other at parties, chat at The Garden...and then there was an attempted double date at your gymnastics meet."

"Oh." My stomach twisted. "That was originally supposed to be a double date?"

"It was..." he said, and I caught the discomfort flash across his face. "Had to take a raincheck on that, though."

Well, at least I didn't have to witness that. That would've been *fun*.

"I guess you could always suggest another double date that night," I said, even though I actually hated the idea. "Then you could both bring your dates to the party."

He chuckled. "Somehow, I'm not sure that's something I really want to do at this point."

Did that mean he didn't want to date? Or just didn't want to date in front of me?

Doing my best to sound casual, I asked, "Okay, so if I'm figuring out the guest list, should I just put you down for one? No plus-one needed?"

He gave me a small smile. "Just me."

I swallowed and nodded. "Okay. Perfect." A beat passed before I added, "Though, of course, if that changes...just let me know."

He held my gaze for a second longer, then said, "I don't

really see that changing anytime soon. I've been just a little...
distracted lately."

And the look he gave me made a whole flock of birds come
alive in my stomach.

"Well...good." I looked down, hiding a smile.

He tapped his screen again. "Do you have a plus-one?" he
asked. "You know...for curiosity's sake. And catering purposes,
obviously."

"No," I said, looking into his eyes and hoping he was on the
same wavelength as I was. "Just Charlotte."

29

———

OWEN

"I SHOULD PROBABLY TAKE you home now, shouldn't I?" I said to Lucy when we were finished with the party plans.

Did I want to take her home?

No. Absolutely not.

If I could have frozen time right there, just kept her curled up on my couch beside me, still smelling like vanilla and whatever heaven her shampoo was made of, I would have. I could've stayed like that for hours—talking about nothing, or everything.

But it was almost eight thirty, and the longer she stayed, the harder it became to remember who she was.

My student.

President Archibald's daughter.

The girl I had absolutely no business entertaining feelings for.

"I guess." She nodded. "I do have strength and conditioning pretty early in the morning."

But she didn't move.

Didn't budge an inch, actually. Just sat there, legs still

curled under her, still close enough that I could feel the warmth coming off her shoulder.

Yeah, she didn't want to leave, either.

Relatable.

Dangerously so.

Because Lucy was...addicting. The sound of her laugh. The way she tilted her head when she was listening. The way her blue eyes lit up when she was fired up about something.

Yep. I had a crush on Lucy Archibald.

And every second we spent like this, the harder it was to pretend I didn't.

Still, I stood—slowly. Forcing myself to be the responsible adult, the responsible *professor* I was supposed to be. I grabbed my keys off the counter and cracked the front door open just enough to point my key fob toward the parking lot and start my car.

I turned back toward her, grabbing her coat from where I'd draped it on the arm of the couch.

She sighed.

Yeah. *Me too.*

She didn't need help putting it on. Of course she didn't. Just like she hadn't needed help taking it off earlier.

But still, I held it out for her.

Just being a gentleman. No ulterior motives.

She stood and stepped into it, slipping her arms through the sleeves. As she flipped her hair out from under the collar, a fresh wave of her shampoo hit me. Light and warm and impossible not to get drunk on. The same scent I'd been lowkey inhaling for the past hour on the couch.

She turned, her eyes meeting mine.

She was so beautiful.

"You should probably put your hood up when we head

out." I swallowed, my chest tightening. "Just...so it's less likely someone recognizes you."

Her lips curved. "Okay."

I reached for my own coat, shrugging it on, then opened the door a little wider. "I'll go out first. Make sure the coast is clear. You can just lock up and follow."

"It's like you've snuck around like this before," she said, a teasing spark flashing in her eyes.

I laughed, the sound slightly more awkward than I meant for it to be. "Not quite."

"Okay," she said softly. "See you out there."

I stepped outside, tugging my hood up against the night air, scanning the sidewalk and parking lot. A couple was just coming up the steps—Carla and Vince, who lived two doors down. I gave them a quick nod and kept moving, trying not to look like a guy sneaking his student out of his apartment.

At my car, I checked the area again, then pulled out my phone.

> Me: Coast is clear. You're good to come out.

And as I hit *Send*, I felt it again.

That tug in my chest.

The one that always came when we had to say goodbye.

I'd liked having her at my house the past two nights—liked the easy rhythm we fell into, the way her laugh filled up the quiet, the way her presence warmed the corners of my life I hadn't realized had gone cold.

It was...nice.

Not being alone.

Having someone like her beside me to help pass the long winter night.

A moment later, she stepped out, bundled in her white

puffy coat like the world's cutest marshmallow. Her hood framed her cheeks, face protected from the cold...and from the gaze of anyone who might walk by.

She climbed into the passenger seat, tugging her seatbelt into place.

"Where do you live?" I asked, clearing my throat.

"Just two streets up," she said, somewhat breathlessly—like she, too, was on edge at the idea of being caught. "I live in Eden Hall."

I nodded, shifting the car into gear and pulling out of the lot.

We didn't talk much on the short drive, just listened to the quiet hum of the heater and the low sound of the tires on the pavement. But it wasn't awkward. It was the kind of quiet that felt full somehow.

"This is it," she said when we reached the building—tan stucco with red brick trim and lights glowing soft behind several windows.

I pulled over to the curb; not too close, not too far. Just enough that I could still watch her make it safely inside.

"Thanks," she said, turning toward me. "For the ride. For dinner. For...everything."

"No problem," I said, meaning every word. *Really.* I'd do it all again in a heartbeat.

I didn't move. Just sat there stealing the moment. Wanting to find an excuse to keep her here beside me a little while longer.

But before I was ready, she reached for her seatbelt and unbuckled it, then leaned into the backseat to grab her backpack. "I'll see you in the chemistry lab tomorrow?"

Her voice was light. But when our gazes locked, I could've sworn the air had shifted.

Could've sworn she felt it, too—the electric charge that had been between us since I first saw her sitting at the bar and tried to keep my cool while serving her a glass of water.

I wanted to kiss her so badly—to lean across the center console and take her face in my hands and see if she tasted as sweet as I remembered.

Just a little kiss. One stolen moment.

But no...I couldn't.

Or rather, I *shouldn't*.

So instead of doing what I very much wanted to do, I offered her a crooked smile that I hoped would mask everything I wasn't saying.

That I wished we didn't have to hide our friendship—or whatever this was.

That I wished things weren't complicated.

That we were just a regular guy and girl enjoying a nice evening together.

"I'll see you tomorrow," I said instead.

"See you." She looked at me for another moment, her eyes full of something my brain really wanted to interpret as longing.

But then, with a sigh, she climbed out and started up the walkway. I watched her go, watched until she slipped inside the glass doors.

Then I exhaled slowly and drove away, telling myself I was doing the right thing.

Even if every cell in my body was screaming for me to call and ask her to come back.

I walked into the science building after lunch, my bag slung over one shoulder and the ghost of last night still trailing behind me.

No texts from Lucy. No accidental run-ins on the quad. Not even a glimpse of her across the dining hall.

And for some reason, the silence had me more in my head than I cared to admit. Which was probably totally ridiculous, since I knew she was busy with classes and training.

But still... Had I said too much?

Maybe I shouldn't have opened up about my mom. My family's losses.

It had felt natural in the moment. Needed. But now, with the daylight sharp and responsibilities settling in again, it was hard not to question whether I'd just trauma-dumped on her and crossed some kind of line.

Not necessarily professionally, but personally. Had I made her uncomfortable? Scared her off?

Which was probably a stupid thing for me to worry about since I should be *trying* to scare her away.

This whole thing, whatever it was between us, didn't have a future. It couldn't. I knew that. Had reminded myself of it a hundred times.

And yet, whenever we were alone...when it was just her and me, like at Ky's party...it was like none of those rules applied. We were just two people talking. Laughing. Connecting.

I climbed the stairs to the second floor, slowing as I neared the lab.

And there she was.

Just like the first week of classes, Lucy stood outside the door. Looking breathtaking as usual, arms crossed lightly over her notebook, her blonde hair falling over one shoulder in a braid.

Waiting for me.

No—waiting for the class she had with me.

"Hey," I said, my chest doing that tightening thing around my heart again.

"Hey," she echoed, a small smile lifting her lips.

I fumbled for my key card, trying to act like unlocking a door wasn't suddenly the most complicated task in the world. After a little more fumbling, the lock finally beeped open, and I gestured for Lucy to step inside ahead of me.

She headed toward her usual table, and I cleared my throat, needing something to say that wasn't *You look really good today* or *I haven't stopped thinking about you since you left my house.*

"I, uh, talked to Evan this morning," I said instead. "He owns The Garden. He's a friend of Theo's, actually. Said they can definitely cater the party."

Her face lit up. "Oh, that's awesome!"

I nodded. "And I also texted my friend Kiara—she owns the bakery next door. She'd be happy to make whatever kind of cake you want. She's got a ton of examples on her social media pages if you want to browse through them."

"Wow," she said, her eyebrows lifting. "How did you already get all that figured out? Because I'm pretty sure I've been stuck in the just-thinking-about-it phase for, like, three weeks."

"I just sent a couple of texts." I shrugged. "It was easy."

"Well, thank you." Her smile was warm. "You're amazing."

Before I could say anything back—or worse, grin like a total idiot—a student walked in. Both of us straightened like we'd been caught doing something we shouldn't. Which, technically, we hadn't. But the way my heart jumped said otherwise.

Lucy busied herself, pulling out her lab manual. I walked over to the front desk and opened mine, pretending like my thoughts weren't still back on the way she'd just looked at me.

More students filtered in. I grabbed my phone, trying to act casual as I typed out a quick message.

> Me: Kiara's handle is @kiarabakes. Check out her cakes when you get a chance. Just let me know a headcount and I'll have Evan work up a catering quote.

I watched as she pulled her phone out from her back pocket. After glancing my way briefly, she typed a response.

> Theo's sister: Thank you! I invited about 15 people and have 10 RSVPs so far. So let's say 20 to be safe. I'm sure the guys in my building will be happy to eat any leftovers I bring back.

Why did the thought of her interacting with guys from her building send an instant pang of jealousy through me?

I was an idiot, that was why. Of course she knew the guys in her building.

Probably had to fight off their advances on a daily basis with how cute and talented she was.

Ugh. I really didn't need to be worrying about that.

Trying to push those thoughts away, I sent her a text.

> Me: Perfect.

Then I slipped my phone into my pocket. As another wave of students walked in, I glanced up, hoping no one had noticed me texting with her.

It wasn't like we were texting anything inappropriate. Just party plans. But...blurry lines were harder to justify when the attraction I had for my student was probably written all over my face any time I looked at her.

"All right, everyone. Lab Three today." I stepped forward when the clock hit the hour. "Instructions are in your workbooks. You'll need your goggles and gloves for this one. If you have any questions, just let me know."

As I glanced around the room, I noticed Lucy still sitting alone.

Today's lab was one that would be hard to do on her own... Should I offer to help her?

My feet twitched like they wanted to move toward her table, but before I could, Brody slipped in through the door.

"Sorry I'm late," he told her. "Had to turn in an assignment."

"It's okay," Lucy said, smiling at him. "I'm just glad you showed up. I would be lost without you in here."

I froze.

The smile she gave him—the ease in her voice—made jealousy hit fast and stupid. I tightened my jaw before I could stop it.

Of course it was irrational. He was just her lab partner. This was school. Chemistry.

I had zero reason to feel like someone had just elbowed me in the chest.

Still, I turned away, trying to look busy.

Trying not to overanalyze the way she looked at him.

Or how different it might be from the way she looked at me. Especially since he was actually Lucy's age.

I exhaled and forced myself into motion, starting my usual loop around the lab. Checking stations. Offering reminders. Pretending like I hadn't just watched her light up for someone else.

I should be glad that she got along so well with her lab partner. That she felt comfortable, since that was what a good chemistry professor should want for his students, right?

Too bad this particular chemistry professor keeps forgetting he's not allowed to want her for himself.

30

LUCY

"ARE you coming to the game tomorrow night?" Brody asked as he adjusted the angle of the beaker in front of us.

"The hockey game?" I glanced up from my lab notebook.

"Yeah." He nodded. "I saw your meet's not until Sunday, so you'll be in town, right?"

"I should be around," I said. "And Nora and I were talking about going to the game."

"Cool. It should be a good one."

We went back to measuring out the solution for the next step in our experiment, our gloved hands moving in near-synchronized coordination. This was our third week working together and we were getting into a rhythm—not just with the lab work, but the easy, banter-filled conversations that helped pass the time.

"If you do make it to the game," Brody added, "then you two should also come to the after-party. It's at my house this time."

"Which means that you and Josh can't get thrown out if

you get into another fight, right?" I smirked, glancing sideways at him.

"Right." Brody chuckled under his breath. "Though, I doubt we'll get in a fight like that again since he seems pretty happy these days."

"Oh?" And before I could stop myself, I asked, "Because of his new girlfriend?"

"Yeah..." He hesitated, the corners of his mouth tightening before he said, "I know that's probably weird for you. But he seems like he's in a good place. Don't think he's even had a drink since our fight."

Relief stirred in my chest, tentative but real. I wanted to believe that. Because the worst parts of Josh—his volatility, the moments that had left bruises deeper than skin—had always surfaced when he was drunk. He'd only ever truly lost control when alcohol was in the mix.

"That's good," I said honestly. And I meant it. I wanted Josh to be happy. I wanted the best for him, really.

Even if there were days I still wondered why he couldn't have been happy with me.

"Anyway," Brody cleared his throat and shifted in his seat, "the party should be fun. Definitely not planning to get wasted like I did last time. So I shouldn't end up in any stupid fights."

"Gotta keep those fights on the ice, right?" I teased, picturing the usual chaos of a hockey game—gloves flying, punches thrown, refs trying to drag players off one another.

"Right."

He started gently swirling the flask, watching the pale blue solution deepen a shade. "Are you excited for your meet against LIU? Didn't you take home the all-around against them last year?"

"I did." I blinked at him. "I-I'm surprised you remembered."

"It's hard to forget..." He shrugged, suddenly looking a little bashful. "Your floor routine was seriously impressive last year. I still don't understand how one of your tumbling passes was even humanly possible."

"Thanks." Heat rose to my cheeks. "That routine was brutal. But it ended up being one of my favorites."

"I could tell," he said, his mouth tilting into a quiet smile. "You always looked like you were having the time of your life out there."

"Did you go to a lot of our meets, then?" I asked, tilting my head. I'd known Brody as one of Josh's teammates, had seen him at parties, but we'd barely exchanged more than a handful of words until this semester.

"I went to most of them," he said softly, almost like he wasn't sure if he should admit it.

"Well...thanks for coming. Home meets are always more fun when there's a big crowd."

His smile deepened, and just for a second, I swore I saw a flush creep up his neck. "It was my pleasure."

And the way he said it, warm, almost hesitant, made me wonder if he'd just revealed more than he meant to.

Was it possible that all the times he'd teased Josh about asking me out hadn't been teasing at all? Had Brody maybe, actually, had a thing for me?

The idea of Brody secretly crushing on me all year—it was sweet. He was a cool guy.

And maybe, in another life—or at least a different semester—I might've even liked him back.

But right now, my heart had set its sights on someone else.

At that thought, my gaze drifted across the lab. Owen was a few rows away, bent over a table, deep in discussion with another pair of students. He didn't seem to be paying attention to us.

Which was probably good. (Even if I secretly wanted him to always be checking in on me the way I was checking in on him.)

"You're having a pretty good season this year, too, right?" Brody asked, pulling my focus back.

"Pretty good." I nodded. "I tied for second at the meet last weekend. Tied with Nora, actually."

"That's awesome." He smiled. "Does it ever get weird? Competing against your best friend and living with her, too?"

"It does sometimes," I admitted. "We both work really hard. And we both want each other to do our best. But...we also both want to win."

"At least they allow ties," he said. "Sounds like that worked out for you both."

"Last week it did, at least," I said with a soft laugh, turning back to our beaker. "You think it's doing what it's supposed to?"

"I'm not sure," Brody said. "Think we should ask the professor?"

"Maybe."

"Professor Park?" Brody raised his hand. "Can we get some help over here?"

Owen looked in our direction and nodded, then after giving the students he was with one last instruction, he made his way over.

"What can I help you with?" he asked, his gaze going to Brody first before peeking at me.

"We're wondering if it looks like this is reacting correctly," Brody said, gesturing to the beaker on the hot plate.

Owen bent slightly to inspect the setup. His shoulder bumped gently against mine with the movement, and I had to force myself to keep my eyes on the experiment and not on him.

"Looks good," he said after a beat. "You'll want to heat it for another couple minutes. Just until the color stabilizes. Then record your final observation."

"Got it," Brody said. "Thanks."

"Of course." Owen gave a nod and turned away, but not before his eyes lingered on mine just a second too long.

It was barely a second.

But it was enough to short-circuit my brain.

Because Owen in professor mode was so freaking hot.

The calm authority.

The quiet confidence in his explanations.

The way he commanded the room without even raising his voice.

There was something steady about him.

Safe.

And that was what drew me in the most.

After years of walking on eggshells with Josh—never knowing which version of him I'd get—being around someone so stable felt like breathing clean air for the first time.

I blinked and turned back to the flask, trying to focus.

But of course, all I could think about was how ridiculous I probably looked in my safety goggles.

Maybe Owen had a thing for the chemistry-nerd aesthetic?

One could hope.

Though, in reality, it probably just reminded him that I was his student.

Ugh.

The crowd at the rink was electric—horns, cowbells, chants, the slap of sticks echoing against the boards. Nora and I had squeezed into the student section near center ice, three rows up from the glass, bundled in puffer coats and school colors, our hot cocoa long gone and our voices mostly hoarse.

The game was nearing the end, tied 3-3, and we were all on edge.

And that was when I saw him.

Directly across the rink, I spotted Owen sitting among a small group—two guys and two women. From this far away, I couldn't make out much, but one of the guys had the confident, relaxed posture of someone who owned the room—or maybe the whole town. The other looked more like a GQ ad come to life.

Unable to resist, I tugged my phone from my coat pocket and shot him a text.

Me: **I see you.**

I probably shouldn't be texting him while we were in such a public place. But apparently, the stretch from Thursday afternoon to Monday was too long for me to go without having at least some sort of contact with him.

I watched Owen as he checked his phone. His head tilted down, the light of the screen lighting up his face. Then, just as he read it, I saw him smile.

He angled the phone downward, like he didn't want the people around him to see, then lifted his head and scanned the stands.

His gaze passed right over me and Nora without a flicker of recognition, so I texted again.

> Me: I'm right across from you. Three rows from the front.

His phone lit up again, and a beat later, his eyes found mine.

And there it was. That smile again. Easy. Warm.

Secret.

Like it was just for me.
My breath caught.

> Me: Who are you here with? I don't recognize the couples you're sitting with.

A few seconds later a text came through.

> Theo's friend: I'm here with my friend Evan and his wife Addie. And Ian and his fiancée Maddie.

> Me: Fun. I'm guessing Evan is the same Evan that owns The Garden?

> Theo's friend: Yep. And Ian is the guy I've been best friends with since we were kids.

> Me: The son of the billionaire?

> Theo's friend: Yep.

> Me: Fancy friends for my fancy professor.

I watched him read it, and sure enough, he seemed to chuckle again. Probably his low, genuine laugh that I loved.

> Theo's friend: Says the girl with the last name Archibald.

I smiled, biting my bottom lip. My fingers hovered for a second before I typed:

> Me: What does the last name Archibald mean to you?

Why would he think it was synonymous with his fancy friends?

I kept my gaze on him as he read it. He didn't smile this time, just stared at his screen a little longer, then looked out at the ice like he was thinking.

Finally, the typing bubble appeared.

> Theo's friend: First, I think of President Archibald and how I'd be in big trouble if he knew I even had your number in my phone.

Fair.

> Theo's friend: Then I think about how, from my conversations with Theo, it sounds like your family has always been involved in high society things. Your dad works for the university now, so I don't know if he's still tied to your grandpa's company or what his inheritance looked like, but knowing how expensive gymnastics is at your level, I'm guessing your family does okay financially.

> Theo's friend: Also…Theo marrying a Vanderbilt, and the way Ky's friends acted like you kissing a bartender was slumming it? I assume your parents probably hope you'll eventually marry someone in a similar social class.

I read it once.

Then again.

Nothing in his words was necessarily judgmental...but I couldn't quite tell how he felt about all of that.

Was he trying to figure out if I thought I was out of his league because of my family's connections and everything that came with the Archibald name?

I knew a first-year college professor—especially one who moonlighted as a bartender—probably wasn't exactly raking it in. But from what I'd seen so far, Owen was surrounded by successful, wealthy friends. So he shouldn't be unfamiliar with my family's world.

Plus, didn't he say he'd grown up pretty well off?

And it wasn't like *I* was rich. My scholarship covered tuition, room, and board. I'd made a little money here and there when a few of my TikToks went viral, and I was hoping to use my future marketing degree to grow that side of things eventually.

But everything else? That still came from my parents.

Which meant, in a lot of ways, I still depended on them.

Very much like I had as a kid.

> Me: Does it bother you that I'm an Archibald?

His reply came a moment later:

> Theo's friend: No. Of course not. I mean...
> aside from the part where your dad scares
> the crap out of me.

I laughed softly, then looked up—just in time to meet his gaze again across the rink.

And suddenly, the meaning behind his words hit me in a new way.

If he was worried about my dad, then maybe...he cared.

Maybe this wasn't just some one-sided fleeting crush. Maybe it meant something.

Maybe despite the obstacles in our way, he, too, was hoping for the possibility of more.

"Who are you texting?" Nora leaned toward me, clearly picking up on the fact that I'd been half-in, half-out of the game for the past ten minutes.

I quickly clicked the side button on my phone, locking the screen and hiding the thread labeled *Theo's Friend.*

But Nora wasn't an idiot. And she *was* someone I trusted.

So I looked at her, smiled, and said, "I'm texting Owen."

"Oooh." Her eyes lit up like Christmas. "That's fun."

"Yeah." I smiled back, warmth blooming in my chest.

It really is.

The sound of skates slicing across ice pulled my attention back to the rink, just in time to see Brody wind up from near center ice and send the puck flying. It sailed past two defenders and somehow slipped right between the goalie's pads.

The crowd went *wild*.

Nora and I jumped up, screaming and clapping, our voices lost in the sea of cheers. I looked toward the ice, heart still pounding, and caught Brody glancing up into the stands.

His gaze swept over our section, and for a second, it almost felt like he was looking for me. And when he smiled my way, I had the feeling he found what he was looking for.

"Okay," Nora said, bumping her shoulder into mine. "I think we might've been right about Brody having a thing for you."

I laughed, breathless from cheering. "I think you're right."

But then, my phone buzzed in my hand. The screen lit up and Nora caught a glimpse of it.

"Too bad Professor McDreamy already stole your attention."

"Yeah..." I bit my lip, trying not to grin too obviously.

The crowd settled down again, and we slid back into our seats as the teams lined up for the last few minutes of the game. I pulled my phone out and glanced at the message.

> Theo's friend: What are you doing after this?

My heart did an immediate little flip as I anticipated why he might be asking.

> Me: Nora and I are going to a party at the hockey house…but I'm not really sure I want to go.

Okay, maybe I only added that last part just in case he's thinking about asking me to hang out...

> Me: What about you?

His response came a moment later.

> Theo's friend: My friends want to grab gelato at The Italian Amigos after this. Then I think I'll watch a movie when I get home.

> Me: Nice. Gelato and movies are always a good idea.

I read my text again, wondering if I should've said something *more*. Something that made it more obvious that I was open to hanging out if he was.

That I didn't care about following the unspoken rules we'd set in place the moment we found out he was my professor.

I mean…I'd already spent time at his apartment twice this week and nothing had happened.

It should be fine for two people who enjoyed each other's company to just hang out, right?

> Theo's friend: I probably shouldn't be saying this but…if you change your mind about the party, I'd love some company.

My breath caught.

I looked up across the rink and found him already looking in my direction.

Our eyes met.

And then, casually, like it cost him nothing and everything all at once, he gave me a small shrug.

Like he knew he shouldn't have said it.

Like he couldn't help himself.

Like he hoped I couldn't either.

My fingers were already moving as I typed:

> Me: Nora drove me here, and I probably shouldn't be seen leaving with you…but maybe I can make a showing at the party and then meet you somewhere.

I hit *Send*.

And for a second, all I could hear was the sound of my heart thudding inside my ears.

> Theo's friend: Sounds perfect. Gelato shouldn't take long. I'll text you when I'm done, and hopefully you'll still want to see me.

31

LUCY

THE BASS THUDDED through the floor at the big yellow house Brody and his teammates lived in, the air warm with too many bodies crammed into one house.

"Hey," Brody said, leaning close so I could hear him over the music, "I'm glad you could make it."

"Of course," I said, stepping in a little, the bass vibrating through my chest. "Thanks for the invite. I always love your parties."

Around us, the house buzzed with post-win energy—voices raised, music thumping, the unmistakable cocktail of sweat, cologne, and cheap beer thick in the air. Hockey players were everywhere. Some were still in partial uniform, others in hoodies and joggers, drinks in hand, grinning like they were the kings of the world.

"I'm gonna miss these parties when we all graduate," I said after taking a sip from my can of sparkling water.

"Me too," he said, nodding slowly.

"But you'll have plenty more parties like this to go to." I

offered Brody a smile. "Since you're playing for the Boston Watchmen next year, right?"

"I guess." He shrugged. "Though...it'll definitely be different." He looked at me, his gaze meeting mine for a beat. "I'll miss seeing *you* there, at least."

"Oh, I doubt you'll miss me for long." I chuckled, somewhat caught off guard by his statement. Trying to play it off, I added, "You know, once you've got all those girls wearing your jersey and screaming your name."

"Maybe." He shrugged but didn't smile. And for a second, I wondered if I'd said something wrong.

Maybe his crush was a little deeper than I'd thought?

I glanced at my watch. I'd been at the party for about thirty minutes. I'd sent Owen my location when I arrived, told him to just text me when he was nearby so I could slip out and meet him. But...had he forgotten about me?

Or maybe he'd just gotten caught up talking with his friends and lost track of time? Not that I expected him to ditch them for me or anything.

Still...how long did it take to get gelato?

I pulled my phone out of my pocket to see if I might have missed seeing a text come through, but there was nothing. Just the wallpaper of me and Nora making silly faces at practice one day.

My disappointment must've shown on my face because Brody tilted his head and asked, "You okay? You just got a look."

"I'm fine." I laughed lightly, tucking my phone back into my pocket. "Just checking the time to see how late it is since I'm feeling a little tired. All those early practices and hours studying must be catching up to me."

"Oh, I feel you there," he said, though something in his expression made me wonder if he sensed there was more.

But it wasn't like he could know...right?

Sure, we were lab partners for three hours a week, but I'd been careful not to let anything slip—only looking at Owen when completely necessary.

Okay. With the *occasional* extra glance.

But still. Pretty sure the only person who *might* have dirt on me was the tall guy who'd been following me Tuesday night.

Not that he could have seen me go into Owen's apartment...right?

It had been dark. I'd been across the street. I was almost certain I had my hood up.

Hadn't I?

I tried to shove the thought away. I was probably fine. Hopefully.

But with all these massive hockey players around me, with their shoulders and elbows and big booming voices, I suddenly felt small. At risk.

A flicker of unease crawled under my skin, and I scanned the room, suddenly needing to find Nora again. Just to anchor myself. Just to breathe.

And then, it happened.

Someone slammed into me—hard. A big guy, laughing with his friends, not even glancing my way. I stumbled straight into Brody, my hand instinctively grabbing his arm to steady myself as a flash of panic surged through me.

Because for a split second, I wasn't here anymore. I was back in that too-small kitchen, slammed into the counter, breath knocked out of me and fear crawling up my spine.

"Hey, man," Brody said, tensing beside me as he turned toward the guy. "Watch where you're going."

"Sorry." The guy raised his hands, still grinning like it was no big deal. "She's so tiny I barely saw her."

A flash of anger lit across Brody's face, and my stomach dropped.

Was this going to turn into another fight? Right here? Because of *me*?

But then, Brody exhaled, jaw tightening as he reined it in.

"You okay?" he asked, looking down at me.

I nodded, willing the tremor in my hands to still—trying to hold onto the present. "I'm fine."

"Are you sure?" He dipped his head low, searching my eyes.

"Yeah..." I said stepping back before he could see all my secrets. "Sorry I'm being so weird. But I-I think I'm gonna head out."

"I can give you a ride if you need," Brody offered, his hand steadying me gently at the elbow. "I only had one drink, so I should be good."

"Um...thanks." I hesitated, since part of me was still clinging to the hope that Owen would text and this night wouldn't be a complete bust.

Then, as if summoned, my watch lit up with a message from *Theo's friend*.

Finally.

I glanced back up at Brody. "Actually, I think I'll just walk. It's not far."

"You sure?" he asked, brow furrowing. "It's not always safe out there."

"I'll be fine," I said, offering a small smile. "But thank you. And thanks for inviting me tonight."

I stepped away and pulled my phone from my pocket, my thumb already swiping up to unlock it before I reached the edge of the room.

I scanned the room for Nora and spotted her across the living room, deep in conversation with the guy she'd been crushing on for weeks.

Instead of walking up and disrupting her, I sent Nora a quick text.

With that, I slipped out the front door and into the cool night air, my heart already picking up speed.

32

─────

OWEN

I HIT the unlock button when I saw Lucy step out of the big yellow house, fully expecting her to slide into the front seat beside me. But instead of doing that, she walked right past the passenger door and opened the back one.

Okay...not what I was expecting.

"Hi—" I said, twisting in my seat to look at her as she climbed in. "What are you doing back there?"

She shut the door, a little breathless as she buckled her seatbelt. "I figured if anyone was watching me leave, getting in the back would be less suspicious since your car looks like it could be from a rideshare service."

"Oh." I let out a quiet laugh and turned back toward the windshield. "That's actually genius."

"I thought so."

"Sorry I took so long," I said, casting a quick glance in the rearview mirror as I eased the car onto the street. "Ian likes to talk."

She smiled faintly. "It's fine."

We drove in silence for a moment. Not uncomfortable

exactly, but not the same kind of ease we usually had when we were together. Did something happen at the party?

Or was she just not as excited to hang out with me as I'd hoped?

"So..." I said, clearing my throat, "you still up for that movie?"

"Sure."

Okay... Not exactly the enthusiastic response I'd been hoping for.

Had something changed within the last hour? Had hanging out with all those people from school made Lucy realize that hanging out with her chemistry professor wasn't actually as cool as she'd thought?

I drummed my fingers once against the wheel, trying to shake the feeling, and turned onto another street.

But I probably should have chosen a different way home because the sight of the sprawling mansion on the corner, with its expansive lawn and stately trees, just brought the reality of what I was doing suddenly into focus.

Because the huge brick home glowing in the warm yellow light just ahead was the president's house.

The house where Lucy's mom and dad currently lived.

My jaw tensed. And for an irrational moment, I wondered if President Archibald had some kind of sixth sense. Like, could he somehow *feel* me driving past with his daughter in the backseat?

Did he have some sort of fatherly radar that told him his daughter was doing something he didn't approve of?

No...that was just my paranoia talking. He was probably fast asleep. Dreaming about the big donation Ian's dad had just made to the university to help build a much-needed parking structure.

"Did you like living there?" I asked Lucy, trying to keep things casual as we drove past the big house.

"It was okay." She followed my gaze. "Kind of strange, though, since it wasn't really our home. Just the house the university gave us."

"I can imagine." I paused. "How long did you live there?"

"Only two years," she said. "I moved into the dorms a few months after I turned eighteen."

"And your dad's been president for, what—five years?"

"Yep." She nodded. "Since I was sixteen."

Which meant that I'd been twenty-three when she was sixteen.

That one realization shouldn't have hit me the way it did, since theoretically I'd known how old she was.

But yeah...with the different scenarios I'd had in my head for how tonight might pan out...it suddenly felt almost wrong.

"When's your birthday again?" I asked. "You told me you were almost twenty-two, right?"

"I'll be twenty-two in May."

"Geez." I shook my head, letting out a breath. *I really am trying to rob the cradle, aren't I?*

There was a small pause. Then her voice drifted forward, calm and knowing. "Trying to figure out exactly how much younger I am than you?"

"Maybe."

"How old are you?"

"Twenty-eight," I said. "I'll be twenty-nine in March."

"So..." She did the math quickly. "You're just over seven years older than me."

"Yeah."

She was younger than Callie would've been. And somehow that hit me harder than the age gap itself.

I tightened my grip on the steering wheel and drew in a breath, wondering—for the hundredth time—what I was doing.

"You're feeling weird about hanging out with me now, aren't you?" she asked. Not accusatory. Just...quietly disappointed.

"I'm sorry," I said, glancing in the mirror again. "I didn't mean to make you feel like that."

"But you *are* feeling weird?" she asked, her voice even softer now.

I hesitated before nodding. "A little. I just..." I sighed. "I don't want to be that guy. The one who crosses a line he shouldn't."

She didn't respond. When I looked back again, her gaze was down, fingers tugging at the edge of her sleeve.

And just like that, the spark I'd been so drawn to—her fire, her lightness—dimmed.

And I hated that I was the reason for it.

I slowed the car at the next intersection, sitting with the weight of everything I wasn't sure how to say.

"Maybe I should just take you home tonight," I finally said.

There was a pause. Long enough for my chest to tighten.

Then she nodded once. "Okay."

No teasing. No protest.

Just quiet resignation.

Disappointment.

And somehow, that made me feel even worse.

I DIDN'T TEXT Owen over the weekend.

Partly because I was busy. But mostly...because I had no idea what to say to him after the car ride on Friday night where he'd panicked about my age and decided he should just take me home.

All weekend I kept wondering if I'd imagined it all—the looks, the tension, the feeling that maybe he actually liked me.

I mean, it had *felt* real. The way he'd opened up to me about his family and everything he'd been through had made me think that we were growing closer and that I was at least somewhat special.

But who knows. Maybe it hadn't actually been that deep. Maybe he was just like that with everyone.

I told myself that I was giving him space.

But the truth?

I was bracing myself for the slow fade.

At my gymnastics meet on Sunday afternoon, I caught myself scanning the crowd, stupidly hoping that I'd see him. That even though he didn't want to hang out in person, he might still show up to support me—or just to hang out with Theo and pretend he wasn't watching me.

But when I panned the crowd between each of my routines, I didn't see him anywhere.

He definitely wasn't next to Theo and my parents.

But hey, at least I'd nailed my routine. Even stuck the landing on my beam dismount, which had the crowd jumping to their feet, their cheers echoing in my ears.

And while I didn't spot the one person I'd been hoping to see in the stands…I did catch Brody, on his feet and grinning, clapping like I'd just won Olympic gold.

That night, as I lay in bed mentally preparing for the week ahead, I convinced myself that whatever Owen and I had shared—whatever attraction or connection had lingered between us since the first time we met—was over.

It was pointless to keep hoping for something that clearly wasn't going to work. Not when he thought I was too young for him.

Because even if we could somehow get around the other hurdles—the fact that he was my chemistry professor and my dad was the president of the university—there was no getting around the age gap. I couldn't magically age several years overnight just to reach whatever number Owen had decided made me acceptable to pursue.

As I stared up at the ceiling, listening to the heater kick on in my dorm room, I made a decision. I'd try to go back to the way things were a few weeks ago. Before the late-night texts. Before I panicked and showed up at his door. Before the dinner where he told me about his mom.

I was just his student now. A girl he'd see in his lecture hall and lab for five hours a week. Nothing more.

So when it came time for my chemistry class on Monday afternoon, instead of arriving early and trying to catch his eye like I'd done the class sessions before, I slipped into the back row just before his lecture began, took careful notes, avoided all eye contact and then slipped out as soon as class was over.

And even though we'd agreed he'd walk me home after my study group, I didn't text to remind him. I figured that door had quietly closed.

When the study session wrapped up at six thirty that night, I grabbed dinner from the dining hall, then zipped up my coat and braced myself for the chilly walk alone back to my dorm.

But when I stepped back into the hall that led to the glass doors, I saw Owen sitting in one of the chairs just outside the student lounge.

Like he'd been waiting for me.

The second our eyes met, he stood up.

And my heart instantly ached at the sight of him. Because even though I was doing my best to avoid him—to not want him—apparently, three days of separation wasn't enough to get over my craving for him.

"Hi," I said, trying to play it cool as he approached.

"Hi," he replied, his eyes cautious as he stepped closer.

We stepped outside together and walked in silence for a bit, the cool night air filled with the faint scent of pine and woodsmoke. I kept my gaze forward, trying not to let my brain run wild.

Had he changed his mind then? Did he regret how we'd left things Friday night?

Did he wish he hadn't taken me home after all?

But instead of asking him any of those things, I turned toward him and stupidly asked, "Aren't you worried about being seen with someone so young?"

The words tumbled out before I could stop them, and I instantly hated how insecure the question sounded.

"I still want to make sure you get home safely." Owen glanced sideways at me, his jaw ticking slightly.

Okay, so...maybe he didn't have any actual lingering feelings for me. Maybe this was just him being my self-appointed bodyguard of sorts.

So I just said, "Okay." And then because I should probably be more grateful that he was going out of his way to still help me, I added, "Thank you. I-I appreciate it."

We didn't talk after that. Just kept walking side by side.

A few times, he opened his mouth like he was about to say something...only to shake his head, seemingly changing his mind and stopping himself.

When we reached the spot where we'd crossed the street to get to his car last time, I slowed, wondering if we might stop there so we could talk with more privacy.

But after only a second of hesitation, he kept going.

Past the intersection.

Straight toward my dorm.

So...no talking needed, I guess. We were just silent walking buddies tonight.

When we reached the sidewalk that led up to my building, I slowed to a stop, about to thank him again and head inside.

But before I could do that, Owen reached out and gently took my hand, saying, "Hey."

My breath caught as he stepped a little closer and guided me off to the side, just behind a tree so we wouldn't be as visible to anyone going in and out of the dorm.

"I'm sorry," he said softly, his fingers still wrapped around mine. "For being so confusing with all my mixed signals. For probably hurting you last weekend."

I looked up at him, and when I met his gaze, the sadness and regret I saw reflected in his brown eyes made my chest ache.

"I didn't mean to end the night like that," he continued. "I'd actually planned on hanging out with you. Watching a movie. Just...being with you. I promise I really didn't plan on getting all weird and freaking out."

I let the words settle in, warm and painful all at once. But after a second, I tilted my head and asked, "But?" Because there had to be another shoe about to drop, right?

"I don't know... There probably *should* be a but." He exhaled slowly, his eyes meeting mine again, conflicted and raw. "But...I guess I'm still at war with myself. And I don't really know how to navigate all of this. I've never been in a situation like this before."

My heart clenched, because *same.*

It was a brand-new world for me, too.

"Well, I appreciate your apology," I said softly, my gaze dropping to where his thumb was brushing gently over mine.

Why did something so small have to feel so impossibly good? Sparking some hopeful, stupid little flame inside me that I hadn't quite managed to smother.

"And I also understand where you're coming from," I added, the words catching slightly in my throat. "This...is complicated. There's a lot on the line if anyone found out."

Having any kind of romantic relationship with me could put his entire career in jeopardy.

And even if we found a way to make it work somehow—if we waited until after I graduated, until we were technically in the clear...

There would still be a stigma.

He'd always be the professor who fell for his student.

We could never tell the story of how we met.

Not without it sounding...tainted.

Not without people wondering how he'd navigated

teaching someone he was attracted to—if it had ever crossed a line. If it might ever happen again.

We stood there for a moment, the quiet stretching between us like a fragile thread.

Like neither of us knew what to say next.

Or maybe we were both just too afraid to say the wrong thing.

A gust of wind came tearing down the sidewalk, slicing through my coat and making me shiver.

"I should let you go," I said, gently pulling my hand back. "It's freezing, and you still have to walk home."

He nodded, but he didn't move. He just lingered, like he wasn't quite ready to leave either.

Then, after a quick glance around—to make sure no one was watching—his arms slid around me, warm and protective, and he pressed a soft kiss to my forehead.

And for a second, the world stilled and I forgot how to breathe.

My chest ached with a deep, hollow longing. Because I wanted this. This little moment right here. I wanted this kind of tenderness, of mutual understanding. This something that felt so right, even if it was completely out of reach.

His clean scent wrapped around me like a memory I didn't want to let go of. I closed my eyes, letting myself feel it. If only for a moment.

But just as quickly as he'd pulled me close, he eased back. Enough for our eyes to meet. And there was something flickering there—quiet, unreadable, and maybe just a little bit heartbreaking.

"Have a good night, Lucy," he said, his voice low and rough around the edges.

I couldn't answer at first. My throat was too tight to speak.

But eventually, I blinked and managed to say, "Goodnight, Owen."

He turned and walked away then, his footsteps fading into the quiet.

I stood there for a moment, my heart thudding in my chest, then slowly turned toward the dorm entrance.

Before I slipped inside, I glanced back one last time.

And there he was—standing at the edge of the property line, watching. Making sure I got in okay.

I lifted my hand to wave.

He waved back.

And all I could think as I stepped inside was, so much for getting over Owen Park.

Because I was pretty sure I'd just fallen even harder tonight.

34

LUCY

THE REST of the week flew by.

I had back-to-back meets—Friday in Upper Marlboro, Maryland, and Sunday in Philly. The energy was electric, the kind of buzz that made every hour on the bus, every team chant, every sore muscle worth it. And on Sunday, after sticking my landings and not second-guessing myself even once, I somehow walked away with first in the all-around. Our team won, too.

It had been a rush. But by the time we made it back to campus Sunday night, I was wiped. The second my head hit the pillow, I crashed—sleeping harder than I had in weeks.

Owen walked me home again on Monday and Wednesday evenings. And things had been...good. Not as flirty as before, but steady. Comfortable. Like we'd settled into this quiet, unspoken understanding that we cared about each other but also knew we needed to stay in the let's-be-careful-and-not-do-anything-stupid zone.

Aside from those short walks, our only real interaction that week was a quick text exchange on Thursday night where we finalized a few details for Theo's surprise party.

> Theo's friend: I'm planning to pick Theo up at 5 on Saturday to grab burgers and go ax throwing. You still want me to bring him back around 7?

> Me: Yes. I was thinking I could call him around 6:50 to say that a pipe broke or something. That way he won't be expecting anything when you guys come in.

> Theo's friend: And he'll hopefully be relieved to see all his friends instead of a flooding house.

> Me: Exactly.

I was in Theo's living room on Saturday evening, building a train track loop with Charlotte, when the doorbell rang. And since I wasn't supposed to know it was Owen, I called out, saying, "Hey, Theo! I think someone is at the door."

But there was no answer.

Which made sense since he was upstairs, probably still scrubbing the carpet with his little carpet cleaner, thanks to Charlotte's naptime rebellion.

I stood and made my way to the front door, pausing just long enough to peek through the side window. And sure enough, it was Owen, standing with his hands in his coat pockets, the late afternoon light casting golden streaks over the sharp lines of his face.

"Hey," I said, slightly breathless as I pulled the door open to let him in.

"Hey." His voice was warm, easy, but something about the way his eyes lingered on mine made my stomach flutter.

"Theo should be down in a bit," I said, stepping aside to let him in. "He's just, uh...cleaning up the carpet Charlotte peed on."

"Oh." Owen winced. "That sounds fun."

"She took off her pull-up during naptime." I chuckled, shutting the door behind him. "She's quite the handful lately."

Right on cue, Charlotte came running into the room, then skidded to a stop when she spotted Owen. Her little hands clutched at my legs as she peeked up at him with wide, curious eyes.

"You remember your dad's friend, right?" I said, scooping her into my arms. "You met him at my gymnastics meet a few weeks ago."

She rested her head shyly on my shoulder and murmured, "Hi."

His whole face softened. "Hi, Charlotte."

And the way he said it, with the tiniest smile tugging at the corner of his mouth, was so freaking adorable I had to stop myself from sighing. Charlotte just stared at him, mesmerized, and I couldn't help but think: *You and me, girl.* Because apparently, Archibald girls just had a thing for Owen Park.

His gaze flicked toward the stairs, as if checking for movement, then he turned back to me. "Do you have everything you need for tonight? Or is there anything else you want me to do?"

"I think I'm good," I said, adjusting Charlotte on my hip. "I've got decorations in my trunk and Nora's on standby to come over as soon as you guys leave. So really, I just need Theo out of here before the caterers show up."

"What time are they coming?" Owen glanced toward the stairs again.

"Not 'til six, so we've got an hour. I don't think cleaning up after Charlotte will take that long."

He smiled and reached out to gently take Charlotte's tiny hand. "Do you like causing trouble for your daddy?"

"Yes," she said matter-of-factly.

We both laughed, and when our eyes met, warmth flickered in the space between us—comfortable, easy, a little charged in a way that made me wonder if he'd felt it, too.

Footsteps echoed upstairs, and just like that, Owen straightened. His hands went back to his pockets, shoulders squared. Professor mode: activated.

"Hey, Owen." Theo appeared at the top of the stairs, his expression sheepish as he jogged down. "Sorry to keep you waiting. Had a bit of a mess to take care of."

"I heard," Owen said, chuckling. "Sounds like Charlotte's a handful sometimes."

Theo ruffled Charlotte's hair as she giggled in my arms. "She's my little tornado." He smiled at Charlotte then, all softness in his expression. "We'll be back in a few hours. Maybe around eight?"

"Sounds good," I said with a smile, knowing full well my emergency call plan would hopefully bring him back a little sooner.

Theo pressed a quick kiss to Charlotte's forehead. "You be good for Aunt Lucy, okay?"

"O-tay," she said in her sweet little voice.

I glanced at Owen just in time to catch his smile at her. And it hit me again—how much I liked that. Not all guys were good with kids, but he seemed to genuinely enjoy her.

He'd probably make a great dad one day.

"Be back soon," Theo said, stepping toward the door.

Owen followed, but just before stepping outside, he said, "Bye, Charlotte." Then his gaze lifted to mine, and when he added, "Bye, Lucy," in that quiet, almost tender way, my heart rose so fast it caught in my throat.

"Take good care of my brother, Professor Park," I managed to say.

"I will." A small smile touched his lips. And in a lowered tone that Theo wouldn't hear, he added, "Good luck getting everything ready."

And then, they were gone.

I exhaled slowly, heart still fluttering, and glanced around the room.

Time to turn this house into party central.

35

OWEN

"BEEN ON ANY GOOD DATES LATELY?" Theo asked, winding up for his next throw at the axe-throwing place on Main Street.

I exhaled through my nose, gripping the handle a little tighter as I searched for an answer that wouldn't give too much away about where my head had been lately when it came to dating.

Because I probably shouldn't count dinner in my apartment with Lucy as a *real* date.

So instead, I went with the truth—just not the whole truth.

"I took a girl named MaryAnn to dinner a few weeks back," I said, watching the blade sail from Theo's hand and land dead center. "It went okay."

You know...right up until I saw his gorgeous sister rushing toward the bathroom and couldn't remember MaryAnn's eye color —or why I'd thought dinner with anyone else was a good idea.

"Yeah?" Theo turned toward me, wiping his palms on his jeans. "Anyone else on your radar?"

"Not really." I shook my head, keeping my expression neutral as I lied through my teeth. "What about you? Any good dates?"

"Not really." He shrugged then tossed the axe again. It hit the outer ring this time. "It's been hard making the time to go out."

"I bet." I leaned against the divider between lanes. "Your job keeps you busy. And then having Charlotte...that's gotta make things more complicated."

"It does." He glanced down for a second before adding, "I mean, I probably shouldn't say this, but...I almost feel guilty trying to go on dates when I've got Charlotte at home just waiting to see me after work."

That had to be rough—balancing work, fatherhood, grief. Trying to open his heart again after losing Alisha. I couldn't even imagine.

And here I was, brooding just because the one woman I actually wanted was technically off-limits.

"You've got a lot to navigate," I said, clearing my throat. "But you deserve to be happy, too. To fall in love again. Find someone to share your life with."

"Thanks. I appreciate that." Theo's eyes softened. "I just wish there was a way to skip all the bad dates and just...find the right girl."

"Isn't that the trick?" I chuckled. "Sadly, the dating apps haven't nailed that perfect algorithm yet."

"Well, they need to get on that," Theo said, managing a smile. "I'm not getting any younger. And Charlotte deserves a mom."

He looked like he was about to say something else when his phone buzzed in his pocket. He pulled it out, glanced at the screen, and frowned.

"Oh, it's Lucy. I better take this. Something might be wrong with Charlotte."

I nodded, trying not to look like I already knew exactly what Lucy was about to tell him.

"Hey, Lucy," he answered, stepping a few paces away as he pressed the phone to his ear.

I checked the time. 6:50 p.m. Right on schedule.

I grabbed another axe and threw it, landing just outside the bullseye as I waited for him to come back.

"Hey," he said a moment later, looking flustered. "Lucy said she started a load of laundry for me and just walked in to find it overflowing from the drainpipe. Water's getting everywhere and she's not sure what to do."

"Oh no," I said, layering in the concern like I hadn't been expecting it. "We better get you home before anything gets damaged."

"Yeah. Sorry, man." He winced. "I hate to cut it short."

"Don't worry about it," I said, waving the thought away. "We can have a re-match another time."

We dropped off our axes and then grabbed our coats to step outside. As we headed toward my car, I pulled out my phone and fired off a quick text to Lucy:

> Me: On our way. See you soon.

It was probably unnecessary since she most likely already knew. But for some reason, I wanted to feel like we were in this together.

———

"The laundry room's just off the kitchen," Theo said as he opened the front door, motioning for me to follow.

"Okay," I said, my pulse kicking up a notch as I stepped in behind him.

And sure enough, we had barely crossed the threshold to the main living area when a dozen people suddenly jumped out from their hiding places and yelled, "Surprise!"

Theo flinched so hard he nearly jumped out of his shoes. "Holy crap," he muttered, his wide-eyed gaze bouncing from face to face as the realization sank in.

Then his eyes landed on Lucy.

She stood in the corner next to us, one arm wrapped around Charlotte, her smile bright, like she'd been waiting all day for this exact reaction.

"So..." Theo stared at her, squinting suspiciously. "My house isn't actually flooding?"

"Everything's fine." Lucy laughed, her eyes crinkling at the corners. "I just needed a good excuse to get you back here."

"And you couldn't have thought of something less stressful?" Theo let out a breath, dragging a hand through his hair. "I was panicking the whole way over, just praying it wouldn't cause any real damage since I really don't have time for a renovation right now."

"Sorry." Lucy shrugged like she wasn't sorry at all.

Theo turned to me next. "Were you in on this, too?"

"Your sister *might* have enlisted my help in getting you out of the house." I gave him a guilty shrug. "Just so she could set everything up."

"And here I thought you just wanted to be besties with me." He gave me a playful nudge. "But thanks. This is fun."

Looking around at the crowd gathering in his living room—friends, family, coworkers—he lifted his voice. "Thank you all for coming to my party!"

A round of cheers echoed back, and Theo made his way

into the mix, offering hugs and high fives as he started making his rounds.

I hung back near the doorway, watching him, then turned to Lucy. She set Charlotte down, who immediately dashed toward the counter with all the food, a determined look in her eye.

"This looks great," I said, nodding toward the decorations strung from wall to wall, the huge, gold three-and-zero-shaped balloons, and the buffet of catered food taking over the kitchen counters. "You and Nora must have been booking it."

"We were panicking just a bit." Lucy chuckled, brushing a loose curl off her cheek. "But Sloan, Ian, and Maddie showed up at the same time as the caterers and jumped in to help. Totally saved our bacon."

"That's awesome." I glanced toward my friends who were chatting with Evan and Addie in the corner and smiled. "It turned out really well."

"Thanks." She looked over toward the kitchen area. Gesturing to the spread, she said, "I hope you didn't stuff yourself at dinner because I'm pretty sure we have enough food in the kitchen to feed an army."

"I saved a little room." I patted my stomach.

"Good."

We stood there quietly for a beat, the hum of the party buzzing around us while I took her in.

At some point between setting the trap for Theo and now, she'd changed outfits. Her dress was light blue and soft-looking, with short, puffed sleeves and a square neckline that dipped just enough to reveal the slightest hint of cleavage.

It was sweet.

Flirty.

Maddeningly sexy in a way that makes it nearly impossible to think straight.

My gaze dipped before I could stop it, drawn to the soft curve just above her neckline—a tease of skin that made my thoughts go places they absolutely shouldn't. I swallowed hard and dragged my eyes away, praying no one noticed just how much I wanted to keep looking.

Her hair framed her face in gentle waves, catching the light as she moved, and her heels gave her just enough lift that she had to tilt her chin slightly to meet my eyes.

She was dazzling—utterly, stupidly dazzling—and I was painfully aware of how much effort it took not to reach for her. Not to close the distance and say to hell with the consequences.

"You look amazing, by the way," I said, my voice lower than I meant it to be. "That dress—it looks really nice on you."

"I'm glad you like it." Her cheeks flushed the prettiest shade of pink as she glanced down, her fingers brushing the skirt of the dress like she didn't quite know what to do with herself. "Figured I should probably wear something besides jeans or gym clothes for once."

"You always look great in those, too," I said. And my gaze must've lingered too long because something flickered in her eyes, like she knew exactly what I was thinking.

That no matter what she was wearing, I always had a hard time not watching her in class.

"Well, that's good to know," she said, the flirty glint in her expression impossible to miss. "Wouldn't want to look like a scrub in front of my favorite professor."

"So, I'm your favorite professor now?" I lifted a brow, unable to stop the grin tugging at my lips. "Does that mean chemistry's finally grown on you this semester?"

She laughed under her breath, a warm, teasing sound. "I said you were my favorite professor. Not that you taught my favorite class."

"Well." I tilted my head, letting my smile linger. "I guess I can't win them all."

Just then, Charlotte came running back over and tugged on the hem of Lucy's dress. "I want cake," she said, wide-eyed and very serious.

Lucy crouched beside her, smoothing a hand over her niece's hair. "We have to sing 'Happy Birthday' to your daddy before we eat the special cake," she said gently. "But we can find you something yummy for now, okay?"

Charlotte nodded, already tugging Lucy's hand toward the kitchen like her tiny stomach was in full control of the evening.

"Guess I'll see you later." Lucy glanced up at me as she stood, a soft smile playing on her lips. "Hope you enjoy the party."

And just like that, she was gone again—swept away by a three-year-old with an agenda and zero patience.

36

LUCY

THEO'S SURPRISE party went off without a hitch. He was happily surprised, the house was packed, and everyone seemed to enjoy themselves—eating, talking, and playing games in different corners of the house.

Once I saw that everyone was having a good time and Charlotte was entertaining Theo and his friends with her somersaults, I slipped away from the main living area and into the big theater room at the back of the house.

When I walked in the back, Miles, Bash, and Ky were sprawled on the tiered seats at the front of the room, playing some interactive video game that involved lots of yelling and arm movements.

Trying not to disturb them, I sank onto a couch in the back row, kicked off my heels, and groaned quietly. My legs were killing me. Coach hadn't exactly murdered us in practice this week, but she'd definitely slow-baked us. Lots of precision drills, balance corrections, and extra holds on beam to "lock in muscle memory" before Sunday's big home meet against Yale.

The result: my body felt like Jell-O. Controlled Jell-O. With a side of bruises.

I leaned my head back, closing my eyes for just a second...

"Let's gooo! Dunk on him!"

The shout came from the front of the room—probably Miles— jarring me out of the edges of sleep.

My eyes fluttered open, and that was when I saw Owen.

Sitting on the couch beside me, maybe a foot away. Casual. Relaxed. Like he'd been there quietly watching his friends play their video game while I was dozing off.

"You tired?" he asked softly, his voice low and close.

I blinked at him, still half-drowsy. "Exhausted," I admitted, letting my head rest back against the cushion. "I just needed to get off my feet for a minute."

He glanced down, eyes catching on my heels now discarded on the floor. "Feet sore?"

"My everything is sore," I muttered with a faint smile, stretching out one leg in front of me.

He smiled, then looked around the room, making sure the guys were still caught up in their game. Then, without a word, Owen reached over and took my foot gently in his hands.

My breath hitched. For a second, I wasn't sure what he was doing. Was he just holding it? About to make a joke? My brain scrambled to make sense of the sudden contact—of how careful his touch was. How warm his hands felt against my skin.

And then he started massaging.

And I nearly melted. Because ohhhh...it felt *so* good.

A sharp breath escaped me—half-sigh, half-moan—and I had to slap a hand over my mouth to muffle the sound.

"Too much?" he asked, his voice low, rougher than usual. Like he, too, was having some sort of internal reaction to touching me like that.

"No." I shook my head, barely able to form words. "That feels...ridiculously good."

He smiled again, and I imagined I saw heat smoldering behind his eyes. His fingers moved in slow, practiced circles over the arch of my foot, making me sink deeper into the couch cushion. Then he slid upward, his thumbs pressing into my sore calf, kneading gently but firmly, coaxing out tension I hadn't even realized I was holding.

Oh. Wow.

I bit the inside of my cheek to keep another groan from escaping. This felt way too good—illegal levels of good.

I let my head fall back for a second, trying to gather myself, but it was no use.

Because then, I looked at him.

And just like that, the focus of my senses shifted—from how good his hands felt on me to how good *he* looked while giving my muscles much needed relief.

His brow was furrowed slightly in concentration, his strong hands deftly moving up and down my calf.

"Thank you," I murmured, my voice husky as heat coiled low in my stomach, unbidden images flickering through my mind of what his hands might feel like on the rest of me. "You're a miracle worker."

"No problem," he said, his eyes locking with mine. "It's the least I could do."

And in that moment, I forgot how to breathe. Because that look...it made me think that if I were to tell him I wanted more, he'd give it.

And boy, did I want more.

So much more.

Wished I could take his hand and pull him into one of Theo's spare bedrooms and pick up where we'd left off in the hot tub all those weeks ago.

To go back to that magical night when the stars just seemed to align perfectly and there weren't all these extra complications.

His hands moved to my other foot, his thumb brushing the curve of my ankle bone, and a full-body shiver rolled through me.

What is he doing to me?

Each stroke, each squeeze, each gentle press of his fingers melted into my skin like warm water on aching muscles. And it felt so good. Too good.

I glanced toward the front of the room where the guys were still hollering at the game. They thankfully seemed oblivious to the fact that we were even in here with them.

When I turned back, Owen was already watching me, his expression unreadable but intense.

What would he do if I lean over and kiss him right now?

He wouldn't be touching me like this if he didn't want more...right?

Would he pull me into his lap like he had that night under the stars? Would he trace his lips along my neck, his breath hot against my skin, sending shivers down my spine as he whispered that he'd been dreaming of doing that since we met?

I studied the way his chest was rising just a little too fast. The way his eyes had darkened to stormy slate, hunger flickering just beneath the surface.

When his gaze dropped to my mouth—and he licked his lips before meeting my eyes again—my heart nearly stopped.

Would it really be so bad if I pulled him away right now? For just a minute. One stolen moment in a quiet corner to take the edge off this unbearable tension simmering between us.

But just when I thought he might actually reach for me, just when it felt like this moment was about to tip into something reckless and unforgettable, Theo's voice broke through the fog with a, "Hey," and I jolted like I'd been electrocuted.

I snatched my foot back from Owen and straightened in my seat, my heart slamming against my ribs like I'd been caught doing something illegal.

"This party has been amazing," Theo said, totally oblivious to the charged moment he'd just crashed. "Seriously, Lucy—thank you for putting it all together. I honestly can't believe you were able to find the time with everything else you have going on."

"You're welcome." I swallowed hard, my pulse still drumming in my ears with the adrenaline of almost getting caught in a heated moment with his friend—my professor. "Professor Park helped a lot, too. Gave me the contact info for the caterers."

Hopefully, using his title in front of Theo would keep my brother off the scent—keep him from realizing just how familiar Owen and I had become these past six weeks.

"Thanks, man," Theo said, stepping in farther and giving Owen a casual fist bump.

"Happy to help," Owen replied smoothly, his voice perfectly neutral again.

But when Theo looked toward the front of the room a second later and I caught Owen's eyes, his gaze seemed to reflect exactly what I was thinking: that we'd been way too close to getting caught.

After the party died down and most of the guests were gone, I stayed behind to help clean up while Theo got Charlotte tucked into her bed upstairs.

I'd just finished putting the leftover cake in the fridge when Owen stepped into the kitchen.

"What can I do to help?" he asked, sleeves pushed up, hands tucked in his pockets.

My heart jumped at the sight of him. I'd assumed he already left after helping the caterers from The Garden load up their van. But here he was.

"If you could take out the trash, that'd be awesome," I said, nodding toward the near-overflowing bin, trying to keep the sudden spike of nerves in check.

Because we are alone.

I mean, Theo and Charlotte were upstairs, so we weren't alone-alone.

But since Charlotte usually took at least thirty minutes to fall asleep—after convincing Theo to read her no fewer than three bedtime stories—it wasn't likely anyone would be joining us anytime soon.

"On it," he said, grabbing the bag and tying it off.

A few minutes later, he was back—liner replaced, water running as he washed his hands at the sink.

I grabbed the stack of paper plates from the counter and opened the pantry door, just as he stepped up behind me with a rolled-up bag of chips in hand.

"Sorry," I mumbled when my arm grazed against his chest, the narrow space making it impossible not to brush against each other.

"It's fine," he said, but I didn't miss the way his voice sounded huskier than usual.

I turned slightly, meaning to make more room, but all it did was bring us closer. His body was just inches from mine, and the air became instantly charged, making my skin prickle.

I could smell him, clean and warm, familiar now, and so stupidly comforting.

"You smell really good," I said, looking up at him through my lashes, suddenly aware of every breath, every heartbeat.

"Thank you," he murmured, looking down at me with his dark eyes that always seemed to see into my soul. "So do you."

And even though now would probably be the time to step out of the pantry...

He didn't move.

And neither did I.

The silence thickened, stretching tight and taut around us, like the air itself was holding its breath.

My eyes flicked up to his.

And that was all it took.

Because the look he gave me wasn't neutral. It wasn't casual.

It was hungry.

His gaze dropped to my mouth, and suddenly, everything in me went still.

Was he thinking what I was thinking?

That maybe it was okay to steal a little moment after all?

Just one.

I mean, it's not like anyone would find out...

As if reading my mind, Owen reached out. His fingers brushed a strand of hair from my cheek, barely touching me, but it sent a jolt of heat straight down my spine.

I didn't breathe. Didn't dare.

One wrong move, and I'd shatter the moment.

But then his hand lingered, his fingertips trailing lightly down my jaw.

I leaned into his touch without even thinking, my eyes fluttering closed for half a second—just long enough to memorize the feel of his skin on mine.

When I opened my eyes again, he was still watching me.

Like I was something fragile. Impossible. Like he couldn't believe I was real.

His thumb brushed across my cheekbone—so gently it made my breath catch—then traced down to the curve of my chin, tilting it ever so slightly.

I lifted my face toward his, only a breath separating us now. Every nerve ending in my body lit up, aching for him to close that space. To kiss me already and put me out of my misery.

Please.

Just do it.

"*Lucy...*" he whispered, my name catching in his throat. Like he was trying to remind himself we shouldn't.

Like he was asking me to stop this before he lost control.

But I didn't want to stop.

Slowly, I turned my head and pressed a kiss to the inside of his wrist—soft, deliberate, and filled with every ounce of longing I hadn't dared speak aloud.

His breath caught before a low, ragged sound escaped his chest—half groan, half surrender.

And then I saw it, the shift in his eyes.

The unraveling.

Like his grip on restraint was loosening, and this time, he didn't want to stop it from slipping away.

His jaw tensed, the muscles in his arm tightening beneath my fingers.

He searched my face, like he was still clinging to the question we weren't saying out loud.

Then he exhaled, low and rough. "Ah, screw it," he muttered.

A second later, his hands were tangling in my hair, his mouth covering mine.

The kiss was rough.

Hungry.

And everything I'd been aching for.

He tasted like heat and tension, like something forbidden that I couldn't stop wanting. So I leaned into him, sliding my hands up his chest, over the steady hammer of his heart.

Man, he was solid—strong in a way that surprised me for someone who spent most of his days in a classroom or a lab. My fingers lingered, exploring the contours of muscle beneath the thin cotton of his shirt. I found myself wondering about his workout routine. Wondering if he'd ever let me tag along, just so I could watch.

His hands found my waist, pulling me closer, anchoring me until we were pressed together. And while he'd hugged me just a few days ago, this—his body against mine, his lips setting fire to my thoughts—was something else entirely.

He slid his hands up my sides, slow and possessive, palms smoothing around my ribcage until they spread across my back. And it felt so good. To be held like this. To be wanted like this. Safe and secure and desired.

"You taste so good," he breathed against my lips. "Feel incredible."

"So do you," I panted, my fingers curled at the hem of his shirt—needing more, craving more. When I slipped them underneath, my palms met warm, unyielding muscle. I traced the lines of his stomach, the ridges of his abs, the rise and fall of his chest with every unsteady breath.

His whole body went still.

Then a groan rumbled low in his throat, and his hands slid down to grip my hips before he lifted me like I weighed nothing.

I gasped softly as he raised me, my legs wrapping around his waist on instinct. He caught me beneath my thighs, steady and sure, as my back pressed against the cool wall of the pantry.

And then he leaned into me.

Every inch of his torso pressed tight against every inch of me.

It was overwhelming in the best way.

His mouth moved against mine with a kind of hunger I felt down to my bones. Like he'd been starving for this. For me.

I couldn't breathe.

Didn't want to.

My fingers curled against his back, digging into the muscles there, feeling the shift and tension of him beneath my palms. Then he deepened the kiss, his lips trailing along my jaw, my throat, until he found that spot just beneath my ear that made my breath catch and my eyes flutter shut.

A sound escaped me. A soft whimper I didn't have time to be embarrassed about.

"*Lucy*," he breathed, rough and low, like it physically hurt him to hold back. His forehead brushed mine. "Tell me if you want me to stop."

But I didn't. The last thing I wanted was for him to stop when I'd been dreaming of this for so many weeks.

So, I clutched him tighter, silently telling him I was right there with him. And when he slid the sleeve of my dress off my shoulder, baring the slope of skin beneath, I still didn't stop him.

He kissed me there—slow, reverent—then let his mouth drift lower, brushing the sensitive skin just above the neckline of my dress. When he sucked gently, a rush of heat bloomed low in my stomach, and my legs suddenly went weak.

It felt so good—his mouth on my skin, warm and intent, like he was memorizing the taste of me. But it wasn't just how he touched me. It was how he wanted me. Like I was something rare. Something to savor. Like I mattered.

And I hadn't realized how much I'd missed being seen like that. A lump formed in my throat, unexpected and aching, because it had been a long time since anyone had looked at me as more than just a warm body, an object to play with until they grew tired of me.

I clung to his shoulders, trying to stay upright, but my legs gave out, and my back hit the wall with a soft thud. Owen's arm shifted quickly to steady me, but in the scramble, his elbow clipped the pantry light switch.

The bulb overhead flickered once...then went out, plunging us into darkness. Only a sliver of ambient light spilled in from the kitchen, casting just enough glow to catch the outline of his jaw and the glint in his eyes as they searched mine.

He started to reach up, maybe to fix it.

But I stopped him with a whisper, "Just leave it."

37
———

OWEN

LUCY and I were pressed together, her back against the wall, my hands firm on her waist. The faint light from the kitchen spilled in behind me, casting her in a soft silhouette. And still, I couldn't catch my breath.

This girl.

I'd spent so many nights imagining what it would feel like to have her in my arms again. But my memory hadn't done her justice. Not even close.

Because kissing Lucy wasn't just electric or intoxicating—it was otherworldly. Like time slowed down just to give me this moment. Like everything else in my life had been in grayscale until she touched me.

After weeks of pretending we were just friends—of stuffing down every glance, every brush of her hand that made my heart beat faster—she was finally here. With me. Her lips swollen from our kiss, her body molding to mine like it was the only place she was ever meant to be.

And I was coming apart at the seams.

I didn't just want her. I *needed* her. Not in a fleeting way.

Not like a fix to take the edge off. I needed her in a way that made it hard to think straight. Hard to remember why we ever told ourselves this was off-limits.

I'd convinced myself a moment ago that this would be enough. That I'd come out on the other side with the craving dulled.

But being this close? Wrapped around her in the dark?

It was doing the exact opposite.

Instead of satiating my need for this girl, it only made me want more. More of her sighs. More of her skin beneath my hands and lips. More of the way she looked at me, like I was something she'd been aching for, too.

I shifted, turning us slowly until my back met the wall. My knees were about to give out, and the last thing I wanted was to drop her. So I slid down, bringing her with me, my hands steady at her waist.

She didn't say a word. Just settled onto my lap like she belonged there—her knees on either side of my hips, her weight warm and perfect against me.

"We probably should've found a less cramped place to do this," I murmured, voice rough as I looked up at her.

"Probably." Her lips curved, the softest whisper of a smile.

But then, as if she didn't actually mind the cramped quarters, she was kissing me again.

Soft at first—testing, teasing—and then deeper. Her tongue tangled with mine, igniting instant heat between us, like a match struck in the dark.

I groaned into her mouth, my hands roaming, sliding up her sides, tracing the elegant line of her spine through the thin fabric of her dress. Every brush of her body against mine made my pulse stutter, made the air in my lungs disappear.

She made a soft, involuntary sound, and I swear, it nearly undid me.

Because that noise?

It wasn't just desire. It was trust.

Surrender.

Like she was as wrecked by this moment as I was.

Like maybe I wasn't the only one who'd fallen so hard.

I curled my fingers into the fabric at her hips. Anchoring her...or maybe anchoring myself. I couldn't tell anymore.

But one thing was clear: I didn't want to stop. I didn't want to go back to keeping our distance. Ever.

She exhaled softly, her breath mixing with mine as her fingers slipped beneath my shirt, slow and searching—as if she was looking for something solid in all this heat and wanting.

"I can't even think when you kiss me like this," she whispered, her voice barely audible, like it had been pulled straight from the center of her.

And that wrecked me.

Because maybe I wasn't the only one losing control.

Maybe she was right there with me.

"I'm having a hard time thinking, too," I admitted.

She leaned forward, her chest pressing flush against mine, and I swear I felt it all the way to my toes. My hands slid lower, finding her thighs, bare and warm beneath the hem of her dress. I curled my fingers there, grounding myself in the feel of her, in this impossibly perfect moment I never wanted to end.

And then—

Footsteps.

Coming down the stairs.

We froze in unison, like someone had yanked the emergency brake on the universe, causing every cell in my body to go on high alert.

Because we were in a dark pantry. Alone. Tangled up. And this was not a moment we could explain away.

Not to Theo.

Not to anyone.

Not without ruining everything.

From outside the pantry, I heard Theo muttering to himself, something that sounded like *"She must be reverting."* And it took me a second to realize he was probably talking about Charlotte.

Lucy's eyes widened. When Theo's footsteps got closer, I worried he was coming down for a midnight snack. But his footsteps continued on, and a moment later, the front door creaked.

"I better get out there," Lucy whispered, already straightening her dress, her voice breathless. "If he doesn't see me, he might come looking."

I nodded, still trying to catch my own breath, and she slipped out the door.

I got myself to my feet and leaned back against the shelves, dragging a hand through my hair.

That was so close.

Way too close.

Seconds later, I heard the door open again—Theo returning.

"Where'd you come from?" His voice came from the other room. "Were you in here when I walked by a second ago?"

"I was just putting some tablecloths in the laundry room," she said, her tone light, easy. "Is Charlotte already asleep?"

"Not yet." Theo grunted. "Had another accident, so she's just getting dressed after her bath."

"Oh, I'm sorry about that."

"Yeah," Theo said. "I don't know what's going on. She's having so many accidents. Has a harder time going to daycare lately, too. I wonder if anything happened that's making her revert."

"I hope not," Lucy said, concern in her voice.

"Me too. I'll have to ask her teachers if they've noticed

anything." There was a brief pause and then he asked, "Hey, is Owen still here?"

"Owen?" Lucy asked, her voice raising a notch.

"Uh, I guess you know him better as Professor Park," Theo said. "I'm pretty sure I saw his car out front just now."

Oh crap.

That wasn't good.

Should I just come out now?

Formulating a quick plan in my head, I stepped out of the pantry, doing my best to look casual and *not* like a man who had just been making out with his friend's sister.

"Hey—sorry," I said, rubbing the back of my neck. "I, uh... realized I left my phone somewhere. Lucy let me back in to look."

"You left it in the pantry?" Theo's brow arched.

I shrugged casually as I could manage. "Must've set it down while I was grabbing something from up high during the party."

Theo studied me for a second, his eyes narrowing just slightly...then he nodded. "Well...glad you found it."

Crisis mostly averted.

"Actually," he added, "while you're still here, I was wondering if you wanted to come to Lucy's gymnastics meet with me tomorrow. It was fun last time. And since we're up against your alma mater..."

My eyes flicked to Lucy, who was working hard to keep her face calm, and back to Theo.

"Sure," I said, mustering a small smile. "That sounds fun."

Yep...yay for sitting beside Theo while watching his sister flip across the mat in spandex, pretending I hadn't kissed her senseless the night before.

38

OWEN

THE ARENA WAS PACKED MORE than usual tonight. Fans from both Eden Falls University and Yale had turned out in full force, filling every row of the stadium. The air practically pulsed with anticipation, the hum of conversation swelling beneath the vaulted ceiling, cheers ricocheting off concrete and steel. I sat beside Theo and Charlotte, trying to act like this was just another Sunday meet. Like I wasn't secretly counting every heartbeat until Lucy's turn on beam.

Charlotte, who'd been sitting quietly with her headphones and a coloring book, tugged on Theo's sleeve. "Daddy, I have to go potty."

Theo looked at the rotation list on his phone, then glanced up at the scoreboard. Lucy's name was next.

He sighed like it physically pained him to miss her routine. "All right, bug. Let's go fast, okay?" He turned to me. "Would you mind filming Lucy's routine for me?"

I swallowed the knot forming in my throat and gave Theo a nod that I hoped looked casual. "Yeah, of course." I pulled my phone from my back pocket, trying not to look like a guy about to commit professional suicide. "I'll get a good angle."

Because what was I supposed to say? *Sorry, man, but filming your little sister feels like toeing every professional line I'm already trying not to cross?*

The announcer's voice cut through the low hum of the arena. "Up next on beam...Lucy Archibald, competing for Eden Falls University."

A round of cheers rose from our section. I angled my phone toward the balance beam and hit *Record*.

Lucy stepped into view, all focus and calm fire, her hair slicked back into a tight braided bun that didn't move an inch. She raised one arm to signal the judges, then turned her attention to the beam, her expression steady and composed. A breath. A beat. Then, before I even had time to register what was happening, she launched off the springboard, twisting midair and landing in a crouch on the beam like it was second nature. No wobble. No hesitation. Just...total command.

She rose to her feet with that quiet confidence that always knocked the breath out of me, arms lifting in a smooth arc, drawing more cheers from the crowd.

But she wasn't even close to being done.

She moved along the beam like it was just an extension of herself. Each movement strong, clean, deliberate. It was that signature mix of grace and grit that was so uniquely her.

I was always impressed by her, but this? This was next level.

She paused at the end of the beam, took a steadying breath, then launched into a tumbling pass—some kind of lightning-fast combo of handsprings that ended in a layout. And when she stuck the landing, the place went wild.

Her smile was radiant. She struck a pose—arms back, chin tilted.

Then her gaze slid toward my section.

Just a quick glance.

But I swear it landed on me.

And that was when it happened.

The shift.

The slow arch of her back. A teasing sweep of her legs. The tiniest wink—so quick it could've been nothing.

And I couldn't be sure since her gaze only landed on me for a brief second before panning to another row, but...was she flirting with me?

I'd seen her do those moves for the cameraman the last time I was here, so I knew they were part of the routine. A way to showcase her personality, connect with the judges, draw the crowd in.

But this time, she was facing my direction.

And I couldn't help but wonder...was she putting on a show for me?

As much as I loved it—loved the idea that maybe she was— it sent a jolt straight through my chest for a whole other reason.

Because her dad was here. Her teammates. An entire arena of spectators.

And if anyone so much as *guessed* what might be going on between us...

It would be game over.

I shifted in my seat.

"Okay, Theo," I muttered, subtly lowering the phone in case anyone was looking my direction, "now would be an excellent time to come back and take this thing off my hands." Because this was dangerous territory.

Also...there was no way I wasn't watching that video again when I got home.

But then I heard it.

A voice from behind me. Male. Low. Way too confident.

"Dang, she's hot. Bet she's a freak in the sheets."

I went still.

"Wouldn't mind seeing that beam routine up close," another guy chimed in, laughing. "With flexibility like that? Yeah, I've got a few ideas."

More laughter.

My jaw tightened and heat crawled up my neck.

Tune it out. Let it go. Don't make a scene, I told myself as I stared at the phone screen, trying to pretend I didn't hear it.

But then the first guy added, louder this time, "Wonder if she's single. I'd let her ride my balance beam—"

And that was it.

"Hey." I turned around before my brain could catch up with my body. "That's President Archibald's daughter you're talking about. Maybe show a little respect."

Both guys flinched, mid-laugh, their expressions shifting fast like they hadn't expected to be called out. One of them muttered something about me needing to take a chill pill.

Then I saw him. Lucy's ex, Josh.

Seated with some hockey teammates two rows up. *Watching.*

His brow arched, eyes locked on mine, and I was pretty sure there was a hint of recognition flashing across his face.

Perfect.

Did he recognize me from that night at The Garden? Or did he know I was a professor here?

Either way, the look he was giving me wasn't good. Because it looked like he was connecting way too many dots.

I forced a slow breath and turned my attention back to the floor.

Lucy was finishing her routine—dismounting with a clean double twist and a small hop.

The crowd roared to life and I let out a cheer of my own,

trying to keep it low-key. Controlled. Normal. Even though inside, pride was flooding me like a tidal wave.

She was unreal.

Strong. Fearless. The kind of performer you couldn't look away from.

A few minutes later, Theo reappeared, carrying Charlotte in his arms. She had her little head tucked into his shoulder, arms looped around his neck.

"Did they announce Lucy's score?" he asked, sounding winded.

"Just barely." I nodded. "She crushed it. Got a 9.935."

"No way." Theo's whole face lit up. "That's one of her best this season. You got it on video?"

"Yep. I'll airdrop it."

He held out his phone, and I sent the file, doing my best to look casual and not like my heart was still racing from watching Lucy dominate that routine.

From hearing those guys talk about her like she was just something to consume.

From Josh noticing how invested I was in her performance.

Yep. Just one more routine to get through and then I could relax again.

39

OWEN

"AND NOW FOR OUR ALL-AROUND DIVISION..." the announcer's voice rang out over the loudspeaker, cutting through the hum of the crowd.

This was it. The meet had wrapped up, the last routines were done, and the gymnasts sat lined up on the floor, waiting.

It had been one of the best meets I'd ever seen—and not just because of Lucy. But yeah...mostly because of Lucy.

"Third place is a tie—Megan Barlow from Yale University...and Nora Miller from Eden Falls."

Okay, I thought, glancing at Lucy. She'd scored higher than Nora in three of the individual events, so this meant that she was either second or first.

I held my breath as I waited for the announcer to continue.

I probably should've tracked the scores more carefully throughout the meet, but I hadn't been thinking very strategically this afternoon. I'd been too busy holding my breath through every one of Lucy's events, too busy feeling like my heart might beat out of my chest every time she nailed a landing.

"Second place," the announcer said. "From Yale University —Zoey Jordan."

A girl in Yale warmups jumped up and waved at the crowd, her teammates cheering. But I barely noticed since my attention was on Lucy and the way her face was lighting up.

Because she knew she'd done it.

She'd won.

And for some reason, just seeing the joy, disbelief, and pride on her face made *me* feel like I'd won something, too.

"And first place in our all-around category..." the announcer said. "From Eden Falls University...Lucy Archibald!"

The crowd roared as Lucy jumped to her feet, immediately swallowed by teammates pulling her into a tangle of hugs. And I couldn't keep the huge grin from taking over my whole face as I clapped for her, resisting the urge to leap to my feet and cheer like a lunatic.

She'd done so well tonight. Such a hypnotizing performance, really.

Theo stood beside me, clapping and shouting, and when a few other students followed suit, I stood, too. Letting myself feel it.

Letting myself be proud of her.

"Go Lucy!" I called, putting my hands on either side of my mouth as I cheered for the girl who was continually stealing pieces of my heart without even trying.

Lucy emerged from the huddle, and when she turned to face the audience again, she smiled hugely in the direction of the student section where Theo, Charlotte, and I were, her eyes holding mine momentarily before scouring the rest of the crowd.

"She crushed it," Theo said, so much brotherly pride in his expression. "Let's go congratulate her."

I followed behind Theo as he navigated his way down to the floor with Charlotte on his hip, trying to keep my expression measured even though I felt like I was practically floating.

Lucy's parents had already made their way down. They'd been sitting a few rows in front of us with Nora's parents this time, which had made it slightly easier for me to breathe throughout the meet.

I lingered back as she hugged them both. Her dad was speaking, his voice low but audible. I listened closely, half-expecting a critique or comment about things she could've done better since that was what he'd done last time. But all I heard was pride. Encouragement. Praise.

Good. She deserved that.

"You nailed it," Theo said, stepping forward next and giving her a side hug. "If you keep that up, there's no way you're not placing top three at Nationals."

"Hopefully." Lucy exhaled softly, a flicker of nerves tightening her smile at the mention of Nationals. "I'm definitely going to give it my best."

A brief silence followed, and then—like some unspoken cue —every eye turned to me.

I cleared my throat, summoning the most neutral, professor-appropriate tone I could manage. "You did really well, Lucy. Congratulations."

Her gaze met mine, eyes shining. "Thank you, Professor Park."

I knew she only said the title to keep up the pretense. But part of me wished we didn't have to pretend. Not in a moment like this. Not when all I wanted to do was wrap her in my arms and tell her just how proud I was. How incredible she'd been.

"This deserves a celebration," Mrs. Archibald said, slipping her arm behind her husband and turning to the group. "What do you say we all go to Jacob's Steakhouse after this?"

"Sounds amazing." Lucy nodded.

"Sounds great to me," Theo added.

"And of course," Mrs. Archibald said, turning to me with a gracious smile, "we'd be happy to have you join us, Owen. As a friend of Theo's."

"Oh—" I blinked, caught off guard by the invitation.

Dinner with Lucy's entire family?

The prospect was positively terrifying.

But also...tempting in a way I hadn't expected. A chance to be near her a little longer. To see her in her element with the people she loved most, riding the high of her win.

Even if it meant navigating the minefield that was President Archibald over steak and mashed potatoes.

Theo clapped me on the back. "You should come."

I hesitated, scanning the group, still weighing the risk.

Then Lucy cut in, her tone casual but her eyes catching mine. "I'm sure my dad would love to hear about that grant you and Dean Harris are working on."

President Archibald's interest visibly sparked. "Oh, you're the professor he's been chatting with me about?"

"Yes, sir." I nodded, not offended that he hadn't remembered which department I worked for during our brief interaction at Lucy's first meet. The man had a lot on his plate.

Everyone was looking at me now. Waiting.

"I'd love to join you for dinner," I said.

"Perfect." Mrs. Archibald beamed, showing me where Lucy had gotten her megawatt smile from. "I'll call to make sure we can get a reservation. How about we plan to meet there around five?"

Everyone nodded in agreement.

And just like that, I was having dinner with the Archibalds.

No big deal.

Right?

I sat in my car in the parking lot of Jacob's Steakhouse, scanning every vehicle that pulled in. When I was younger, this was the place my family came to celebrate my dad's work wins, Asher's piano recitals, Callie's soccer goals, and my own science-fair ribbons.

I adjusted the cuffs of my button-down, running a palm down the front to smooth the fabric. After texting Theo earlier to ask what he was wearing—because who knew what the Archibalds wore to dinner—I swapped my usual weekend attire for slacks, dress shoes, and a collared shirt. Casual but presentable. Trying to blend in. Maybe impress.

Impress Lucy's parents enough that they might see me as the kind of guy they might want their daughter to date.

You know, one day...after she'd graduated and we'd let enough time pass that people wouldn't question the right or wrongness behind how we got our start.

Okay, yeah...so that was definitely a tall order. Especially since I had no idea if she was even interested in anything like that.

Not when we still hadn't had a chance to talk about last night's kiss.

A sleek black Mercedes turned into the lot, headlights sweeping across the windshield of my car. Sure enough, I spotted President Archibald behind the wheel, his wife in the passenger seat, and Lucy in the back, her golden hair catching the light.

Theo pulled in right behind them in his Volvo, and I took that as my cue to get out. I straightened my tie, smoothed the front of my shirt, and walked toward the restaurant, nerves buzzing beneath the surface. I needed to make a good impression. Even if, officially, I was just Lucy's professor tagging along as a friend of her brother's.

Everyone smiled in greeting as I joined them, and I had to look away for a second when my eyes landed on Lucy. She was wearing a pale-yellow dress under her coat paired with strappy heels that did wildly distracting things to her legs. I swallowed the surge of attraction, shifting my gaze to the pavement before anyone could notice.

The hostess led us to a round table near the back when we stepped inside—cozy and private, just big enough for six. Charlotte climbed into her booster seat beside her grandfather. Theo took the seat next to her, and Lucy settled between her mom and the empty spot that was apparently meant for me.

I pulled out the chair and slid in, aiming for the perfect middle ground. Not too close to Lucy. Not too far either. Just comfortably centered between her and Theo like the totally professional, not-at-all-sweaty professor I was trying to be.

But then my knee brushed hers under the table.

I froze for half a second. Shifted away casually. Or...what I hoped read as casually. Only to accidentally nudge her again a second later.

Seriously?

I adjusted again, clearing my throat and pretending to be extremely invested in the placement of my napkin. Meanwhile, my entire body was suddenly hyperaware of the six inches of space to my right. And how utterly impossible it was to pretend that space wasn't occupied by the girl I shouldn't have a major crush on.

Gosh. I wasn't even two minutes into dinner, and already, my nerves were getting the best of me.

The waitress handed us menus and water glasses. I took a long sip, trying to cool the heat already crawling up my collar.

"Have you been here before, Owen?" President Archibald asked, glancing at me over the rim of his menu.

"Yes." My fingers toyed with the corner of my napkin, and I forced myself to meet President Archibald's eyes, hoping I didn't look as stiff as I felt. "My family came here a lot when I was younger. It was my dad's favorite place for celebrations."

"So your family's from the area?" he asked, interest flickering across his expression.

"Yes," I said, catching the subtle way Lucy went still beside me at the mention of my family. "Lived in Eden Falls most of my life—except for the four years I was at Yale."

"It's a lovely town. We've grown quite fond of it." President Archibald paused, then asked, "And what does your father do? Does he work here in town?"

"He used to work in New Haven, actually." I cleared my throat. "For Hastings Industries. He and Joel Hastings were close. But...he passed away about ten years ago."

"Oh." Mrs. Archibald's brow creased. "I'm sorry to hear that."

"What was his name?" President Archibald asked after a beat. "We used to work with Hastings Industries quite a bit when I was still with my father's company. Our office was just down the street from theirs."

I hesitated for half a second before answering, "Hyunwoo Park."

"Hyunwoo?" Recognition flared in his eyes. "Yes. I did know him." He looked away for a beat, like he was replaying something in his head. "We worked together a few times. He was sharp. Fair. He had this way of putting people at ease, which always made our negotiations smoother. That's rare."

A small smile tugged at my mouth, then fell away. "That sounds like him."

Mr. Archibald nodded slowly. "I remember hearing about the accident. It was awful. Such a loss."

And just like that, my chest tightened.

Because I knew what else they would have heard.

The aftermath. The headlines. My mother's arrest. How quickly our name stopped meaning what it used to. How fast people's perception of me changed once they knew the kind of woman I'd been raised by.

A drug addict. A woman in prison for killing half her family.

I felt Lucy shift beside me, just slightly. Like she'd sensed it, too. The moment right before the conversation turned.

I kept my eyes on my glass, bracing for it.

The subtle distance. The silent judgment. The pity.

But then, President Archibald's voice cut through.

"I'm sure your father would be very proud of the man you've become," he said, his tone softer now. "Everything you've accomplished—it's awesome to see such a passion for one's vocation, especially from such a young professor. I know Dean Harris thinks the world of you and that's no small feat."

His words hit harder than I expected. I had to blink a few times before I looked up, trying to pull myself together fast enough to nod.

"Thank you," I said, appreciating his kindness after all the years I'd spent wondering if anything I did would ever be enough to outshine the shadow my mom's mistakes had cast. The black mark on my father's once-respected name.

President Archibald's expression shifted, the corners of his mouth lifting like he was ready to steer the conversation somewhere lighter. "Though I suppose the real test of your teaching skills is whether our Lucy thinks you've been doing a good job." He turned his sharp blue eyes toward her. "So what do you say,

Luce? Would you agree with Dean Harris's glowing review of your professor?"

She froze for just a second, like she hadn't been expecting to be put on the spot. Her gaze flicked to mine briefly before she found her voice.

"I'd say it's pretty fair," she said. "I've actually been able to understand most of what he's taught so far, so...that's a plus."

"Definitely." Her dad chuckled. "Especially considering how frustrated we all got with your chemistry assignments in high school." He looked at me with a sheepish expression. "I'm afraid neither my wife nor I were much help when it came to science. Poor Lucy was on her own."

"Yeah." Lucy rolled her eyes fondly. "It was pretty much a disaster."

"Well, she's been a great student so far." I smiled, hoping it wasn't obvious how great of a student I thought she was. "No complaints from me."

Definitely not.

40

OWEN

I'D JUST STARTED my car after my dinner with the Archibalds and was waiting for it to warm up a bit when my phone buzzed in the cupholder beside me.

> Theo's sister: Do you have plans for the rest of the night? I was thinking we should maybe touch base about what happened last night.

I stared at the message, my pulse instantly picking up speed.

Because I knew exactly what she was talking about.

Our kiss.

The moment when I'd officially crossed over the line and kissed my student.

Not just kissed...but passionately made out with in her brother's pantry.

> Me: I was just planning to hang out at home. And since I can't exactly be seen going to your place without raising suspicions...do you want to come to mine instead?

> Me: You know, unless we're going full sketchy and meeting in a dimly lit parking lot somewhere.

When I looked up, her parents' car rolled past mine, and there she was—Lucy in the backseat, her profile illuminated as my headlights caught the window. Her head was tipped back slightly, lips parted in a quiet smile, like she'd just laughed at the ridiculous parking lot joke I'd texted her.

And being the simple man that I was, I smiled too. Because there was something deeply satisfying about being the reason her face lit up like that.

> Theo's sister: I'll come to your place.

The moment I got home, I moved like a man on a mission. Clothes I'd dropped on the bedroom floor before dinner were shoved into the hamper. I wiped down the bathroom counter, brushed my teeth, reapplied deodorant, and gave myself a light mist of cologne. Just enough to smell good. Not enough to seem like I was trying too hard.

As I passed my bedroom, I paused in the doorway.

Should I tidy that up more?

Fluff the pillows? Straighten the comforter? Maybe light a candle?

No, that was definitely too much.

Lucy wouldn't be stepping foot in my bedroom.

At least...I wasn't planning on it.

I shook my head, trying to steer my thoughts away from every scenario that involved Lucy and my bed.

This was just a check-in.

Two adults having a conversation.

Totally innocent.

You know...unless she was open to picking up where we'd left off last night.

And before I could stop it, the scene played out in vivid detail in my mind—

Lucy sitting on the edge of my bed, that yellow dress riding up just enough to make me shaky.

I'd kneel in front of her, my hands skimming up her calves as I slowly unfastened those strappy heels—slow and reverent—because helping her undress would feel like a privilege.

She'd watch me with a hunger in her blue eyes that would fill me with an ache of hope and longing.

I'd press a kiss to the inside of her knee, and her breath would catch.

Then I'd rise, pull her gently into my arms, and kiss her—deep, slow, and hungry. Until the world outside the room faded away.

Her fingers would fist the fabric of my shirt, tugging it up with quiet urgency, and I'd help her pull it over my head and toss it aside.

Then her hands would roam—tentative at first, then bolder—fingertips tracing along my chest, my ribs, my back, like she wanted to memorize the shape of me.

And through it all, her laugh would slip between kisses—soft and breathless—like she already knew exactly where this was headed...and couldn't wait to get there.

I'd lay her back against my pillows, crawl over her, and feel her arch into me as our bodies pressed together, her thighs framing my hips. Every inch of her, soft and warm and mine.

I blinked hard. *Okay. Time to stop.*

I dragged a hand down my face and forced the scene out of my head before it went even further.

This wasn't that kind of night.

Probably.

But...maybe.

Get it together, Park.

I shut my bedroom door before I could entertain any further thoughts.

Just as I started pacing, my phone buzzed.

> Theo's sister: Just pulled in. Coming up.

I texted her back:

> Me: I left the door unlocked. Just come in.
> Less risk of being spotted that way.

Then I settled onto the couch, doing my best to give the impression of someone who looked cool and casual and definitely not like he was a complete ball of nerves.

A gust of cold air swept in as the door opened, and I looked over.

Then looked again.

"Are you wearing a wig?" I asked after Lucy stepped inside and shut the door, flipping the hood off her coat and revealing a cascade of glossy dark curls that definitely hadn't been there at dinner.

"Thought it might be smart to show up in a disguise." With a playful toss of her head, she asked, "Do you like it?"

I took her in, the unfamiliar look stealing my words for a second. She looked gorgeous—just different. Still her, but not.

"It's cute," I said honestly, then added with a half-smile, "but I think I prefer your natural hair."

"Well, technically, my hair isn't natural since I bleached it. So..." She raised a brow.

Crap.

"I, uh..." I cleared my throat. "Sorry, I didn't mean that the way it sounded."

"Don't worry." She laughed, shaking her head. "This is just the cheap wig I got for Halloween last year. I get what you meant."

"Okay, good." I exhaled. "Because honestly, you're gorgeous no matter what you're wearing. Or how your hair is done."

Her gaze softened. "Thank you."

"You were incredible today, by the way." I stood, suddenly too restless to sit. "I didn't really get to say it earlier, with your parents and Theo right there, but you honestly blew me away, Lucy."

"Thanks." Her smile spread, soft and a little bashful. "It really was a good meet."

I hesitated, the urge to pull her into my arms suddenly tugging at me. But instead of doing that, I cleared my throat and asked, "Can I get you something to drink?"

"Let me guess." She arched a brow, teasing. "Water or ice water?"

"Actually, I've upgraded." I chuckled. "There's sparkling water in the fridge now, too."

"Oooh, fancy."

"So…" I said, giving her a look. "What will it be?"

"Well, since the tall drink of water I was trying not to stare at in the crowd all afternoon doesn't seem to be on the menu…" She smirked. "I guess I'll go with ice water."

She'd been staring at me during her meet?

The idea landed like a spark across my skin.

But trying to play it cool, I turned toward the kitchen and said, "Maybe we can do something about that tall drink of water a little later."

41

LUCY

"MY PARENTS WERE TALKING about you on the ride home," I said as I curled one leg beneath me on Owen's couch, angling toward him.

"They were?" His brow lifted. "What'd they say?"

"That they really like you." I gave a small shrug. "I mean, it was definitely in the *'he's a good friend for Theo to have'* kind of way, but still...they think you're a cool dude. So that's good."

"A 'cool dude,' huh?" A smile tugged at the corner of his lips. "Somehow I can't picture those words coming from either your mom or your dad's mouth?"

"You know what I mean," I said, nudging his arm playfully. "They were impressed. Everything you've accomplished, the way you carry yourself...they like you."

"Well, that's good to hear." He leaned back slightly, his arm brushing mine.

I hesitated, then asked, "What did you think of the dinner?"

"It was really good." He gave a small chuckle. "Your mom is

super sweet, and your dad was way cooler than I expected. Honestly, I was kind of surprised by the things he said. Especially after hearing the critique he gave you after your first home meet."

"That's because you're not his kid." I sighed. "You don't have the Archibald family legacy to live up to."

He gave a soft exhale, his tone gentler when he said, "But he seemed proud of you today. Did he say anything else when I wasn't around?"

"No. He was good. Proud." I shook my head. "But...I took first place. So, you know."

"So he didn't have anything to complain about."

I gave a small shrug, my fingers absently running along the seam of the cushion. "Maybe I'm being too critical. I guess I just don't want to disappoint him."

Owen's voice was steady when he said, "If he's disappointed in you, he's the one with the problem."

I swallowed and smiled, those words hitting deeper than I expected. I set my glass of water on one of the coasters on his coffee table. Then, on impulse, I scooted a little closer and leaned into his side.

His arm came around me, warm and solid, and I let myself sink into the feeling of him. His chest rose and fell beneath my cheek, calm and steady, and I breathed in the quiet comfort of just being close.

After a moment, I reached for his tie and played with the silky fabric between my fingers. "I like this on you, by the way," I said. "The purple."

"Really?" he asked, glancing down. "Doesn't look too... feminine?"

"Nope." I smiled. "It looks good on you. Brings out your eyes."

His gaze met mine, the smallest flicker of vulnerability there.

"You have really nice eyes," I added.

A soft smile pulled at his mouth. "So do you."

For a second, we just looked at each other.

I let my eyes wander over his face, taking in the little details I hadn't noticed before. The sharp cut of his jaw. The faint shadow of stubble along his skin. The way his dark hair fell across his forehead like it was too soft to stay put.

He looked older than the guys I usually hung out with—not in a bad way. Just in a *he-knows-who-he-is* kind of way. A little more serious, a little more guarded. Like someone who'd learned the hard way not to let people in too easily.

But it was his eyes that had me hypnotized.

That rich, warm brown that always looked thoughtful, measured.

Like he was trying to memorize this moment. Or maybe memorize *me*.

And I couldn't help but wonder if he saw me differently now. Not just as Theo's little sister. Not just as the student in his one p.m. lecture.

Just...me. Lucy.

His eyes dropped to my lips, and I felt the tension rise between us, last night's kiss hanging in the space between us like a secret we couldn't stop replaying.

"So..." He cleared his throat. "You wanted to talk about what happened last night?"

I nodded. "I just wanted to check in...see how you were doing." I looked down at my hands, my heartbeat pulsing in my temples. "I know yesterday was kind of unplanned, and I really don't want to put you in a weird position or mess with your job or anything, but..." I took a breath, nerves bubbling up as I added, "In case it's not obvious, I kind of have the teensiest bit of a crush on you."

"I've been thinking about that a lot, too—" Owen let out a soft breath, his gaze holding mine. "My job, the rules, what could happen if we're not careful." He paused, his voice quieter as he added, "But the truth is...I'm not really sure I'm able to stay away from you at this point."

"Really?" My chest tightened as I searched his face. "You mean that?"

"I do," he said, his voice low, his eyes searching mine. "And in case it wasn't obvious...I might have a little crush on you, too."

"Just a little crush?" I tilted my head up at him, giving him a look.

His grin widened, making his eyes crinkle at the corners. "Maybe a little more than a little."

Warmth bloomed in my chest, soft and bright, like sunlight breaking through a cloudy sky. "Me too."

We were quiet for a bit, the moment filled with tenderness and something undefined. Something that made it hard to look away, but also hard to speak. Because what else could we really say? We were tiptoeing through uncharted waters—something we never should've started—but neither of us had the strength to stop.

Owen sighed and looked at me for a long moment, then gently pulled me closer. His hand slid along my back, grounding and warm, as he pressed a soft kiss to my forehead.

"We'll figure this out," he murmured, his voice low and steady against my skin.

I exhaled, my eyes fluttering closed as I rested my head against his chest. His heartbeat thudded steadily beneath my cheek, the faint scent of his cologne lingering in the fabric of his shirt. And for that moment, I let myself just melt into him.

Enveloped.

Warmed.

Wanted.

Because no matter where we went from here, for tonight, just having him hold me like this was enough.

42

LUCY

OWEN and I were both swamped over the next few weeks. He was buried in his lecture load, lab hours, and the mountain of grant paperwork he was tackling with Dean Harris. As for me, I was juggling midterms, a pile of marketing projects, and trying to add a higher-difficulty pass to my floor routine—something that could boost my score enough to (hopefully) qualify for Nationals on my own, in case our team didn't make it.

Instead of traveling for meets those weekends, we lucked out with the last two of February being close to home—a tri-meet in New Haven and a home meet against George Washington. The break from travel gave me a little more breathing room...and a few more chances to see Owen on the weekends, even if we still had to keep things careful.

At school, we kept our distance. Not that it stopped my stomach from flipping every time our eyes met across the lecture hall or chemistry lab. But at night, after study sessions or late practices, he'd walk me home.

And even when the wind bit at my cheeks and my backpack dug into my shoulders, those walks were my favorite part of the day.

Because even without holding hands or stealing kisses in public, I loved being with him. Talking. Laughing. Listening to him share his hopes for his research project with that quiet, focused kind of excitement that made me feel lucky just to witness it.

Did I understand all the chemistry jargon? Not even close. But I loved the way his face lit up when he talked about it. The way his voice took on this low, animated tone, almost giddy in a still-totally-masculine kind of way, like he couldn't help but be swept up in what he loved.

On the first Wednesday in March, after another long day, we were walking side by side in the quiet chill, the sidewalk shimmering faintly from the earlier rain.

"Do you have more homework waiting for you tonight?" he asked, bumping his shoulder gently into mine like it was second nature.

"A little." I yawned, tugging my sleeves over my fingers. "But I was thinking of taking a break. Give my brain a rest."

"Want to come over?" He smiled. "Watch a show or a movie?"

"That actually sounds really nice."

We paused at the corner near his apartment. I checked around us, tugged my hood up over my head like I was avoiding the paparazzi, then we darted across the street to his place, laughing quietly the whole way.

Inside, he motioned toward the couch. "How about you pick something to watch while I pop some popcorn?"

He disappeared into the kitchen while I scrolled through the streaming apps. I settled on the newest romcom I'd been meaning to watch, then glanced over my shoulder to see him at the stove, turning the handle on some contraption I'd never seen before.

"Is that a...popcorn machine?"

"It's a stovetop popper," he said proudly. "Tastes better than microwave."

The smell was amazing—salty, buttery, warm.

When he joined me on the couch with a big bowl in hand, I leaned in to grab a handful and curled into his side.

"You did well on your test today, by the way," he said, draping his arm around me.

"You already graded it?"

"I did." He nodded. "And I know you said you and chemistry don't get along, but if you keep telling people that and they see your grades, they might think I'm inflating your scores."

I laughed. "Does this mean I've officially surpassed my high school B-plus?"

"You had an A-minus when I checked today."

"Well, imagine that." I grinned. "Not the straight A's my dad prefers, but...pretty good."

"It's more than good." He looked at me like he meant it. "You're doing really well."

"I guess there's something to be said for being interested in the professor's lectures."

He chuckled. "So, I'm not boring you to death with all my talk of reaction kinetics and molecular orbital theory?"

"I mean, I do occasionally get distracted by how your biceps flex when you write on the board," I joked. "And how good you look in your button-downs and ties..."

He laughed, shaking his head, but I could see the pleased flush on his cheeks.

"Let's just say I didn't nickname you Professor Heartthrob for nothing." I winked.

"Wait...is that my name in your phone?"

"No." I smirked. "You're still 'Theo's Friend.'"

"Smart. Less suspicious." He chuckled as he picked up a few pieces of popcorn. "Don't need your dad seeing your phone and wondering who Professor Heartthrob is."

"Exactly."

"So..." Owen glanced at the TV screen. "What movie did you decide on?"

"It's a romcom," I said, giving him an innocent look. "About a girl who goes off to college and falls for her hot professor."

"Seriously?" He blinked, then gave a soft laugh. "That feels...suspiciously on theme."

I shrugged, fighting a smile. "It's a total coincidence."

"Mm-hmm." He tugged me closer, his tone warm and teasing. "Well, hopefully it has a happy ending."

"Hopefully."

I pressed *Play* on the remote, and the movie started to roll. Owen leaned back against the couch, legs propped up on the coffee table, and I curled against his chest, tucking myself beneath his arm. It should've been the perfect way to unwind—movie, popcorn, warm boyfriend beside me.

But I barely registered the opening scene.

Because all I could focus on was him.

The rise and fall of his chest beneath my cheek.

The soft scent of his aftershave clinging to his skin.

His fingers trailing lazily up and down my side...then slipping under the hem of my shirt, brushing bare skin.

My breath caught in my throat.

Oh.

I liked that.

The quiet intimacy of it. The way it made my heart stutter and my body ache for more.

He pressed a soft kiss to my forehead, and I tilted my face

up to look at him. His gaze dropped to my mouth, lingering there, and for a second, we just stared at each other.

We'd had a few kisses since that night in the pantry—sweet, fleeting moments stolen in private corners—but nothing quite as reckless and uninhibited.

And right now...I wouldn't mind forgetting everything else again. Especially since we were actually alone in his apartment and no brothers could come downstairs and interrupt.

Owen's fingertips trailed along my side again, slow and featherlight, following the curve of my back and gliding up my spine. I shivered, that simple touch making my breath hitch. And yeah, it had been a long time since anyone had touched me like that.

With care.

Purpose.

Want.

He shifted beneath me, laying flatter against the couch until his head rested comfortably against the leather armrest. I moved with him, instinctively adjusting so my body settled more fully on top of his, our chest and hips gently aligned. It wasn't necessarily the most optimal position for movie-watching, but it was definitely perfect for other activities I hoped he might be up for...

His other hand reached up, fingers tracing the edge of my temple before skimming down the curve of my cheekbone, then along the line of my jaw. When his thumb brushed across my bottom lip, I had to bite down gently just to steady myself against the shiver that rolled through me.

When I glanced up, he wasn't even pretending to watch the movie anymore. Instead, his eyes were locked on me, dark with hunger and something deeper. Something that looked a lot like longing.

I shifted, scooting up just enough to nestle my face into the warm curve of his neck. He smelled so good—faintly of his cologne that had faded over the day, but mostly just...him. Clean, warm, familiar. I pressed a kiss to the hollow of his throat, and then, unable to help myself, I let my teeth graze lightly across the tender skin.

"Maybe we should try watching this movie some other time?" he asked, his voice husky.

"Good idea." I laughed softly, then murmured against his skin, "Since the professor in real life is way more interesting than the one on screen." I lifted my head slightly and added with a smirk, "Tastes better, too."

"Pretty sure the real-life student is way more interesting, too." His smile curved, slow and wicked. "But...I might need a refresher on how she tastes."

"Guess you better refresh your memory then," I whispered.

That seemed to be all the encouragement he needed for him to let his hand slide beneath my chin and guide my lips to his.

His lips brushed mine—once, twice.

Then again and again. Each brush of his lips growing firmer. Somehow slower. Like he was determined to savor every second, memorizing the exact feel of my lips and imprinting it somewhere he could never forget.

My fingers curled into the soft cotton of his button-down, needing something to anchor myself as I shifted over him, aligning my body more fully with his. He was all solid strength beneath me—warm, hard muscle—and when his hand slid to my lower back and pressed, guiding me closer, the sensation of our bodies fitting so tightly together knocked the breath from my lungs.

"Yeah," he murmured, "this is definitely better than watching the movie."

I couldn't have agreed more.

His tongue swept gently across my bottom lip, coaxing my mouth open. And I let him in.

The kiss deepened, slow and sure, like nothing else in the world mattered but the way we moved together. Like he'd been thinking about this—about me—all day.

His other hand slipped beneath the hem of my shirt, fingers gliding over the bare skin at my lower back, and I sighed into his mouth. The rest of the world fell away as we kissed again and again—long, slow, breathless kisses that made me forget everything but him.

His lips drifted from mine, trailing along the curve of my jaw before finding the sensitive skin at the base of my throat. When he kissed me there—soft and open-mouthed—I couldn't stop the quiet sound that escaped me. A whimper of need.

"You feel way too good, Lucy," he murmured against my skin, his warm breath grazing the curve of my neck. "Too good for me to think straight."

"You too," I whispered, struggling to draw in a full breath.

That earned me a groan—a deep, rumbling sound from his chest that vibrated against mine—and the next kiss he gave me was rougher around the edges. Less controlled. Like something inside him was on the verge of snapping loose.

I slid my hand up the center of his chest, fingers brushing the crisp fabric of his button-up until I reached the knot of his tie. With a teasing smile, I hooked two fingers beneath it and gave it a slow, deliberate tug to loosen it.

"The sexy professor is officially off duty," I murmured. "You don't need this anymore."

His mouth curved against mine in a low chuckle. "Fine by me."

And then he kissed me again—deeper this time. Hotter. His tongue slid against mine in a slow, sensual rhythm that made my stomach twist and tighten, heat blooming low and warm in my core.

My hips shifted instinctively, pressing more fully into him, every inch of me aching to be closer.

And then he moved.

With a smooth, fluid motion, he rolled us gently onto our sides, his arm cradling me as my back pressed into the cushions. Our legs tangled together, bodies flushed, my chest pressed tightly to his.

And I suddenly wasn't sure where I ended and he began.

His hand skimmed farther up beneath my shirt, warm against my bare skin, rough fingertips exploring the ridges of my ribs. I gasped softly at the touch, and he pulled back just enough to look at me, his eyes dark with something that made my breath catch.

"Is this okay?" he murmured, his voice low, like he was barely holding on to whatever restraint he had left.

"Yes." I nodded, barely finding my voice. "More than okay."

He could touch me anywhere and I'd literally be just fine with it.

Want it, actually.

His mouth claimed mine again, more urgently this time, more needy. One hand cupped the back of my neck, tilting my face to his as the kiss deepened, then slowed, then deepened again. Like he was savoring it.

Savoring me. Every soft sound I made. Every subtle shift of my body into his.

I moved instinctively, hooking one leg over his hip as our bodies locked together. His fingers dug into my waist, anchoring me to him, like he didn't want to let me go for even a second.

Heat curled low inside me as I reached for the hem of his shirt, untucking it with slow, deliberate fingers. I slid my hand underneath, brushing over the hard lines of his stomach and ribs—nothing but muscle and heat and barely leashed tension. He was a work of art.

One I wouldn't mind studying a little more closely.

Especially to see if my memory from the hot tub held up.

My hand slid higher, palm landing flat over his chest right where his heart pounded hard and fast beneath my touch.

"Your heart's racing," I whispered.

He glanced down then looked up at me, his eyes a little dazed. "Kind of hard to stay calm with such a beautiful girl wrapped around me like this."

I smiled, then reached for his hand, guiding it to my chest and placing it gently over my own heart. "Mine's going just as fast."

He stilled.

His gaze dropped to where our hands rested, his palm warming my skin. And for a breathless moment, he just stayed there—like he was trying to anchor himself to the beat beneath his hand.

Then his fingers twitched, moving ever so slightly to graze along the neckline of my blouse.

Just enough to let me know he might be thinking about exploring more than just my heartbeat.

"Lucy..." he said, my name low and rough, like it physically ached to hold back.

Like restraint was slipping with every second.

"Owen..." I breathed, dragging my nails down the sculpted line of his back, tracing the dip between his shoulder blades.

I wanted more.

More of him against me.

More of his skin on mine.

He might've been playing the gentleman tonight... But I wasn't sure I wanted to be that good anymore.

So I reached for his buttons, undoing them one by one, my fingertips grazing the warm skin of his torso as the tension between us thickened.

"I want this off," I whispered, my voice low and sure as he watched me slowly undress him.

As if he'd just been waiting for permission, he didn't hesitate—just shrugged out of the shirt, tugged it down over his broad shoulders, and tossed it aside.

My breath caught.

Yeah...he was definitely a work of art.

All hard muscle and golden skin, like he'd been carved from pure temptation and somehow didn't even know it.

And when his mouth found mine again, there was nothing careful about it.

It was messy.

Breathless.

Wild.

Like every stolen glance across the lecture hall, every brush of his hand against mine, every night we'd spent pretending this wasn't real had finally broken open something neither of us could hold back anymore.

Something we couldn't close again.

My palms slid along the curves of his shoulders, squeezing his biceps, and I felt him shudder beneath my touch.

"Lucy..." he whispered again.

And this time, it didn't just sound like my name.

It sounded like a plea.

Like he was right on the edge of falling.

He kissed along the line of my collarbone, breath hot against my skin, and I tilted my head back, giving him more space to explore. And when his lips found a spot just a little lower, I couldn't stop the soft moan that escaped. Because it felt just too good...made everything else disappear.

The rules. The risk. The consequences.

All that mattered was this moment and the way he made me feel—the undeniable way we fit together perfectly.

My hands threaded into his hair, tugging just a little as I pulled him back to my mouth. And the way he kissed me then...I could get so lost in him.

I wanted to.

And that scared me more than I wanted to admit.

Because I'd never felt seen the way Owen saw me. So wanted.

And the temptation to keep going—to feel more and give him everything—was so strong I had to will myself to breathe.

But I couldn't breathe.

So I pulled back, just enough to press my forehead to his and draw in a steady breath.

We were both panting, chests rising and falling like we'd just run a race.

A race that could take us somewhere we might not be quite ready for.

Was I ready for more?

I wasn't sure.

It had been a long time since I'd felt safe enough to even ask myself that question.

But maybe...

If things kept going the way they had been—if he kept being Owen, steady and patient and real—we might get there.

And the thought of that didn't scare me the way it might have a month ago.

In fact, it felt kind of...inevitable.

Because sharing that part of myself with him—when I was ready—would be something sacred. Something special.

Because that was who Owen was.

I drew in another breath and looked down, my gaze catching on where my hands rested on his bare chest.

I exhaled slowly, grounding myself in his warmth. In his steady breathing. In the soft rasp of his fingers still drifting along my back.

And that was when I really saw it.

The tattoo—two eagles, one smaller than the other, wings outstretched as they soared toward the edge of a solar eclipse.

The moon was swallowing the sun, a dim halo of light outlining the shadow. Stark. Haunting. And beautiful.

I reached up slowly, my fingers brushing along the shaded curve of a feather that had broken free.

"What does your tattoo represent?" I asked softly. Because knowing how intentional Owen was, it had to mean something. This striking tattoo had to have a deep meaning to him.

He hesitated, swallowed. Then his gaze found mine and held it.

"It's for my dad and my sister," he said, vulnerability etched in his voice. "The eagles are them...still fighting to fly, even as the light faded." There was a slight hitch in his voice as he added, "I got it shortly after we lost them. As a reminder that they'll always be in my heart. Even if they were taken from us too soon."

I blinked against the sudden sting behind my eyes and slid my hand down his chest, right over his heart. "That's a beautiful tribute."

His throat worked as he swallowed, and for a second, all I could do was watch him, completely undone by this sweet, tenderhearted man.

"You care so much," I whispered. "Feel things deeply. I love that about you."

A flicker of surprise crossed his face.

"You love with all of you," I added, my voice steadier now. "Deep and true. I can feel it in the way you talk about them..."

Maybe even in the way you are looking at me right now.

Did Owen love me?

No. Probably not—not yet. This thing between us was still so new.

But when his hand came up to cradle the back of my head, his thumb brushing lightly along my cheek like he didn't quite know how to say what he was feeling...it made me wonder if he was getting close.

And that thought?

It made something in my chest go quiet and full at the same time.

Because I was already on my way there.

To loving this man I wasn't supposed to fall for.

He kissed me again and I kissed him back, pouring every beat of my heart into it.

I let my fingers trail over his tattoo again, tracing not just the shape of the ink but everything it stood for. His losses. His loyalty. The way he gave himself so completely when he let someone in.

And all I could think was how beautiful it would be to be loved like that by Owen Park one day.

43

———

OWEN

I CLICKED through the last slide of the lecture and glanced toward the back of the room, scanning the rows of students as they started to pack up.

Still no sign of Lucy.

I'd been looking for her since the second I walked into the room. I kept telling myself she was probably just running late, that maybe she'd sprint through the doors with that breathless smile and flushed cheeks. But the hour passed. No Lucy.

Had something come up?

Had she gotten hurt at practice?

Was she sick?

I finished the lecture with more autopilot than focus, my brain already drafting a text by the time I shut my laptop.

> Me: Hey, I missed you in class today. Hope everything is okay.

I stared at the screen for a beat, waiting for the typing dots to pop up.

Nothing.

I had another lecture starting in ten minutes, so I slipped my phone back into my pocket and hoped she'd get back to me soon. We hadn't been able to see each other yesterday—both of us buried in school and work. But still...this was the first time she'd ever missed class.

Halfway through the second lecture, my phone buzzed. I kept speaking, barely missing a beat as I pulled my phone out of my pocket and casually glanced down at the message.

> Theo's sister: Sorry. Had a bad fever and threw up last night. Thought it was the sushi Nora brought home. But then the sore throat kicked in and it turns out I have strep.

Ah, dang.

Strep wasn't just a casual sick day. I'd had it a few times in the past and it always knocked me flat—fever, chills, the fire-in-your-throat kind of misery.

But at least Lucy was alive and able to text... which was more than I could say for some of the scenarios that had been running through my head during the past hour.

Ones involving dark alleys and hulking, nefarious men.

Yeah...apparently, I still wasn't over what happened to her a month ago.

I wanted to text her back right away. Ask if she was okay. Offer something—anything. But I was still mid-lecture, standing in front of a lecture hall full of students with all eyes on me.

The second I got back to my office, though, I shut the door and fired off a response.

> Me: Do you need to go see a doctor? Get an antibiotic?

> Theo's sister: Just got out of the doctor's office. My mom took me. She's in the pharmacy picking up my prescription right now.

> Me: Thank goodness for moms who live close by and can help.

> Theo's sister: Seriously.

And I knew I shouldn't be disappointed that she hadn't called or texted me first...but part of me was.

Not because I thought she *should* have since I understood why she went to her mom.

Mrs. Archibald struck me as the nurturing type. The kind of mom who'd drop everything to take care of her kid, even if that kid was technically an adult.

Besides...it wasn't like I could do much.

I had lectures to teach. Labs to run. And there was still the inconvenient truth that I was her professor.

Taking care of a sick student didn't exactly fall under my job description.

Still...I couldn't shake the ache in my chest that wished I was the one sitting beside her.

Holding her hand.

Making her chicken noodle soup.

> Me: Are you going back to your dorm to rest?

> Theo's sister: My mom is taking me home with her since it'll be easier to take care of me there.

> Me: Sounds like a good plan. I hope you get feeling better soon.

Theo's sister: Me too. Hopefully, the
antibiotics will kick in fast. I don't have time to
be sick. (I may be panicking slightly about
missing practice and all my classes. I really
can't miss the Nebraska meet on Saturday.)

She was probably spiraling. All week, she'd been stressing about how slim the odds were of her team making Nationals.

Sure, she and Nora had been rock solid all season, but the team had lost some really great gymnasts last year, and the team wins weren't coming like they had the year before.

Lucy had been pushing herself to the brink trying to carry the weight of that pressure, saying that if the team didn't make it, she at least wanted to qualify on her own for the all-around.

But with her getting sick, I wondered if she'd been pushing herself too hard.

Her body could only do so much, and she was running herself ragged.

I'd say that at least we have spring break next week and she could hopefully have some time off to relax. But when I'd asked her if her coach might lighten their load in honor of spring break, she just laughed and said that with only one meet between spring break and the conference championships, there was no chance of that.

But hopefully this forced rest would at least let her body catch up on some sleep.

Even if I knew her mind was probably racing, trying to keep all the spinning plates from crashing down.

Me: Just get your rest. I know it's easier said
than done, but I'll help you catch up on your
chemistry assignment and tomorrow's lab. So
no need to worry about either of those things.

At least I could help her with one of the stressors in her life.

Theo's sister: Thanks.

I was updating grades at my kitchen table on Thursday night, staring blankly at my laptop screen, when a knock sounded at the door.

I glanced at the clock. It was too late for deliveries. And being a hermit professor, I didn't have too many friends showing up unannounced these days.

Maybe someone knocked on the wrong door?

Curious, I stood and made my way to the door. When I checked the peephole, I had to angle my gaze down. And when I saw who was there, my heart thudded.

Because it was none other than Lucy—bundled up in an oversized hoodie and knit beanie, her cheeks flushed, either from the cold or the fever that still lingered.

I opened the door fast and tugged her inside.

"What are you doing out in the cold?" I asked, wrapping her in a hug the second the door clicked shut behind her. "Aren't you supposed to be resting?"

"Probably," she said, melting into me, her voice still raspy. "But I was sad you couldn't come to me. So I decided to sneak over."

"You must really like me to brave the cold like this," I mumbled, kissing the top of her head. "But I'm glad you did. I missed you in lab today."

"I wanted to be there." She groaned. "But the doctor said no public places until twenty-four hours after starting the antibiotic. Technically, that was around three, so I could've come an hour late...if my mom hadn't held me hostage."

"You're not really great at staying down when you're sick, are you?" I asked, liking her determination even though I knew she needed the rest.

"I don't have time to be sick," she muttered. "I can be sick after I win Nationals and graduate."

I chuckled and tugged her farther inside so we could sit on the couch. "So...did you really come here as soon as your mom dropped you off at your place?"

"Pretty much." She nodded, scooting close to me on the couch. "She fed me homemade chicken noodle soup, made me promise to go straight to bed, then let me go."

"And instead of resting, you came here?" I arched a brow.

Hopefully, she drove here instead of walked. It was the second week of March, so it was warming up a bit as the earth was slowly transitioning from winter into spring, but still, not something a person with strep should be doing.

"Nora wasn't home, and I already slept most of the day." She gave a shameless shrug. "So I thought I'd come bug you. I even have my backpack in my car in case you'd want to help me figure out the chemistry assignment I missed." She studied my face. "That is, if you're not too busy."

"I could do that." I nodded toward my laptop on my kitchen table. "I was just finishing up some grading."

"Let me guess. My lab grade went down today?"

"Just for now," I said, smiling at the cute way her nose scrunched up. "But once you make it up, it'll be back where it belongs."

"If only you were the kind of professor who made special accommodations for the girl he was sneaking around with," she said, narrowing her eyes playfully.

"I'm just a mean professor, aren't I?" I gave her a teasing look.

"Totally..." She grinned. "But better a mean professor than a mean boyfriend, I guess."

The moment the words left her mouth, she froze, her smile faltering, like she hadn't meant to say that part out loud. Like something had slipped.

Had it?

I studied her, quieting the urge to joke back as a knot slowly formed in my chest.

Better a mean professor than a mean boyfriend.

Not a joke. Not really.

Especially not when I thought about the things I'd seen—Josh's temper at The Garden, his fight with Brody, the way he'd shouted at the refs on the ice.

Had he hurt her? Was that why they'd broken up?

"Have you had a mean boyfriend before?" I asked quietly. "Someone who...didn't treat you well?"

Her gaze dropped as she twisted the edge of her sweatshirt between her fingers. Then, after letting out a soft sigh, she said, "Yes."

A sharp ache settled in my chest. "Did Josh hurt you?"

I tried not to tense, not to betray the way my pulse suddenly surged. But I already knew. The hesitation in her silence said enough.

"I, uh...haven't really told anyone," she said, voice barely above a whisper. "Wasn't sure what might happen if I did. But...things got physical a couple of times. The worst being right before Nationals last year, when he pushed me really hard and I got bruised ribs."

I went still as a wave of shock rolled through me. Followed by a sharp wave of fury that locked up every muscle in my body. But I needed to keep my anger in check. Seeing me become too upset might trigger her, and the last thing she needed to worry about was my reaction.

So I took in a few deep breaths before I asked, "Are those the same bruised ribs Nora mentioned when you were talking about gymnastics injuries in the hot tub? Were they not actually from gymnastics?"

"They're the same bruised ribs." Her big blue eyes met mine, raw and weary. "I told the doctor, and everyone else, that I got hurt from a bad dismount on bars. But...it happened at Josh's apartment when he was drunk. I said the wrong thing, I guess...and he slammed me into the counter."

"I'm so sorry, Lucy," was all I could say as a sick heaviness settled in my stomach. "I'm sure that was terrifying." To have someone who claimed to love her treat her like that.

She nodded, and when her hand came up to wipe away tears, she gave a self-conscious smile. "Sorry. I always get more emotional when I'm sick."

"Come here," I murmured, drawing her gently into me.

She hesitated. "I might give you strep, though."

"I'm not worried about that."

She let herself lean into me, and I wrapped my arms around her. We sat like that for a while—her curled against my chest, her heartbeat soft and steady beneath my hand, the weight of her confession sinking deeper into my bones.

I never would've guessed she'd been through something like that.

That someone so strong, so talented—a ray of sunshine who lit up every room—could be carrying the kind of scars no one ever sees, left by the person who was supposed to love her most.

But that's how it was sometimes. Abuse doesn't care how bright someone burned.

"I broke up with him for good after that," she said eventually, voice muffled against my shirt. "Finally realized we were actually too broken to fix. That I deserved better."

"I'm glad you did," I said. "Not everyone has the strength to walk away. Especially not with love tangled up in the pain."

"Yeah..." She let out a soft breath. "I still wonder sometimes...if I should've told someone. Reported him." Her fingers fidgeted with the hem of her sleeve. "Because...what if he hurts someone else?"

"I get that," I said quietly. "That fear's real."

She nodded slowly. "But Brody said Josh stopped drinking after their fight. That he seems to be getting better. So I want to believe that. That maybe he realized what he was doing hurt me and ruined us, and maybe he'll try harder to avoid that in his future relationships."

"I hope so," I said, meaning it, too.

"But...do you think I should've reported him?" She looked up at me, eyes wide and vulnerable.

"I don't know," I said honestly. "It's hard. Especially when it's someone you care about. It's human to want to believe they'll change. That it won't happen again."

She gave a small, solemn nod.

"But you did the most important thing," I added. "You got out. You protected yourself. That's not nothing."

"Thanks," she whispered.

After a beat, she pulled back just enough to meet my gaze. Her eyes were still watery but steady now. "And thanks for not freaking out. I haven't told anyone before. And it was...nice. To just say it out loud. Without having to manage someone else's reaction."

"I'm glad you felt safe telling me." I gave her a soft smile. "That means more than you know."

She nodded again, then curled back into me, her body sinking into mine like she was finally letting herself be held.

As we sat there, I considered suggesting she tell her family, since I was sure it had been hard keeping it a secret from them.

But that conversation could wait for another time.
Right now, she didn't need advice.
She just needed comfort—maybe even *me*.
And I wasn't going anywhere.

44

LUCY

"THANKS FOR HELPING me with the assignment," I said as I zipped my backpack shut and glanced up at Owen with a tired smile. "Hopefully, my chemistry professor gives me a good grade on it."

"If he doesn't, then Professor Park has officially lost his mind." He winked.

I laughed. "Well, I know he's still got all his faculties...so I'll take that as a guaranteed A."

He chuckled, his brown eyes crinkling. "Guess you'll just have to wait and see."

"Guess I will." I reached for my backpack strap, ready to sling it over my shoulder, then paused. "Actually...mind if I use your bathroom before I head out?"

"Go ahead." He stepped aside and nodded toward the hall- way. "Second door on the left."

I slipped down the hall and into the bathroom, flipping on the light and closing the door behind me. When I moved to wash my hands, something on the wall caught my eye. A small shelf beside the mirror, lined with a few personal development books and a stack of science and technology magazines.

I smiled to myself.

Of course he had those.

He really was such a nerd. A smart, thoughtful, deeply lovable nerd.

And to think he'd let me believe he was just a bartender when we first met.

After drying my hands, I opened the door and paused in the doorway.

Owen was standing by the table, zipping up my backpack.

He straightened a little too quickly, his expression casual in a way that made me instantly suspicious. "Just making sure you had everything for tomorrow."

"Uh-huh." I crossed my arms as I stepped toward him. "You're not sneaking in surprise quizzes, are you?"

"Never," he said, with just enough mischief in his voice to make me squint. "Just something...for later."

"For later?" I lifted an eyebrow. "What kind of something?"

He didn't elaborate, just gave a mysterious little shrug.

"Well, I guess I better head out so I can find out what you did to my backpack."

"Yes." He chuckled softly, his eyes holding mine. "You better."

But even as he said it, neither of us moved. And all I wanted was to sink back into the couch with him and let time stretch a little longer between us. But I sighed and reached for my coat. "I should probably get back to my place before my mom checks my location and sees I'm not there."

He froze. "Your mom checks your location?"

"Sometimes," I said. "Usually only if I don't answer her texts or if she knows I'm traveling. It's not, like, constant."

"Still..." He rubbed the back of his neck, and I could see the wheels turning. "That could be a problem. If she realizes you were here...and knows this isn't student housing..."

I swallowed. He was right. And even though I didn't think my mom was currently tracking me, the possibility still stirred a sense of unease.

We hadn't officially defined what was going on between us —whether we were a real couple or not—but we'd definitely stepped into the gray.

"Do you get nervous about us spending so much time together?" I looked up at him. "About what might happen if someone saw us?"

"Yeah." He rubbed the back of his neck. "I mean, we've been careful. And I don't think we're doing anything morally wrong. We're both adults. But..."

"But since we haven't exactly been forthcoming with the dean," I said slowly, "it could get...complicated."

"It could." He nodded, the corners of his mouth tightening. "Which kind of makes it feel a little wrong."

"Wrong?" I tilted my head, not loving the sound of that.

"Maybe *forbidden* is a better word," he said, softening his tone. "It's exciting. And obviously I'd rather be with you than not. But I also know how it might look to someone who doesn't understand how we got here. I mean, I *am* a lot older than you..."

"In years, maybe," I teased, bumping my shoulder into his. "Maturity, though? That's still up for debate."

"Okay, fair." He chuckled, the tension in his expression easing.

"Though, maybe I still have a little catching up to do there, too."

"You're just the way you're supposed to be," he said, his voice gentle as he leaned in to press a kiss to my forehead. "Just perfect for me."

My chest fluttered, a sweet ache blooming beneath my ribs.

"Do you think we should tell Dean Harris about us, though?" I asked softly. "Would that make you feel better? More secure with your job since professors are supposed to disclose relationships like ours?"

He narrowed his eyes. "You think we could do that without your dad finding out?"

"Probably not." I wrinkled my nose. "They're pretty good friends."

"And what do you think the chances are of us telling your dad without him completely freaking out?"

I winced. "I mean...he *might* surprise us."

Though we both knew he wouldn't.

Even if my dad was magically okay with me dating my professor, the fact that Owen was seven years older than me would be an issue for him. He'd already been freaked out too much by stories in the news several years back about gymnasts being abused by a man in a position of power whom they'd thought they could trust.

So if he had the slightest concern that Owen had used his position and age in any way to influence me, that would definitely trigger his worst fears.

Owen chuckled. "So maybe we think about it over spring break and hope a solution magically appears."

"Yes." I grabbed my backpack and slipped it over my shoulders, fluffing my hair out from under the straps. "Are you still going to New York to see your brother next week?"

"I am," he said. "I thought I might spend a couple of days there, but..." His gaze lingered on me, like he was thinking something through. "I know you don't get the full week off, since it's crunch time, but...I was wondering if there might be an evening you could slip away from Eden Falls. Maybe catch a Broadway play with me?"

"Beauty and the Beast?" I asked, hope blooming in my chest.

"Of course." He smiled. "I already talked to Asher and he said he could get me two tickets. And if you wanted, I could introduce you to him and Elyse backstage."

"A Broadway date with my boyfriend," I murmured. "Where we can hold hands in public and don't have to hide how we feel about each other... That sounds amazing."

"So, I'm your boyfriend?" He smiled wider.

"I mean...I've been calling you that in my head for weeks." I laughed. "I know we never really put a title on it, but..."

"I like it," he said. "I haven't been anyone's boyfriend in a long time. And being Lucy Archibald's boyfriend... Well, that's even better."

"Well, good." I checked the time and sighed. "I really should go now."

"Yeah. You need your sleep." Tilting his head, he asked, "Are you going to take it easy tomorrow?"

"I'll rest as much as I can between classes and practice. But I need to be ready for Saturday's meet in Nebraska."

"That's fair." He nodded. "I'm glad you're feeling at least a little better today."

"Me too." I smiled faintly. "Tuesday night was rough. I don't know if I'll ever be able to eat sushi again."

He pulled me into a hug, warm and grounding. "Sleep well, okay?"

"You too." I met his eyes as we parted, a little more softly this time. "And...thanks for being so great about what I told you earlier."

I'd been so nervous to share what happened with Josh, but Owen had made me feel safe. Seen. Believed.

"Of course," he said. "I appreciate you feeling safe enough with me to open up."

We said our final goodbyes, and I stepped out into the cool night air. Once I made it to my car and waited for the engine to warm up, I couldn't stop thinking about how Owen had zipped up my backpack earlier.

Curious, I unzipped it and peeked inside.

And nestled beside my laptop was a small, plush cow.

I pulled it out slowly, my brows lifting. The fabric was minky soft, and as I held it to my chest, I caught a gentle lavender scent.

The plush cow had a bit of weight to it, too, like it was filled with more than just the usual stuffing.

And then it hit me.

I'd seen these before. A microwavable stuffed animal, filled with flaxseed and dried lavender. Designed to soothe sore muscles and help you sleep.

My heart melted.

Owen.

Tucked just beneath the cow was a small envelope with my name on it. I opened it, my fingers already trembling.

Inside was a note written in Owen's familiar, steady handwriting.

TO MY FAVORITE OVERACHIEVER:

IN CASE YOU START TO PANIC ABOUT ALL THE THINGS YOU'RE NOT GETTING DONE WHILE YOU RECOVER, DR. PARK PRESCRIBES THE FOLLOWING "TO-DON'T" LIST. (AND YES…HE KNOWS THAT HAVING A PHD IN CHEMISTRY IS NOT THE SAME AS BEING A MEDICAL DOCTOR. BUT LET'S JUST PRETEND FOR A BIT…)

1. DON'T TRY TO CATCH UP ON EVERYTHING (THE WORLD CAN WAIT. YOUR BODY CAN'T.)

2. DON'T APOLOGIZE FOR RESTING. (YOU DON'T HAVE TO EARN YOUR WORTH WITH EXHAUSTION.)

3. DON'T MEASURE YOUR VALUE BY WHAT YOU GET DONE. (YOU ARE JUST AS LOVABLE WHEN YOU'RE CURLED UP IN BED DOING NOTHING.)

4. DON'T WORRY ABOUT DISAPPOINTING ANYONE. (THE PEOPLE WHO TRULY LOVE YOU WON'T BREAK IF YOU TAKE A DAY OFF.)

5. DON'T SCROLL. DO NOT STUDY. DO NOT STRATE-GIZE. (DRINK WATER. NAP. STARE AT THE CEILING. THAT'S THE ASSIGNMENT.)

6. DON'T TRY TO BE PERFECT. (I'M NOT IN LOVE WITH YOUR RÉSUMÉ. I'M HERE FOR YOU.)

7. DON'T FORGET THAT YOU'RE ALREADY ENOUGH. (EVEN IF THE ONLY THING YOU DO TODAY IS BREATHE AND BE HERE—THAT'S STILL ENOUGH.)

LOVE,
THE GUY WHO COULDN'T STOP FALLING FOR YOU JUST AS YOU ARE.

I read the note a second time, then a third, tears gathering at the corners of my eyes as I read his simple, yet profound words.

It wasn't that his "To-Don't" list was revolutionary or poetic or the kind of thing people posted online to go viral.

It was the fact that somehow...he knew.

In the short time we'd known each other, Owen saw me more clearly than anyone else ever had.

He saw past the medals and the GPA and the relentless schedule I clung to like armor. Past the performative smile I wore when I was exhausted but didn't want to disappoint anyone.

He saw the part of me that believed I had to earn love. That unless I was achieving something remarkable, I ran the risk of not quite measuring up.

That if I wasn't impressing my parents or chasing the next big goal, I might not be worth sticking around for.

I'd spent years hustling for my worth, piling more and more onto my plate because if I was ever caught just sitting around doing nothing, maybe my friends and family would finally realize I wasn't actually all that special. Sitting around and "just being" wasn't a luxury I could afford to take.

But with Owen...he made it feel possible.

Like, maybe I didn't have to do anything to deserve love.

Like maybe I could actually take a break—stop striving for just a moment—and still be worth loving.

I curled the little cow into my chest, the weight of it settling over my heart.

I'd never been one for stuffed animals before, but I suddenly knew this cute little brown-and-white cow would be traveling with me to all my meets and sleeping in my bed every night.

My phone was still sitting on the passenger seat. I reached for it and opened a new message to Owen.

> Me: I just found the surprise in my backpack. I don't even have words right now. But thank you. For seeing me. For reminding me I'm more than what I achieve.

> Also…this little cow? Definitely my new emotional support animal. 🤍🐄

I hit *Send*, pulled the cow in close again, and let myself sit there in the quiet car, breathing in lavender and love and the strange, wonderful calm of finally being seen.

My phone buzzed in my hand a moment later.

Theo's friend: I'm glad you liked it. I just wanted to give you something small to hold onto when your world gets loud. Something to remind you that you don't have to earn peace or rest or love. You already deserve it just by being you.

Another buzz.

Theo's friend: Also, I had to resist the urge to buy the entire barnyard. There was a lamb, a sloth, and a ridiculously smug-looking penguin. But the cow just felt like you. Soft. Strong. A little unexpected. And completely lovable.

A tear slid down my cheek and I smiled so hard it hurt.

Me: Okay, stop. You're going to make me fall in love with you or something. 🫠🩶

His reply came instantly.

Theo's friend: That's kind of what I'm going for.

45

___

OWEN

"THAT WAS INCREDIBLE," Lucy said, looking over at me after the cast of *Beauty and the Beast* did their final bow. Her eyes were wide with awe; her cheeks flushed in a way that made it very hard not to lean over and kiss her right there in the middle of the packed theater. "Asher and Elyse were just... I don't even have words. I think I forgot to breathe during the 'If I Can't Love Her' scene. Your brother's voice is unreal."

"He's truly talented," I said, a smile tugging at my lips as I studied her face. "I'm glad you enjoyed the musical."

"I loved it," she said, glancing up at me, eyes bright. "Thanks for inviting me. This was seriously a dream come true. This whole day has been magical, really." And when she leaned her head against my shoulder, my heart swelled.

"I'm glad you could make it work." I slid my arm around her, tugging her a little closer. "I know how busy you are."

It was the Wednesday of spring break, but even though classes were out, Lucy's schedule hadn't exactly slowed down. She still had training sessions in the mornings—thankfully pushed back to ten instead of the usual crack-of-dawn start, since her coach wasn't completely heartless. But even with the extra hours of sleep, she was still knee-deep in the chaos of competition season and juggling big class projects.

She'd flown to Nebraska over the weekend for a meet—taking second in the all-around despite still recovering from strep. And after the home meet she had coming up this Sunday, only three meets remained: the Conference Championship in Philadelphia, NCAA Regionals two weeks after that, and then the big one—the NCAA Finals.

It was such an important final stretch in her gymnastics career, the kind of moment she'd been working toward her whole life. And the fact that she'd carved out a day to come to Manhattan with me? That meant something.

Made me hopeful that maybe I wasn't the only one really falling here. That maybe...once we figured out how to bring our relationship into the light, we might actually have a shot at something real and lasting.

Which I wanted so badly.

These past few weeks with her had been so good that I couldn't help but want more.

Not just weeks. But months. Years.

Maybe forever.

"Are we still going backstage to meet them?" Lucy asked, glancing up at me with a flash of nerves in her blue eyes.

"If you're up for it," I said, slipping my fingers through hers. "Asher told me how to get backstage to his dressing room."

"Okay, cool." She nodded, blowing out a breath. "I'm just a bit nervous, since they're like...famous. But yeah, I'd love to meet your family."

And there was something about the way she said it that made my heart shift in my chest.

Because I was about to introduce the girl I was falling for to my family. Which was actually a pretty big moment since I couldn't even remember the last time I'd done that.

Had I ever?

Giving Lucy's hand a gentle squeeze, I led her toward the backstage entrance Asher had mentioned. And as our hands swung casually between us, I couldn't get over the fact that I was actually able to do this—hold her hand in public.

It was a seemingly small thing to most people in a relationship...but for us—ever since that kiss on New Year's—this was the first time we hadn't had to hide. There were no shadows to keep to, no ducking out of sight when someone walked by.

Here in a city full of strangers, we could be a regular couple. Just me and Lucy, hand in hand, enjoying a spring night out in town.

The whole day had been amazing, actually; the kind of day I wanted to bottle up and keep forever. I'd picked Lucy up from the train station earlier this afternoon, and we'd wandered through Manhattan, letting the city buzz around us as we walked hand in hand through Central Park.

Crocuses and daffodils had just started blooming, dotting the grass with color and promise. Everything smelled like fresh air and street pretzels.

Dinner had been at a cozy little Korean restaurant tucked into a side street—dim lighting, soft music, the kind of place that made you lean in closer without realizing it. Lucy had stolen bites off my plate, told me my chopstick skills were "hot," and laughed in that effortless way that always made something in my chest loosen.

And then tonight—watching her glow under the theater lights, fingers laced with mine as she sat completely captivated by the show—it had felt...real. So good. So blissfully uncomplicated.

Like I wasn't her professor and she wasn't my student.

Just a guy falling for a girl who made the world brighter.

Sitting there, soaking in the music and the magic and the way Lucy leaned her head against my shoulder like she belonged there, I found myself wanting more moments like that.

Moments where I could walk up to her on campus and kiss her cheek without worrying who might see. Moments where I could find her after a meet, wrap her in a hug, and tell her how proud I was.

Just...the little things. The freedom to feel what I felt out in the open. To stop hiding the happiness she gave me.

And I knew that we were less than two months away from her graduation. If we could just keep things quiet until then, we might actually be in the clear.

But part of me didn't want to wait.

Not because I couldn't. But because I didn't want to miss her big moments. I wanted to be at her last meets. To watch her at Nationals in Texas next month and not spend the whole time ducking behind a program, terrified her dad would spot me in the crowd.

Which meant I probably needed to talk to President Archibald and Dean Harris. Tell them I was dating my student.

And hopefully, when I walked out of those conversations, I'd still have a job.

Lucy and I reached the backstage entrance, and I knocked. As we waited, I gave her hand a gentle squeeze.

"You nervous at all?" she asked, glancing up at me.

"A little," I admitted. Then, with a smirk, I added, "Mostly just hoping my brother doesn't completely embarrass me. He's kind of a dork sometimes."

She laughed, her eyes catching the light. "Somehow, I doubt your Broadway star brother who just crushed it in front of a sold-out crowd could do anything that embarrassing."

"You never know," I said with a wink.

A stagehand opened the door a few seconds later, giving us a quick once-over before I introduced myself and told him who we were. He gave a nod and motioned us inside, leading us through a maze of narrow backstage hallways that smelled faintly of sweat, sawdust, and old makeup.

Lucy's hand stayed tucked in mine the whole time, but I could feel the hum of nervous energy radiating from her the closer we got. *Excited nerves*, I thought. *The good kind.*

"Ready?" I asked, giving Lucy's fingers one more reassuring squeeze as the stagehand knocked on Asher's dressing room door.

"Ready," she said, her voice soft but steady.

A moment later, we stepped inside and found Asher and Elyse cuddling on a small couch, still in costume from their last curtain call—he in his velvet Beast coat, she in her glittering Belle gown, the stage makeup giving both of them a slightly surreal glow.

"Owen!" Asher said, standing the second he saw us. "I'm so glad you guys made it." He pulled me into a quick hug, clapping my back.

"Yes, it was so fun seeing you in the audience tonight," Elyse said warmly, wrapping me in her own hug.

I stepped back and slid an arm around Lucy's waist. She looked a little wide-eyed but kept smiling—and for a second, I wasn't sure how to introduce her. My brain scrambled for words that felt right...and didn't make me sound like I was twelve.

I turned to Lucy, gesturing at my brother and his wife. "Uh...this is my brother, Asher, and his wife, Elyse." Then I looked back at them and motioned toward Lucy. "And this is Lucy..." I hesitated a beat before awkwardly adding, "My girlfriend."

Okay...not exactly the most polished delivery of my life. But it got the job done.

"It's so nice to meet you," Lucy said, letting out a soft laugh as she stepped forward, giving each of them a quick hug. "You two were amazing. I've wanted to see *Beauty and the Beast* on Broadway ever since I was a kid and they couldn't have picked more perfect leads."

"Thank you," Elyse said warmly, her brown eyes glowing at the praise. Even though she and my brother had been playing these roles to sold-out audiences for a year and a half, she was still the same level-headed girl she'd been when they first met. "We're so glad you could come with Owen."

Lucy nodded and looked between the two of them. "Wow, you're all so tall in real life." They chuckled, and Lucy quickly added, "But I guess that's probably because I'm just really short."

"No, I'm five foot nine, so I am pretty tall for a girl." Elyse laughed, linking her arm through Asher's. "Luckily, I got my six-foot-two guy to make me still feel dainty."

"Well, you two look super cute together," Lucy said, beaming at them. "And your chemistry—it seemed so real on stage." She let out a little laugh, then added, "It's like you're really in love or something."

Asher and Elyse just smiled at each other, and watching them, I felt a quiet happiness swell in my chest. Not many high school couples made it, but these two were proof that young love could grow into something deep and lasting. Real.

Lucy turned back to them. "I actually have this weird thing," she said, tucking a loose strand of hair behind her ear. "I watched one of my married cousins in a play once, and when it came time for him to kiss the female lead, I was just cringing the whole time, thinking, '*Please* don't kiss her, you're married to someone else.'" It stressed me out so much." She gave a little laugh. "So it was nice not worrying about that tonight. I don't know how actors and their spouses handle that. I would be so jealous."

Gosh, she's so cute. The way she was nervously rambling.

But also, the sentiment behind what she was saying was refreshing to hear. Showed the kind of life partner she'd be. Loyal. Devoted.

"We're definitely lucky that it's worked out for us to work with each other on those scenes." Asher laughed, reaching for Elyse's hand. "But back in high school..." He shot a look at Elyse. "Let's just say I was *extremely* jealous when another guy was playing the Phantom to her Christine during the 'Point of No Return' scene in *Phantom of the Opera.*"

"And the fact that you and the guy playing the Phantom hated each other at the time didn't exactly help." Elyse smirked.

"Very true." Asher chuckled.

"But now you're best friends, so it all worked out," Elyse said.

"Right. Plus, I got to marry you, so that helps, too." Asher winked.

We all chuckled at that.

"But enough about us," Asher said, turning back to Lucy. "We already peppered Owen with about a thousand questions when he told us he was bringing someone special tonight, but we'd love to hear more from you."

"Yes," Elyse said, her eyes warm. "He's already gushed about what an accomplished gymnast you are. How smart and driven you are as well, in addition to being excellent at keeping him on his toes. He's clearly completely smitten. But..."

"...what is it that you see in my brother?" Asher asked, picking up the thread with a mischievous grin. "Because as far as I'm concerned, he's just a boring chemistry nerd who gets his kicks and giggles from balancing chemical equations."

"See, I told you he'd try to embarrass me," I said, looking at Lucy with mock embarrassment.

"We might need to sit down for this," Lucy said, hooking her arm through mine. "Because I've got a whole list of things I love about your brother and it might take a while."

46

LUCY

THE TRAIN ROCKED GENTLY beneath Owen and me as we headed toward New Haven, the hum of conversations and the occasional squeak of wheels on tracks filling the quiet space around us.

"I had the best time tonight," I murmured, curling into Owen's side and letting my head rest against his shoulder. "Your brother and Elyse are seriously so cool. I was so nervous to meet them, but they were...just easy to talk to. It felt like hanging out with friends."

"I'm glad you liked them," he said, his voice low and relaxed. "I'm pretty sure they liked you, too. Which is good..." He paused, his gaze dipping down to mine. "Because I kind of like you a lot, too."

"Oh, really?" I asked, a slow smile pulling at my lips.

"Yes." He looked down at me, the intensity in his brown eyes making my stomach flutter. "Definitely."

"Well, good." I snuggled closer, letting the weight of his arm and his steady presence melt away the last bits of anxiety I'd been holding onto. "Because I'm quite fond of you, too."

He chuckled under his breath, his fingers brushing lightly along my arm. "Looks like we're the perfect match then."

"I think we are." I shifted just enough to look up at him. And when our gazes locked, a quiet understanding seemed to settle between us. Like we both were feeling the same things. That what started as a flirty night at a New Year's Eve party had turned into so much more. Not a fleeting crush, not a fun escape, but something *real*. Something that might even last.

"Thanks for coming back with me tonight," I said, rubbing his forearm that was bracketed over my chest. "I know you originally planned to spend the whole week with your brother, so... it really means a lot. I was slightly terrified of the prospect of traveling home alone this late."

"I'm happy to come back with you," he said, the sincerity in his voice telling me he meant it. "I wanted to make sure you got home safely. Plus, this way I get to see you tomorrow night, which is always a treat."

"Don't forget you get to help me with that lab I missed tomorrow afternoon," I said, smiling as I peeked up at him.

"How could I forget?" He smirked. "An afternoon with my cute little chemist? Talk about a fantasy come to life."

"So, the safety goggles and lab coat really do it for you, huh?" I laughed, arching a brow.

"You have no idea," he said, waggling his eyebrows.

"Good to know." I gave him a playful look. "Maybe I'll add *sexy chemist* to my Halloween costume idea list."

"As long as I don't have to return the favor by wearing one of your leotards, I'm all in."

I snorted at the mental image of a tall, broad-shouldered Owen trying to squeeze into a spandex leotard. "Pretty sure it was you in that fitted black T-shirt that hooked me at first sight."

"Guess I better put more of those back into the rotation."

He chuckled, and I felt his thumb trace a lazy line over my hand.

"Speaking of us looking our best..." I reached for my bag with a grin. "Do you mind if we take a quick photo together?"

"Right now?" he asked, glancing around with a smile. "On a train?"

"We forgot to get one earlier," I said, unlocking my phone. "And I mean...you're looking so hot, and I spent all that time finding the right outfit..."

"Of course I want a photo with you," he said, his tone softening before he pressed a kiss to my temple. "I want to remember tonight."

I pulled up the camera app on my phone and switched it to selfie mode. As I leaned in, Owen shifted closer until our cheeks brushed, and I snapped a few photos.

I zoomed in on one of them, studying it with a little grin. "Our first photo," I said, showing it to him. "Don't we look so good together?"

"We totally do."

I tucked my phone back into my bag and leaned into him again, settling in for the rest of the ride. When we reached the train station in New Haven a while later, we climbed into my car and drove back to Eden Falls. The roads were quiet at this hour, and by the time I pulled up in front of Owen's apartment, the silence between us had settled into something warm and full—like neither of us needed words to know how good tonight had been.

He glanced over at me with a soft, contented look that made my heart flutter. "I'm really glad we did this," he said. "Tonight was kind of perfect."

Then he leaned across the console, his hand finding my cheek, his fingers warm against my skin. And when his lips met mine, the kiss was sweet and slow. I melted into the moment, eyes falling closed, my fingers curling lightly around his wrist as I let my lips and tongue explore his.

When he eventually pulled away, I blinked, slightly dazed, trying to catch my breath.

"Hey, before I forget," he said, a little smile tugging at his lips as he met my eyes in the dark car, "can you send me that photo you took? I'd love a copy."

"Of course." I reached for my phone, tapping the screen. *Nothing*. I hit the power button, but still no response. "Uh... well, maybe not since I guess my phone died."

"Sounds about right," he said, an amused look in his eyes.

"I'll get some charge in it when I get home and text it to you," I promised.

"Sounds perfect," he said. Then he leaned in for one more kiss, slower and deeper this time, making my stomach swoop.

"Gosh, I could just kiss you all night," he said, pulling away with a quiet groan.

"Me too," I said, letting him go even though I didn't want to.

If it weren't already so late and I didn't have practice in the morning, I probably would've asked to go inside with him.

But I needed to be responsible.

Even if spending time with this gorgeous man was way more fun than sleeping.

"I'll see you in the lab tomorrow afternoon," I said instead.

"Okay," he said, opening the passenger door to climb out. "See you then."

"Someone looks happy," Nora's voice sounded in the doorway of my room after I'd gotten home and changed into my pajamas. "I'm guessing your Broadway date with Professor McDreamy went well."

"It was so good," I said, looking up at my best friend after putting my phone on my charger so it could come back to life. "It was just so nice having a real date with him. One where we could just have fun and relax and not worry about who might see us."

"I bet," Nora said, stepping farther in to sit on the chair I had in the corner of my small dorm room. "Did you get to meet his brother?"

"I did," I said, smiling as I thought about how that had gone. "He's awesome. Both him and his wife are. Just really cool and down-to-earth."

"That's awesome." Nora smiled. "Too bad you guys couldn't stay longer, though, right?"

"Yeah," I said, thinking that twelve hours of downtime with Owen wasn't nearly long enough. "But we'll have to take another day trip like that again soon."

"Maybe take Theo's sister-in-law up on that hotel stay she offered." Nora wiggled her eyebrows suggestively.

"Ahhh," I said, covering my cheeks as they instantly flushed with her implication. "I really shouldn't be thinking about *that*."

Nora laughed. "You don't want to spend the night with your sexy professor?"

"No..." Then shaking my head, I said, "I mean...yes..." I shook my head again. "I mean...I don't know. I guess with everything feeling so forbidden with us, taking *that* step just..." I let my words trail off, not really knowing what I was trying to say since I wasn't really sure what my thoughts were.

"You're just a little confused?" Nora said for me.

"Yeah," I said. "I mean, I've definitely been tempted to go there already since our chemistry—no pun intended—" I laughed at my own accidental joke. "Is definitely off the charts and I'm sure it would be amazing with him."

"It's okay to take things at a pace you feel good about, though," Nora said. "And I'm glad he's not, like, pushing you into anything, since you know how guys can be sometimes."

"Oh yeah, he's definitely a gentleman," I said. "If anything, I'm probably the one who has been pushing things further in that direction."

"Well, at least one of us is having some fun with a guy," Nora said, and I caught a hint of disappointment in her tone.

"Things with you and Cash not going anywhere?" I asked.

"No," Nora said, shaking her head. "I mean, he seems flirty in our study group, but aside from that, we've just been texting. And I kind of feel like we've landed in that no man's land where maybe we're just texting buddies and he's not actually interested in anything more."

"Oh, I'm sorry," I said, sympathy tugging at my heart. "That sucks."

"It's okay." She let out a long breath and sank deeper into the chair. "Maybe I'm just not meant to have a boyfriend this year."

Just then, my phone lit up on the nightstand.

"Sorry, I need to send something before I forget," I said as I reached for it, the screen finally alive with a gentle glow. I quickly opened my photo app to the photo I'd taken on the train, then clicked the arrow to send it to Owen. After typing out a quick message, thanking him for the magical day and that I hoped he'd sleep well, I hit the send button.

Then, setting my phone down again, I turned back to Nora.

"Well, if the guys at school aren't working out..." I said with a sly grin, "then you should copy me and try going for an older guy. Turns out, they're kind of the best."

Nora laughed. "Is this your sneaky way of trying to set me up with your brother?"

"Not necessarily," I said. "But...he *is* still looking. And I'm pretty sure I caught him smiling while you were playing that game with Charlotte at his surprise party."

"You're funny, you know that?" She let out a soft chuckle.

"Just saying." I shrugged.

"Well, I better get to bed." Nora stood and stretched. "I'm glad you had such a good night."

"Thanks," I said, watching her go, my heart still full from the day.

Once the door closed, I reached for my phone again and tapped the screen, just in case Owen had responded. But there was nothing new.

Still, I couldn't help smiling as I set it down.

As I headed into the bathroom to wash my face, my body still buzzing from the perfect night, I couldn't help but feel that after everything I'd been through last year, life was finally falling into place.

And for the first time in a long while, I wasn't waiting for the other shoe to drop.

47

LUCY

THE SCIENCE BUILDING was so quiet today. No distant footsteps. No professors chatting in the halls. No students laughing in study groups. Just the low hum of fluorescent lights and the faint clink of glassware as Owen set up the station for my makeup lab.

"Is it weird that I kind of love how empty it is in here?" I leaned against the counter, my voice sounding louder than expected in the silence. "It's like the whole place belongs to us."

He paused, glancing around the lab before meeting my eyes with a smirk. "Kind of makes you feel like you could get away with anything in here, doesn't it?"

"Exactly." I smiled, liking that we seemed to be on the same wavelength. "Makes you feel like you could...break a few rules."

"Now that..." his eyes brightened, a slow smile spreading across his face, "is a dangerous thing to say."

"And why's that?" I asked, leaning in closer and looking up at him with innocent eyes.

He switched the burner on and then stepped a little closer.

"Because I've imagined having you alone in this lab way more times than I should probably admit."

"Oh yeah?" My eyebrows arched, suddenly intrigued.

Has he actually thought about kissing me in here?

Because yeah, all those stolen glances we'd shared across the lab this semester had definitely given me a few ideas of my own.

"Definitely." He nodded. "Like right now…" His eyes darkened as his hands slid to my hips. "I could set you up on that counter," he murmured near my ear, stepping closer until I could feel the heat radiating off his body, "and take my time with you."

His gaze dipped to my mouth, then dragged slowly back to my eyes, like he was already imagining every detail.

"I'd lean in slow," he said, his thumbs brushing slow, measured circles against my sides. "Close enough to touch, but not quite. And I'd just…breathe you in. Let the anticipation build."

And when he leaned in closer, I swallowed, suddenly overcome by his presence.

Was this leading where I hoped it was?

To that forbidden kiss I'd been imagining ever since the first day I walked into this lab?

"And then, after teasing you just long enough, I'd kiss you," he said, pressing his lips to my neck, then my jawline. "Deep, steady. Until you're clutching the edge of the counter because nothing else feels solid."

My breath caught. He was *way* too good at this.

"You'd really kiss me right here?" I barely managed to say, pulse kicking up at the look in his eyes. "A-aren't you scared of getting caught?"

"Just a little," he admitted, his voice dipping low as his face hovered near mine again. "But…" His hands tightened at my hips. "I haven't kissed you properly in days, so I'm just a little tempted to take the risk."

Then, without a word, he effortlessly lifted me onto the counter, the cool surface making me gasp. "Have you ever kissed anyone in a chemistry lab before?" I asked, already light-headed from the heat boiling between us.

"In real life? No." He pulled back just enough to meet my gaze, a wicked smile on his lips. "But in my daydreams..." He gave me a look that told me his fantasies may have been every bit as forbidden as mine had been. "In my daydreams, I've kissed you in here a time or two."

"Just once or twice?" I arched an eyebrow, feigning control even though I was completely breathless.

"Okay..." He chuckled, the sound low and rough. "So maybe it was more times than I can count."

"Good." I grinned. "Because I've totally imagined it, too."

His eyes burned into mine for a beat, then flicked toward the door.

A quick check.

As if reassured that we were in fact alone, he slid his hands along my thighs. Then stepping between my knees, he said, "Then maybe we can fulfill just a *tiny* bit of that fantasy while we wait for the solution to heat up."

"Deal."

He kissed me then, hard and hungry. Like he'd been waiting all day to do this. His hands skimmed higher along my thighs, anchoring at my hips as my legs wrapped around him on instinct.

And because I actually *did* need something to hold onto, I fisted the back of his lab coat with one hand and tangled the other in his hair, tugging just enough to make him deepen the kiss. And when he responded by teasing my mouth open, he completely stole the breath out of me.

And wow, I didn't think I could ever get enough of this man and the way his kisses made me feel.

Electric.

Alive.

Desired.

His lips found my neck, brushing lower with every pass. And each time his lips pressed against my skin, I felt his restraint lessen more and more.

"You're going to ruin me," he murmured against my throat, the words barely audible but soaked in heat.

And when one of his hands slid beneath my shirt, his thumb curling gently against my ribs, I knew he was indeed barely hanging on by a thread

"You know..." I mumbled when his lips found mine once more, "we could always slip into your office for a few minutes. Come back to the experiment later."

"Such a tempting thought..." He groaned softly, his grip tightening against my ribs.

"It could be fun..." I said, hoping to tempt him even further. "We could find another use for your desk."

His breath caught, then he groaned again, low and rough, like the idea physically hurt.

But just as his tongue flicked against mine, a muffled voice echoed in the hallway.

We froze.

Just for a second.

Breaths locked. Bodies still tangled.

Then we broke apart.

I slid off the counter, heart hammering, as I reached for my safety goggles with shaky hands. Owen adjusted his stance, breathing hard, eyes darting toward the door.

A second later, a shadow passed the frosted glass window. *Someone is here.*

We both held still, barely breathing as we waited for what might come next.

When the steps continued down the hall, growing more distant, we both let out sighs of relief.

"That," I whispered, trying not to laugh as adrenaline fizzed through me, "was *way* too close."

Owen ran a hand through his hair, looking slightly shell-shocked. "We seriously have to stop pushing our luck."

"Maybe we should get back to the experiment?" I asked, slipping my goggles on like I hadn't just had my legs wrapped around him five seconds ago.

"Yeah," he agreed, passing me a fresh stir rod. "But when this lab is over, we're definitely finishing that...conversation. Somewhere more private."

A warm ache bloomed low in my belly. "Looking forward to it."

"Speaking of things I'm looking forward to..." he said. "Think you could airdrop that photo of us now that your phone is back from the dead?"

"You didn't get it?" I blinked up at him. "I texted it to you last night."

"I didn't see it." He frowned and pulled out his phone. After scrolling through it for a moment, he turned the screen so I could see our text thread. Our texts from yesterday morning were there, but nothing after that.

"That's strange." My brows pulled together. Had I just imagined texting him then?

I opened my photo app, selected the picture again, and hit share, choosing his name from the airdrop list.

A second later, his phone buzzed.

"Got it," he said, showing me the photo of us on his phone.

"Glad it worked," I said, setting my phone on the tabletop. "Though I could have sworn I sent it last night."

"Hopefully, you didn't accidentally send it to some random stranger," he teased, tucking his phone back in his pocket. "It could be bad if a photo of us got out."

We both froze as soon as his words were out.

Oh no.

I felt the blood drain from my face as I picked up my phone again and opened my messages. And even though I hadn't texted my brother for a week or so, at the top of the list was Theo.

A contact name *so* close to "Theo's friend."

No, no, no, no, no. My stomach dropped as I tapped the thread.

And there it was. The photo. Me nestled against Owen's chest on the train, both of us smiling.

"I'm so sorry, Owen." My voice came out in a whisper as I turned the screen toward him. "I must've tapped Theo instead of Theo's friend."

Owen's eyes flashed wide with panic, and he leaned in, studying the screen. "Okay, wait. It says 'Delivered' but not 'Read.' So that means he hasn't seen it yet, right? So we might still be okay..."

"Yeah." I nodded quickly, grasping onto that thought like a lifeline. "He was probably already asleep when I sent it. And he's probably been busy in court today. So maybe we have time to fix this..."

Which was how? I didn't know.

I stared at the photo like it had the power to explode everything we'd been careful to protect.

"I wish there was a way to magically delete the photo from his phone," I said when no other ideas popped into my mind.

"That would certainly come in handy right now," Owen said, dragging a hand through his hair. "Is there any chance you could, I don't know... sneak into his office and delete it?"

"You want me to drive to New Haven and Mission Impossible his phone?"

"If it saves our lives and my career, it's worth a shot, right?"

But before I could respond, a bubbling hiss behind us made us both jump.

"Oh shoot—" I rushed back to the experiment, turning down the heat beneath the beaker just as Owen grabbed the flask beside it and added a splash of water to bring the reaction back under control. A few seconds later, the bubbling slowed.

Once it stabilized, I looked at Owen and said, "Maybe I could text Theo's assistant. See if she could get into his phone and delete it. I think she likes me."

"Might as well try, at least." Owen nodded.

I pulled up my messaging app, scrolling to find a text thread with Theo's assistant. I was sure I hadn't deleted it after planning his surprise party.

But before I could get to it, a new message popped up on my phone.

From Theo.

> Theo: Uh, I think you sent that to the wrong number, sis.

> Theo: Also...what the hell are you doing in that photo with Owen? Have you been sneaking around with him?

"*No!*" I let out a strangled gasp. "He just saw it."

"What?" Owen looked over, his voice tight.

I held up the screen for him to see, then before Theo could do something impulsive like call my dad, I hit the button to call him.

"Hello," Theo's voice came through the earpiece a moment later.

"Hey, so before you freak out or call Dad," I blurted, my hand shaking as I held my phone to my ear, "can you please just let me explain?"

Silence.

Then, "I'm listening."

"Okay, so, just so you know, this thing with Owen started before I knew he was my professor," I said, my words tumbling out frantically. "As you know, we met that night I saw you at The Garden, and for all I knew, bartending was his only job. I thought he was super cute and interesting, but I had no idea he taught chemistry at my school."

"Okay…" Theo exhaled loudly through the phone.

"Anyway," I continued, "nothing happened that night, but then we ran into each other again the next weekend at Ky's New Year's Eve party and hit it off. And I think it's also important to note that at that point, Owen had no idea that I was your sister, or that I was still in college, since I *might* have let him believe I was already done with school…"

Theo groaned. "Lucy…"

"I know. My bad for wanting an older guy to stay interested," I said. "Anyway, when midnight rolled around and everyone was kissing, we had our own little kiss, too."

As well as a super-hot make-out session that I'm definitely not going to mention.

"We left that weekend still not knowing a ton about each other. But then, on the first day of class, I was sitting in my chemistry class when Owen walked in. And because I still thought he was just a bartender, when I first saw him, I honestly thought he was a student."

"He's *my* age, Lucy."

"I know," I said quickly. "I just thought he was a non-traditional student who had figured out what he wanted to do a little later on."

I mean, it wasn't *that* big of a stretch. I'd had a bunch of older classmates over the years.

I sighed. "As soon as we realized who each other was and how off-limits a relationship would be, we tried to keep our distance. I promise."

"Clearly not hard enough," Theo muttered. "Since you look pretty cozy in that photo."

"Okay, yeah," I admitted, rubbing the back of my neck. "So that didn't last as long as it should have. But...we made it all the way to your birthday party without any slip-ups."

"Something happened at my party?" Theo's voice shot up an octave. "Is that why Owen was in my pantry?"

Ugh. My mouth seriously needed a filter.

"Uhh..." I hesitated. "I didn't mean to say that out loud."

"Lucy—"

"I know it sounds bad. But I swear we were trying to do what was right. Owen's a good guy. He treats me well. He's respectful, kind, even-tempered, mature...and things just...happened."

I glanced behind me to where Owen was watching the beaker. He looked calm, but something in his jaw told me he was tense.

Was he mad at me for saying too much?

Upset this had spiraled out?

Theo didn't say anything for a moment, and the silence stretched until I wanted to scream.

"I know Owen is a great guy," Theo finally said with a sigh. "And if it weren't for the fact that he's so much older and, you know, your professor, I probably would've tried setting you two up myself."

"So...are you going to tell Dad?" A breath I hadn't realized I'd been holding slipped out. "Because I know we're definitely in a gray area here," I added. "But I really don't want Owen's job to be in jeopardy. I promise he didn't use his position to seduce me or anything."

"Ew," Theo said. "You did not just talk about being seduced by my friend."

I let out a laugh, covering my face with my hand. "You know what I mean."

"And you expect me to be okay with that?"

"For what it's worth," I said gently, "we've only, um...kissed. And stuff. He's been a total gentleman."

Not that I would've turned him down if he wanted to be a little less gentlemanly...

"Well..." Theo made a noise like he was trying to unhear me. "I guess that's good."

"So...are you going to tell Dad?"

"Not right now." He exhaled slowly. "But you probably should, since it would be better coming from you than someone else you might accidentally send another selfie to."

"Yeah..." I groaned. "Sorry about that."

At least it was just a cuddle pic on the train and not anything more incriminating.

"I'll try to figure out how to tell Dad," I said. "I mean, he seemed to like Owen when we all had dinner together. So hopefully, he'll remember that when I tell him that I like him quite a bit, too."

Theo let out a low chuckle. "Good luck with *that* conversation."

"Thanks," I muttered.

After the call ended, I slowly turned back toward Owen, my heart beating like it already knew how this would go.

I wasn't sure what I expected. Frustration. A raised voice.

Something sharp.

Something I'd learned to brace for.

My pulse jumped as I met his eyes, already tensing for the fallout.

But instead of reacting the way Josh would have, Owen just arched a brow, his expression dry and unreadable.

"So...is Theo calling your dad now?" he asked, nodding toward the door. "Should I start looking for jobs in another state?"

A laugh caught in my throat. Half relief, half disbelief.

"Not yet." I shook my head, my shoulders easing the tiniest bit. "But...I'll probably have to tell him about us now."

48

OWEN

THE SUN HAD DIPPED below the rooftops by the time I parked outside Theo's house. I sat there for a second, watching the porch light flicker on as the motion sensor caught me.

I didn't know if showing up here was a terrible idea or a smart one, but I couldn't shake the feeling that if I wanted to prove myself to Theo—and to Lucy—I needed to do this in person.

So, after giving myself a little pep talk, I climbed out of my car, walked up the front walkway, and knocked. A few seconds later, the door opened.

Theo stood in slacks and a dress shirt, sleeves rolled up, his tie tugged loose. He looked tired but not surprised to see me.

"Hey," I said, clearing my throat. "Mind if I come in and talk?"

"Sure." He stepped aside. Which was...probably a good sign.

The house smelled like takeout. When we walked into the kitchen, a half-eaten container of noodles sat on the table in front of Charlotte's booster seat. A second container with the remnants of a salad sat where Theo must have been earlier.

I glanced around, half-expecting to see a three-year-old with pigtails running circles around the room. But the faint sound of cartoon voices filtering in from the living room told me Charlotte must be in there, winding down before bed.

"So," Theo said as he moved to the kitchen island and poured himself a glass of scotch. "You decided to show up for the big-brother interrogation?"

"I did." I rubbed the back of my neck, a sudden swell of anxiety filling my chest. "Figured you deserved more than a phone call or text."

"Don't forget the photo." He gave me a wry look, lifting the bottle slightly in my direction. "Want one?"

"No, thanks." I shook my head. "Figure I should keep a clear head for this."

Theo studied me for a beat, then took a sip. "I'm guessing Lucy told you what we talked about?"

"She did." I nodded. "Said you weren't planning to call your dad right away, which...I appreciate. A lot."

"Didn't feel like stepping into that minefield just yet." Theo chuckled, then took another drink. "But in all seriousness, after hearing what Lucy had to say and taking some time to think about it...I guess I can see that you two just got stuck in a really tricky place. And while I'm not exactly thrilled that my baby sister is dating a guy my age...I know you're a good guy. And..." He let out a slow breath. "If Lucy picked you—even while knowing the wrath she might face from my dad—then there's got to be something real there. She's not exactly known for letting people in."

"She's kind of amazing," I said quietly.

"I know." Theo's mouth pulled into a wry smile. "Which is why I've spent the last few hours trying not to picture the two of you doing anything that makes me want to set myself on fire."

I choked out a laugh. "We've kept things in the, uh, PG-13 realm."

"Well, that's a relief," he said with a sigh. "I mean, I know you're a good guy and I'd like to think you're interested in her because of who she is and not just the physical stuff. But you never know. And I know in her past relationship, she wasn't always cherished the way she deserved to be."

"I know." I met his eyes. "And I swear I'd never do anything to hurt her. I care about her. Way more than I planned to."

"I hope so." Theo's mouth pressed into a line, but then a flash of amusement crossed his face as he added, "Because if you do hurt her, even by accident, it's not just my dad you'll have to deal with."

Then he shot me a look that said he might be joking, but also...maybe not.

"Noted," I said, my throat going dry. "So...any advice for how I tell your dad that I've been secretly dating his daughter? While also being employed by his university?"

"Just, uh..." Theo huffed a quiet laugh. "Good luck with that."

"Thanks, super helpful."

"Okay, fine." He sobered, crossing his arms. "Honestly? I think it's best for you to just lead with the truth. All of it. Especially the part where you didn't know who she was at first. And that when you did find out, you both tried to take a step back."

"I promise we did," I said, needing him to believe it.

"I know. And that's going to matter." Theo leaned back against the counter. "And while I'm sure my dad will be mad and will possibly lash out a bit when you guys first tell him, he's not completely unreasonable. So as long as you can get him to understand that you weren't trying to mess with his baby girl's heart, he'll hopefully take a breath and hear you out."

"I hope so." I let out a slow exhale, tension slipping from my shoulders. "Because I'd really love to keep my job *and* still have a chance at dating your sister."

"I'll be crossing my fingers for you," Theo said. Then, with a smirk, he added, "But maybe just don't mention the pantry."

I winced. "Don't worry. That part's already been wiped from my mental script."

"Good." He chuckled as he rinsed out his glass and set it next to the sink. Looking back at me, he said, "Also, I guess I know why you stopped going on dates."

"Yeah..." I scrunched up my nose. "It was *slightly* difficult to think about other women when your sister was in my classroom three days a week."

He gave me a long look. "She really did a number on you, huh?" His voice was soft, more curious than teasing.

I shrugged. "I tried not to fall for the temptation. I mean, I'm not exactly known for being reckless. But..."

"But my sister weaseled her way into your heart and refused to let go," he said, a knowing look in his green eyes.

"Basically."

"Well," he said, a hint of a smirk tugging at his mouth, like he couldn't decide whether to be annoyed or amused. "She's worth all the drama that might come your way. So just...don't screw it up."

"I'll try not to."

He stood and walked me to the door, then paused. "Oh, and when you do talk to my dad?"

"Yeah?"

"If you and Lucy want...you can do it here on Saturday." He shrugged and gestured to the living space behind him. "A dinner in neutral territory. No crowd, no pressure. And if things go south, you can bail without any onlookers watching."

I blinked. "You see this ending with me running away?"

"I'm not ruling it out." He gave a shrug. "Just remember: the front door's easy to access, and the back patio's even faster if you need to make a run for it."

I laughed and held out my hand. "Thanks for the heads-up."

He shook it. "Take care of her, Owen."

"I will."

Then I stepped back out into the night, the porch light flickering on again like it was saluting me for surviving the first real test.

One hard conversation down. One very big, very intimidating conversation to go.

49

LUCY

I OPENED Theo's front door on Saturday evening before Owen had a chance to knock, heart already thudding like I'd just sprinted up a flight of stairs.

He looked...way too good for someone about to walk into a lion's den. Dark jeans. A button-down rolled at the sleeves. That steady, calm expression on his face I wished I could borrow for five seconds.

"Hey," I said, stepping back to let him in.

"Hey," he echoed, voice low and warm. But beneath the calm facade, a flicker of nerves showed in his eyes.

Which was understandable. In the very least, it showed that I wasn't the only one feeling like my insides were made of wet tissue paper.

"They're already in the dining room," I whispered as I closed the door quietly behind him. "Charlotte's being adorable. My dad's already a glass of wine in. So...we'll see how this goes."

He leaned a little closer. "You okay?"

"Not even a little." I gave a breathy laugh. "But I keep

reminding myself that we haven't actually done anything wrong."

"That's true." He nodded, his voice calm and grounding. "We met outside of school. We didn't know each other's full identities at first. And when we figured it out, we did everything we could to step back."

"Exactly." I forced a smile. "And it's not like we've been hiding some grand affair for years. It's still early-ish."

"Right." His lips curved slightly. "Besides, it's not unheard of for professors to date students…"

"Yes." I nodded. "It's totally normal. Just two adults falling in lo—"

I stopped myself before the big "L" word could slip out. Then, with an awkward shrug, I added, "Uh, I mean, you know…"

"I do." And when his brown eyes met mine with a meaningful look, I knew that he really did understand.

I exhaled and glanced toward the hallway, listening for voices. Then I looked back at him, and my chest pinched with something sweet and sad.

Hopefully, when this conversation with my parents is over, we'll still have a chance at saying the big "love" word to each other one day.

But just in case…

"Can I have one last kiss before everything potentially explodes?" I asked quietly, my voice barely above a whisper.

"Last?" Owen's brows lifted.

"I'm hoping it's not," I said, trying to smile. "But if my dad flips out and bans me from ever seeing you again…I'd rather not regret missing the chance."

A range of emotions crossed his features. But then, instead of saying anything, he just leaned in and pressed a soft and grounding kiss to my lips—a silent promise that we'd find our way through, no matter what.

When we pulled back, he rested his forehead against mine and said, "Not the last."

I nodded, swallowing down the anxious bubble in my throat.

We looked at each other for just a beat longer. Deep breath in. Deep breath out.

And then squeezing his hands one last time, I whispered, "Here goes nothing."

I stepped into the dining room first, heart hammering hard enough I was surprised it didn't echo off the walls.

"Where did you disappear to?" Mom said, looking up from cutting the roast already dished up on Charlotte's plate. And when she recognized Owen trailing behind me, she said, "Oh!"

My dad turned, eyebrows lifted in surprise. And then Theo, who was standing behind his chair, shot me a quick look that seemed to say, *Good luck.*

"You guys remember my friend Owen, right?" Theo said casually, pulling out the chair between his seat and mine. "We're hanging out later so I figured I might as well invite him over for dinner as well."

"Good to see you again, Owen," Mom said, giving Owen a polite smile as he took his seat.

"Yes, yes, of course," Dad added. "Welcome."

"Glad I could join you." Owen nodded and smiled like a pro. Acting completely opposite of me, who was sweating through her blouse and trying not to look like I was heading into battle.

I just hoped my parents would still be happy to see Owen by the end of the night.

"Well," Theo said, clapping his hands together. "Let's dig in, shall we?"

Everyone began passing dishes, Charlotte singing softly under her breath, delighting in her little plastic fork. I should've been grateful for the normalcy, for the fact that nothing had exploded yet. But my appetite had gone completely MIA.

While my mom chatted happily about the trip she and my dad had just gotten back from, I poured myself a glass of wine. I probably shouldn't be drinking since I had a meet tomorrow afternoon, but I took a few sips anyway, hoping it would settle the storm brewing in my head.

Then as the Mississippi roast made its way around the table, Owen and I exchanged a few glances, each one a silent question.

Should we rip off the Band-Aid now?

Or wait?

Yeah...we should probably wait. Theo had clearly worked hard on this dinner, and as much as my stomach was in knots, I wanted to give everyone a few moments to enjoy it. Or at least pretend to.

My dad turned to Owen as he buttered a roll. "So, are you looking forward to the rest of the semester now that spring break is almost over?"

"Yes, definitely," Owen said smoothly. "My classes have been going well. Students seem engaged. As a first-year professor, I'm still figuring out the rhythm of the year, but I'm grateful for how welcoming the department's been."

"That's good to hear." Dad nodded, clearly pleased by the answer.

"Oh, I'm sure you're staying busy," Mom said. "But have you had time to date at all? I know Theo mentioned you two were thinking of going on a double date at some point?"

Owen's expression froze for a heartbeat. Then he glanced at me.

I gave a helpless shrug. I had no idea if now was the moment or not.

"Yeah," Owen said slowly, setting his fork down. "Dating has been...interesting."

Mom chuckled. "That's what Theo keeps saying about his love life, too. But I'm sure there's a sweet girl out there who would love to date a handsome, young college professor like yourself. In fact, I have a few friends with daughters about your age. Maybe I could set you up."

Theo choked on his water before saying, "Playing matchmaker for me isn't enough, Mom?"

She waved a hand, smiling. "Not when you're as picky as you are."

"Picky?" Theo scoffed. "Pretty sure it's more the fact that it's actually quite difficult to find a woman who wants me *and* the responsibility of being an instant mom right off the bat."

"I know," Mom said with a sympathetic glance. Then she turned back to Owen, oblivious. "So, is there a type of woman you're looking for? Age? A certain look? Interests? Personality?"

Owen hesitated, eyes darting from her to Theo to me, clearly unsure of how to escape the interrogation.

I swallowed and set my napkin down.

"Actually, Mom," I said, voice a little shakier than I wanted, "Owen's already seeing someone."

"Oh?" She blinked. "Really?"

"Yeah...um..." I reached over and covered Owen's hand with mine, heart beating in my ears. "We just started seeing each other."

For a full second, the room went dead silent.

All eyes turned to us.

Then my dad's face went rigid—his jaw clenched, brows

pulled tight as he looked at Owen like he'd just watched him commit a felony.

"You?" he barked, pushing out of his chair with a sharp scrape. "You've been sneaking around with my daughter? While she's your student?" His voice dropped. Low and lethal. "You have sat at her meets like a supportive friend of Theo's, and as a professor at our school, but all this time you've been preying on her?"

50

———

OWEN

"IT'S NOT LIKE THAT, DAD," Lucy said, standing so fast her chair scraped against the hardwood. "Just let me explain. Please."

She seemed ready to take this on herself, but every instinct in me still wanted to absorb her dad's fury instead. I looked to Theo for guidance. He gave me a subtle nod. Lucy needed to do this.

So, I stayed quiet.

But I was ready to step in if she needed me.

"I know how this looks," Lucy continued, her eyes locked on her dad's angry eyes. "But it's not what you're imagining. It's nothing like those stories. Owen never pressured me. We met before the semester started. At a New Year's Eve party in the Hamptons. I didn't know he was a professor. He didn't know I was a student. I let him believe I was older." Her voice trembled slightly, but she didn't look away. "When we figured it out, we tried to back off. I even looked into switching classes, but nothing else worked with my schedule. And I know you probably think he used his position to manipulate me, but that's not what happened. He's not like that." She swallowed. "He's a good man. You even said so yourself just a few weeks ago."

"Yeah, well..." Her dad barked a bitter, humorless laugh. "That was before I realized he was buttering me up so he could get in your pants."

"*Richard!*" Mrs. Archibald gasped, reaching for his arm. "That's enough—"

"No." He pulled away, fury radiating off him. "You're defending this? A grown man sleeping with our daughter while she's still in his class?"

"We never said we were sleeping together, Dad." Lucy's voice cracked, but she stood her ground. "And even if we were, I'm not a child. That would still be my choice."

His gaze cut to me. "And how old are you exactly?"

"I'm twenty-eight," I said evenly.

"Twenty-eight. You've got to be kidding me." He shook his head, then turned to me fully. "My daughter is twenty-one. Did you even stop to think about the consequences? About what kind of fallout this could cause? Did you talk to Dean Harris about the ramifications of dating a student? Of course not. Because you knew it was wrong. You knew once he found out, he'd be on the phone with me before you could blink."

"We're not doing anything wrong," Lucy said before I could say anything. "We've been careful."

But he wasn't hearing it.

He wasn't seeing us.

"Yeah, well, say goodbye to that grant money," he snarled. "You'll be lucky to have a job by the time I'm done with you. You took advantage of my daughter. She's barely an adult."

"I've been an adult for almost four years, Dad," Lucy said, her voice trembling at the edges.

He scoffed. "You stopped acting like one the second you dumped Josh for some fantasy fling with your professor."

Lucy flinched. And pain instantly flickered across her face, raw and visible.

"That's enough." I stood, my voice rising despite the tight lump forming in my throat. "You can hate me all you want, but don't you dare talk to her like that. Your daughter is smart and capable of making her own choices. So am I."

"Oh, don't flatter yourself," he spat, eyes sharp. "You're just the rebound. You think she knows what she wants? She stopped making good decisions the second she threw away someone who actually gave a damn about her future."

"Stop," Lucy pleaded, voice cracking. "Just...please stop." She faced her dad more fully, eyes glassy and blazing. "You have no idea what you're talking about, Dad. You think Josh was a better choice than Owen?" she asked, a bitter laugh escaping her lips. "Then you don't know what dating him was actually like." She took a shaky breath. "He hurt me, Dad."

"He hurt your feelings?" President Archibald shook his head, clearly missing her meaning. "That happens. We all get our hearts broken. It's part of being an adult."

"No." Her voice broke, and she cut him off. "He hurt me. *Physically.* Remember those bruised ribs I had last year? That wasn't from a bad dismount on the bars. That was from Josh. He was drunk. Furious. I said something he didn't like and he threw me across the kitchen—so hard I couldn't breathe for a full minute."

"What?" Mrs. Archibald gasped, a hand flying to her mouth.

"What the hell?" Theo said, pushing up from his chair, wide-eyed.

"He—" President Archibald asked, his voice barely above a whisper as the color drained from his face. "He hurt you?"

"Yes," Lucy said, the word coming out strangled. "He hurt me and made me feel worthless."

And then she broke.

The dam burst.

Tears spilled down her cheeks as years of silence and shame cracked wide open.

I wanted to reach for her. To pull her into my arms and hold her until the storm passed.

But the air in the room had shifted as her family sat frozen, grappling with the truth that shattered the fairy tale they'd always believed about Lucy's past relationship—a reality they'd never thought to question.

And sweet little Charlotte, who'd been silent through the storm, sat wide-eyed at the end of the table, her fork suspended in the air, as she tried to make sense of why everyone she loved suddenly looked so broken.

I reached for Lucy's hand and gave it a gentle squeeze.

She turned to me, her eyes watery and vulnerable in a way that made my chest ache. "So sorry for all of this," she whispered, her voice barely audible.

"Don't be." I leaned in, my lips close to her ear. "I just want you to be okay."

Her eyes closed briefly, as if anchoring herself with those words.

Then, turning toward Theo, I said, "Want me to take Charlotte into the other room? Give you guys a minute?"

"Yes, please," Theo said, his nod quick and grateful. Then, glancing at my mostly untouched plate, he added, "You can take your food in there if you'd like to finish."

But I didn't have an appetite anymore, so I just took Charlotte's plate and offered her a soft smile. "Wanna build something with blocks? Or maybe watch a show?"

She blinked up at me and nodded. "Otay..."

At the doorway, I looked back.

Lucy's eyes found mine, and I hesitated—torn between the instinct to stay and shield her, and the quiet truth that my presence might only be making things worse.

"I'll just be in the other room, okay?" I said.

She nodded. "Okay."

51

LUCY

"I SHOULD GET Charlotte ready for bed." Theo stood and rubbed a hand down his face, the shadows beneath his eyes deeper than usual after the difficult conversation my family and I had just waded through.

"Good idea." I nodded, my chest tight as I took a moment to breathe after the intensity of this evening.

I'd told my family everything. Not just about Josh and the night that left me bruised and breathless, but about the months I spent convincing myself it wasn't that bad. About the ways I shrank inside myself. How I stopped trusting my own instincts.

And to their credit, they set aside their adoration for Josh and the pedestal they'd put him on long enough to listen.

Even my dad, who had been Josh's biggest cheerleader and longtime friends with Josh's dad, had sat in humbled silence while I spoke, his expression slowly crumbling the deeper I went into something that looked a lot like heartbreak.

And while I knew pulling back the curtain of my past wouldn't automatically fix the issues my dad had with me dating an older guy, it was hopefully a start.

I found Owen sitting cross-legged on the floor beside Charlotte when I walked in the living room, patiently listening to her explain the elaborate storyline behind whatever she'd built with the blocks.

He stood the moment he saw me. "How are you doing?" he asked, a look of gentle concern passing over his face.

"I've been better." I gave a small, exhausted sniffle.

"I bet," he said, opening his arms for me to come to him.

I sank into him, letting my head rest against his chest, the steady rhythm of his heart grounding me.

This.

This right here was what I needed.

Not answers. Not explanations. Just this feeling of safety. Of knowing someone was on my side.

We stood there like that for a long moment, wrapped up in quiet.

Eventually, I pulled back, just enough to look up at him. "Sorry about how that went. I really didn't think it would be that bad."

"It's okay." His lips twitched with a faint, wry smile. "Definitely not the best family dinner I've ever been to, but...I get it. Your dad's just trying to protect you from the big bad wolf."

"I know." I sighed. "And I hope he'll come around once he's had more time to process, but...in hindsight, I probably should've talked to him one-on-one. Eased him into the idea of us more since I'm sure this felt like an ambush."

"We did our best," he said, pressing a gentle kiss to my forehead.

I nodded, the ache behind my eyes creeping back in. "I'm going to keep talking with them, and since I don't know how long it'll take, you should probably head on home."

"You sure?"

"Yeah." I managed a weak smile. "And...sorry again for all the things my dad said."

"It's okay. I know he loves you and is just trying to keep you safe." He cupped my face for a second, his thumb brushing lightly along my cheekbone. "And if I still get to be with you in the end, it will all be worth it."

"That's what I'm telling myself, too." I hugged him again, tighter this time, wishing I could disappear into his arms and stay there. Just for a little while longer. Long enough to forget everything else.

He nuzzled his cheek against mine. "Text me later, okay?"

"I will."

When the door clicked shut behind him, I didn't move. I just stood there, letting the weight of everything settle deep in my bones.

Finally, after drawing in another breath to steady myself, I walked back into the kitchen to where my dad was pacing.

"I sent Owen home," I said, looking between my mom and dad.

My dad's expression flickered, something subtle shifting behind his eyes. And I knew it was time to start bargaining.

"I know you're still upset about all of this," I began carefully. "About me dating my professor. So...if it helps, I'll switch out of his class. And if that's not enough—if you're worried his feelings might've affected my grades—I'll delay graduation and retake chemistry next fall." I swallowed hard, the reality of what I was offering hitting me like a brick. "Graduation's only a month and a half away. But I'll do it if it means he can keep his job."

My dad's steps slowed, but he didn't speak.

"Owen loves this job. He's worked so hard to get there. He's an incredible teacher." I kept going. "Just ask any of his students. You said it yourself. He's passionate. Kind. He actually cares about doing things right." My voice cracked, but I pushed through it. "He doesn't deserve to lose everything because of me. I should've tried harder to get out of his classes. Should've made something else work. But I didn't. I—" I paused, my voice thick. "I didn't really want to. I liked the idea of seeing him every week."

My dad didn't speak right away. He just looked at me like he was searching for some trace of the little girl he used to understand.

Finally, he let out a long, steady breath and dragged a hand down his face.

"You can stay in his class," he said gruffly. "You've come this far, and it's too late in the semester to shift everything around. But Lucy—" His gaze met mine, hard and unwavering. "You need to cut off all personal contact. Completely."

I flinched, like the words had shot me straight in the chest.

"You've got championships coming up. You're on the edge of something big. This is your last year, your last shot. I won't stand by and watch some...forbidden fling blow it all up."

"It's not just a fling," I whispered.

But he didn't seem to hear me. Or maybe he just didn't want to.

"You'll have your whole life to figure out relationships. But this—your future, your gymnastics career—it needs your full attention right now. So, no more secret meetups. No more texts. Whatever's been happening outside of class ends now."

"But he's not a distraction," I said, my voice breaking. "If anything, he's helped me. Just knowing he's cheering me on has kept me going on the hard days."

Dad's expression didn't soften. "This is how it has to be.

I turned to my mom, grasping for a sliver of support. "Do you agree with him?"

She met my eyes, her expression sad and conflicted. After a

moment, she gave a helpless shrug. "I don't know what the right answer is, honey. But...he is so much older than you. That makes me nervous."

"He's a good guy," I said, my throat burning. "He's not some predator."

Helplessness swept over me like a wave.

But when I looked into both their faces, I knew they wouldn't budge. They'd read too many horror stories about gymnasts being taken advantage of over the years, and to them, me falling for a man in a perceived position of power was one of their worst nightmares coming true.

But Owen wasn't like the guys from those news stories. He would never do those kinds of things to me. He'd never hurt me like that.

If my dad didn't hold power over Owen's future, I'd tell them to get over it. That I was an adult now and not a teenage girl anymore. I could make my own choices.

But he *did* have power.

And unlike Owen, he wasn't above using it to get the outcome he wanted.

I swallowed hard. "If I do what you're asking...if I break things off with him...will you promise not to fire him? Will you let Owen keep his job? And still get his grant?"

My dad didn't answer right away. His jaw flexed. And then, with a heavy exhale, he said, "If you agree to end all personal contact, outside of what's absolutely necessary for class, I won't interfere. I won't bring it up to Dean Harris, and I won't touch his position."

It wasn't what I wanted. But it was probably the best offer I'd get.

So instead of thinking of myself, I thought of everything Owen had worked for. Of how much this job meant to him.

How hard he'd fought to build something stable out of a life that had been anything but.

"Okay," I whispered. "I'll break things off with him tonight."

Even if it shattered me.

Even if it meant walking away from the man I loved.

I'd do it.

For him.

52

OWEN

THERE WAS a knock at my door just after ten.

Lucy was here.

I'd left her at Theo's house two hours ago, giving her space to talk things through with her parents. In the time since, I'd done nothing but pace my apartment, nursing a mug of chamomile tea I'd reheated twice and barely touched.

When I'd driven home, it was with the hope that she'd come back with good news, a glimmer of hope in the mess we'd found ourselves in.

But the second I opened the door, I knew better.

Because instead of looking like the ray of sunshine she'd been in my class all semester, she stood there, eyes rimmed in red, her arms wrapped tightly around her middle like she was holding herself together by sheer will.

She looked like she'd been through a war...and lost.

And the moment I looked in her sad and swollen eyes, I knew what was coming.

She was here to end things.

My stomach turned, a slow, hollow ache curling through me like I'd just been punched in the gut.

"Hey," I said, gripping the edge of the doorframe, wishing I could freeze time right here, hold her on the threshold, and stop everything from falling apart.

"Hey," she whispered, not quite meeting my gaze. "Can I come in for a second?"

"Sure." I stepped aside, nodding, even as dread thickened in my throat. She walked in slowly, like every step hurt, and I shut the door behind her.

"So..." She stood in the middle of the room, still and silent, like she was waiting for her courage to catch up to her. "I talked to my dad after you left."

"You did?" I swallowed. "Was it a long talk?"

"Not really," she said, looking down at the floor. "I, uh, I've actually been sitting in your parking lot for over an hour."

"Oh..."

That...wasn't a good sign.

"Yeah..." She sighed, her fingers knotting together in front of her. "And well, I guess the good news is that my dad said I could stay in your class. And that he wouldn't go to Dean Harris...or try to get you fired."

"That's good," I said, a small hit of relief blooming in my chest.

Could we just stop this conversation there? Pretend there wasn't anything else? No real reason for her to look as sad as she did?

But then she looked up at me, her beautiful blue eyes breaking my heart as she said, "There's just one little thing he asks in return."

"There is?" I gulped.

She nodded. "He says he won't do anything to interrupt your career as long as I...promise to end things. With you."

And there it was.

The words I'd seen coming the second I opened the door. The ones I'd hoped I was wrong about.

"Oh."

It was all I could manage.

"I'm so sorry," she whispered, her eyes welling fast. And seeing the same heartbreak I was feeling reflected in this fierce, vulnerable girl I'd fallen for wrecked me.

"I didn't want it to be like this," she said. "But I...I couldn't let him take your career from you. You've worked too hard, Owen. You *belong* here. Your students—"

"You matter, too," I cut in, the words rasping out harder than I meant. "This wasn't just..." I broke off, trying to swallow the lump forming in my throat. "I thought this was something real. Something rare. The thing I'd been hoping to find and never could."

"It was." Her voice cracked. "It is. But we have to think about your future. And if that means stepping back...then I'll do it."

Her words hit me like a blade to the chest.

A sharp, twisting pain that stole the air from my lungs.

Like my heart was being ripped apart from the inside—slow and merciless.

I couldn't breathe through it.

Couldn't look at her without wanting to fall to my knees and beg her not to go.

But I didn't. I just stood there.

Because how could I ask her to stay when she was already tearing herself apart to protect me?

She glanced up, and our eyes locked. And in that look was everything.

Everything we didn't have the words for.

Everything we were about to lose.

And suddenly, I couldn't hold back anymore.

I reached for her, pulling her into my arms like I could memorize the feel of her before she slipped away.

And then she was holding me, too. Desperate. Clinging.

Her face buried in my chest. My hands cradling the back of her head.

"I don't want to lose you," I whispered into her hair, the words muffled and broken.

"I don't want to go," she breathed back, her fingers fisting the fabric of my shirt.

"Then don't," I pleaded, even though we both knew that wasn't an option anymore.

She shook her head against my chest, her shoulders trembling. "We don't have another choice."

And she was right.

So, for another long moment, neither of us moved. We just stood there, grief pressed between us, holding each other like we could freeze time, like maybe if we stayed like this long enough, the rest of the world would forget how to pull us apart.

But the seconds still ticked by, regardless. And goodbye didn't stop coming.

"Tell your dad...thanks," I said eventually, the words bitter on my tongue. "For sparing me my job, I guess. Even if it cost me everything else."

"I will."

She took a step toward the door.

At the threshold, she paused and turned back, eyes shimmering. "I guess I'll see you in class, Professor Park."

And just like that, I was no longer "Owen" to her. Not even "Theo's friend."

Just a guy standing at the front of her classroom three times a week.

I swallowed hard and managed a single nod. "See you in class."

What else was I supposed to say?

She lingered there, her hand hovering near the doorknob, like maybe she wasn't ready to end this either. Then, in a swift, almost desperate motion, she stepped closer and pressed a trembling kiss to my cheek.

"Thank you," she whispered, her voice splintering. "For showing me what it's like to be loved by someone safe. Even if it was only for a little while."

My throat burned as I tried to hold myself together.

And then she slipped out the door, quiet as a heartbeat, the soft click of the latch feeling final in a way I wasn't ready for.

I stood there frozen, my stomach twisting like something vital had been ripped out of me.

Because the truth was, everything I wanted had just walked away.

And just like that night ten years ago, when I lost my dad and Callie...I couldn't follow.

53

———

LUCY

WHEN I GOT HOME, I barely made it three steps inside before Nora looked up from the couch.

Her eyes widened when she took in my puffy face, the slump of my shoulders, the way I couldn't quite breathe right.

"Oh no, baby," Nora said, her voice cracking the second she saw me. "It didn't go well?"

"No—" I shook my head, but the word sounded more like a wounded sob. "I had to break up with him."

"Oh, Lu…" Her expression crumpled with heartbreak on my behalf.

Then she just opened her arms.

My bag hit the floor with a thud. I walked straight into her hug, folding into her like I was a kid again.

She wrapped me up tight, her arms a cocoon, and I cried.

Hard, ugly sobs that wracked through my whole body and left me empty.

"I'm so sorry, Lucy," Nora whispered into my hair as she rocked me gently. "I'm so sorry."

The music was loud in the arena the next afternoon. Every corner of the arena buzzed with energy, with pride, with celebration.

It was Senior Day.

The last home meet of my gymnastics career.

A farewell to four years of grit and glory. A time to look back and feel proud of how far we'd come. Eden Falls had shaped us, broken us, built us, and now—this meet was our final bow.

"Just one apparatus at a time, okay?" Nora squeezed my hand before we were announced, her eyes shimmering with a mix of nostalgia and nerves. "We'll get through this together."

"Okay," I said, still unsure how today would go when I was a complete wreck.

The announcer called my name first, so I jogged onto the floor as the audience clapped and whistled, holding up signs with glittered letters and inside jokes from over the years.

I smiled.

Waved.

Even managed a laugh when the announcer reminded everyone about my freshman debut and how I'd tripped during the march-out, tried to save face with a front handspring, and definitely didn't land it.

But even though I was doing my best to look happy, on the inside it felt like I was trying to stand on a balance beam in the middle of a hurricane.

Because the pit in my stomach hadn't left since last night. Since saying goodbye to Owen.

And now, as I bowed in front of the audience and turned to scan the stands, the ache hollowed out again.

Because there it was.

The empty seat.

Right beside Theo.

Like a placeholder for what could have been.

I blinked hard, forcing my smile to stay. Because even though it would have been hard to see him today, knowing he could never be mine, it also felt wrong for him not to be here at the same time.

But he wasn't here.

Because my dad made me pick Owen's future over my heart.

When it was time for floor, I stood at the edge of the mat, hands on my hips, breathing deep. My coach gave me a nod. I gave her one back, barely feeling my legs as I moved into position.

The music started. I moved on instinct.

Twist. Leap. Smile.

Push through.

And I didn't know how, but somehow my body found its rhythm. The muscle memory and hours I'd put in through the years took over. Each pass sharper, more powerful than the last. I danced like my heart hadn't cracked in two. Tumbled like I hadn't spent all morning fighting back tears.

And when I landed that final tumbling pass, knees steady, chest high, the crowd exploded.

My coach's face was pure joy. Nora screamed my name.

And me?

I smiled.

Because I had to.

But as I raised my arms in salute to the judges and glanced back at the stands, that one empty seat made my eyes sting.

Because while I was pretty sure I'd just nailed a career high on floor...maybe even secured first in the all-around...the one person I wanted to celebrate with wasn't here.

The next week blurred by in a haze of survival.

I switched on autopilot. Forced myself through classes, through practices, through life, because the alternative was lying in bed all day crying into the lavender-scented stuffed cow Owen had once tucked into my backpack.

My appetite was non-existent, replaced by a permanent knot in my stomach that refused to untangle. My whole nervous system felt frayed—jumpy, short-circuited, completely out of sync.

All Monday morning, my anxiety over facing Owen for the first time since our breakup built in slow, pounding waves as the clock ticked toward one o'clock.

By the time I stepped into the science building, my body revolted, and I had to duck into the bathroom while I lost the few bites of toast I'd forced down at lunch.

I stayed in there for a while, leaning over the sink, staring at my reflection as I debated skipping class altogether. Maybe I should just drop the class. Come back as a fifth-year senior in the fall to finish it.

It would be easier than facing him every day.

Easier than pretending the man I loved was just my professor now.

Easier than knowing he could never be mine as long as my dad was still sitting in the president's office.

But no. If Owen had to still show up... If he had to go about life like nothing had happened over the weekend, then I would, too.

Even if it killed me.

I slipped into the back of the lecture hall ten minutes late, hoping no one would notice—especially him. But the second I sat down, I felt it.

His eyes.

He glanced at me once, the alarm flashing across his face so briefly I might have imagined it, before he forced his gaze away.

And then he kept teaching.

But every word he said, every movement he made, hit me like a jolt. Like the air between us was wired with everything we weren't allowed to say anymore.

And it hurt so much more than I expected.

By Thursday, I was running on fumes.

I'd made it through several drills at practice, but my legs were shaky. My head felt floaty. Like I was about to tip over and fall straight off the beam during a drill I could normally do in my sleep.

"Lucy, what's going on?" Coach Chambers blew her whistle and walked over, eyes narrowing. "You sick again?"

My chin trembled.

But before I could even attempt a lie, Nora stepped up beside me, her voice quiet but steady. "She had a bad breakup over the weekend. Hasn't been able to eat or sleep."

"Oh, honey. I'm sorry to hear that." Coach's expression softened as she pulled me into her side. "Really. Breakups are rough. Especially with how much pressure you're under."

I nodded, swallowing the lump in my throat. "Yeah."

"How about you take ten. Go sit. Try to eat something if you can. Then if you can, we'll just have you run through your floor routine and call it good, okay?"

"Thanks, Coach," I whispered, even as guilt clawed at my insides.

This was the worst possible time to have a nervous breakdown.

Conference Championships were on Sunday. The team was counting on me.

Still, I grabbed my water bottle and sat down on the edge of the floor mat, my muscles aching and my head pounding.

It wouldn't be much of a break, though. Because in a few hours, I had Owen's lab.

And the thought of walking into that room—watching him stand at the front, so close and yet so impossibly out of reach—made my stomach twist all over again.

54

OWEN

THE NEXT FEW weeks were what could've easily passed for normal as the semester wound down.

I showed up to teach my lectures. Held office hours. Graded the usual stack of labs.

I even got the official notice from Dean Harris that the grant we'd applied for had been approved and I'd be promoted to research professor.

I should've felt proud. Excited, at least.

But I didn't feel much of anything.

Just...numb. Like I was moving through my life in grayscale again.

Sure, I smiled when I was supposed to. Chatted with students and colleagues. Answered questions in the lab the same way I always had.

But underneath it, I was completely miserable.

And like clockwork, every Monday, Wednesday, and Thursday, Lucy was there in my classes—sitting in her usual spot.

On the surface, we probably seemed fine. Normal. Since

throughout the semester, we'd become experts at hiding the feelings we had for each other from everyone else.

But even if no one else could see it, we knew each other better than that.

Every brief flicker of eye contact was a silent reminder of everything we weren't allowed to feel anymore.

There was a cloud hanging over us now. A heaviness that hadn't existed before.

And the sparkle in her eyes—that bright, hypnotic energy that used to light me up from the inside out—was gone.

How was she holding up?

Was she sleeping okay?

Eating enough?

Keeping her strength up for training?

I knew it wasn't my place to worry about her anymore. But I couldn't help it.

Because unlike chemistry—where you could balance an equation and watch everything cancel out—feelings didn't dissolve that cleanly.

They lingered.

Burned.

Made you do reckless things.

Which was exactly why I'd driven to Pennsylvania the first weekend in April to watch the NCAA Regional Gymnastics Championships Lucy had qualified for.

Was it smart? Probably not. Especially with the chance her parents might see me in the crowd.

But I couldn't not show up.

Because even if Lucy and I weren't speaking—if there was even the slightest chance things could still work out between us someday—it would've been a shame not to witness this moment.

To not be there for her, cheering her on.

Even if it had to be from the shadows.

And while Lucy was a force on the floor, the competition that weekend was brutal. Gymnasts from all over the region were trading near-perfect scores like punches and every decimal point mattered.

So by the time the final rotation ended, I was practically holding my breath.

And when they announced the all-around results, my heart was pounding like I was the one being judged.

"And in second place, Lucy Archibald from Eden Falls University."

So close to first. Just a tenth of a point behind the leader.

Still, it was good enough to continue to the finals in Texas.

"*Good job, Lucy,*" I whispered under my breath as she accepted her medal and waved at the crowd. "*I'm proud of you.*"

I pulled out my phone, wondering if I could text her. Just to let her know I'd seen her. A little sign that I still cared.

But I didn't know if I had the right to even text her anymore —we hadn't shared a single message since our breakup a month ago.

In fact, the only real personal interaction between us had come on the last Thursday of March when she'd walked past me at the end of her lab and quietly said, "Happy birthday, Owen," before slipping out the door with Brody by her side.

It had happened so quickly I hadn't even had a chance to thank her before she was gone.

I sighed and opened my messaging app to look at my previous text thread with Lucy.

The last message from her still sat there: **Can I come over to talk?**

I stared at it for a long moment, thumb hovering before I

typed out a new message: *You did amazing today*. Only to backspace every word.

I shook my head and slid my phone back into my pocket. Then, before the crowd could get too thick, I made my way toward the exit.

I was just rounding the corner near the bathrooms when a familiar voice stopped me.

"Owen? Is that you?"

I froze, my heart jumping before I turned to find Theo approaching, his expression unreadable.

"Hey," I said, trying not to look guilty. "Didn't expect to run into you."

"Yeah, same." He studied me for a second, and I briefly wondered if he was going to get after me for showing up where I wasn't wanted. But instead, he asked, "You doing okay?"

"About as good as I can be, I guess," I said, pushing my hands into my pockets. "Not fired yet, at least."

Theo chuckled, then threw an arm around my shoulder. "You're a good guy. I know my dad's a bit hotheaded, but he knows it, too. Even if the age thing makes him nervous."

"I get it," I said quietly.

"Lucy's his baby girl. Always has been." Theo looked away for a beat, then added, "And after hearing what Josh did to her...my dad's just feeling a lot. Guilt. Fear. Helplessness. He's in full-on protective mode."

"I know." I nodded slowly, the ache in my chest tightening again. "And I would never purposely hurt Lucy. That's the last thing I'd ever want. Maybe I am too old for her... I don't know. I don't really know the rules anymore."

Theo gave me a look. "You're not too old. I mean...sure, seven years is a lot. But it's not unheard of. At least you two are in the same decade of life. That's more than I can say for

Alisha's grandpa who had a thing for twenty-somethings when he was seventy."

"Well, at least I can't say I'm trying to be a sugar daddy." A breath of laughter escaped me before I could stop it. "Hard to do that on a chemistry professor's salary, anyway."

Theo snorted. "Seriously."

We both chuckled, a lightness threading between us, and for a moment, I felt...almost okay. But then I scrubbed a hand over my face, the weight of it all catching up again. "Man, I sure made a mess of things, didn't I?"

"Not too big of a mess," Theo said, a slow smile tugging at his mouth. "I mean, at least you didn't get her pregnant. Unlike another science teacher we know."

"Go me!" I lifted a hand in a mock cheer as I remembered exactly who Theo was referring to—a previous science teacher at Eden Falls Academy. The one I'd been hired to replace.

Yeah. At least I hadn't crossed *that* line.

Though...waiting to be a professor in a college setting before I fell for a student hadn't exactly turned out much better.

"It's good to see you here, though." Theo clapped me on the back, his voice gentler now. "I don't know if Lucy noticed you in the crowd, but...I'll tell her I saw you. Anything you want me to tell her?"

"Just that..." I hesitated, my throat tightening since there were about a hundred things I wanted to say. "I'm so proud of her." I cleared my throat. "And that...she's incredible."

Our eyes met again, and when I saw the shift of understanding in his expression, I knew that Theo knew.

He knew I was a goner for his sister.

"I'll tell her," he said quietly, patting me on the back.

"Thanks," I managed to say, suddenly feeling choked up for some reason.

Which was kind of ridiculous.

But I guess not being able to be with the person you love in their biggest moments just kind of sucked.

55

OWEN

I WAS DRYING glasses behind the bar the next night, trying not to stare when Lucy walked into The Garden with a group of friends.

What is she doing here? I wondered, my stomach dropping like it always did whenever she was near these days.

Had she heard I'd been picking up extra shifts on weekends —my pathetic way of staying busy now that I couldn't spend my downtime with her?

Had Theo mentioned spotting me at her meet yesterday, and this was her way of returning the favor? Showing up in my space, teasing me with even more of her presence.

Only this time, instead of showing off her power and talent on the gymnastics floor, she'd get to show me just how desirable all the guys in the club found her, too. Since yep, right behind Lucy and her girlfriends, were Brody and several guys from the hockey team.

Great. A knot tightened in my gut. *I get to spend the evening watching other guys try their luck with her.*

At least The Garden closed at ten on Sundays, so I'd only

have to endure watching the guys fight for Lucy's heart for two hours max.

The group of college athletes made their way to the same corner where Lucy had been sitting the first night we'd met. Lucy slid in between Nora and a petite brunette, laughing at something one of them said. And I allowed myself to study her for a moment, careful not to be too obvious about it.

Maybe Lucy didn't know I was working tonight.

Maybe she'd only come here on a Sunday because she knew I usually worked Saturdays.

She shrugged out of her jacket, and when her black corset top came into view, my pulse didn't just stumble—it crashed hard. Because it was the kind of top that turned heads. The kind that would have every guy in this place taking notice.

Had she dressed like that for the guys with wandering eyes and practiced smiles who'd line up to buy her a drink?

The thought made my stomach churn.

But then her gaze found mine, like she knew exactly where I'd be, and when she sent me a soft smile, the tightness in my chest loosened.

So maybe she hadn't dressed up for the other guys after all. Maybe she'd dressed up for me.

She turned back to her friends, and I forced my gaze away from her table, trying to shake off the feelings of desire as I set the glasses on the shelf.

When I turned around again, Brody was at the bar with another hockey player.

"Can I get a whiskey and Coke?" he asked casually. Then, doing a double take, recognition lighting up his eyes, he added, "Oh, hey, Professor Park. I didn't realize that was you."

"Hi Brody," I said, managing a smile. "Good to see you." Then, deciding to keep the focus on this job and not my other one, I asked, "You want that on the rocks?"

"Yes, please."

I started making the drink, and when I asked if he wanted to keep his tab open, he nodded, saying, "Yeah. And whatever Lucy gets, put it on my tab, too."

He handed me his card, and when our eyes met, there was a flicker of satisfaction in his expression.

Are they an item now? A spark of jealousy hit my chest, fast and hot. *Has he managed to win her over now that I've been forced out of the picture?*

I'd always known he wanted her. The guy had never exactly been subtle about it.

But did Lucy want him back as well? Had she moved on to someone closer to her age?

Was it too late to ask Theo not to pass on my message after all?

Because if she was dating Brody, for me to still pine after her suddenly felt a lot less romantic and a lot more pathetic.

I slid Brody's drink across the bar. "Enjoy your night," I said, opening his tab.

"I will," he said, lifting his glass in a mock toast. "Hopefully, I'll be doing another kind of chemistry experiment with my lab partner tonight."

And when the wink came next, I had to clamp down hard on the urge to wipe that smirk off his face.

Lucy and Nora broke away from their group and headed toward the bar about fifteen minutes later.

There were two other bartenders standing at the bar and available to help, so they could easily walk over to Malik or Irina to avoid any awkwardness that might happen with me.

But instead of heading to the other end of the bar, they stepped up to the counter in front of me.

"Can we get two waters?" Nora asked, speaking for the both of them.

"Sure," I said, my gaze sliding to Lucy and wanting to stay there. "Coming right up."

I grabbed two water glasses from beneath the bar and started filling them.

The silence that followed was loaded as I searched for something to say. But nothing was coming.

"So, Owen," Nora said, thankfully coming to our rescue, "did you hear our team's going to Nationals after yesterday's meet?"

"Uh, yeah," I said, glancing at Lucy. "I heard."

"Theo said he saw you there," Lucy said softly, her gaze meeting mine.

"Yeah, I was there." I sighed as I started filling the second glass. "Couldn't miss it."

Her eyes caught mine, and for a moment, the rest of the bar seemed to fade as something unspoken passed between us.

Was she happy I'd been there? Was there still hope for us?

Nora chuckled awkwardly. "Is this the first time you guys have spoken since...?"

"Yes," Lucy said.

"Okay, cool, cool." Nora's gaze flicked between us, eyebrow raised. "Should I leave you two alone for a bit?"

Please.

"You better not," Lucy said quickly. "Can't have word somehow getting back to my dad about us breaking his rules."

Right...

"Want me to grab you anything else?" I cleared my throat and slid their waters across the bar. "Food, drinks, whatever. Brody said to put anything you order on his tab."

I knew them ordering water wasn't necessarily about saving money, since with their strict diet plans, they were only occasional drinkers. But if they wanted food, I might as well have Brody pay for it... Who was I to stand in the way of that?

The girls exchanged a look I didn't understand. Then Nora, playing buffer for us again, lifted her glass of water with a nod and said, "We're good, thanks."

I was just about to ask the girls how they planned to balance the end of the semester and the National Championships happening around the same time—just for an excuse to keep Lucy here another thirty seconds, but then Brody appeared at her side, sliding a hand to the small of her back. "I'm ready to cash in on that dance you promised me."

"Right now?" Lucy's laugh was awkward, her eyes darting to mine like she hated that I was seeing this.

"This song's too good to pass up."

She hesitated, then after seeming to take a breath, she nodded and said, "Okay." She handed her drink to Nora next. "Can you watch this for me?"

Nora took it, and as Brody led Lucy away, she turned back to me with a sigh. "Don't worry," she said, like she could read the jealousy I was trying to hide. "I'm pretty sure she only sees him as a friend."

"Good to know," I said.

Though, being *pretty sure* wasn't the same as being certain.

56

LUCY

"HEY, I'm gonna go grab a tampon from my car real quick," I told Nora, stepping up to the bathroom sink in The Garden's restroom after discovering that my period had started. "I'll be right back."

"I can grab it for you if you want," she offered, grabbing a paper towel to dry her hands.

"That's okay." I shook my head. "It's not too heavy yet, so I should be fine to head outside."

What I didn't tell her was that I was more than happy for the excuse to slip out for a few minutes—away from the heat, the noise, and Brody.

He'd been a little too touchy on the dance floor for my taste tonight, hands at my waist, hips pressing closer than I wanted, his *"Don't be shy"* whisper in my ear every time I tried to put some distance between us.

Yeah, I needed a moment to breathe and regain my bearings.

The night air was cool when I stepped outside, a welcome change from the humid press of bodies inside.

My car was parked toward the back of the lot, away from the streetlights, so I clicked the key fob to make my headlights flash and give me a target to walk toward.

That was when a dark figure stepped beside me out of nowhere.

"Hey, where are you headed?" a familiar voice came from the tall figure.

"Oh, Brody!" I gasped, putting a hand to my chest. "You scared me."

And something about the sudden appearance of a tall, broad figure in the dim parking lot sent me straight back to that night I'd run to Owen's apartment, a stranger's footsteps pounding behind me.

"You leaving already?" Brody asked, stepping closer, oblivious to the spike in my pulse.

"Not yet." I pointed toward the row of cars where my headlights had just flashed. "Just grabbing something from my car."

"Cool." He exhaled like he was relieved. "I'll walk you there. Never can be too safe."

"Thanks," I murmured, and I meant it. The shadows felt heavier out here than they had a minute ago.

"You having fun tonight?" He shoved his hands into the pockets of his jeans.

"Yeah." I wrapped my arms around myself, wishing I'd grabbed my jacket. Because even though it was technically spring, it was still chilly at night.

"Good." Brody's eyes flicked over me, the intensity in his eyes making me suddenly aware of every inch of skin my corset top left bare. "I am, too. Way better than the last time we came here, right?"

"Yeah." I gave a small laugh. "A lot nicer without you and Josh trying to beat each other up."

"True." He smirked. "Plus, I got to dance with you this time."

And while I knew he was trying to be playful, I got the feeling that he was hoping for more than a few dances.

Should I tell him I wasn't in a place for anything romantic right now? That my heart was still wounded—tangled up in someone else?

I didn't know.

We reached my car, and I opened the door, bending across the driver's seat to grab my purse. I found it easily and took a quick peek inside to make sure I had a tampon in there.

But when I straightened to stand, Brody's solid form was right there—much closer than I expected.

"Sorry—" I startled, trying to take a step forward even though there was nowhere to go.

"Don't be," he said. Then before I knew it, his hands were on my hips and he was turning me so my back was pressed against my car.

"Hey! What are you doing?"

"Since I finally have you alone..." He grinned, leaning in. "I was thinking we could do a little chemistry test."

"Oh—" I braced my hands against his chest, heat and panic tangling in my veins. "I'm...not really in the science mood right now."

"Come on, Lucy." He bent down, his breath brushing my ear. "You've been teasing me all semester. Just give me one little kiss. I promise I won't tell anyone."

"Sorry." My stomach knotted. "I just...don't feel that way. I thought we were just friends."

"That's only because you haven't kissed me yet." His hot breath hit my face, laced with cinnamon whiskey. "Believe me, I'll rock your world."

Before I could respond, his hands came up, fingers

clamping along my jaw, thumbs grazing my cheeks like he thought this was tender. Like this was something I wanted.

"Stop, Brody—" I shoved at his chest.

But he didn't budge.

My pulse roared in my ears, and the smell of alcohol, the scrape of his calloused fingers against my skin, and the way the cold metal of my car door pressed into my back all closed in until I could barely breathe.

"Just give me a chance." He tilted my face higher, his grip firm, insistent—like he expected me to melt into him if he angled me right.

And then—

"Get away from her!" Owen's voice, sharp and furious, cut through the dark like a lifeline.

Brody twisted toward the sound but didn't let go, his fingers still clamped to my jaw, hot and unyielding.

"She said no," Owen growled. And the next second, he wrenched Brody back by the collar.

Brody stumbled, boots scuffing against the pavement. For a split second, I thought that would be the end of it. Until he spun around and shoved Owen hard, sending him back a step.

"You've got a problem with me kissing Lucy?" Brody sneered.

"You heard me." Owen's tone was ice. "Back. Off."

"What?" Brody's eyes narrowed, his mouth curling into an ugly grin. "You don't want to share?"

I froze, pulse thundering in my ears. *Share?* What was he talking about?

I only had to wait a beat for the answer.

"You two thought you were so sneaky," he spat, eyes wild. "But I've been onto you all semester—caught Lucy running up to your place back in January. Didn't even know who she was meeting until I followed her again."

Followed me?

A cold chill swept through me, locking up my spine. Was he the one who'd shadowed me that night, the reason my skin had prickled all the way to Owen's door?

All this time, I'd thought his crush was harmless. Sweet, even. But this…this sounded a lot like stalking.

"Then at her meet," Brody went on, "when you were *filming* her. Going off on those guys behind you for a couple of crude comments? That was hilarious considering you were already living out their fantasies."

"You need to stay the hell away from her," Owen said, his jaw tight, voice like steel. "If you so much as look at her again, President Archibald will make sure you regret it. He doesn't take risks where his daughter's safety is concerned."

When Brody let out a short, sharp laugh, Owen stepped forward, his fists curling at his sides.

He's seconds away from putting Brody on the ground.

But before Owen could wipe the smug look off Brody's face, another deep voice cut in, "What the hell is going on here?"

I turned toward the sound, and my breath caught. Because my ex was storming toward us.

I hadn't even seen Josh tonight, but suddenly there he was, shoving Brody back and stepping between us.

"You really want to do this again?" Brody asked, holding up his fists.

"I'd *love* to," Josh said. And, strangely enough, I didn't mind seeing his temper flare for once.

"Save it for the ice," Owen said, stopping the two hockey players from going at it. Then, looking back at Brody, Owen said, "Leave now. Or I'm calling the police."

Brody backed away slowly, an arrogant smirk lifting his lips before he turned and disappeared into the dark.

And yeah, I was definitely switching lab partners this week. If my dad didn't expel him first.

"You okay?" Owen's voice softened as he pulled me into his chest.

And it was then that I realized how badly I was shaking.

"I will be," I said, clinging to the safety of his arms. "Thanks to you."

57

LUCY

"THANKS FOR STEPPING IN," Owen told Josh once Brody's taillights disappeared from the lot.

"No problem," Josh said. "Glad I was here."

"What were you doing out here, anyway?" I asked, still trying to piece together how both of them had managed to appear at exactly the right moment.

I understood Owen since he'd probably seen me leave the club alone and his protective side had kicked in.

But Josh? I hadn't even spotted him inside tonight.

"I was here to pick up some of the guys." Josh gave a half-shrug. "Tried to go in for a few minutes, but..." He rubbed the back of his neck, a sheepish smile tugging at his mouth. "Turns out I'm blacklisted. Guess the bouncer hasn't forgotten about my fight with Brody in December."

"Oh." I hesitated, unsure which response fit best. "Should I say sorry you're blacklisted...or thank you, since it meant you were outside?"

"Not sure." He chuckled. "Yeah, fun times. But I deserve it." His smile faltered, his voice dropping a notch. "And well...I know it's way too late for this, but...I really am sorry for every-thing that happened when we were together. I was a terrible boyfriend, and you didn't deserve any of it."

"Thanks," I said, somewhat surprised he was bringing it up now.

My instinct was to follow it up with an *it's okay* since the people-pleaser in me practically trained for it.

But it wasn't okay. Not even close.

So instead, I asked, "I heard you stopped drinking. Is that true?"

"It is. Took me way longer than it should have but...I finally realized it was turning me into someone I didn't like."

"I'm glad you were able to realize that." Even if he'd hurt me, I still cared and wanted what was best for him...even if it couldn't be with me.

An awkward beat passed between us before he cleared his throat. "And sorry for not warning you about Brody. I always knew there was something off about him, but...I didn't know why until tonight."

"Yeah." A shiver crawled up my spine. "He took me by surprise, too."

We exchanged a few more strained pleasantries before Josh tipped his head toward Owen. "It's good to know Lucy's got someone else looking out for her now."

"Yeah," Owen said, skirting the fact that we weren't exactly allowed to be together right now. "Maybe we can talk sometime about getting you off the club's blacklist."

"That'd be great." Josh managed a small grin. "Mocktails only, though."

"Sounds good to me." Owen chuckled.

Josh headed back to his car and Owen turned back to me, his arm still warm and solid against my lower back, that touch the only thing keeping me steady at the moment. "Want to go back inside?"

"Not really." I shook my head. "Would it be too much to ask you to take me to my parents' house?"

"Definitely not too much," he said. "Just let me tell Malik he's closing up."

We walked inside together, Owen staying close by my side. After speaking with the other bartenders, Owen and I made our way to the corner where my friends were.

"Lucy! What happened?" Nora shot to her feet the moment I reached the table for my jacket. Her gaze flicked over me, then to Owen, then back to me. "Are you okay?"

"I'm okay now." My hand trembled as I held out my keys. "Can you drive my car home? I...I'm not up for it."

"Of course." She took the keys without hesitation. "Do you want to go now?"

"Owen's going to take me to my parents' house," I said, already feeling the weight of the conversation I'd need to have with them. "I'll call you later, okay?"

"Okay." She hugged me, quick but firm, not pressing for details even though I could see the questions in her eyes.

Owen's car was parked close to the back entrance. The ride was quiet, the hum of the engine the only sound between us. I kept my gaze on the dark streets sliding past, the glow of street-lights smearing into golden streaks, fighting the replay of Brody's face in my mind.

When we stepped into my parents' living room, Mom was curled up with a book, Dad scrolling on his phone.

"Mom. Dad." My voice came out small and shaky, like it belonged to someone younger.

They both looked up immediately.

"What's wrong?" Dad rose to his feet, his gaze locking on

Owen like he assumed Owen was responsible for my distressed appearance.

"This isn't what you think," I said before we could have a repeat of the last time we were all in the same room together. "Owen drove me home from The Garden. He was just making sure I got home safe after a hockey player tried to—" My throat closed around the words, but I forced them out. "—tried to assault me in the parking lot."

Mom's book slipped from her lap. Dad's expression shifted in an instant, all that heat redirecting away from Owen and into something colder, harder—dangerous.

"Who?" he asked, voice clipped.

"His name is Brody," I whispered.

Dad's jaw clenched like he knew exactly who I was talking about. "Did he hurt you?"

"No. Owen got there just in time." My voice wavered. "But...apparently, he's been stalking me."

A wave of insecurity slid over me as I realized the security blanket I'd thought I had—my sense of who I could trust—was gone.

I'd thought Brody was my friend. But after this betrayal, I wasn't sure how many other smiling people in my life were hiding something I couldn't see.

"Come here, sweetheart." Mom crossed the room, wrapping me up in her arms, her familiar perfume grounding me. "You're safe now."

Dad's expression shifted from barely restrained fury as he stepped in and pulled us both close.

"We'll make it so he can't hurt you again," he said, each word clipped like he was already running down a list of exactly how to make that happen.

When we finally stepped back, my gaze went to Owen,

who still stood by the door, his shoulders squared in a way that said he wasn't leaving until he knew I was really okay.

"Thank you for bringing her home." Dad turned toward him, his protective energy redirecting like a spotlight. "I know you probably have classes early in the morning, so we'll take it from here."

"If it's all right," Owen said, his eyes flicking to mine before returning to Dad, "I'd like to hear about your plans for keeping Lucy safe. I know you have your opinions about me and my intentions with your daughter, but I want her safe just as much as you do."

For a beat, Dad just looked at him, like he was deciding whether to bristle at the intrusion or recognize the fact that whether he liked it or not, he wasn't the only protective man in my life now.

"Okay," he said with a sigh, something in his stance easing. "Have a seat."

58
———

OWEN

I WAS HALFWAY through grading last week's labs when a knock sounded on my open office door.

My head lifted, and the air in my lungs stilled when I saw none other than President Archibald standing there.

I'd been half-expecting he'd stop by at some point today after showing up at his house with Lucy last night. But still, my pulse picked up.

Was he here to thank me again? Or had he stopped by to remind me that, despite what happened with Brody, nothing had changed about his opinion of me?

"Do you have a minute?" he asked.

"Of course." I cleared my throat, keeping my voice even as I gestured to the chair across from my desk. "Have a seat."

He stepped inside, closing the door quietly behind him.

He sat, posture as controlled as always, but there was something different in his eyes when he looked at me today. Less steel. More kindness.

"I wanted to speak with you because..." He paused, letting

out a breath that felt almost...regretful? "I owe you a big apology."

He *what?* My brain snagged on the words, not sure I'd heard him right.

I blinked. "Y-you do?" For some reason, even after coming to a truce of sorts last night, I hadn't expected an actual apology from this seemingly stubborn man.

"Yes." He nodded, then paused like he was choosing his words carefully. "I probably should have done this a month ago, but...I would like to apologize for the way I reacted when you and Lucy told me about your relationship. I should have stopped to think about it and maybe let the idea sink in first. I should have listened to what the two of you had to say before jumping to my own conclusions and concocting worst-case scenarios in my head."

Was I actually hearing him right? Or was I having some sort of hallucination right now?

Had I inhaled too many chemicals in the lab today?

But after studying his face a bit longer and seeing something like humility reflected in his sharp brown eyes, I decided that this must actually be happening.

So, letting the words soak in, I swallowed the lump in my throat and said, "I appreciate you telling me that. Really." And then, offering an olive branch of my own in return, I added, "And I do understand some of where you were coming from. Lucy's your only daughter and I am several years older than her. You felt blindsided." I licked my lips and shrugged. "And there was probably a better way we could've come to you. We just... Well, it was a tricky situation. Hindsight's always twenty-twenty, but—"

"That's no excuse," he said, cutting me off. His voice wasn't sharp—just certain. "I was out of line in calling you a predator and assuming the worst. I had my reasons for being wary...and we both saw one of those fears play out just last night. But that doesn't excuse the way I treated you. I'm not proud of it. In fact, I'm embarrassed by it. And I hope you'll accept my apology."

For a second, I just sat there, stunned.

I hadn't expected that. Not from him. Not after the way he'd looked at me that day in Theo's dining room—like I was the big bad wolf who'd seduced his daughter.

"Thank you, President Archibald," I said finally, something uncoiling in my chest. "I do accept your apology. And I hope we can move forward without too many hard feelings."

"That's my hope, too." He nodded slowly. "And whether or not I like how this started, it's clear you care about my daughter's well-being as much as I do. Which means," —his gaze held mine— "we're in this together now."

This was good, right?

He leaned forward. "Anyway, my wife and I ended up with an extra ticket for Nationals next week. If you're open to it, we'd really like you to join us in Texas."

I stared at him for a second, unable to find words.

This man, who not long ago had looked at me like I was the worst thing that could have happened to his daughter, was now offering me a seat beside their family.

"It would mean a lot to us." He offered a faint, sincere smile. "And more than that...it would be a shame to keep Lucy from sharing that moment with the man she's clearly in love with."

"I...would be honored," I said finally.

And for the first time since we'd started this, it felt like he finally might see me as someone who belonged in his daughter's life.

59
___

LUCY

IT WAS MONDAY EVENING, and I was nestled into the far corner of the student lounge with my marketing study group, a notebook open in my lap. The energy in the room was the usual mix of caffeine and tired ambition, with the faint hum of vending machines near the back wall.

"I'm thinking bold colors and a tagline like *Hydrate Harder* for my final project," Quincy said, tucking her braids behind her ears as she scrolled through mock-ups on her tablet. "That way, it might look like it could sponsor a championship but still be trendy enough for TikTok."

"I like that," I said with a smile, trying to stay invested in the conversation despite being distracted with everything from last night. "That would definitely fit in with the vibe of other sports drinks I've seen, while also being fresh and new."

"You think so?" she asked, her brown eyes brightening.

I nodded.

"You could even do a social campaign around athletes who train late at night," Beckett, another group member, added. "Like 'Hydrate Harder After Dark.' Boom."

"Okay, Dracula." Quincy snorted. "But I actually kind of love that."

The group chuckled, but my attention was soon distracted by the soft buzz of my phone in my lap.

> Theo: How'd your chem class go today? Still the same with Owen?

I typed back quickly.

> Me: Same as it's been all month. Why?

Just because Owen had come to my rescue and been included in my parents' "keep Lucy safe" conversation last night didn't mean my dad's opinion of us had magically changed.

As far as I knew, he still expected my only interactions with my chemistry professor to be the occasional eye contact during his lectures and maybe a question or two if I was stuck on an assignment.

> Theo: Sorry. I guess I was hoping that after everything last night, something might have shifted.

Yeah...me too.

I was staring at our text thread, trying to figure out what to say when movement from across the way caught my eye.

As if my spiraling thoughts had conjured him up, Owen stepped through the glass doors.

My breath stalled.

Because how many Monday and Wednesday nights had this exact thing happened?

Owen walking into the student lounge just as my study

group was winding down...pretending to look busy while waiting to walk me home.

My heart squeezed as I watched him. And I didn't know whether I wanted him to look my way or not.

Until he did, his eyes finding me immediately. Like he'd been hoping to see me all along.

And when our eyes caught, instead of looking away like he'd done all month, he...smiled.

A real smile. The kind of smile you give a person you're close to.

One I hadn't seen since that night everything between us cracked.

And even though I was slightly thrown by his sudden, almost carefree demeanor, my stomach still flipped. I gave him the smallest smile before quickly turning back to my group, pretending like I wasn't seconds away from unraveling.

Had anyone noticed the flush on my cheeks?

Probably not. Quincy was still flipping through her tablet, Beckett was deep in his notes, and I was doing my best impression of someone who hadn't just made accidental eye contact with the man I hadn't stopped thinking about for three months straight.

But I could only pretend to focus for so long before my gaze slid back to Owen.

Where was he going tonight?

Dinner in the dining hall? Meeting someone?

He looked...different. Not just physically—though he definitely did. But there was something more relaxed in the way he moved, like the tension he usually carried around his shoulders had temporarily been let go.

Had he changed clothes?

Earlier in class, he'd been in a button-up and slacks. Now, under his light jacket, he wore a fitted black T-shirt and a pair of jeans. The outfit he'd worn the night we first met at The Garden. The shirt I'd once told him he looked amazing in.

Was it the same one?

Why had he changed?

Was he meeting someone? The thought struck me before I could stop it.

Possibly for...a date?

It was around dinner time. Maybe he had a date with someone who worked in this building.

The idea twisted in my chest, and I blinked down at my notebook, the words on the page suddenly blurring together as I tried not to feel sick.

Sure, it had been a month since we ended things, and he probably had already set up said date before everything that happened last night at The Garden. But was he really ready to move on?

Because I certainly wasn't.

Ever since Theo had told me he'd seen Owen at my meet on Saturday, I'd been holding on to the ridiculous hope that maybe once I graduated, my dad would come around and we could try again.

Once I was no longer Owen's student or even enrolled at this university, maybe...just maybe...we'd be in the clear to pick up where we'd left off.

Yes, it was probably delusional. But still...I'd hoped.

Was it possible he'd simply gone to my meet because he'd fallen in love with the sport and...I don't know...just wanted to see what the regional championships looked like?

And the only reason he'd followed me outside at The Garden and saved me from Brody was because it was the "right" thing to do?

I hoped not.

Because I really liked the fairytale idea of my prince being patient enough to wait for me.

But maybe it had been just that. A fantasy. One that I'd told myself to get through the ache.

I forced myself to glance in his direction again, bracing to see him walking toward another woman. But instead of disappearing down the hall or joining someone for dinner, he sat down.

Just twenty feet away. In the seat he used to claim on Monday nights like it belonged to him.

Like he belonged here.

And then, as if he could feel my gaze on him, he looked up again.

Our eyes met.

And this time, the smile he sent me wasn't just friendly—it was soft. Open.

Hopeful.

My heart thudded, and I tried not to jump to conclusions about why he was here. But if he was here—if he was smiling at me like that—it must mean something had changed, right?

When my study group finally disbanded for the evening, I packed up slower than usual, pretending to fish for a missing pen so no one would notice the way my hands shook. Quincy, Mason, and Beckett waved their goodbyes, and I gave a quick "good luck on your projects" as they filtered out.

But even as I pretended to be focused on packing up my things, my eyes kept flicking toward Owen. Because even though ten minutes had passed since he'd first walked in, he was still here, sitting in the same chair. Like he belonged to the rhythm of my Mondays.

I adjusted the strap of my backpack over my shoulder and walked toward him—each step slow and hesitant, like I was tiptoeing across thin ice.

When I stopped in front of him, I swallowed. "Hi."

"Hey," he said, his expression warm as he stood. "Can I talk to you?"

"Um..." I glanced around quickly, suddenly nervous that my dad might have spies watching me before nodding and saying, "Sure."

The student lounge was dimly lit and relatively deserted at this time of day, but it wasn't exactly private. And just down that corridor, maybe fifty yards away, was my dad's office.

I had no idea if he was still working or if any of the administrative staff were lingering late, but I wasn't about to risk it.

"Let's just go somewhere else," I whispered, brushing Owen's arm as I passed him. "This way."

I led him into a side hallway, then kept going until we turned into a tucked-away alcove nestled between the campus theater and the faculty lounge.

No one should see us here.

"What did you want to talk about?" I finally turned to him, my heart pounding. "Does it have anything to do with today's test? Did I completely bomb it?"

"No, nothing like that." He exhaled like he'd been holding it in for a while. "I just wanted to, uh, touch base after my conversation with your dad this afternoon."

What? My stomach dropped. "You talked to my dad again? Why?"

A dozen questions raced through my mind at once.

Had my dad stopped by to tell him about the restraining order we were trying to get against Brody? To let him know he didn't need to keep such a close eye on me anymore?

Or worse—had this been some kind of warning to back off completely?

"Your dad stopped by my office." He stepped closer, his eyes locked on mine. "Said he wanted to apologize."

"Wait—" I blinked, stunned. "My dad wanted to apologize?"

He almost *never* did that. Only if he really knew he was in the wrong about something.

What did this mean?

Was he rethinking everything he'd said about Owen and me?

Was this...permission? Acceptance?

Would he be okay with us being together now? Or at least in two and a half weeks, when I finally graduated?

"He said he had time to think things through." Owen gave a faint smile, like he was just as shocked as I was. "That he over-reacted. And then he..." He let out a breath, almost like he still couldn't believe it. "He said he won't stand in our way if being together is what we really want."

"What?" My voice came out barely above a whisper. I couldn't tell if I was breathing. "You're serious?"

"As serious as I've ever been." He reached for my hands, lacing his fingers with mine. "After talking in my office, your dad and I went to Dean Harris together and told him every-thing. About the timeline of how we met and everything that happened after that. He said they'll still need to talk to you and do an official review to make sure everything was handled ethi-cally—your grades, the lab—but based on what we shared, since we talked to your dad shortly after we became official and then ended things when your dad asked...he thinks we'll be fine."

"So..." I blinked. "He won't keep us apart?"

"No." A slow smile tugged at Owen's lips. "He's not going

to fight it. He even invited me to join your family in Texas next week."

My jaw dropped. "You're coming to Nationals?"

"Yes." He laughed softly. "I'll be there to cheer you on."

"So...this is real? I'm not dreaming?" My heart swelled, a lightness pushing out the fear that had been wrapped around my chest since last night. The shadows Brody had left behind disappearing now that I was safe with Owen. "We won't be breaking any rules in being together? We won't have to sneak around anymore?"

"This is really happening." He stepped closer, his voice dropping, softer now. "If you still want to be with me..." He tucked some hair behind my ear. "Then yes, Lucy. We can be together."

Emotion surged so fast and so fiercely, it nearly took me under.

His hand slid into my hair, and after making sure I was okay with it, he kissed me—soft and warm and reverent, like he didn't want to rush it. Like he'd been hoping for this moment just like I had.

I kissed him back, gripping the front of his shirt like if I let go, he'd vanish again.

When we broke apart, we paused, breath mingling. And when I looked into his brown eyes, his expression flickered with something that looked a lot like love.

And with that one look, I knew I wasn't alone in all the aching and missing and *wanting*.

He pressed me back gently against the wall, hands anchoring at my waist. "I missed you so much." He groaned low against my mouth.

"Me too." I nodded, swallowing. "I couldn't stop thinking about you."

"I couldn't sleep." His lips found the corner of my mouth,

then my jaw. "I hated walking into class and pretending you weren't everything to me."

I laughed. "You were so good at pretending."

"Not really." His hand found mine and threaded our fingers. "You should've seen me after class."

My eyes suddenly stung with emotion, the idea of him still loving me even when things had seemed hopeless completely undoing me.

I leaned in, kissing him again, slower this time. My arms circled his neck, his slid around my back.

"You have no idea how many nights I've dreamed of this," he murmured, voice low and rough against my neck as his mouth traced a slow path along my jaw and down the column of my throat, lips warm and open, breath hot enough to make my pulse trip. "Needed this."

"I think I have an idea," I breathed, more moan than words as my hands slid beneath his shirt, palms flattening over the firm planes of his back. "Since I've been dreaming about it, too."

A groan rumbled from his chest, and my heart pounded so hard I was sure he could feel it. When his lips found mine again—slow, reverent, full of everything we'd been forced to hold back—I melted into him completely.

One of his hands gripped my hip, drawing me closer, while the other slid higher along my spine. The contact pulled a soft whimper from me—so intimate, so familiar, yet still new enough to steal my breath.

We were just getting even more lost in the moment when the sharp slam of a distant door cut through the haze.

We froze, still pressed together, panting. His forehead rested against mine, his thumb tracing absent circles at my hip like he couldn't bring himself to let go.

"We should probably take this somewhere else," I whispered with a shaky laugh, brushing my thumb along his jaw. "Don't need anyone discovering what Professor Park is like behind closed doors."

His low chuckle vibrated through me, and I saw the moment he came back to his senses. "You're probably right." Then, softer, "You hungry?"

"Starving," I admitted, my heart still thudding against his.

"I was thinking we could go out to dinner."

I tilted my head. "Like...to a drive-thru?"

"No." That slow, sure smile curved his mouth—the one that made me want to kiss him all over again. "I was thinking more like a sit-down place with a cozy booth."

"You want to get dinner in public?"

Could we actually do that now?

"I do." He grinned, taking my hand in his as he led me back down the hall. "I want to show you off and let everyone know you're finally mine."

60

LUCY

THE ENERGY inside the Dickies Arena in Fort Worth, Texas, was everything you'd expect from the NCAA Gymnastics Championships—loud, pulsing, alive. We were in the final rotation of the semifinals—the meet that would determine who took home the all-around title and which four teams would advance to the finals on Saturday.

And I had one event left.

Floor.

The crowd was still recovering from the routine just before mine. Oklahoma's star gymnast—last year's all-around champion—had just nailed her landing with the kind of grace that made your stomach twist. Her final all-around score?

39.675.

Which meant that if I wanted the all-around title...I would need a perfect 10 on floor.

A near-impossible feat.

Especially because it would be my third perfect 10 of the night.

Bars. Beam. And now floor?

It was insane. Unreal. Practically unheard of.

But if any event gave me a shot, it was this one. Floor had become my strongest event this season. I'd poured everything into it: refining every leap, every line, every tumbling pass. I knew this choreography like I knew my heartbeat. Every beat, every transition, was muscle memory now.

If I could channel the same fire I'd brought to the gym this week...I might actually have a chance.

I might actually do what I couldn't do last year.

A twinge of nerves flared in my stomach.

Please. Let me hit this routine.

"You've got this, Lucy," Coach Chambers' voice cut through the noise as she stepped up beside me, setting her arm on my shoulder. "You've done this routine a hundred times. Just hit your landings. Sell your performance. And no matter what the scoreboard says...I'm proud of you. We all are."

I nodded, emotion rising like a tide I wasn't ready for. "Thanks, Coach."

Because I was proud, too.

Proud of how far I'd come.

How far we all had.

This whole year had been a climb. A fight. A string of near-misses, long practices, taped ankles, and early-morning lifts. We'd battled for our spot here at Nationals. And we'd made it.

Now I was about to close it out.

I walked to the edge of the spring floor, then paused, letting myself take one last look into the stands.

My heart surged when I spotted Owen sitting with my family.

He was smiling, waving, and when he mouthed, *"I love you,"* my chest swelled so full I could hardly breathe.

We'd fought for this moment, too. For each other.

And somehow, after everything, my dad hadn't just invited Owen to be with my family today. He'd accepted him.

Even telling me earlier this morning that he was looking forward to golfing with Owen and Theo at the Hastingses' private course in Eden Falls next week.

Which was something I *never* would've believed a month ago.

I turned to the judges, and when they gave the signal that they were ready, I walked to the center of the floor and drew in a long, centering breath.

It's go time.

The music kicked on—"Fireball" by Pitbull—and I struck my opening pose.

The crowd roared as the beat pulsed through the arena. I let the rhythm settle into my body, my feet already moving as I launched into my dance elements—confident, flirty, controlled.

The choreography pulled me across the floor like a current, and I played it up. Flashing smiles, hitting clean lines, throwing in that little shoulder shimmy that always got a reaction.

Then I hit the first corner.

Deep breath. Run.

Front double. Punch front.

Stick it.

The floor caught me clean and solid. I hit the landing and threw my arms up.

The crowd exploded, and I powered into the next section of choreography, feeding off the energy. My body and the music were in sync. Every movement felt precise. Intentional. Alive.

But as I danced across the floor toward the final corner, my focus narrowed. One pass left.

Roundoff. Back handspring. Double full.

The pass that had haunted me earlier this season.

The one I couldn't stick in January to save my life.

But not today.

I sprinted forward.

Pushed hard off the floor.

Launched into the twist.

And I *stuck it*.

No wobble. No hop. No hesitation.

Just *perfect*.

The arena erupted. It was a roar so loud it buzzed through my limbs. And while I could hardly hear the music as I finished the final few counts of choreography, my body knew what to do.

Tears blurred my vision before I even hit the final pose.

Because I knew I'd done it.

Not only had our team secured a spot in the finals, but I was pretty sure I'd just clinched the all-around national title.

I'd come back from an injury. From heartbreak.

From self-doubt and mental blocks and almost walking away so many times.

And I hadn't just pushed through. I'd triumphed.

I struck my final pose as the music faded, holding it a breath longer than necessary before lifting my chin and looking up into the crowd again.

To my family.

To Owen.

I'd done it.

And everyone I loved was here to see it.

I barely made it off the floor before my teammates swarmed me with cheers and hugs, crying right along with me. But even with all the noise and adrenaline rushing through my body, there was only one thing on my mind.

The score.

Had I actually done it? Because nothing was sure until the score was announced.

My teammates, coaches, and I all linked arms at the edge of the floor, staring up at the giant scoreboard to see if my routine had been enough to take the title and secure us a spot in the finals.

The arena fell strangely quiet, as if the entire place was holding its breath with us.

Then the scoreboard lit up.

10.000

The arena erupted.

Screams. Cheers. Arms thrown around my shoulders. My feet left the ground as my teammates lifted me, and the announcer's voice boomed over it all:

"With a perfect ten on floor, Lucy Archibald is your NCAA All-Around Champion!"

I laughed and sobbed at the same time, adrenaline crackling in every cell. Coach Chambers and Nora were hugging me. The rest of my teammates were jumping. And when I turned toward the stands to search for my loved ones, Owen was already on his feet, one hand in his hair like he couldn't believe what he'd just seen, the other pressed to his heart as he grinned down at me.

I had to stay in the corral for photos and quick interviews, my medal hanging solid and bright around my neck. My cheeks ached from smiling, my voice felt raw from cheering. And inside, my heart was pounding like it was still mid-routine.

When the last flashbulb popped and the final handshake

was done, I glanced toward the stands and saw my family making their way down the steps.

My mom reached me first, her arms coming around me, with a sob that shook us both as she whispered, "I knew you could do it."

My dad was right there, too, folding us into his arms. "We've been waiting for this moment your whole life, Lu. You earned every bit of it, and we couldn't be more proud."

I stayed there, eyes squeezed shut, soaking in their warmth and the pride in their voices. Because after years of early mornings, long drives, and so many sacrifices, we were finally here.

And I couldn't have done it without their support.

"Congrats, sis," Theo said next, giving me a tight side hug with Charlotte on his hip. "I'm so proud of you."

"Thanks," I said, appreciating that my big brother had been able to make time to come to so many of my meets throughout the year, even though he was so busy with his demanding career and raising Charlotte on his own.

When Charlotte reached over to give me a hug, I spotted Owen standing just behind Theo, still holding back until my family had had their moment. His smile was all pride and awe, and when I finally stepped up to him, his arms were already open.

And the second his arms wrapped around me, I was airborne, his laugh rumbling against my ear as my feet left the ground.

"You did it, Lucy" he whispered. "You were unreal out there."

"I can't believe I stuck the double full," I said, grinning through the tears on my cheeks.

"You did more than stick it." His hands framed my face, thumbs brushing the edges of my smile. "You made the whole world stop. I don't think I've ever seen anything more beautiful."

And then I kissed him—right there at the barricade, in front of my family, fans, cameras and whoever else might have been watching.

Because I wanted to.

And I could.

THEO

BOOKING an eight a.m. flight after a weekend of nonstop gymnastics was definitely not my brightest move. Especially when said flight was with an overtired three-year-old who thought "sitting still" was a suggestion and not a requirement.

Though, I couldn't take *all* the blame for the chaos that was sure to happen on this four-hour flight. At least I'd tried to make it better by booking first-class seats for both Charlotte and me.

But when the airline oversold them, my grand plan went out the window—leaving me trudging down the narrow aisle of the main cabin, clutching our carry-ons and silently praying our seatmate wouldn't hate kids.

Charlotte was adorable. Obviously. But not everyone shared my bias.

We made our way down the aisle—me angling our bags so they didn't smack anyone in the shoulder, my daughter dragging her sparkly unicorn backpack.

And when I spotted our row, I found a familiar shock of reddish-brown hair by the window.

Lucy's friend, Nora.

Thank goodness it's someone I know, I thought as relief loosened my shoulders. I'd been sure we'd be sharing our row with a grumpy old man who hated kids.

But Nora had always been nice to Charlotte the handful of times they'd met, so hopefully, she'd still like us by the time this plane landed in New Haven.

"Hey," I said, stopping beside my seat.

"Hey." She pulled out an AirPod and smiled at me, seeming just a little surprised. "Are you guys sitting here?"

"Guess so." Then directing Charlotte to the middle seat, I said, "Okay, honey, this is your spot."

And miracle of miracles, she offered a shy smile up at Nora before climbing into her seat.

Well, that was easier than expected.

"Want me to help with your seatbelt, Charlotte?" I heard Nora ask as I fussed with putting our carry-ons in the overhead bin.

And when I was ready to sit, I saw she was all secured and ready to go.

"Thank you for helping her," I said, reaching around for my seatbelt.

"No problem," Nora said. "Though, I could have sworn I heard that you and your parents were flying First Class."

"That was the plan." I chuckled. "But apparently, they oversold seats, so...here we are."

"Slumming it with the rest of us," she teased.

"Yep, lucky you," I said, nodding down at my daughter who was most definitely not going to be keeping to the bubble of her seat. "I hope you don't mind kids."

"Oh, I love them," she said. Then patting Charlotte's leg, she added, "Plus, Charlotte and I are already buddies, aren't we?"

"You're *Lucy's* friend," Charlotte said matter-of-factly.

"You're right." Nora smiled. "But you and me can be friends now, too."

"Okay." Charlotte shrugged, seeming to like that idea.

"See, Charlotte and I are going to be just fine on this flight." Nora said, her brown eyes smiling. "It's you I'm worried about."

"Me?" I furrowed my brow, wondering why she'd be worried about me. "I'll be fine. Just a little more cramped is all."

"Uh huh." She smirked, her eyes skeptical. "I heard you used to fly on the Vanderbilts' private jet back in the day. This must be rough for you."

Okay, so she thought I was a snob.

But I wasn't the only one here with fancy people in my life.

"Funny hearing you say that," I said, arching a challenging eyebrow. "Weren't you flying all over Europe in your famous pop star brother's private jet last summer?"

"Okay, so I wasn't planning to mention it since I didn't want you to feel sorry for me," she said with a grin. "But if I start crying into the complimentary pretzels later, you'll know why."

And I couldn't keep my own grin from lifting my cheeks because this was actually kind of fun.

But before I could think of anything to say back, Charlotte suddenly piped up, "Daddy cries sometimes, too."

I groaned. "Thanks, kiddo."

Nora laughed, but when her eyes met mine again, there was a softness there. Like she understood why a widowed father might get emotional from time to time.

And while the thought of anyone knowing I sometimes cried when the grief of losing Alisha suddenly hit would have embarrassed me a few years ago, I just had to shrug and embrace it since letting the emotion out was better than keeping it bottled up.

About an hour into the flight, after the fiftieth request from Charlotte for fruit snacks, Nora pulled out her phone to look at something.

"What's that?" Charlotte leaned over, curiosity lighting her face.

"It's a game where you match the colors in bottles," Nora explained.

"Oh fun!" Charlotte gasped. "I can help!"

Two minutes later, she was perched on Nora's lap, chubby fingers pointing at the screen like she was the official strategist.

"Sorry," I murmured, reaching to pull her back. "She can be a little overbear—"

"She's just fine." Nora glanced at me with a conspiratorial little smile. "We're a team now."

***

By the time we were halfway home, the team was out cold.

Charlotte had begged Nora to trade her for her window seat, only to curl across Nora's lap shortly after that. And somewhere in the rhythm of Nora absentmindedly running her fingers through Charlotte's curls, Nora had drifted off, too, her head resting against my shoulder.

So with a quiet moment to myself, I pulled out my phone and opened the stack of applications I'd received for Charlotte's new nanny.

Yep, daycare wasn't working out, and I was hoping more one-on-one care might be better for her.

But after reading the same paragraph three times and not retaining anything, I knew the warmth of Nora pressed into me was making it impossible to focus on résumés and reference lists.

Especially since she was holding my daughter like she was made for the job I was trying to fill.

It had been almost two years since Alisha passed. Two years since I'd had a woman beside me like this. And the weight, the quiet trust. Well...it was doing things to my chest I hadn't felt in a long time.

And when I glanced down at the way a loose strand of reddish-brown hair had fallen across her cheek, I noticed something I probably should have seen a long time ago—what a natural beauty Nora was. The faint spray of freckles over her nose. The fullness of her lips. Her petite frame, perfect for tucking beneath my arm like she belonged there.

Okay, you are not *getting a crush on your little sister's friend.* I shoved the thought aside immediately.

Because, *geez.* I'd thought Owen was too old for Lucy and here I was, even a year older than him.

I sighed and went back to my phone, forcing my eyes to read the details of the application before me.

I was just skimming over the section that stated the candidate had a degree in early childhood development when the plane hit a pocket of turbulence. Nora stirred beside me, her lashes fluttering just a second before her eyes slowly opened. It took a beat for her to register where she was, and then she sat up straighter in a hurry.

"Oh, I'm so sorry." She looked up at me, embarrassed, as she started to shift away.

"Don't be," I said quietly. "I don't mind. Small quarters and all."

"We did already establish how cramped it is back here." She gave me a small, almost shy smile.

"That we did," I said.

But instead of resting her head back on my shoulder like I

secretly hoped, she settled farther back into her seat, putting her AirPods into her ears.

And when she closed her eyes again, I let my gaze linger for a second, taking her in.

Just because I knew I couldn't act on anything didn't mean it was illegal to look.

EPILOGUE
OWEN

Six years later

I PULLED along the curb in front of the EFU gymnastics practice facility a few minutes after picking up Tate and Lennon from daycare. No matter how long the workday might have been, seeing Tate's mop of dark hair and Lennon's toothy grin were always enough to boost my spirits.

The second I unbuckled them from their car seats, my four- and two-year-olds were off like rockets, little sneakers pounding down the hallway of the gymnastics facility. I jogged behind at a slower pace, smiling at the trail of laughter they left in their wake.

By the time I reached the open doorway to the gym, I caught the best kind of scene—my kids sprinting across the mats like they owned the place, Lucy crouched down to their level, arms wide.

She'd been mid-conversation with a brunette in an Eden Falls warm-up jacket—one of the new freshmen this year—but the second Tate launched himself at her and Lennon followed, she laughed and caught them both in a hug.

Six years ago, when Lucy had been fresh into her gymnastics retirement and still trying to figure out what to do with her life after college, Coach Chambers had asked her to stick around and help. Now, with her sixth season in the assistant coach position coming to an end, she was ready to step in as head coach.

It was something she'd never even thought to dream of back when we first met, but after only a few practices her first year coaching, it became obvious she'd been born for it.

After hugging each of the kids, Lucy's gaze lifted over their heads, finding me in the doorway. The moment our eyes locked, her smile softened. And yeah, seeing her look at me like I was still her home after all these years just did something to me every time.

We'd been together six years, married for five of those, and I somehow fell more in love with her each day.

I shoved my hands in my pockets and made my way across the spring floor, weaving around balance beams and chalk dust. When I reached Lucy and the kids, I bent to give her a quick hug and a kiss on the cheek. "You smell good," I murmured.

"Really?" She chuckled. "Hard to believe since I've been in the gym all day."

"Well, you do. You always do," I said. "Must be the smell of victory in the air."

"That's what we're hoping for." Her bright blue eyes sparkled as she glanced toward a group of gymnasts packing up for the day.

Conference championships were two weeks away, and while the program hadn't had a year quite like her own senior season since she graduated, this team was showing some really great promise. And if they kept nailing their routines and putting in the hard work, we were hopeful they'd at least make regionals.

"Think Coach Chambers will loosen up and give these girls the spring break of their college dreams?" I asked, tossing her a wink as the memory of *our* spring break experience—New York, Broadway, and a very ill-timed relationship reveal to Theo—made me grin.

"If you mean keeping the regular practices just at a slightly kinder hour of the day, then you know it," she said, smirking.

I slid my arm around her waist, tugging her closer. "One of these years, we're going to take a spring break trip somewhere fun."

"I think that's out of the cards for us as long as I'm a coach, baby." She smiled sweetly at me, catching my mock pout before shoving me playfully in the chest. "Lucky for us, we both have all summer off to more than make up for it."

"True." I grinned, leaning down to kiss her temple. "Definitely a better trade-off."

Spending the summers with my family, especially when the kids were so young and constantly changing and growing, was definitely a gift I didn't take for granted. We were particularly looking forward to spending a week in the Bahamas with my mom and Asher's family—something I never would have imagined back when everything fell apart.

It was a reminder that even after loss, you can still build new traditions worth holding onto. And after spending so many years watching other families make memories together, it was a dream come true to finally have a family of my own like that.

Were we perfect? Of course not. But our life was pretty dang good.

Lucy and I walked hand in hand out of the gymnastics facility with Tate insisting on carrying Lucy's bag for her and Lennon bouncing along at my side, chattering about the "big jump" she was going to show Mommy when she was "big like Tate."

The drive home didn't take long as we wound through the familiar streets of Eden Falls and into the neighborhood right next to where I'd grown up. Pulling into our cul-de-sac still gave me that odd mix of nostalgia and gratitude. Nostalgia for all the years I'd spent here with my family and friends. And gratitude that now, my own little family lived here, too—in the house right next door to my childhood best friend and his own little family.

I hit the garage door opener and pulled in, shutting off the engine as Tate and Lennon scrambled out. Lucy grabbed her bag from the back, while I took my time, just watching her in the late-afternoon light.

When I stepped into the house, I was instantly hit with the smell of the lasagna soup I'd tossed into the crockpot this morning. Since Lucy and I both worked, dinner duties rotated. Tonight was officially my night, but since I still had a salad to chop and throw together, I knew she'd be right there helping me out.

Which was always a nice reward at the end of the day.

While Lucy got the kids settled with their playdough at their little table in the corner, I washed my hands and pulled the lettuce, tomatoes, cucumbers, and feta cheese from the fridge.

"Want some help?" Lucy asked, stepping up beside me at the counter.

"I'd love it."

We chopped in sync, sliding veggies into the big wooden bowl between us. Every so often, we bumped elbows or shoulders, and since I was still addicted to my wife, I didn't bother pretending it was accidental.

"Careful, Coach," I said, brushing past her to grab the salad tongs. "You keep getting in my way."

"Whatever." She smirked, not looking up from slicing tomatoes. "Pretty sure you're the one in my way."

"Hmm," I murmured, stepping right up behind her so my chest brushed her back. "Guess we'll have to work this out."

I slid my arms around her waist, and a soft laugh escaped her lips. "Oh, is that your plan?"

I kissed the side of her neck, slow and lingering, then just under her ear. "That's part of it."

She tilted her head slightly, giving me better access. Then, knowing we needed to practice safety first, I carefully removed the knife from her hands, setting it on the counter.

"Knives and kisses don't mix."

Her breath caught, and a spark lit her eyes when she looked at me. "Guess we'll finish the salad later."

"We're just taking a little break." I turned her toward me, trapping her between my body and the counter, my hands resting on her hips. She giggled when I kissed her and then her fingers curled into my shirt.

"Got any plans for after the kids are in bed?" I asked, my mind already entertaining a few ideas of its own.

"I don't know..." She caught my bottom lip gently between her teeth before letting it go. "Probably shower." Her shrug was casual, but the slow lift of her gaze was anything but. "Maybe put on something lacy after that."

Her words had barely left her lips when heat hit me like a match to kindling. "Careful, darling," I murmured, leaning close enough that my lips brushed her ear, my voice pitched for her alone. "Because I'm already getting ideas about what I can have for dessert."

"Maybe we can get that shower together then..." She bit her lip again in that way that wrecked me.

I forced my gaze away for a beat, willing my pulse to slow. When I looked back, I scanned behind us to make sure we were out of the kids' line of sight. "Maybe we should sneak upstairs right now?"

Because yeah, dinner could *definitely* wait.

"Not so fast, mister." She patted my chest, a wicked smile curving her lips. "Dinner should always come before dessert, right?"

While Lucy loaded the dishwasher, I got the kids bathed, jammied, and tucked into bed with their favorite stories. Lennon conked out halfway through the picture book. Tate took a little longer, insisting I check under his bed for monsters twice. By the time I closed his door, the house had settled into that rare, perfect quiet.

I found Lucy in our bedroom, hair down and damp from her shower, wearing one of my old Eden Falls University hoodies that hit mid-thigh. She was standing by the bed, folding laundry.

"Need help with that?" I asked, leaning against the doorframe as I drunk her in.

Her lips curved in a slow smile. "You're offering to fold towels?"

"If that's what you want." I crossed the room in three long strides. "But if you're still up for other activities...we can do that, too."

"I guess you did get the kids to bed..." Her laugh was soft. "You probably deserve a reward for your hard work."

"Just so you know, my intentions were completely pure in going the extra mile with kid duties tonight," I murmured, sliding my hands to her hips. "I definitely wasn't expecting anything in return."

"Sure." She laughed. "I know how you work by now. No one likes putting the kids to bed *that* much."

"Okay, fine. So maybe our conversation in the kitchen gave me just *a little* motivation."

"I bet it did."

She tipped her head back as I kissed her, deep and unhurried this time, tasting the faint sweetness of the wine she'd had with dinner.

My hoodie was loose on her petite frame, but I could still feel the warmth of her through the fabric, and it made me want to strip away every barrier between us.

Her hands skimmed under my T-shirt, palms warm against my skin. "You smell like basil," she said against my mouth.

"It's better than playdough at least, right?" I asked.

"Much."

We ended up tangled in the sheets after shoving the laundry off the bed, laughter giving way to the kind of quiet that felt like home.

Every touch was as familiar as my own heartbeat and still electric enough to leave me breathless.

Outside, the world could have been chaos, but here—wrapped around the girl of my dreams—everything was steady.

***

To stay up to date on news, sales, and releases from Judy, join her newsletter here: https://subscribepage.com/judycorry

While you wait for Theo's book to release, read Owen's brother Asher's book: *The Ruse.*

. . .

Are you just discovering the Kings of Eden Falls series? If so, don't miss Addie and Evan's Brother's Best Friend/Mafia romance: *Hide Away With You.*

Dear Reader,

I want to thank you for taking a chance on *Wish You Were Mine,* and for giving me the opportunity to share this story with you. I couldn't do my dream job without you!

I would also be so grateful if you could take the time to leave a review. It's amazing how such a little thing like a review can be such a huge help to an author! Even a sentence or two counts!

Thank you so much!!

-Judy

ALSO BY JUDY CORRY

<u>Eden Falls Academy Series:</u>

The Charade (Ava and Carter)

The Facade (Cambrielle and Mack)

The Ruse (Elyse and Asher)

The Confidant (Scarlett and Hunter)

The Confession (Kiara and Nash)

<u>Kings of Eden Falls:</u>

Hide Away With You (Addie and Evan)

Say You Remember Me (Maddie and Ian)

Wish You Were Mine (Lucy and Owen)

<u>Rich and Famous Series:</u>

Assisting My Brother's Best Friend (Kate and Drew)

Hollywood and Ivy (Ivy and Justin)

Her Football Star Ex (Emerson and Vincent)

Friend Zone to End Zone (Arianna and Cole)

Stolen Kisses from a Rock Star (Maya and Landon)

<u>Ridgewater High Series:</u>

When We Began (Cassie and Liam)

Meet Me There (Ashlyn and Luke)

Don't Forget Me (Eliana and Jess)

It Was Always You (Lexi and Noah)

My Second Chance (Juliette and Easton)

My Mistletoe Mix-Up (Raven and Logan)

Forever Yours (Alyssa and Jace)

<u>Standalones:</u>

Protect My Heart (Emma and Arie)

Kissing The Boy Next Door (Lauren and Wes)

ACKNOWLEDGMENTS

After years of dreaming about writing a forbidden romance featuring a college gymnast, I was thrilled to finally bring Lucy and Owen's story to life. They truly were such a fun couple to hang out with this past year and I absolutely loved watching their story unfold.

To my husband, Jared, and my kids—James, Janelle, Jonah, and Jade—thank you for being my biggest supporters. I wrote a huge portion of this book during summer break, and I appreciate your patience when I had to hide away for a few hours each afternoon instead of filling every moment of free time with you. You are my reason for pushing through on the hard days, and I wouldn't be where I am without each one of you.

Meredith Logan, Crissy Holland, and Sarah Constable—you're the real MVPs for reading the chaos draft and helping me shape it into something worthy of swoons. Thank you for the pep talks, sharp notes, and reminding me why I love telling stories like this.

To my incredible editor, Precy Larkins—thank you for once again going above and beyond, not only for working with my deadlines but for pushing me to dig deeper when I wanted to take the easy way out. Your notes make my stories stronger, and I'm so thankful I get to work with you.

And to my sharp-eyed proofreader, Jordan Truex—thank you for catching all the little things I miss and giving me the peace of mind that my words are polished and ready to be sent into the world.

To my ARC and Influencer teams, I can't thank you enough for cheering this book on from the beginning. Your excitement, messages, and posts are a constant source of encouragement, and I wouldn't make it to the finish line without you.

To every reader, Bookstagrammer, BookToker, blogger, and reviewer—thank you for picking up my books and sharing them with others. Every post, every review, every recommendation means the world to me. You are the reason I get to keep writing love stories.

And finally, thank you, dear reader, for taking a chance on Wish You Were Mine. Because of your support, I get to live my dream every single day, and I'll never stop being grateful for that.

ABOUT THE AUTHOR

Judy Corry is the Amazon Top 12 and *USA Today* Bestselling Author of Contemporary and YA Romance. She writes romance because she can't get enough of the feeling of falling in love. She's known for writing heart-pounding kisses, endearing characters, and hard-won happily ever afters.

She lives in Southern Utah with the boy who took her to Prom, their four awesome kids, two dogs and a cat. She's addicted to love stories, dark chocolate and chai lattes.

www.ingramcontent.com/pod-product-compliance
Lightning Source LLC
Chambersburg PA
CBHW031641200726
48289CB00004BA/1065